YOU
DESERVE
TO
KNOW

ALSO BY AGGIE BLUM THOMPSON

I Don't Forgive You
All the Dirty Secrets
Such a Lovely Family

YOU DESERVE TO KNOW

AGGIE BLUM THOMPSON

TOR PUBLISHING GROUP
NEW YORK

YOU DESERVE TO KNOW

A Forge Book
Published by Tom Doherty Associates / Tor Publishing Group
120 Broadway
New York, NY 10271

www.torpublishinggroup.com

Forge® is a registered trademark of Macmillan Publishing Group, LLC.

The Library of Congress Cataloging-in-Publication Data is available upon request.

ISBN 978-1-250-89201-0 (hardcover)
ISBN 978-1-250-89203-4 (trade paperback)
ISBN 978-1-250-89202-7 (ebook)

Our books may be purchased in bulk for promotional, educational, or business use. Please contact your local bookseller or the Macmillan Corporate and Premium Sales Department at 1-800-221-7945, extension 5442, or by email at MacmillanSpecialMarkets@macmillan.com.

First Edition: 2025

Printed in the United States of America

10 9 8 7 6 5 4 3 2 1

For my father, Martin,
who, when I was a child, took me to the library
on Friday evenings and let me check out
as many books as I could carry

YOU
DESERVE
TO
KNOW

TRANSCRIPT FROM NBC'S *DATELINE*

INTERVIEWER: Your book has been a sensation. An international bestseller. The subject of several podcasts. It's being turned into a movie as we speak, there's a documentary about the whole affair in the works—but what is *You Deserve to Know*, exactly? Fiction? Memoir?

GUEST: I call it autofiction—personalized reflection based on facts.

INTERVIEWER: The fact is that you had a front-row seat to a horrific crime, or series of crimes I should say, that shook your quiet suburban neighborhood to its core. But what you've written is not a piece of journalism, is it?

GUEST: Absolutely not. Autofiction is when an author recounts their life in a fictionalized manner, but modifies significant details and characters, invents subplots, and imagines scenarios with real-life characters in the service of a search for self. Of course, I didn't witness every scene in the book, and even with as much research as I did, and even though I was there, I am still unable to truly know what other people were thinking. So, no, it's not journalism and it's not technically a memoir, but obviously one of the points of view is based on me, and I think that gives it authenticity.

INTERVIEWER: Are you worried readers might think the book is a completely accurate account of what happened?

GUEST: A lot of what happened is available in the court records— like the murders. Some readers will assume that every single word is true. But I caution readers right at the beginning. I've changed details here and there and taken poetic license. Still, the essence of the story is true. The court records will back that up.

INTERVIEWER: How do you respond to the criticism that you've written yourself as a hero in the story when you were anything but?

GUEST: *You Deserve to Know* is my version. And I don't let myself off easy. If you've read it, you know what I mean. But everyone is welcome to their own version of the truth. That's what's so beautiful about the world today. Everyone has their own truth. What right has anyone to deny mine?

INTERVIEWER: Are you concerned about being liable for defamation?

GUEST: No, this book has been vetted by many lawyers. As you know, the bar for libel when it involves a public figure, or a dead one, is very, very high.

INTERVIEWER: But putting aside the legal issues, what do you have to say to friends, even family members, who feel you've exploited their pain and profited off a tragedy by writing a book about them?

GUEST: I'm going to paraphrase one of my favorite writers here, Anne Lamott. She said *if you wanted me to write warmly about you, you should have behaved better.*

DISCLAIMER

You Deserve to Know is a work of autofiction.

It is a result of much research, as well as of my own memories—and, like most people, my memory is imperfect—as well as my imagination. I have tried to capture my lived experiences, although some details have been changed.

If you recognize yourself in one of these characters, that's between you and your therapist.

1

She has a sneaking feeling that her friends are talking about her.

Anton and Lisa, outside on the patio, keep glancing at her through the kitchen window, where Aimee stands at the counter, dressing the salad. They're sitting at the large patio table, too close together, too close for other people's spouses, that is. What are they whispering about?

Her.

Aimee is sure of it. Probably talking about that stupid argument that she had with Lisa earlier, and the way she stormed off. Not stormed, exactly, but Aimee stood up so abruptly that her chair scraped the flagstone in an earsplitting screech as she announced, "I'll get the salad."

From where she stands inside her kitchen, Aimee has a good view of the two of them at the table. Through the large sliding doors to the right, she can see the whole of her backyard. At one end, all six of the kids are running around, jumping on the trampoline, chasing the dog. A plume of smoke curls from around the side of the house where her husband, Scott, and Lisa's husband, Marcus, are presumably manning the grill, a behemoth of a thing she gave to Scott for Father's Day a few months earlier.

Lisa and Marcus.

Gwen and Anton.

And Aimee and Scott.

The three families live on the same cul-de-sac, Nassau Court, in East Bethesda, just outside Washington, D.C. The five younger kids are all close in age and attend the same school—both sets of twins in first grade and Noa in fourth grade, while Lisa and Marcus's son, Kai, has just started middle school. The three families have spent so much time together in the past year that Aimee can read Anton's and Lisa's body language even thirty feet away.

Gwen appears beside her with a bowl of potato salad.

"I think that salad is ready, girl," she says. "You're whipping it like it's egg whites."

Aimee looks down at the metal salad servers in her hands. She drops them in the bowl and sighs.

"What were you staring at?" Gwen asks.

"I was watching Anton and Lisa. I think they're talking about me."

"Hmm. Knowing Anton, he's telling her to calm down, maybe not be so judgy?"

"Or maybe he agrees with her," Aimee says. "That my mothering leaves something to be desired."

Gwen sucks in her breath. "No. You're an amazing mother. She was being a—"

"Don't say it." Aimee turns to smile at Gwen. Three-way friendships are tricky. She was friends with Lisa first. For a few years, they were the only families with kids on the cul-de-sac. When Gwen and Anton moved in next door a year ago, the three women formed a trio. Aimee loves having two close friends on her block that she can count on. Loyalty is everything to her. Sometimes, though, she senses an undercurrent of competition between her two friends.

"I appreciate your coming to my defense, but I'm fine," Aimee says. She doesn't want to encourage Gwen to say anything negative about Lisa. She loves Gwen, considers her one of her closest friends, but she can be a little sharp.

Still, Aimee is a bit stung by Lisa's earlier sanctimonious outrage. Her tone was nasty. *You let your daughter do what?*

Gwen snorts and pulls open the sliding door to the backyard, and Aimee follows her, clutching the large wooden salad bowl as if it might protect her from incoming arrows.

This is their Friday night ritual. The three families pile into one of the backyards and either grill or order takeout. In the cooler weather, they build a fire and roast marshmallows. Sometimes they drink too much. Sometimes people say things they shouldn't. But mostly they have fun.

"It's getting chillier, but I'm so glad we can still eat outside." Aimee puts the salad down and takes a seat across the table from Anton. The air has the slightest crisp to it, a hint of the autumn to come.

These cloudless September days are her favorite time to be working. In the fall, her landscape design business does not have to deal with the frantic panic of homeowners who want instant flowers in the spring, impatient with the pace at which most plants grow. In the fall, she gets a different sort of client. The ones interested in reshaping their yards, preferably with native plants—her specialty. She'd like to transition to only native designs, but the market isn't there yet. People love their boxwoods and crepe myrtles.

"What's this?" Gwen sits down next to Anton and picks up his glass, which contains one large square ice cube sitting in a golden-brown liquid, before taking a sip.

"Blandon's."

"Anton. Really. You brought your own?" She smirks at Aimee as she says this, her tone halfway between teasing and mocking. Ribbing her husband is a regular thing for Gwen, which sometimes leaves Aimee uncomfortable at the obvious underlying tension. She wouldn't do that to Scott, nor he to her. They made a promise to each other to never become a publicly bickering couple. On the surface, Gwen and Anton seem perfect. Anton, the successful writer and university teacher, their beautiful twin boys, and sophisticated Gwen, who works part-time at a Georgetown PR firm and directs her excess creative energies into complicated holiday displays, interior design, and her own flawless appearance.

Aimee always feels slightly unkempt around Gwen. Probably because her own wardrobe consists of Carhartt jackets and cargo pants, and her hair is always up in a messy bun. Not that Gwen has ever said anything to make Aimee feel less than. Gwen can't help it if she's one of those moms who makes every other woman feel slightly inadequate.

Anton reaches into a bag at his feet and pulls out a bottle shaped like a large glass grenade, a wide grin on his face. His contribution to Friday nights has been to introduce everyone to expensive alcohol. Aimee chalks this up to his being a writer. She pictures him at home every day, sitting in front of an old type-writer, surrounded by books, sipping bourbon. She once shared this flight of fancy with Gwen, who laughed and said that when she gets home from her work, she often finds Anton in his under-wear playing *Fortnite*.

"Want some?" Anton asks as he holds the bottle in the air.

"I'll take an old-fashioned," Aimee says.

He cringes in exaggeration, pulling at his clipped beard. "I can't let you pollute my Blandon's, but I think Scott's got some Maker's Mark in there I can use." He stands up.

"He definitely does," Aimee calls after him. "On his beautiful bar cart."

Once Anton is out of earshot, Aimee turns to Lisa. "Did you see the bar cart Scott bought? It was made in Denmark in 1960 and he's very, very proud of it."

"Ooh, mid-century modern," Gwen says. "Who's the de-signer?"

Aimee shrugs. "Beats me." Her husband's fascination with Scandinavian mid-century modern furniture is a passion she doesn't begrudge him, but one she doesn't share. It seems all the men she knows in their forties and fifties have developed some strange hobby. Anton and his top-shelf liquor—he's always traveling far distances to pick up some limited-edition bottle—or Scott and his hours spent online hunting down some Danish chair. And Lisa's husband, Marcus, took up cycling during the pandemic and now heads off every weekend at the crack of dawn in some neon spandex outfit.

"Of course, we're going to have to trade that thing of beauty in for a locked liquor cabinet at some point," Aimee says. "I found Noa pouring apple juice into a martini glass from the shaker the other day."

Gwen laughs. It's supposed to be a funny, self-deprecating *look-at-the-things-our-kids-get-into* story. That's what mom friends are for, to make you feel less alone in your parenting challenges. But when Aimee looks over at Lisa, her friend's face is frozen in a neutral mask. Aimee feels an uncomfortable twinge in her stomach. The way she parents her nine-year-old daughter has become something of a sore subject with Lisa. Leaning across the table to touch her hand, Lisa smiles. "Listen, I'm sorry about what I said earlier."

Aimee shakes off Lisa's hand and tucks a loose curl back into her top bun. "Oh, it's okay, I get it." She doesn't get it. Why Lisa lit into her like that, *in front of everyone*, for letting Noa visit one of her clients. But she's trying to avoid a repeat of the conversation.

"You're an awesome mother," Lisa says, gathering her long black hair and pulling it over one shoulder.

"Yes, she is!" Gwen says. "In fact, I think we're all killing it."

"It's just, how well do you know this woman, Aimee?"

Gwen groans. "Unbelievable," she says. "Just drop it."

"Look, I know you mean well, but I've got this, okay?" Aimee stares into Lisa's almost-black eyes. She is not about to relitigate why she's been letting Noa spend time visiting one of her clients. The woman, a retired elementary school teacher named Cathy, is perfectly harmless in her baggy Eileen Fisher clothes and chunky black glasses. She wants to hire Aimee to replace the azaleas on her sprawling front lawn with native plants to attract butterflies and birds. When Aimee first went out there to brainstorm design ideas about a month ago, she hit it off with Cathy. On her second visit, she brought Noa, who discovered Cathy had not just a cat, but three newborn kittens, after which she insisted on coming back whenever Aimee went. And yes, over the past few weeks, Aimee has let Noa spend a few hours here and there at Cathy's to play with the cats. Aimee doesn't tell Lisa and Gwen that Noa's fourth grade is off to a rough start, that words like *ADHD* and *sensory processing issues* have been bandied about. That being around those kittens makes Noa's face light up, a welcome contrast to the defeated state in which she comes home from school every day.

Aimee isn't ready to admit to herself what challenges Noa might have, can't even bring herself to open the psychologist's report that arrived in her inbox a few days ago.

And why should she have to say any of this to Lisa? To Gwen? Why should she have to justify herself?

She doesn't have to. Anton comes back with drinks, followed closely by Scott and Marcus carrying trays laden with burgers, sausages, and grilled corn. Any further conversation is impossible, about Aimee's parenting choices or anything else. Smelling the meat, the children converge on the table. Lisa and Marcus's son, Kai, hangs back with Noa, but the four younger kids swarm the food.

"Slow down, boys!" Gwen stands and begins delivering commands while Marcus struggles with the tongs, distributing the slippery hot dogs. Finally, the boys step back and Kai and Noa hold out their plates.

"You two are so patient," Lisa says to Kai and Noa. "Thank you for letting the younger boys go first."

All the parents pitch in to get the kids settled with condiments and bean salad, with napkins and forks. This shared sense of responsibility, that they are all helping to raise each other's children, has created a tight bond. Aimee's heard people complain that the D.C. suburbs are cold and unfriendly, too transient to make any real connections, so she feels extra lucky to have this circle of friends. They seamlessly step into and out of each other's lives—picking up one another's kids at school, for example, or checking if anything is needed before going on a Costco run.

Scott sits next to her, slipping his hand behind her neck and giving it a little rub.

"How's Bethesda's most innovative gardener doing?"

She laughs. That accolade was bestowed upon her company by *Bethesda Magazine* last spring, and he's called her that ever since.

"It's been a long week." She needs to tell him about Noa's psycho-educational report. They usually sit down after dinner on Sundays to go over important things. She can tell him then.

"Then drink up!" Anton says. "How's the old-fashioned?"

Aimee takes a big swig, catching the cherry in her teeth. It's delicious, and as the bourbon does its job, her stress begins to melt.

After dessert, as everyone is getting ready to leave, Aimee hunts for a book on gentle parenting that she found useless but promised to lend Gwen. She remembers leaving it in the laundry room, and heads there to look. A little buzz from the bourbon has her a bit fuzzy but in a good way. Behind her she can hear the chaos of kids and adults, who have all moved from the backyard through the house and into the large foyer. As she grabs the book from a basket of random things, Aimee senses someone behind her and looks up to see Anton standing there.

"Hey." She straightens up and holds out the book. "Gwen asked for this."

He doesn't take it, but he wobbles a little, and Aimee realizes he's drunk. It's not the first time she's seen him this way. Last winter break, when the three families went to Vermont together, Anton drank so many IPAs that he passed out in the snow outside the Alchemist Brewery in Stowe.

"Listen—about before, you know with Lisa . . ." His voice trails off. He witnessed the worst of Lisa's nasty comments about Aimee's parenting.

Aimee waves her hand. She doesn't want Anton getting involved. She can handle Lisa. "I'm fine. No hurt feelings here."

"Yeah, that's not it," he says, irritated, vibrating with nervous energy. He glances behind him as if to make sure no one is listening and turns back.

"Anton?" Gwen calls from the foyer.

"I think Gwen's looking for you." Aimee puts her hand on his arm, gently nudging him in the direction of the front door.

Gwen appears. "There you are! Didn't you hear me calling? We have to go. The boys are really tired." The tension in her voice is evident. Gwen doesn't like to let the ugly parts show. It's all about control with her. Tidy house. Twins in matching clothes. Job at a prestigious PR firm with high-powered clients. The only thing that refuses to bend to her will is Anton.

He's a hot mess.

And tonight, he is messier than usual.

Gwen maneuvers around her husband and gives Aimee a hug.

"Thanks for bringing the potato salad," Aimee says. "Here's the book I told you about. It just ended up making me feel guilty, but maybe you'll get more out of it."

Gwen takes the book and turns to go, but Anton doesn't follow her. Not right away. He leans into Aimee, as if for a goodbye hug, but instead he hovers, his mouth inches from her ear.

Aimee can feel his hot breath on her neck, smell the bourbon. The intimacy of someone else's husband so close unnerves her. She instinctively pulls back, but not before he whispers something in her ear.

"You deserve to know."

2

NOW

Gwen marches her boys to their house next door while Anton trails behind. Inside, the boys kick off their shoes and run upstairs. Anton enters, stepping over the mess on his way to the kitchen while she bends down to pick it up. She misses the mudroom in their old house, outside Boston. She never wanted to leave, but after what Anton did, she had no choice.

"I'll get them in pj's and their teeth brushed," she calls to Anton as she begins to climb the stairs. "When I call you, come up and read a story."

She doesn't wait for a response. She's not supposed to do this. Treat him like an incompetent employee. Bark demands at him. She learned that at marriage counseling. That was where she learned that it was her fault he had cheated. She had *emasculated* him. She had made him feel small.

She has tried in the past few years to be a different kind of wife, and most of the time she succeeds. But sometimes, when he does something to embarrass her, like get drunk in front of their friends and then come home and ignore the mess right in front of him, she can't help herself. She reverts to her old ways.

Gwen is very good at corralling the boys. She's always considered herself one of those moms who has no problems with boundaries and routines. She feels she could handle an entire squad of children and had always wanted that. That had been the plan. Enough kids to fill a baseball team. It was only her and her sister, older by five years, growing up. It was lonely in their large, beautiful house outside Richmond. Her parents had bought her a horse named Shadow, whom she rode throughout high school. But a horse is no substitute for the love of a close-knit family.

But she lost so much blood during delivery of the twins, she almost died. Another pregnancy was too risky. Besides, her marriage might not survive the stress of another child.

Rafi and George share a room even though there are two more spare bedrooms. They are inseparable. No matter how much they fight, they always find their way back to each other. It felt like a gift from the universe when they moved here a year ago and it turned out the family next door had twin boys, too. Another mother who would get it, that feeling of observing an alien culture developing before your own eyes. Sometimes the boys let her in, but other times Gwen is acutely aware of being on the outside. Rafi and George share a special language, a shorthand, with each other. Their large brown eyes contain a multitude of meanings decipherable only by a pair of matching eyes. Sometimes she feels lonely in her own family. She is more than a little jealous that Aimee also has a daughter. All she has to turn to in her loneliness is her dog, Sababa.

The boys climb into their bunk bed, George into the single above and Rafi in the double below, although she knows there's a good chance that in the middle of the night George will find his way into his brother's bed. She often finds them together in the bottom bunk in the morning, a tangle of blankets and limbs.

"Daddy will come read you a story," she says.

"First do tuck-tuck," George says.

"Okay." Gwen begins the ritual of tucking the blankets around his slim body, stepping on the lower bunk so she can reach and press the fabric up against him, saying "tuck" with every push.

As she continues, her mind flits back to Aimee's laundry room. What was going on back there? Was Anton hitting on Aimee? Would he do that? Anger surges through her. Sometimes she feels she could kill him.

"Tuck, tuck, tuck."

The rage burbles up inside her. Things have been off for at least a month, maybe even all the way back to the beginning of the summer. But she doesn't want to believe that it could be happening all over again.

"My turn!" Rafi squeals.

Gwen sits on the bottom bunk and begins the process again.

She longs for someone with whom she can talk this through, but there's no one. She hasn't even told Aimee about her past marital trouble. It's the one thing she hasn't told her since they became friends. All those shared drinks and laughs and late-night talks on vacations. She's told Aimee the whole grueling story of the boys' birth—how close she was to death, the twenty-eight-hour labor, the postpartum depression—but she's never shared anything about Anton. Because Gwen knows that once you tell people that your husband cheated on you, they will never look at him, or you, the same way again.

She knows that from experience.

After the boys have been put to bed, Gwen walks downstairs to the foyer and calls Anton's name. When she hears him approaching from the living room, she turns to walk the other way through the dining room toward the kitchen, so their paths won't cross. It's awful to be so angry that you don't even want to face your husband. She'll wait in the kitchen to confront him, but first he needs to read to the boys. He needs to do something useful around here.

She passes by a pair of antique pewter candlesticks, which Anton gave her for their tenth anniversary, and hesitates. Gwen finds them hideous, tall and heavy, but she keeps them out because they remind her of Anton's promise to recommit to the marriage. In the kitchen she takes a half-empty bottle of wine out of the fridge and fills a coffee mug. Anton's things—his laptop, a few books, notebooks, pens—lie in a haphazard pile on the kitchen counter.

He's supposed to be writing a second book. His first, published years ago when they were newlyweds and Anton had recently graduated from a well-regarded MFA program, was a massive hit. It was the rare book that managed to be both the darling of the literary world and an international bestseller. The movie rights were sold before *The Last Cyclamen* hit the bookstores, although the adaptation seemed stuck in development. The book received fawning coverage from legacy media like NPR and *The New York Times*, but was also a book club favorite.

Those first few years of marriage were shaped by Anton's literary success. Wherever Anton went—to speak at festivals, to sign books—she tagged along as well. She felt so proud, like her longshot bet had paid off. Anton's success was something she could show to her parents, who had never approved of their union. She sent them every positive review, every write-up she could find. When the one millionth copy of the book sold, she made it clear to her parents that their financial support was no longer needed. Anton wasn't just an award-winning author, he was making real money.

The book detailed one summer in the life of a young French-Lebanese woman who has a torrid affair with an older man in the sophisticated world of Beirut before the civil war. The book had an innocence and immediacy that was all the more poignant when you realized the horrific war that was about to break out in Lebanon. At the end, the heroine is forced to flee her childhood home and come to America, where she settles near Boston, leaving behind her lover and her beloved city. It was a love story and a tragedy. The writing was lyrical, the imagery evocative. Anton told everyone it was inspired by his late mother's experience emigrating to America. She had died when he was in college, and his father had retired to France.

The problem was Anton hadn't written a book since.

Oh, he tried. He started many projects, hoping they would turn into his second novel. But he never finished.

She's read some of his attempts over the years—short stories, first chapters. He would be the first to admit he was floundering. The writing was flat, false. Without any real emotion or depth. He hadn't published a thing since *The Last Cyclamen*.

Gwen sips from her mug of wine and flips open one of the several Moleskin notebooks. It's an act of violence to open someone else's journal and read from it without permission. Gwen can't deny the slight pleasure she takes in violating his privacy.

She wore her grief like a cloak, heavy on her shoulders, and like a cloak her grief hid her. Her son's murder had done the seemingly impossible, made a middle-aged woman even less visible to the world. For what is a childless mother? A nonentity. Deep inside the pain, an ember of anger burned red-hot, calling out for vengeance.

She flips ahead in the notebook. The writing's not terrible. A little overwrought. What does Anton know about being a middle-aged woman? Or losing a child? He grew up in the suburbs of Boston, the spoiled only child of two accountants who were determined that their son should never want the way they once had. But whatever. At least he is actually writing something. Sometimes Gwen worried that he did nothing all day long while she was at work and the boys were at school.

She flips ahead until she comes to a scene about a writer named Tony who is in New Orleans at a conference and begins to read. *Tony.* Could Anton be more transparent? Instead of eating dinner with his fellow conference attendees, this Tony is taking a *nubile* young woman, an aspiring writer and fan of his, to one of the nicest restaurants in New Orleans. During this ostensible business dinner of oysters and champagne, the young woman seduces a powerless Tony, who, try as he might, is simply unable to stay faithful to his wife back home.

Gwen feels like she is going to throw up. And not just at the hackneyed plot. She remembers that writing conference, only it was in Tampa, not New Orleans. It was over the summer, and she later caught an expensive charge at a restaurant on their credit card bill. What was the name of that place?

When she had asked Anton about it, he exploded.

"Do you begrudge me a single nice dinner on a work trip?" he spat. "Do I have to ask your permission before I eat a meal?"

But it was more than two hundred dollars, she protested.

"It was with two other writers. They gave me cash so I could get the credit card points. Do you want their names and emails? One's an aging lesbian poet and the other a sci-fi nerd at the same imprint as me."

Gwen dropped it, ashamed of who she had become—a snoop, a nag, jealous, insecure. Of course he was entitled to a meal with colleagues.

Rage brews in her now. She reads a bit more—there is no aging lesbian or sci-fi nerd in these pages. It's the story of a brilliant writer, misunderstood by his cold, heckling wife, redeemed only by the forbidden love of another woman.

The sex in the following scene is intense, the details too vivid even for Anton to have made up. His first book was nothing like this. That language was poetic, the imagery dreamlike and bittersweet. This reads like soft porn.

He traced his finger across the tattoo of a barbed wire heart centered on the left cheek of her luscious ass.

Gwen screams, a half howl, so guttural and raw she can feel it in her chest. She throws the notebook onto the floor. Then, with the sweep of her arm, she knocks everything of Anton's off the counter.

Bastard. So he *was* sleeping with someone at that conference.

Thump, thump. Anton's footsteps on the stairs are clumsy and uneven, as if he is determined to broadcast his drunkenness. Her heart galloping in her chest, Gwen rushes to gather up his notebooks and papers and put them back on the counter the way she found them. She's not ready to confront him, not until she's figured out what all this means. In the seconds before he enters the kitchen, she composes herself, stuffing her emotions deep down into the darkest part of her. She'll unpack them and examine them later when she has both time and privacy.

"I better take Sababa for a walk," Anton says as soon as he walks into the kitchen. He steps out the back door, which leads to the side yard that abuts Scott and Aimee's property. There's a gate that will take him out to the street, where he can head deeper into the neighborhood or turn left toward a footpath that leads into downtown Bethesda. Gwen suspects that Anton sometimes "walks" the dog into town to go to a vape shop, or even get a drink.

Gwen follows him out onto the back patio, clutching her coffee mug of wine. "You don't have to walk him." Her voice quivers with suppressed rage. She wonders how Anton can not sense the fury emanating off her. "He got plenty of exercise running around with the kids tonight."

"I don't mind."

"What were you whispering to Aimee? Before we left?"

"What?" He stops and turns, the moonlight catching his face. He's more handsome now than when she first met him. Back then he was a skinny boy, dark half-moons under his eyes giving him the moody look of a post-war existentialist. He's filled out now, and his close-cropped beard has a few streaks of silver. He looks like a man.

"What did you say to her? She looked weirded out."

"Nothing." The catch in his throat, a half laugh, is his tell. It's the same half laugh she heard when she asked him three years ago if he was cheating.

"Please." She shuts her eyes for a second. Inside she is roiling, but she remembers how it went three years ago when she confronted him. He denied everything. He made her feel like she was crazy. She became what he said she was—hysterical, unreasonable, paranoid. Only months later, when she had irrefutable evidence, did he come clean and admit it. But the damage had

been done. Those months of denial had wrung out her soul like
a wet rag.

This time she will stay calm. If she accuses him, he'll get defensive and there will be a fight. She won't get answers and that's
what she wants. "Just tell me, Anton. I know you. I know when
something is up."

To her surprise, he doesn't deny it. He drops Sababa's leash.
He brings his hands up to his face.

"I fucked up, Gwen," he says. "I fucked up big-time."

3

THE BEGINNING OF LAST SUMMER

Lisa took one look at this new Gwen woman and realized in her gut that things were about to change, and not for the better.

For the past two years it had been just Lisa and Marcus, Aimee and Scott—#SLAM. As in, *Let's have some SLAM time this weekend.* Or in the captions beneath the many posts on Instagram and Facebook, #SLAM #SlammingGoodTime.

She and Marcus had moved into the East Bethesda neighborhood toward the end of the pandemic. She had wanted to do it sooner, but Marcus was reluctant to leave their row house on Capitol Hill, so close to where he worked as a lobbyist on K Street, and a short drive from where his mom still lived in Calvert Hills. But for Lisa, living in those cramped quarters had become unbearable, no matter how cute the nineteenth-century molding was. The combination office-slash-living room-slash-family room just wasn't working. During the pandemic, when Kai was home trying to attend first-grade class online and Marcus was taking calls, Lisa found it increasingly difficult to run her life-coaching business in the crowded house. The spirit of her coaching business was summed up in her motto, written across the top of her website in pink script: *I am allowed to do what's best for me, even if it upsets others.*

So, she took her own advice and insisted they decamp for the suburbs. Bethesda offered the promise of a backyard for Kai to play in and what seemed like an endless number of rooms to hide out in, and all within walking distance of downtown Bethesda and the metro. Even if the commute was farther for Marcus, the public schools were great. Meeting Aimee and Scott had validated that this was the right move. Not only would Kai flourish, but Lisa could also start over socially. She had few friends on the Hill, and she felt lucky to have hit it off with Aimee.

But now the delicate ecology of the cul-de-sac was being threatened. She could see it in Aimee's face, the way it lit up when Gwen waltzed through the gate with her two little boys in tow. Lisa had to stifle a snort. Gwen with her blond hair in a low bun, in white linen pants and a linen tank that showed off her tan. What kind of woman wore white linen to a backyard barbecue? What mom of twins even *owned* white linen? And the two boys in their matching clothes. It was all so desperate, so inauthentic. As if she were the star of her own reality TV show.

Aimee, who ran her own landscaping business and, as hard as she tried, never seemed able to scrub all the dirt from her hands, would see right through this woman's phoniness, wouldn't she?

Aimee was her best friend. Her FP—favorite person. After years of struggling to befriend women, Lisa finally had found someone worthy of her intense loyalty. Aimee was *good*. And she had never felt so secure in a friendship before. Ever since college—even before that, if she was being honest with herself— female friendship had eluded her. She knew how to attract guys. That started early. By seventh grade she had a full C cup and her first boyfriend. Yet connecting with girls her age did not come naturally. She might make a friend, but then there would be some blowup that left her baffled and hurt and alone. Her freshman roommate, Ruth, was the most extreme example of this, but there had been other, less-dramatic incidents.

But Aimee was different. Aimee didn't just like Lisa, Aimee needed her. A bit frazzled and overwhelmed by work and kids, Aimee valued loyalty and reliability above all else, above cleverness, or wit, or a fancy wardrobe. And Lisa could provide that reliability. She made sure of that. She loved to be there to scoop the kids up from school if Aimee was delayed at work, or to offer to grab something at Whole Foods while she was shopping. She had made herself indispensable to Aimee, and in return Aimee had offered a kind of automated friendship. They sat next to each other at school events, they trick-or-treated together. She would never be alone again, thanks to Aimee.

But on this Friday night, prime #SLAM time was being interrupted by this Gwen woman and her twin boys, who just showed up in Aimee's backyard.

The way Aimee beamed at the woman, Lisa knew she was fucked.

"Gwen! I'm so glad you could come." Aimee took the bowl Gwen was carrying and put it on the table. "This looks amazing!"

Lisa peered inside the bowl. A caprese salad, the kind a child could throw together with a basket of cherry tomatoes and a container of mozzarella balls. "And you must be Anton!" Lisa looked up to see an unsmiling man with a salt-and-pepper goatee standing there holding a four-pack of beer in one hand while his other was jammed into his pocket. Aimee turned to Lisa. "Anton and Gwen, this is my friend Lisa. She lives two houses down, the one with the orange door. And that's Marcus, her husband, next to Scott over there."

Friend? Not best friend. Not even dear or close. Just friend. Lisa seethed. She held out her hand. "So exciting."

"They have twins also! The same year as Benji and Max." Aimee gestured toward her two boys huddled over some rocks at the edge of the yard.

"Isn't that just nuts!" Gwen said and held out her hand. Lisa took it. How could she not?

Anton put down the four-pack of craft beer. Scott came over and started oohing and ahhing, and soon Marcus joined them, the three of them back-slapping and debating the merits of different types of IPAs. Such simpletons. All it took was good beer.

Lisa turned her attention to Gwen and Aimee. It was like watching the scene in a movie when the main characters meet and fall in love. They were standing a foot apart, beaming at each other and going on about their twins. *Twins, twins, twins.* As if giving birth to twins gave them some magical connection. Lisa kept her smile pinned to her face, watching in real time as she shrank smaller and smaller in Aimee's universe.

An anguish bloomed within her—she was being replaced. Aimee would leave her. Fade her out. She was already nervous that Kai starting middle school this fall would weaken one of the bonds between her and Aimee. When the kids were little, the two-year difference, and the fact that Noa was a girl and Kai a boy, hadn't mattered at all. They were happy to hang out together and go to the zoo or the park, or watch animated movies. But that had changed last year. Kai had started making comments and pushing back when asked to socialize with Noa. It would only get worse once he was in middle school. Would Aimee pivot away from her?

No. She wouldn't do that to Lisa. And Lisa wouldn't allow it to happen, not again. She wouldn't make the same mistakes of her freshman year all over again. She had learned a lot since then.

Now, she knew that fighting too hard for a friendship could actually cause you to lose it. It was like that book *Of Mice and Men*, the way that big guy petted the puppy too hard and killed it accidentally. She had held on to Ruth's friendship too tightly and squeezed it to death. She had learned that you had to be subtle. Work back channels. Not be obvious. Lisa plastered a huge smile on her face.

"Well, welcome to the neighborhood," Lisa said. "You're going to love it here."

4

NOW

Scott is in with the twins while Aimee goes into Noa's room. They used to rotate, switch nights, but in the past few months, without either saying it out loud, it has become clear that Noa can't go to sleep without Aimee.

Not won't, but can't.

Aimee begins by checking for nightmares in the closet, then spritzes lavender-scented water under the bed to get rid of monsters, and finishes by reciting a short prayer her mother used to say to her as a child.

If Aimee isn't home, or is busy, Noa will simply refuse to turn off the light and go to sleep until she comes and performs these rituals. The psychologist they visited said it wasn't unusual, but a sign of anxiety.

But what is their little girl anxious about?

Noa pulls the covers up to her chin, so just her little face sticks out, as Aimee finishes the prayer. "May the angel Michael be at your right, and the angel Gabriel be at your left." Here she slides her hand under Noa's pillow. "And in front of you the angel Uriel, and behind you the angel Raphael—" She stops short, pulling something hard from beneath the pillow.

"What's this?" She examines the object. It's a pen, black and heavy, not cheap, with the words *Le Cannu* written in gold. A heavy sensation settles on her heart. "Where is this from?"

"I found it."

Aimee bites her lip. This isn't the first time something of unknown provenance has shown up in Noa's possession. "Honey, this is a really nice pen." She turns it over in her hand. There's no address or phone number. Whatever Le Cannu is, it's fancy. "Where exactly did you find this?"

"At Lisa's." The words emerge as barely a whisper.

"Lisa's, huh? You found it there?"

"She has so many pens."

Aimee smiles and makes a show of examining the pen more closely. She weighs it in her hand. "It's a cool pen, all right. But that doesn't make it okay to take it. Remember how we talked about this? You know we're going to have to give it back to her."

Noa's eyes fill with tears. "No, Mommy, don't make me." Noa rolls over and buries her head in the pillow.

Aimee rubs her daughter's back. "Shhh. It'll be fine. Lisa is very understanding."

She hopes this is true. It's just a pen, after all. But Lisa showed tonight how judgmental she can be. Kai seems like the easiest kid in the world. Last year, in fifth grade, he won the Community of Caring award. He probably never stole a pen in his life. So much of parenting was turning out to be luck.

Aimee slips the pen into her back pocket. "Don't cry, honey. It's going to be okay. People make mistakes, but when they do, they have to acknowledge them and make it right." But Noa won't turn around and look at her. Instead, she lets out a little growl. She's embarrassed, Aimee thinks. She's learned that pushing a topic of conversation when Noa needs to be alone usually leads to a meltdown.

Aimee stands up quietly, turns out the light, and leaves without a kiss or hug. Noa is so unlike her boys. Neither can stand it if Aimee is even a little annoyed with them. Neither can go to sleep without hugs and kisses. But Noa is stubborn.

As she walks to her sons' room to kiss them goodnight, she knows it's not the pen that's bothering her, or even Lisa's judgment. It's that damn report. It's the fear that something is wrong with Noa, that she's wired in such a way that will make life hard. And Aimee doesn't know if she is the right person to shepherd her through. There is Scott, of course, who is endlessly patient. But losing her mother at such a young age seared into Aimee's soul the desire—no, the *need*—to be there for her kids.

After kissing both boys goodnight, Aimee heads downstairs. She ducks her head into the living room, where Scott holds up a finger. He's on a call, probably with one of his investors in Hawaii. He has been working on an algorithm-based software that can automate insulin dosing for diabetics and has partners around the globe. His work week is scattershot throughout every day, including weekends—a few hours here, a few hours there.

Aimee steps out onto the back patio to grab a few dishes that have been left behind from dinner. She is gathering them up when the sound of raised voices startles her. She freezes, realizing that she can hear Gwen and Anton arguing. They are close, separated from her by a tall hedge of euonymus. She has always wanted to remove the shrubs, not just because they are prone to a white powdery mildew, but because as the owner of a landscaping business whose focus is native plants, she feels a little guilty about them. Who is she to persuade clients to switch out their non-native plants and trees for native ones if she can't be bothered to do it herself? The plan is to replace them with American hollies—evergreen, with berries that will be eaten by more than eighteen species of birds. But the thought of ripping out the eight-foot shrubs is daunting. And tonight, Aimee is grateful for their cover.

Anton's and Gwen's voices are strident but their words unintelligible. It's always embarrassing to Aimee to witness other couples fighting. Overhearing Anton and Gwen argue makes her realize how little she knows about what really goes on inside her friends' marriage. Or any couple's, for that matter. And it makes her grateful for what she has with Scott. They rarely argue and have never had a big blowout. He's never yelled at her or called her names. Nothing has ever been thrown in the heat of anger. Aimee has never liked conflict, and she's happy to be in a marriage free of one. Not that they don't squabble or get on each other's nerves, but nothing like what she is overhearing now. She wonders if Gwen and Anton are arguing about Anton's behavior, how drunk he got this evening. Aimee recalls that cryptic comment: *you deserve to know.*

She starts to head back inside but stops at the door when Gwen's voice, angry and shrill, cuts through the night air. Her words are as clear as the stars in the night sky.

"I'm not going to let you ruin my life, Anton."

Aimee tiptoes back into her house, afraid to make any sound that might reveal her presence. Once inside, she shuts the door and locks it, as if slipping the bolt will keep the marital discord next door from seeping into her home. She stands there shaking. She has never heard Gwen speak like that. She could be sharp, sarcastic, but there was real rage in her voice just now.

Ruin her life? What could she have meant by that?

A part of her wants to reach out to Gwen, ask her if she is all right. Her hand hovers over her cell phone. But what could she text? She begins typing.

Everything all right?

She deletes it. It implies that something might be wrong. It would reveal that she witnessed their fight. It might embarrass Gwen. *It's really none of my business*, Aimee thinks. Some couples fight, don't they? And she doesn't want to appear smug, as if she and Scott were perfect.

If Gwen wanted her to know something, or if she needed support, she would reach out.

Wouldn't she?

Benji appears, rubbing his eyes. "Didn't you hear me calling? I want a glass of water."

"Oh, sweetie." She gets a glass down and fills it. "Let's get you back to bed." She walks him upstairs, past Scott, who is still on his call. After she resettles Benji, she gets herself ready for sleep.

Tomorrow she will talk to Gwen, feel her out, make it clear that her friend can tell her anything.

They are more than neighbors.

More than mommy-friends who happen to have kids at the same school.

They are real friends. Found family.

*   *   *

Aimee awakens to the gleeful chaos that is Saturday morning in her house.

From below she can hear the twins racing through the house and yelling, not out of distress, but because they are seven and probably hopped up on maple syrup and orange juice. She loves it. As an only, her own childhood was quiet. Even more so after her mother died. Her father quickly remarried, and had three boys with her stepmother, Deb, but Aimee was away at college by then.

In the kitchen, she pours a big mug of coffee and clears off some of the Lego Ninjago figurines on the island.

"You excited for your day of rest and relaxation?" she asks Scott. "Tim is expecting me at eleven. We're installing a row of blueberry bushes over at that house in Glen Echo."

Scott flashes a smile. "I have bad news."

"No, do not tell me." She shakes her head and puts down the mug. "I'm not listening—"

He holds up his hand. "I have to go in to work."

"Scott, no." Her perfectly planned-out weekend schedule blown to bits. "You told me you'd be available today to watch the kids."

"Can you reschedule?"

"I can't. Those bushes need to get into the ground today."

"But you don't have to be there for that, do you? Tim can do that, right?"

Technically, he's right. Tim Romero, her number two, can oversee any installation. She trusts him implicitly. But Aimee likes to be there. Issues come up. It's her name on the company and on the side of her truck—Stern Landscaping. "That's not the point. We had an arrangement."

"Lisa or Gwen can watch the kids, right?"

"All three?"

"I don't need to be watched," Noa says, running into the kitchen. "I can go see the kittens."

"Kittens?" Scott frowns.

"I told you, a client of mine. Has cats?"

"Right, right." He nods, but Aimee can tell it doesn't ring any bells. He's been so preoccupied with work recently that not much she's said has gotten through. She reminds herself that his work is about helping people with diabetes live better lives. His own mother died from complications of the disease his senior year in high school, and the success of this software launch is personal. "Seeing the kittens sounds like a great plan to me."

"Yay!" Noa jumps up and down, convinced she has won.

"Right, but . . ." *But it's not a plan*, Aimee thinks. It's her scrambling to find childcare, leaning on her friends, her clients, while Scott has not offered any solutions. "I don't love this. Having to call up people and ask them to watch my kids. Rearrange my day."

"But that's what friends are for, right?" he asks.

Aimee narrows her eyes, but doesn't respond.

"Look, I'll reach out to Gwen," he says. "Tell her it's my fault. Would that make it better?"

"A little." She watches him take out his phone and send a quick text.

"Done," he says. "See? That wasn't so hard."

After breakfast, Aimee and Scott get the kids dressed and ready to head out. She's halfway out the door when she pauses. "Did you hear back from Gwen? She knows we're coming, right?"

Scott looks at his phone. "Actually, she didn't respond."

Aimee hesitates a moment. Gwen is one of those people who always texts back immediately. She *could* just pop in. *Surprise!* Gwen is a close enough friend that she will roll with it. If the situation were reversed, Aimee would happily take George and Rafi.

Still, as she heads down her walkway, she feels uncomfortable in a way she can't quite articulate. When she notices a car parked outside Gwen's, the feeling intensifies. She knows every car on this cul-de-sac, and this dark, late-model sedan does not belong here. Something is up. She walks up to Gwen's front door and rings.

"I don't want to stay with all the boys," Noa says, appearing at her side. "It's too loud. I hate it." She puts her hands over her ears.

"You can listen to music. You can use Gwen's iPad."

"I don't want the iPad. I want to be with the kittens. I want to feed them with the bottle."

Aimee's heart sinks; she feels like a terrible mother. The kind that works on Saturdays and tries to talk her kid into using a screen instead of doing something healthy like playing with animals. If only Scott hadn't changed the plans this morning. The twins run around the side of the house and unlatch the gate, letting themselves into the backyard.

"Go with your brothers," Aimee tell Noa, who glares at her in response, her lower lip trembling ever so slightly. For a millisecond, Aimee fears her daughter might collapse into one of her epic tantrums. But then Noa runs down the path, after her brothers. Aimee watches until she disappears into the backyard and then looks back at the street, where the sedan is parked. She counts four antennas—is it an unmarked police car?

She thinks of the fight she overheard last night.

The anger, the yelling—*I'm not going to let you ruin my life.*

She shakes the thought away as footsteps inside the house grow closer. This is Gwen and Anton. They're lovely people. Flawed, yes, but fundamentally good. She's been on vacation with them twice now—once in Vermont at Gwen's parents' place and over the summer at the Outer Banks. They're not the type of people who get visits from the police.

The door opens. Gwen's eyes are red-rimmed and moist, and she is holding a tissue to her nose.

"Honey, what is it?" Aimee asks. "What's wrong?"

"It's Anton. He's dead."

5

Gwen sits curled up, her knees pulled to her chest, across from a man in a maroon dress shirt and black tie. His thick black hair is pulled off his face, reminiscent of an old-time crooner, the kind her grandparents listened to on their record player.

According to the card he gave her, he's Detective Jay Salazar from the Montgomery County Police Department. And she guesses that he's dressed in a tie and jacket because he's been tasked with breaking the bad news to her.

Anton's body was found in an alley in downtown Bethesda. He'd been hit by a car.

"Let me ask you . . ." he starts, but Gwen holds up a finger to pause him while Aimee walks through the living room like the Pied Piper, followed by all five kids.

Aimee stops at the door. "I'm going to take everyone over to Lisa's, and then I'll be right back."

Gwen nods, waving goodbye to George and Rafi, who are jostling each other and seem oblivious to this strange man in a suit in their living room. They haven't noticed that Anton was not here when they woke up. But she will have to tell them what's happened at some point. The thought seizes her, and she starts to tremble. This will crush her sweet boys. How could it not? Their lives will forever be divided into two—before their father died, and after. The enormity of it all looms in her imagination. Gwen chokes back a small sob.

"Can I get you something?" the detective asks. "Water? Tissue?"

Shaken from her thoughts, Gwen looks up at the man in front

of her. His dark eyes are fixed on her, as if he can see straight into her thoughts. Discomfited, she looks away, her gaze settling on the chevron pattern of the rug under the coffee table. "No, no thank you. I just don't want them to hear any of this. I want to tell them later. I want them to have one last morning of a normal childhood, before everything changes."

"Of course, I think that's smart. You're lucky to have such good neighbors."

"Lucky," Gwen repeats. She feels anything but lucky right now.

"Poor choice of words. I'm sorry, Mrs. Khoury."

Gwen hugs her knees tighter. *Mrs. Khoury.* She wills herself to stay focused, but she can feel her mind pulling into itself, going into protective mode. A trick she learned as a child when her parents would rage at each other, or at her. A kind of dissociation that allowed her to endure what was happening without letting any of it in. It did get in, though. And years of therapy have taught her that the coping skills of childhood can sabotage you as an adult. She blinks twice and tries to focus on the detective's black tie, made of some kind of fabric that catches the light streaming through the living room window. "What were you saying? I'm sorry, where was Anton found?"

"In an alley next to a bar on Wisconsin Avenue. Villain & Saint. Are you familiar with that establishment?"

Gwen nods. "Sure. It's kind of our local hangout." The dive bar is an anomaly in Bethesda, dark and smelling of beer, complete with sticky floors and a bathroom that screams *cooties*. A stark contrast to the nearby rooftop bars with their twenty-dollar mixed drinks, offering Instagram-perfect views. "One of the dads at our boys' school is in a cover band called the Trophy Husbands, and sometimes they play there. So, yeah. We've been. Was Anton there last night?"

"We're not sure if he ever went inside the bar or not," Salazar says. "Did he mention heading there?"

"No." A vivid image of Anton stumbling down the alley between the Bethesda Farm Women's Market and the bar springs to her mind. "So, someone hit him with their car in the alley? Was it a hit-and-run?"

The detective shifts in his seat. "It looks like he was hit deliberately."

She tries to swallow, but her throat refuses. "How can you tell that?"

The detective shakes his head. "I'm not at liberty to go into the details, but he was struck more than once. I know this is incredibly upsetting to hear, but your husband's death is being investigated as a homicide."

"Homicide." Gwen repeats the word, a numbness settling on her. "You mean he was murdered."

Gwen grabs a throw pillow and squeezes it to her chest. *This can't be real.* She rocks back and forth, trying to stay here in this room, in this moment, when every fiber of her is screaming for escape.

The detective flips open a small notebook. "Do you have any idea what he might have been doing in that alley last night? Was he headed to the bar?"

"Umm, I don't know." She looks up at him, wondering how he can do this, sit in people's living rooms and talk about death so calmly. *Focus*, Gwen tells herself. "Maybe he went there to get a drink. I went to bed right after the kids did."

"Did he do that often? Head out to drink after you and the kids have gone to bed?"

Gwen detects a hint of judgment in the man's voice. She glances at his hand, at the gold band on his ring finger. He's married. Does he cheat on his wife? Lie to her? Do they get into knock-down, drag-out fights? Or is he one of those insufferable types who calls his spouse his best friend and who never goes to bed mad?

"Sometimes," Gwen says. "Like I said, there's a band we like that plays there. Anton likes live music." She's repeating herself. And it's not even true. Why did she say that? She was the one who dragged him out to see the Trophy Husbands last fall. A large group of parents from the school went. But Anton sulked in the corner, nursing a drink while she, Aimee, Lisa, and some other moms danced to covers of the Police and Matchbox Twenty.

"Was that band playing last night?"

"I don't think so," she says. "But I'm not sure."

"We can check on that. Might he have been meeting someone?"

"No. I mean, not that I know of. I didn't even know he had gone out." Her first real lie. She almost expects the detective's head to pop up, as if he might be a human lie detector. But he keeps scribbling in his pad.

"Your husband taught creative writing at American University. Could he have been meeting a student? Or another faculty member?"

Gwen is startled that Salazar knows about Anton's job. But why should she be? A quick online search of Anton Khoury brings up his book and his position at the university. It might have been the first thing the detective did when they found his body and his ID. Isn't that what everyone does when they meet someone? Google them. Why would the police be any different? She wonders what else they could have gleaned from their online search.

"I doubt it."

"And everything was all right at work, no run-ins? No disgruntled students?"

Gwen shakes her head. "No. His students love him. And he gets along with everyone at work."

"What about money?" Salazar looks around the room, taking in the minimalist but expensive décor. He can't know they are sitting on a modular sofa that costs fifteen thousand dollars. She had bought it when Anton was at the height of his fame.

Gwen hadn't been careful about money when they were flush. She never imagined that they might run out.

"What about it?"

"Writing isn't exactly lucrative, is it, Mrs. Khoury?"

"Not for most writers, but my husband wasn't most writers. His first book was a massive hit." She knows she sounds defensive, and is surprised that a part of her is still invested in everyone seeing Anton as a success. She's not willing to tell him that there had been no second massive hit, that they had run out of money and were now relying on her parents for their car and mortgage payments.

"I see."

"It's sold more than two million copies worldwide. *The Last Cyclamen.* That's the title."

"Never heard of it." Salazar shakes his head. "But I'm not much of a reader, to be honest. I think the last book I read was in high school. What about you? Do you work?"

"Part-time. At Blue Dot Public Relations in Georgetown." Gwen unfolds her legs and stretches them out. She doesn't like this topic. When she and Anton were first dating, she worked at a public relations firm in New York City. Her parents had subsidized her; the pay was abysmal. She hoped to one day make partner, maybe even open her own shop, but marriage and motherhood derailed those plans. She continued working, doing PR in Boston, but when they moved to D.C. she had to take what she could get, part-time work, freelance. She had finally scored an entry-level position at a boutique PR firm in Georgetown, mostly writing press releases for nonfiction authors and public speakers. It had been a major step down for her.

"So, money was not an issue?"

Gwen chews the inside of her mouth, remembering all those fights about Anton's spending. It's how she discovered he was cheating three years ago—an unknown charge on the credit card bill during a weekend when she was out of town with the kids, visiting her parents in Virginia. When she looked into it, it turned out to be for a couple's massage at a spa at a luxury hotel in Boston. Taking control of the finances was one of the conditions Gwen insisted on if he wanted her to stay. "No, money was not an issue."

"Did he like to gamble?"

"Gamble?" The word comes out shrill. "Of course not. Why would you even ask that?"

The detective's eyebrow shoots up. "These are standard questions. No offense intended."

Aimee lets herself in the front door, looking sheepish. Gwen speaks to her, past the detective. "The boys all set?"

"They're all at Lisa's," Aimee says. "It's no problem."

The detective stands. "Again, Mrs. Khoury, I am very sorry for your loss." He writes something on a piece of paper. "If you call this number, you can arrange a time to view your husband's body and collect his things. I'll be in touch."

He walks to the door and Aimee opens it for him. Once he is gone, Aimee shuts it and rushes over. Gwen stands and lets Aimee embrace her. "Oh my God, Gwen, this is so awful."

Gwen pulls back. "I'm in shock."

"What happened?"

"He was hit by a car, last night, in the alley next to Villain & Saint. They think it was intentional."

"You mean murder? Who would want to kill Anton?"

Gwen's mind goes blank. She can't do this. Not right now. "I'm sorry, Aimee. I've got to go. I have to call people." She holds up the piece of paper the detective gave her like some kind of morbid hall pass.

"That's fine. I should probably make an appearance at work, anyway," Aimee says and then pauses. "Unless you want me to cancel and stay with you?"

"No. Don't. I appreciate it, but I have so much to do."

"Just text me if you change your mind and want company.

Lisa will watch the kids and when I come back, I'll handle dinner."

Together they walk toward the front door. Aimee stops and frowns. "I think I stepped on something." She bends down and pulls something from her shoe.

"Don't worry about it," Gwen says. But it's too late. Aimee straightens up, holding a ceramic shard. Gwen was so sure she had cleaned everything up last night.

"Is that blood?" Aimee asks, holding the shard up to the light.

Gwen lets out a halfhearted laugh. "I broke a coffee cup in the sink the other day. I must have cut myself. Here, give it to me, I'll throw it away." She holds out her hand and watches Aimee drop the jagged piece into her palm.

"Thank you for everything." She embraces Aimee before her friend can speak, and then just as quickly opens the front door.

As she watches Aimee leave, she curses herself for that stupid lie. If she broke the cup in the sink, how did the shard get on the living room floor? She just prays Aimee didn't notice. The last thing she needs is for her friend to start prying.

6

NOW

"What is going on?" Lisa answers her door, clutching an immense mint-green water bottle with a straw sticking out. "Is everyone okay?"

Aimee steps inside the foyer and looks around. "Where are the kids?"

"Everyone's out back. Now tell me."

"Even Noa?"

"Even Noa. What is going on, Aimee? I'm dying here."

"We're not sharing this news with any of the kids yet, okay?" Aimee asks. "Gwen's going to want to tell her boys, and I'd like to break it to my kids myself later. Let them have fun today."

"What news? What's happened?"

"It's Anton. There's no easy way to say this, but he's dead. His body was found early this morning in an alley in Bethesda."

Lisa's mouth opens in disbelief.

"The police think he was hit with a car," Aimee says. "But they're not sure of anything yet."

"Like a drunk driver?"

"Maybe. They don't know much. But Gwen said the police called it a murder."

"A murder? That's insane. Are you saying that someone hit him with their car on purpose?" Lisa shakes her head. "I can't believe that. Who would do such a thing?"

"I don't know, but Anton is gone. And now we have to focus on George and Rafi and Gwen. Those poor little boys."

"Do they know? They didn't seem upset."

Aimee shakes her head, annoyed. "No. I told you, none of the kids know yet, so please don't say anything."

"You can count on me," Lisa says. "Poor Gwen. How is she holding up?"

"As good as can be expected, which is not great. I think she's in shock. I'm sure the reality will hit her later. We're going to need to be there for her."

"What can we do? My heart breaks for George and Rafi. Can you imagine?"

"I think just pitching in, like watching the kids today, is a huge help. I have to go to work for a few hours, but I'll pick up pizza on the way home. Do you mind keeping the kids until then? Scott had work, too. Otherwise I wouldn't ask."

"Don't give it a second thought. I'm here for you, Aimee. And for Gwen, and for those sweet little boys. Whatever I can do to help. Should I put something on the Listserv?"

Aimee flinches. "No. Like I said, no one knows about this yet. I know it will end up on the news and on the Listserv soon enough but I think we should all try to keep this quiet until Gwen has a chance to break the news to the kids. We don't want them hearing it from some random neighbor. So keep the TV off, okay? No news."

Noa emerges from the shadows of the darkened dining room. "I don't want to stay here. I want to go to Cathy's."

"Noa, honey, I didn't see you there."

"I want to see the kittens."

"Don't you want to stay here with your brothers?" Lisa asks in a singsong voice, bending forward, hands on her knees. "We can do all sorts of fun things."

Noa scowls. Aimee knows that Lisa is just trying to help, but Noa hates when adults talk to her in sugary voices. She touches Lisa's arm. "Give me a minute, okay?"

"Sure." Lisa looks hesitant. For a moment Aimee fears Lisa

is going to start in again on her parenting. On more than one occasion she has implied that Aimee was coddling Noa, almost blaming her for the child's social anxiety. She'd even begun forwarding Apple News stories about anxious kids, which Aimee had taken to immediately deleting. She is grateful when Lisa heads to the back of the house. She's not in the mood for sanctimommy nonsense.

"It's okay with Cathy if I come."

"And how do you know that?" Aimee asks. Noa pulls out a phone that Aimee recognizes as her own. "You have my phone?"

"I took it from your pocket when we were at Gwen's." Her voice is full of regret, but it lasts all of two seconds before she perks up. "But Cathy said I could come. She said any time before four o'clock was fine."

Aimee plucks the phone from her daughter's hand. "What did I tell you about taking my phone without asking?"

"But you were busy," she wheedles.

"You shouldn't take my phone, Noa."

"Sorry." Noa lowers her head.

Aimee looks at her messages and sure enough, there's a back-and-forth with Cathy. She inhales sharply.

"Noa Helen Crowder, you cannot do that. Ever." Aimee's tone is angrier than she intends. Her daughter recoils.

"But you said you would ask her," Noa says, quiet but determined.

"No, I didn't say that. And that still doesn't give you the right to text people on my phone."

"Yes, you did," Noa says with the confidence of the righteous. "You said so. You said, *I'll ask her.* You said it this morning in the kitchen."

Did she? Aimee can't remember. Maybe she did say that, just to get Noa to stop badgering her. This morning in the kitchen seems a world away. A chaotic, normal world where the biggest problems were childcare, not murdered husbands and fatherless children.

"Anyway," Noa says. "She doesn't mind. She said so."

How can she explain to her daughter that even when people say they don't mind, they might actually mind? A lot. Noa can be so literal. *Literal. Rigid.* Those were some of the words that Noa's teacher had used to describe her.

The youngest of her three half brothers was the same way as a child, and it had befuddled her family until he was diagnosed with being on the autism spectrum. The diagnosis helped him get services at school and opened up new ways for her dad and Deb to support him, but it didn't change him. He is in his thirties now and still lives at home, in a tiny house they built for him on the back of their property. He works in the family nursery business, in the billing department, and by all accounts is excellent at what he does. But he isn't independent by any means. Life's responsibilities, what some people call *adulting*, just elude him. Her dad and stepmom pay his utilities, shop for his food, and send in a cleaner once a week to make sure things haven't gotten too bad.

Is that what is in store for Noa?

Aimee shakes the thought from her head. She's getting ahead of herself. She hasn't read the report yet. Lots of kids are literal or have impulse issues, and they grow up to live full, independent lives. The news of Anton's death is affecting her, scaring her. Something so terrible and violent happening in such a safe place has shattered her sense of security. The sound of boys screeching from the kitchen echoes through the house and Noa flinches. She has always been sensitive to loud noises and bright lights. Spending the day here with four boys and with Lisa, who would just tell her to get over it, would be brutal for her. Cathy was a former teacher. She was good with kids. Her house was serene, set on several acres.

"Fine, get in the truck. You can go to Cathy's."

"Really?" Noa runs outside toward the truck without waiting for a response. Aimee calls out to Lisa that she is taking off, and that Noa is coming with her. She doesn't stick around to hear what Lisa has to say. Once outside, she watches Noa climb in on the passenger side. She is halfway to the truck when someone calls out to her. She turns to see the detective emerging from the sedan parked in front of Gwen's.

"Hey, hold on a minute!" He waves at her, and she stops, only a few feet from her truck.

"Can I help you?" She is alarmed that he was clearly waiting for her.

The detective looks past her at Noa. "Sorry, I don't mean to hold you and your daughter up, Ms. Stern, but I meant to ask you this earlier. We'll be canvasing the neighbors to see if anyone has security footage of last night. You know, Ring cameras, that sort of thing. Trying to figure out exactly when Mr. Khoury might have left the neighborhood. Do you have a camera at your house?"

Aimee nods. "We have a doorbell camera."

"Great. Is it accessible from your phone?"

"You want me to look now?" She glances over at Noa in the front seat.

"If you don't mind," the detective says. "I'm interested in nine o'clock on."

Aimee doesn't feel she has a choice. She pulls up the app on her phone and then angles the device so the detective can see it. "It records any motion detected," Aimee says, feeling vulnerable, as if she is about to expose some terrible secret about herself. She clicks on the video from the night before and starts it at nine.

The two of them watch a man Aimee does not recognize walk up the street with a small dog, whom he allows to come up onto their lawn and take a dump.

"That's not right," the detective says.

The video skips ahead, showing a man turn up their front path, a little unsteady on his feet. He keeps touching the side of his head. Aimee swallows a gasp. "That's Anton," she says. He steps closer to the front door and turns slightly, revealing a bloody gash across his forehead.

A moment later, Scott steps out onto the front stoop. His coat is on, and he pulls the door behind him. Together the two of them head back down the path and disappear out of the camera frame, somewhere on the darkened street.

Then, time-stamped an hour later, the video picks up again with Scott returning. Alone. Aimee is stunned, but she tries to keep the surprise out of her face. Her gut tells her she needs to play it cool. Showing this video to the detective may have been a mistake, but she won't make it worse.

"Did you know that Anton had come to your house last night?" the detective asks, straightening up.

Aimee shakes her head. "No. I must have been asleep by then."

"Was that your husband who left with him?"

"Yes."

"Any idea where they went?"

Aimee jostles the keys in her hand. "I'm sorry, no. Look, I have to drop my daughter somewhere, and then be at work."

"That's fine." He holds his hands up and smiles. "Is your husband at home now?"

"He had to go into work."

"No problem, I can stop by later. In the meantime, mind emailing that video to me?" He pulls out a card and passes it to her. "My email is in the corner."

"Sure." She takes the card.

"Would you mind doing it now?" His tone is gentle, but she gets the message. What choice does she have?

7

LAST WINTER BREAK

Lisa tried to hide the smirk she felt spreading across her face as soon as she entered the condo in Stowe. The walls, the enormous lounging couch, the fluffy rug in front of the roaring fire were all shades of oatmeal, beige, and blond—just as boring and basic as Gwen was.

"What a beautiful place!" She dropped her bag on the floor to let herself be embraced by Gwen. Behind her, she could hear Marcus muttering under his breath as he struggled with the skis. Gwen had told her that her parents had "gifted" her and Anton a ski cabin as their wedding present. The word *cabin* made her think of some rustic dump with dark wood paneling and drafty windows. She wasn't expecting a luxury modern chalet.

She disentangled herself from Gwen's embrace. Gwen smelled like pine. *She probably has a special Vermont perfume that she only wears up here*, Lisa thought.

"Come in, come in! You must be exhausted. How was the drive?"

"Oh, fine." She followed Gwen into the heart of the large A-frame condo, where she was accosted by two stories of glass overlooking the village center and Mt. Mansfield. It was like peering out at an Alpine village covered in freshly fallen snow. She gasped, despite herself.

Gwen appeared by her side. "I know. Every time we come up here, I just pinch myself. We're just so lucky to have this." She squeezed Lisa's arm. "And so blessed to be able to share it with friends."

"Yes, you're so blessed." *What a phony*, Lisa thought. Gwen was a classic Libra. So obsessed with how she looked to the world. The whole reason people thought Gwen such a great hostess was because of her ability to pretend to like people she hated. But Lisa wasn't fooled. As an Aquarius, she saw right through Gwen's games.

"Oh, wow. This is amazing." Marcus headed toward them, passing the roaring fire. "And the ski lifts are right there? It's like a fairy tale!"

Gwen pointed. "Yup. Ski lifts are right there."

Marcus walked right up to the plate glass window and stretched. "Sure beats skiing in the Poconos like when I was a kid. Magical."

Lisa clapped her hands, as if the noise might break the spell her husband was under. Why was everyone so easily seduced by this woman? "We better get Kai settled."

"Of course!" Gwen said. "The kids are all downstairs in the bunk room. Hope Kai doesn't mind being with the younger kids. If he hates it, he is welcome to sleep up here in the living room. And you and Marcus are down there, too. Don't worry, you have your own bathroom."

"Are all the bedrooms downstairs?" Lisa asked.

"There are two upstairs, and two down below."

"Great!" Message received. Gwen and Aimee would be on the top floor, no doubt enjoying spectacular views and privacy, while she and Marcus were relegated to the basement with the kids. Gwen was really enjoying this, Lisa thought. She had wondered why she was invited at all, and now she realized it was simply to humiliate her. "Marcus? Bags?" Lisa grabbed one small bag while he took the rest. As soon as her feet hit the lower steps, she could feel it was a few degrees chillier down here, and there was a dank smell.

"I can't believe she stuck us in the basement," she said as soon as they entered the large bedroom.

"It's not the basement." Marcus pointed to the sliding door that led to an outside patio. "You can walk out to the back."

"It's so cold down here." Lisa began to put her things away. She hadn't even wanted to come. She hated the cold, and she didn't like to ski.

The past two years, her family and Aimee's family had enjoyed a lovely little routine during their winter break. After Aimee returned from a holiday visit to her family's house outside Baltimore, the two families would spend the days leading up to New Year's ice-skating in Georgetown and seeing the lights at the National Zoo.

But not this year.

This year Gwen announced they could all join her and Anton and the boys up in Vermont. They could ring in the New Year on the slopes. Aimee had jumped at the chance. What was Lisa supposed to do? Let Aimee go up there without her? Vacations, weekend trips, these were when people bonded. And she could only guess what kind of poison Gwen might pour into Aimee's ears if she wasn't around. Imagining the shared jokes, the inside lingo, the memories they would later laugh over sent her heart racing.

"Try to be positive," Marcus said amiably. "This will be fun. You can learn to ski."

"Excuse me for noticing that we're being treated as second-class."

"Don't be like that. It's really nice of them to invite us." He headed into the bathroom and started putting away his toiletries.

"Whatever," Lisa hissed. Marcus didn't see what she saw. And the more she sensed things, the less sensitive he became, as if there were some algebraic equation in their marriage that always had to equal zero.

That evening was painful for Lisa. She should have anticipated that she would be on Gwen's turf, and that her hostess would lord it over everyone. She tried to connect to Aimee, but Aimee was clearly overwhelmed with tending to the needs of her three kids. Not for the first time did Lisa wonder if Aimee hadn't made a mistake having the twins. During dinner, she plastered a smile on her face while returning to a favorite fantasy—that Aimee had stopped having kids at Noa. That the two of them had bonded over being parents of onlys, and that when Gwen moved in with her boisterous twins, their joint rejection of her became one more tie that bound them together. In this fantasy, Marcus and Scott often watched the two kids while she and Aimee traveled together having adventures.

She crashed back to reality when she heard her name.

"Earth to Lisa!" Scott said. "Hello?"

"What is it?" She looked around the table. The dishes had been cleared.

"Where did you go?" Gwen asked. "We were talking to you, and you were lost in la-la land."

Lisa's stomach clenched. She was always embarrassed to be caught out during a daydream. Teachers would humiliate her in class for not paying attention. Her mother used to berate her for being a *space cadet*. But in a family of five kids, delving deep in her own imagination was often the only chance she had at privacy. If she had to share her toys, her clothes, even a bedroom—at least she could keep her imagination locked away. No one could access her thoughts.

"Oh, she's probably just tired. It is a long drive," Aimee said and smiled at her. Lisa felt her friend's warm affection bathe her. That kindness was what drew her to Aimee in the first place. Aimee might be the only person she had ever met who made her feel that she was good enough. Her whole body relaxed when she was around Aimee—her pulse steadied, her breathing regulated. How nice this trip would be if it were just the two of them.

Gwen held up a deck of cards. "Pitch?"

Lisa winced. She hated cards, especially this game that Gwen had taught them all with its complicated rules about jacks and trumps. Aimee had never been a card player before, and neither had Marcus, but now they all acted like they couldn't think of a better way to spend their time together.

"Oh, yes!" Aimee said, heading to the living room. "This time you guys are going down!" The other adults took their beverages and gathered around the coffee table in front of the fire while the children headed down to the basement. Lisa hesitated in the kitchen. No one asked her what she thought, what she wanted. She wasn't sure what an ideal end to the evening might be, but it wasn't this. "I have a headache. I think I'll go to bed early."

"Ohh." Aimee made a frowny face. "Do you need some Advil?"

"I have some, thanks." She turned and walked downstairs. She knew it was abrupt, that she sounded curt, that another woman would have kissed her husband goodnight. But she wanted them to know she was displeased. She wanted her disapproval to hang over the evening like the smell of burnt food. Maybe Aimee might even come down and probe her for what was really the matter. Or at least Marcus.

But no one did.

She peeked in on the children, who were involved in a game called Assassin and completely ignored her pleasant inquiries. Even Kai was having fun. Feeling useless and unloved, she got into bed, where she seethed. Occasional peals of laughter wafted downstairs. They were having a good time without her, even her own husband. Traitor.

She hadn't felt so alone in years. She thought of Ruth, her college roommate. Ruth had been a shy slip of a girl, afraid to go to the dining hall alone the first day. Lisa had accompanied her, watching how her roommate trembled slightly when confronted with the chaos of the cafeteria. Their friendship bloomed almost overnight and soon Ruth had become her *favorite person*. Everything about Ruth seemed wonderful to Lisa, from the way she held her hand over her mouth when she laughed because the gap between her front teeth embarrassed her, to how she drenched herself in drugstore body spray that smelled like honeysuckle.

They stuck together that first month, meeting up for all their meals, touching base between classes to tell each other funny little anecdotes, whispering their dreams and hopes to each other as they lay in their dorm beds at night. Lisa had been euphoric. Finally, she had a friend all to herself. It had been a little difficult to keep the other girls on the dorm floor away, but she was able to with a nasty comment or a rude look. People avoided them that first month. They developed a routine on Friday nights. While their floormates would pile on makeup and down shots of cheap liquor before going out, she and Ruth would tuck themselves into a little cocoon on one of the single beds and eat ice cream and watch TV on the tiny television that Ruth had brought from home.

But all that changed in the second month. Ruth started to pull away, to venture out further into the school. She began to make other friends, first a girl from her Spanish class, then a few members of the Film Club. Sometimes Lisa couldn't find her at lunchtime, and when she did, she'd be sitting with those new friends, halfway through her salad.

The rejection had been unbearable.

In the dark, Lisa flinched at the memory of what she had done in response.

She had been hurting, and like a wounded animal she had lashed out. It wasn't her fault.

A line from a book that she had read came to her: "Pain and suffering are always inevitable for a large intelligence and a deep heart."

But she knew better now, in her forties, than she had at eighteen. That even though pain and suffering were her lot in life, she had control over her actions. She wouldn't repeat the mistakes of the past. A judge would not be so understanding this time.

But Lisa also couldn't ignore the truth: if Gwen were gone, everything would be better.

Lisa squeezed her eyes and imagined herself and Aimee at Gwen's funeral. The grieving friends, holding hands, leaning on each other for support. They would find succor in each other over their mutual loss. It would cement their friendship even more. Lisa would become Aimee's *favorite person* again. After all, Aimee would turn to her whenever she wanted to remember Gwen. Lisa frowned. That could get exhausting. Having to pretend indefinitely that she was devastated that Gwen had died. She was sure to slip; a crack in her façade would show eventually. Besides, she didn't want to mourn Gwen. No, the more she thought about it, the more she realized Gwen dying would be a disaster for her. The whole neighborhood would glorify her; she'd become a saint in death. It would be nauseating. Knowing the women in her neighborhood, they would probably start some kind of charity in her name. She would never escape Gwen then.

She rolled over on her side to face the window that she had cracked to let the cold Vermont air whisper in.

No, killing Gwen was out of the question.

There had to be another way to destroy her.

8

NOW

Aimee grips the wheel of the truck and stares straight ahead, determined to keep her emotions from showing on her face and freaking Noa out. The traffic is light on River Road as she passes over the Beltway and continues toward Potomac, where Cathy lives. After she drops Noa, she needs to oversee the installation of the blueberry bushes, and then she can circle back and see what Gwen needs. Her friend's entire world has just been upended and Aimee wants to be there for her, the way she wishes someone had been there for her when her mother died. As for Scott, she knows he will be able to explain what she saw on the video. She didn't hear him leave or return, for that matter. Where could he have gone?

There's a perfectly reasonable explanation, she tells herself.

"Mom, there, turn!" Noa points at the entrance to the driveway. Aimee slows and turns. She was caught up in her thoughts and almost missed it. Cathy's old farmhouse, with a wraparound porch, has somehow survived being torn down and replaced by the fairy-tale mansions all around it. It sits on about two acres, and there's even an old barn off to the side that looks like it could use a good renovating. There used to be several horse farms in Potomac, and Aimee wonders what kind of farm this once was.

As soon as the truck comes to a stop, Noa rushes out and runs to the front porch.

Cathy comes to the door and opens it wide. "Come on in." Noa runs inside, gives Cathy a quick hug, and then runs off, Aimee guesses, to find the kittens.

"I am so sorry to impose on you like this," Aimee says, wishing she could leave without chatting. But she doesn't want to be rude. Cathy has been very generous to allow Noa to come over.

"No imposition at all." Cathy starts walking to the kitchen. "Coffee?" she calls over her shoulder. "I just made a fresh pot."

Cathy's house is a mix of heirloom quality antiques and bohemian touches. A framed old map of Block Island hangs next to an abstract watercolor. Aimee follows her to the large, airy kitchen, where Cathy is puttering around. Her long silver hair is wound in a neat bun at her neck, and she wears an oyster-gray top with a darker gray long skirt. She's very chic for an older woman, Aimee thinks, and then admonishes herself for her assumptions about aging women. She wonders, as she sometimes does when she's around women this age, what her own mother would be like now. She died when Aimee was in high school, not even forty-five years old. Would she be a chic sixtysomething like Cathy? Or would she be like her stepmom, Deb, practical in her sweatpants, turtlenecks, and Crocs?

Cathy hands her a cup of coffee.

"Thank you," Aimee says, taking it. "But I can't stay long. I don't want to be late for an installation, and this has been a crazy morning."

Cathy's face creases with concern. "Oh dear, is everything all right?"

"Not really." Aimee brings the mug to her mouth and inhales. She notices a slight tremble in her hands. So much for keeping her emotions in check until later. "A friend of mine, her husband was found dead."

Cathy sucks in her breath, places a hand on her chest, right over a large green jade pendant. "My goodness. How awful. What happened?" She steps back, pulls out a stool from under the counter, and pats it. *That's the former teacher in her*, Aimee thinks. Her ability to connect right away. And like a good pupil, Aimee takes a seat. She sends Tim a quick text telling him she's on her way but running late, and tells Cathy what she knows. It feels good to have someone to talk to. "I'm still just processing the whole thing. It's so awful. The police think . . ." Her voice trails off. Why is she being so cagey? Is it because saying it aloud makes it true?

"They think what?" Cathy cocks her head.

"They're treating it as a murder investigation." She fidgets with a small wooden bowl in front of her, filled with stone hearts. She pulls out a pink quartz one and worries it with her hand.

"How awful for you. And your friend." Cathy's gaze falls to a framed photo next to the bowl of hearts. In it, a young woman holds the hand of a little boy who grins at the camera. "That's me and my boy. I lost him when he was young."

"I'm so sorry. I didn't know you had a son."

"That was taken a long time ago. He was only three."

"He was very cute."

She presses her lips tight. "He was a wonderful boy. The light of my life. He would be about your age now. I think that's one of the reasons I enjoy having Noa come visit. He was my only child, and when I lost him, well . . ." She gives Aimee a sad smile. "I'll never know the joys of grandchildren."

"But you had your students."

Cathy smiles. "True. I do so love having little people about."

It touches Aimee deeply. "That makes me feel a little less guilty about how much we've been coming over. I lost my mother when I was a teenager. She died of cancer when I was sixteen. Actually, it was the medicine that killed her, not the cancer. But that's a story for another day."

"Oh, Aimee, I am so sorry. I had no idea."

Aimee is struck by how genuine Cathy's concern is. "My dad remarried right away, and my stepmom is perfectly nice." Aimee pauses. Because it's true. Deb is nice. "But she never really accepted me as her own. She got pregnant right away and had three more kids with my dad. So, there were three new kids for my father to focus on. I left for college the next year, and well, I just never . . . I miss my mom."

"Of course you do. Look, if you need me to watch Noa or help out while you look after your friend, please don't hesitate to ask. I know what it can be like to lose a loved one. It's world-shattering. Be there for her." Cathy stands and opens her arms.

"Thank you," Aimee says, stepping into Cathy's hug. She is curious about how Cathy's son died but doesn't want to pry. It would probably be too painful.

Her phone pings. It's Scott finally responding to her text.

"I'd better get this. Thanks again. I'll come back for Noa in a few hours?"

Aimee walks outside and stops in front of the azalea bushes Cathy wants to replace. She's been out here several times discussing the merits of spice bush and clethra, viburnum and native hydrangeas that will support the local insect and bird populations. At first she thought that Cathy was another one of her wealthy, indecisive clients, but now Aimee realizes all those long talks in Cathy's kitchen weren't because Cathy is high maintenance. Cathy is lonely. Leaving Noa here for a few hours feels like she is helping them both, and that makes her feel good.

Inside the truck, she dials Scott as she drives to her Glen Echo client. Tim has been working the ground for a few weeks now, making sure the soil is acidic enough for the finicky blueberry bushes, and installing drip irrigation so the bushes have the consistently soggy soil they prefer. Now she just has to make sure all the bushes look healthy and the spacing is right, and to answer any questions from the client.

"That was me, don't worry," Scott says as soon as he answers.

A shiver runs through Aimee. "What? What was you?"

"The money. You're calling about the money, right?"

"I don't know what you're talking about. What money?"

He laughs. "I thought you saw the email from the bank about

the withdrawal, and I didn't want you to worry. We weren't hacked. That was me."

They have an alert system on their accounts that withdrawals over a certain amount trigger an email, but Aimee hasn't checked her email recently. "How much did you take out?"

"Fifty thousand."

"Fifty thousand!"

"I can explain. I'm just moving some money around."

"That's a lot of money to move around without telling me."

"Yeah, sorry, the deadline to buy these bonds was coming up, and I had to move to catch the current interest rate. Starting next month—"

"Okay, okay, I get it. You can give me all the details later. Listen, that's not why I called."

"Is everything all right? Is Noa okay?"

"Yeah. She's fine, she's visiting the kittens, and the boys are at Lisa's." She takes a deep breath. "I don't know how else to say this except straight-out. Anton's dead. He was hit by a car last night."

There's a long pause before Scott answers. "Oh my God, that's horrible. Where did this happen?"

"Downtown Bethesda, but listen." She pulls into the driveway and sees Tim's truck. He waves at her. Standing next to him is the client, a woman a bit older than Aimee, with a scowl on her face. Aimee's stomach sinks. The last thing she needs is a disgruntled client. This is a straightforward job. She picked out the bushes herself a week ago when she was at the family nursery outside Baltimore.

"I have to go, but you should know the police are going to come by and talk to you."

"Me? Why me?"

"Because Anton came by the house last night."

Scott lets out an awkward laugh. "What? Why do you think that?"

"Scott, I saw it on the doorbell camera. And so did the detective."

"So now you're checking up on me?"

Aimee frowns. Scott is not usually defensive. "Of course not. The police asked me to look. They're trying to solve a murder."

"You know that you didn't have to show them, right? Not without a warrant."

Aimee is stunned. "I didn't think we had anything to hide." Tim begins to walk over to her truck. "I saw you walk out with Anton. Where were you going?"

"He was drunk. And bleeding from his head. He said he fell. He wasn't making any sense. I took him home."

"But you didn't come back right away." Aimee holds up a finger to Tim and then points to the phone. She needs an explanation before she can get off this call. "You were gone for more than an hour. Where did you go?"

"I can explain everything. But not on the phone."

A knock on the window startles her, and she turns to see Tim standing there. Flustered, she flashes him a smile. "I have to get to work, but this isn't over."

Aimee hangs up, but is left with a heavy sensation in the pit of her stomach. She and Scott have never kept secrets from each other. They weren't like those other couples, where the women hid their shopping habits and the men lied about weekends in Vegas.

But for the first time in their marriage, she gets the feeling that Scott is *managing* her. It's the same feeling she gets when one of her employees has a too-elaborate explanation about why they didn't show up for work.

It almost always means they're lying.

9

NOW

Gwen awakens around noon, feeling groggy and hungover. The silence in the house is deafening. Without George's and Rafi's voices bouncing off the walls, or Anton's narration as he moves through the house—*guess I'll get some more coffee now* or *where did I put that notebook?*—the only sound is the clicking of Sababa's nails on the wooden floor.

Gwen sits up, the morning's events flooding her mind. Beside her sits a pad of paper with the list she started of things to be done. *Contact the funeral home. Draft an email to send to Anton's colleagues and work. Reach out to his father—best time to call France?*

That's as far as she got this morning after Aimee left until she felt a full-blown panic attack creep up on her. Her heart began to pound at an alarming rate and she couldn't steady her breathing. She quickly took a Xanax and then wrapped her arms around her knees and rocked back and forth, moaning, waiting for it to kick in. When she didn't feel better after a few minutes, she popped another.

Now it is two hours later, her head feels full of cobwebs, and she feels no less ready to tackle the list.

The thought of picking up Rafi and George from Lisa's, bringing them home, and breaking the news to them fills her with dread. She has no idea where she will find the words to tell them their father is never coming home. Whatever marital problem she and Anton had, they always presented a unified front with the kids. She was the disciplinarian, the one who enforced rules. He was the one who would crack a joke to ease the tension or tickle a kid to make him laugh if the mood felt too heavy. But she will have to do this one without him. She'll be doing it all without him from now on.

All of a sudden she longs for her boys. It's a physical ache deep in her. She throws off the covers and gets up. Putting her hair in a messy bun, she tosses a sweater on and rushes downstairs. At the front door, she slips on some shoes and peers outside first. Her neighbor Paola, an older Argentinian woman who lives alone, is walking a geriatric poodle. Gwen waits for the woman to exit the cul-de-sac, hoping to avoid being cornered by her aimless conversation. The woman repeatedly confuses her with Aimee and asks for advice on her plants, a subject Gwen has no knowledge of or interest in.

At Lisa's house, Marcus answers the door and gives her an enormous hug. She has to pull back before she starts weeping. He apologizes that Lisa is in the shower, but Gwen is grateful not to have to interact with her. She likes Lisa in small doses, and she can be really helpful, but Gwen knows that if it weren't for Aimee she would never be friends with her.

"She'll be sorry to have missed you," Marcus says. He is wearing a bright-yellow pair of biking shorts and a half-zip top, clearly having just come back from a ride.

Gwen makes a noncommittal noise and then waits for Marcus to get the kids. On the walk home, Gwen thinks about the day she and Anton first stepped foot onto Nassau Court. They couldn't believe that something so quiet and peaceful lay just a few minutes from the busiest parts of downtown Bethesda.

She could never have imagined that such a bucolic setting would be the scene of her husband's death.

"And the high school is just a few blocks that way!" the Realtor enthused, so certain that they were a family looking for their forever home.

The Realtor could have no idea that this would be their third home in five years.

That Anton always did something to force them to move. But three times was a charm. Gwen had really believed that. A new start.

A fresh beginning. That's what was so appealing to her about the D.C. area. Not just that no one here knew them, or about their past, but that the whole region was made of transplants. She had scoured mommy boards for different cities, and she kept coming back to D.C. and the complaints that it was too transient, because people moved in and out all the time for their jobs.

It sounded perfect to Gwen.

As she turns up her walkway, the boys zipping ahead of her, Gwen flashes back to last night. How she threw that coffee mug, hitting him in the head. How it landed on the tile floor, shattering, and he stormed off. She was so sure she had cleaned up every last bit of broken ceramic. She must be more careful in the future. All eyes will be on her.

"Gram!" George yells as soon as they are inside the house.

Gwen is startled to see her mother standing in the middle of her living room, fully made-up, her short wheat-colored bob shellacked into place.

"Mom, what are you doing here?"

Her mother steps forward and hugs her stiffly. Gwen can smell her mother's Yves Saint Laurent perfume, the heady scent she has worn continuously since the 1980s.

"Darling, you poor, poor thing," she whispers in Gwen's ear. "I came as soon as I heard."

Gwen pulls back, trying to do the math. It's about a two-and-a-half-hour drive from her parents' house outside Richmond. "But how did you hear?"

"Your friend told me. Lisa something?"

"Lisa called you?"

"Are you staying, Grammy?" George asks, running into the room. "I want to show you a magic trick. Stay there." He runs off.

"I take it they don't know?"

Gwen shakes her head. "So, Lisa told you? About Anton?"

Barb looks around the room, as if she is a Realtor assessing the place. "I texted the boys to ask them about Christmas presents. You never responded to that email I sent—"

"Because it's September."

"—and she responded. Apparently, Rafi had taken off his watch thingamajig. Not sure why boys that age need a device at all." She glares at Gwen pointedly. Barb had been opposed to letting the boys have Apple watches, had deluged Gwen with articles about the dangers of screens, even when Gwen explained it would make her feel safer letting them go down to the playground if she could track them.

"But you're the one who texted them."

Barb waves away the inconsistency. "And I'm glad I did. When this Lisa person called me and told me what was going on, well, you can imagine my reaction. I tried you immediately, but you didn't answer."

"I've been busy. It's been a horrible morning."

"What I don't understand is how could I not be the first call that you made, Gwendolyn?"

The old familiar mix of anger and embarrassment burbles within her. "Because I just found out a few hours ago that my husband is dead, so sorry I didn't call you right away." She storms off into the kitchen, noting that it took less than five minutes in her mother's presence for her to revert to an impertinent teenager. She grabs the electric kettle and fills it with water, making sure to bang it around the sink a bit.

Barb follows her in, tsk-tsking. "Oh sweetie, my poor sweetie, I didn't mean to accuse you. Don't be upset. Come to Mommy." She comes around the island, arms open, and envelops Gwen in a hug. "My poor little baby." Barb pulls back and holds her at arm's length. "How can I help? Let me help you. What happened? Tell me everything. I'll take that. You sit down."

She takes the kettle, puts it back on its base, and switches it on.

Gwen sits down, stunned by the power of Barb. She's never been able to keep a secret from her mother, so what makes her think she can now? She sits and watches Barb make tea and then lets her mother lead her back to the living room, where she plumps up some pillows and orders Gwen to sit. Barb takes a seat beside her.

Gwen tells her everything, only stopping once George and Rafi return to perform some clunky card tricks they've been obsessing over the past few weeks.

"We need to practice more," Rafi says.

"I think you were both wonderful!" Barb says.

After the boys leave, she turns to Gwen.

"Come back to our house for the weekend. You're in no condition to be here by yourself. It'll be good for you to let us take care of you. Daddy can take the boys to the club—did I tell you they upgraded the golf carts? The boys will like that. And I'll look after you. You need your family at a time like this."

"I don't want to leave." The house her parents live in isn't even her childhood home. As soon as she left for college, they sold their house in Richmond proper for an immense one farther out in the country. Who buys a bigger house when their kids leave? Her parents, that's who. More room for her dad's cars and boats. More rooms for her mother to decorate.

"If you don't want to come, at least let me take the boys for the weekend."

"Take the boys?" The idea alarms her. First her husband, then her boys. "I'll be all alone."

"Then come. Gwen, honey. There's bound to be media attention. You don't want to expose them to that. Imagine the things they will say. The probing. It could get very ugly."

Gwen lets out a choked sob. Maybe her mother is right. She needs to protect George and Rafi.

Barb opens her purse and pulls out a compact the size of her hand.

"Look in the mirror, honey." Her mother holds up the compact. All Gwen can see is one of her eyes, swollen from crying and smudged with mascara. "Look at yourself. Is this how you want those boys to see you? Give yourself a few days to get it together."

"I need to tell them. I can't keep the truth from them, as much as I might want to." She stares at her one eye in the mirror. It's the eye of a stranger, a disintegrating woman. Is her mother right? Does she owe it to her boys to be pretty and pulled together? Barb can confuse her this way, the way no one else can.

"It's just for a night or two," Barb coos, stroking her arm. "You don't want them seeing police coming and going, their mother in tears. Give them one last weekend of pure innocence before it's all snatched away. Once they learn what's happened to their father, once they *know* about their father, well, they can never unknow it, can they? Give them this weekend. It's a gift to them, believe me."

"Fine." Gwen relents. Maybe her mother is right. Maybe by letting them go she is allowing them one last gasp of their childhood. And if she's being honest, she doesn't have the guts to tell them. Not yet. Dealing with their grief on top of her own seems unfathomable right now. She'll be better in a few days, stronger. She'll use the weekend as a respite, the chance to think, the quiet time to process what has happened, so that when they return she can be the mother they deserve.

Is that terrible? Is she a terrible mother that she doesn't want to have to be pulled together in front of her boys? Maybe a better mother would plaster on a smile and make dinner from scratch the night after she found out her husband has been murdered. But Gwen feels like she's wearing one of those weighted blankets, pulling her to the ground.

"Smart girl." Barb stands up, smoothing out her slacks. "I'll just pack up a few things. I've got bags in the car. I'll be right back."

"Wait, what?" Gwen's spine stiffens. "You brought bags with you? I didn't agree to anything until just now."

"I knew you'd see sense." Her mother is unfazed. She's heading outside.

"You brought your own suitcases?" Gwen calls after her.

Barb pauses at the door. "I wasn't sure if you had yours easily accessible and I was trying to make less work for you. Stop trying to make it sound nefarious. Not everyone is out to get you."

She watches her mother leave the house and return a few moments later with two matching navy carry-on bags, and then take them up the short flight of stairs with the efficiency of a seasoned flight attendant. She disappears into the boys' room, and moments later Gwen hears drawers opening and closing. She's filled with a strange sense that her mother has come to take her children away forever.

Her mother is not an ally, has never been. How Gwen wishes she was. How she wishes she could unburden herself to Barb, and spill the poisonous, inky secret that is seeping into every corner of her soul.

Not her secret, but Anton's. The one he told her last night.

She could use some real advice. She's going to be navigating treacherous waters soon and Barb would know what to do. But telling Barb what Anton told her would come with too high a price. Her mother would use it to manipulate Gwen forever.

No, Anton's secret is one that Gwen must manage all by herself.

10

Aimee is drawing on every last ounce of patience to assuage her client, who is upset because she has learned she will have to net the blueberry bushes in the summer.

"But netting will destroy the aesthetic." The woman crosses her arms over her chest. In leggings and a fleece with the crest of a local private school embroidered over the chest, her blond hair pulled into a tight ponytail, she looks like an average suburban mom. And while Aimee is not intimidated, she knows these Washington moms can be vicious. She will have to thread the needle between accommodating her demands and setting boundaries so this woman doesn't walk all over her.

"Well, you can leave the bushes unnetted," Aimee says. Her tone is gentle, considering she went over these details with the woman and her husband a few weeks ago. "But the birds will pick most of the berries. Birds love blueberries."

"But I didn't plant them for the birds." The woman narrows her eyes. "I planted them for the antioxidants. You told me this would be an edible hedge."

"And it will be!" Aimee's chipper response does nothing to wipe the scowl off the woman's face. "But for about one month out of the year, you will have to net them. Don't worry, they make very unobtrusive green netting. You won't even notice it."

"I feel duped. I really do." The woman shakes her head, looking at Tim nearby as if he might confirm this, but Tim is looking at his phone, trying to ignore the whole thing. Aimee feels jealous. Being the boss means having a lot of these conversations.

"I mean, what do farms do?" the woman asks.

"They use netting." Aimee employs the same voice she uses with her kids when they are on the verge of spiraling into a tantrum. "Or walk-in cages."

"Cages? Oh no." The woman shakes her head. "I don't want my front yard to look like a factory."

Behind her, Tim lets out a quiet chuckle. Aimee tries to keep her face neutral.

"Well, then you can let the birds have the berries. That would be very environmentally conscientious of you. And you'll probably be able to get a handful of berries."

"I have to say I am really disappointed. I thought a bird, maybe two." She exhales. "But *birds*? Plural? This is really unacceptable."

Aimee looks at the thousand dollars' worth of mature blueberry bushes that need to go into the ground today. What she'd really like to do is tell this woman to suck it. That her friend's husband was just murdered. That she should be back at her house now, comforting that friend. Instead, she digs deep, trying to channel her father, who never lost his patience with a customer. "How about we put in one or two very elegant bespoke netting *boxes* on the ones closest to the house." She points to the end of the trench that Tim dug. "We'll paint them green, you'll hardly even notice them, and leave the rest of the bushes for the birds? That way, from the street you won't notice the box, the greenery will hide it, but you'll have one or two bushes right near your kitchen door so you can pop out in the morning and have fresh blueberries with breakfast?"

"Netting boxes, huh?" The woman nods as if imagining those fresh blueberries in her yogurt. "How many blueberries are we talking?"

"Pounds. When these mature, you're looking at three to nine pounds each year. Each."

"Really? Wow. I had no idea. Two bushes should be plenty. All right, go ahead, put them in."

Finally, she and Tim can get to work. She is grateful for the physical labor—it's always been a way for her to work off any bad energy, ever since she was a child helping at her dad's nursery. In the years after her mother's death, the nursery was a refuge from the home she no longer recognized without her mother there. And then Deb moved in, making her feel even more uncomfortable. Aimee sprinkles soil acidifier into the trench and hauls a four-foot bush into it.

But even with the task at hand, her mind keeps looping back to what happened this morning. Anton is dead. She'll need to clear some time to help Gwen. She knows Gwen has a sister, but they aren't close. She thinks she's the closest friend Gwen has. She can organize a meal train, get the other moms in the neighborhood to help out. She won't let Gwen go through this alone.

Aimee steps back to see if her spacing is correct, that the bush has enough room to spread out. She wants it to blend into the bushes that will be planted next to it, but at the same time they all need enough room to avoid becoming entangled in each other's limbs, which can spread disease. She adjusts one bush that is lilting to the left, trying to focus, but a horrible thought pops into her head. *Scott was involved in Anton's death.* Aimee's body stiffens. Where did that come from? She banishes the thought, attributing it to the stress of everything going on. Scott could never be involved in anything as sordid as a murder. *He'll explain everything later*, she reassures herself.

After she and Tim have finished the job, she heads back to Cathy's to grab Noa. She texts Cathy once she's outside her house and then waits in the truck, going through her missed messages. Her phone is blowing up with the news about Anton. Random groups texts, like one among parents in Noa's class about bringing in hand sanitizer and tissues to school, have been repurposed to spread the news. Her feed is filled with wild stories and speculation—a robbery, a drug deal gone wrong, gang activity.

She just wants to get home and have a face-to-face conversation with Scott. They communicate best in person. On the phone he might be distracted, looking at a screen while he is talking. Over text she could never figure out his tone. She needs to be looking at his face, his body language, when he explains everything about last night.

Noa jumps in the truck. "It was so cool, Mom. They are getting so big. And they're brave, too. Miles tried to leave the closet."

"Miles, huh? He's the adventurous one?" Aimee turns back toward Bethesda. "We're going to grab Ledo's for everyone—all three families."

"Mommy, I don't like that pizza. I only like Da Marco."

Aimee sighs. Ledo's is closer, and cheaper. But Noa is underweight. In the second percentile for her age. At the last visit, the pediatrician admonished her and Scott to get food into Noa any way possible. *Don't worry about a balanced diet right now*, she said. *Noa needs to gain weight.*

Aimee has seen her daughter skip meals too many times. Deb told her that Noa will eat when she is hungry, but it is turning out not to be the case. The pediatrician said if she didn't gain weight, they would have to go to an eating specialist. "Da Marco's it is."

They pick up enough pies for all three families, along with a few salads, and head back to the house. Noa offers to run down to Lisa's and get all the boys while Aimee pulls out plates, cups, and napkins, preparing for everyone to show up at once. She lifts a box lid and inhales the scent of tomato, cheese, and basil. After all that physical work, she's starving. She pulls out a slice and starts eating while standing at the counter. With her other hand, she texts Gwen.

Pizza if you're interested.

Then she deletes it. Too casual. This isn't a typical Saturday night. Aimee tries calling instead, but it goes straight to voicemail.

What should she do? Everything she thinks of sounds too

vapid to say to someone whose husband has just been murdered. Anton's death has opened a gulf between her and Gwen, and she doesn't like it. The kids burst through the door yelling for pizza, with Lisa and Marcus trailing behind them. Marcus hoists a six-pack of beer. "Scott here?"

"He's on his way home. Kids, wash hands!" Aimee directs the kids to the downstairs bathroom. It's then she realizes Gwen's kids are not here.

"Where are George and Rafi?"

"They're probably with Barb. Gwen's mom." Lisa stops putting slices on plates and faces Aimee. "I spoke to her earlier today. I didn't mean to be the one to break the news to her, but I just assumed she knew."

"When did you speak to her mom?"

Lisa's hands flutter to her neck. "Oh, I saw she was texting the boys. Well, Rafi. But he had taken his watch off to go on the trampoline. And I thought it might be urgent, so I called her."

Aimee searches Lisa's face for any sign that she realizes she may have crossed a boundary. But Lisa's face, perfectly made-up as always, cheeks and lips ever so slightly plumped by filler, reveals nothing of the sort. "I'm sure you were trying to help," Aimee says. She's always had a soft spot for Lisa's clumsy attempts at intimacy. She's seen how hard it is for her to blend in with the other moms in the neighborhood.

"Oh, I was! Absolutely. Anyway, she said she was going to come up and grab the boys. Take them back to Virginia for a few days."

"Without Gwen?"

"I didn't ask. How is Gwen doing?" Lisa says. "I can't imagine how she feels right now."

Aimee takes a few slices and puts them on a platter. "I'm going to take this over there now. She was in shock this morning. Can you keep the fort down? I won't be long, and Scott will be back soon."

"I can come with you," Lisa says. "Marcus can watch the kids."

"I think it's better if it's just me. For now."

"Oh. Fine. Sure. I'll stay here. Whatever you need, Aimee."

Aimee is just pulling the front door closed behind her when Scott pulls up in his car. She stops in the street and waits for him to get out.

"Is that for me?" he asks as he approaches. "Nice of you to come greet me."

"Ha ha." She pulls the pizza out of his reach. "This is for Gwen. Lisa and Marcus are inside with all the kids."

"Are you annoyed about something?"

"I don't know. I just, I'm feeling weird, Scott. You went out last night—where did you go? Make me understand this."

Scott rolls his eyes. "It's no big deal. I went for a drink. That's all."

"A drink?"

He mimes bringing a glass to his mouth. "You know, a drink? Why is that so hard to believe? You were asleep, I wasn't tired, I was feeling kind of restless, so I went out."

"Where did you go?"

"Downtown Bethesda."

"Where?"

"What is this, the third degree?" He shifts his messenger bag, restless. "I went to Villain & Saint. See, this is why I didn't tell you. I knew you would give me a hard time."

"Wait, Villain & Saint? With Anton?"

"Of course not. Why would you even think that?"

"That's where he was found. In the alley behind Villain & Saint."

Scott frowns. "That's crazy. I didn't see him there. I left Anton on his front stoop."

"What were you doing there?"

"It was Friday night. I had a long week. I wanted to get out of the house. I don't go to bed at ten like you. I was antsy, so I went and had a glass of whiskey. Is that a crime?"

"No. It's not a crime."

"Now I'm going inside to eat. I'm starving. And I hope Marcus brought beer."

"He did."

"Go check on Gwen. You can continue grilling me later if you want." He gives her a kiss on the top of her head before walking to the house. But she is not mollified. Her heart thumps in her chest as she turns toward Gwen's house. Scott doesn't go out to bars after she goes to bed. That's not his thing, so why is he pretending it is? And the first time he does, it just so happens to be the night that Anton is murdered. It doesn't add up. Scott is being evasive. She believes him that he didn't see Anton at the bar, that didn't seem like a lie. But he's keeping something back. After all these years, she can tell when he isn't being completely honest with her. No, it's not a crime to go to a bar and have a drink. But if he hasn't done anything wrong, why is he acting so guilty?

11

NOW

Gwen opens the door to Aimee on the front step, still wearing her work clothes, her pants streaked with dirt. "Pizza?" Aimee asks, offering a wan smile. She steps inside without waiting for a response.

Gwen shuts the door and locks it. After her mother left with the boys, someone from a TV station came by and rang the bell. Gwen hid in the living room, hunched down, like a scared rabbit. Now she follows Aimee into the kitchen, where a small flat-screen TV mounted on the wall is paused on the news. She likes to watch TV while she cooks dinner or cleans up.

"Look at this," Gwen says and picks up the remote, rewinding it a bit.

A news reporter stands on the sidewalk outside Villain & Saint, as yellow crime-scene tape flaps in the wind.

"I'm standing in front of the alley where police say Anton Khoury was struck by a car in the late hours of last night. His body was dragged behind a dumpster and was not discovered until early this morning when a vendor at the Farm Women's Market arrived around six-thirty to open up for the day. Police are asking anyone who saw anything unusual or suspicious to contact them."

Gwen pauses the TV. "They came here, you know, and knocked on the door. That woman, right there"—she waves her wineglass at the TV—"She called out, *Gwen, Gwen, are you in there?* As if we were friends."

"Oh yeah?" Aimee's eyes dart to the half-empty bottle of wine, and Gwen feels a shiver of resentment go through her. Who is

Aimee to judge? Gwen picks up the bottle and makes a show of refilling her glass, emptying the bottle, holding it upside down until the last drop is out, daring Aimee to challenge her. "Want a glass? There's plenty more where that came from."

Aimee hesitates and then shrugs. "Sure, why not? I've had a stupid day. Not as bad as yours, but I'll take a drink."

"Scott's got the kids?"

"They're at my place. Everyone's there—Lisa, Marcus, Scott."

"Barb swooped in and took the boys back to Virginia."

"I know. Lisa told me. She said she spoke to your mom earlier today. Something about her wanting to allow the boys a few more days without having to learn the awful truth."

"Huh. Lisa sure likes to talk about me. She's great at spreading news." Gwen reaches into a cabinet to get another glass before crouching down in front of the wine fridge. "Sauvignon, chardonnay, Riesling?"

"You have that green one I like?" Aimee asks. "Was that your idea to wait to tell the boys?"

Gwen is grateful her face is hidden, below the counter level, so Aimee can't see her reaction. She can feel her lip curl as she reaches into the back of the fridge for the bottle of Hugl Gruner Veltliner. "No, it was my mom's. She doesn't want the boys to *see me* like this. You know, as a human being. God forbid I show any messy emotion. I mean, my husband is dead. He was killed." She stands, unscrews the bottle top, and fills both their glasses. "She doesn't care. She's already in spin mode. How will this all look to her friends at the club? She hasn't asked me how I'm feeling. How I'm handling this. She won't let me have any feelings. It's all checklists."

"That's hard." Aimee takes the glass. "I'm sure she's just trying to help in her own way. People don't know how to act when terrible things happen. They get weird."

"I mean, maybe it is good that they won't know for another

few days. Because once they know the truth it's going to destroy them. I mean, how am I going to tell them their dad is dead? They're so young. It's so unfair."

"It's not fair. How are you feeling?"

Gwen takes a gulp of wine. "Empty. In shock. Scared. Furious."

"Furious? You mean at whoever killed Anton?"

"Yeah, of course. But I also mean at Anton."

Aimee puts her glass down with a *thunk*. "Oh, Gwen, you don't mean that."

Gwen narrows her eyes at Aimee. She picks up her glass and the bottle and heads into the living room, where she takes her position on the sofa next to Sababa, who hasn't moved in hours. The cushions are still indented and warm from Gwen sitting in the same spot all afternoon.

Aimee sits down in a chair across from her. "I'm sorry. I shouldn't have said that. I can't even imagine what you are going through."

"No, you can't." The words are sharp, and they slice through the goodwill between them.

"You have every right to all your feelings," Aimee says. "I am not here to judge you. I love you, Gwen. I want to help."

But she will judge, Gwen thinks. Her friends back in Boston certainly did. Her family did. The people in her life were evenly split when they found out that Anton had cheated on her. Again. Some thought she was a doormat for staying with him, a loser, a failure as a feminist. She had made the mistake of confiding in her group of mom friends in her neighborhood. She hadn't planned to, but at book club, she burst out crying. The pain after discovering Anton was cheating was so real, so raw, she couldn't hide it. The marriage was surviving on a day-to-day basis, and she thought her friends would support her.

But they pulled away, one by one, as if infidelity was a virus that was catching. As if whatever Gwen had done to make her husband betray her could be passed on to them like an invisible germ that they might carry home to their own husbands.

I could never stay with a man who cheated . . .

A woman who doesn't respect herself . . .

One friend dropped a book at her front door called *Finding the Courage: How to Learn to Love Yourself Enough to Walk Away.*

Her own family was in the opposite camp. Her older sister, whom she had never gotten along with, said, "Welcome to the club. Marriage is hard work."

Her parents had met as freshmen in college and married one year after graduation. *There are good years and bad years*, Barb had said. *Heck, there are good decades and bad decades.*

They implored her to forgive. They even had their pastor call her and offer counseling.

"Think of what you will be doing to those boys if you break this marriage up," the pastor said.

He's the one, not me! Gwen wanted to shout. Her mother emailed articles about desperate single mothers, about how boys growing up without fathers were at risk, about the long-lasting trauma of divorce on children.

Gwen deleted them, along with the inspirational takes from her neighborhood friends—first-person narratives of women who had found their true happiness after divorce, pieces on children's resilience and the risks to kids of growing up with unhappily married parents. She threw them all away, finding it nearly impossible to isolate her own voice in all the noise. What did *she* want?

Slowly, with the help of a marriage counselor, she began to set the terms. Terms she could live with. Complete control of their finances. Access to all his tech. No secrets. They would move far away from the judgment of their so-called friends. Anton would leave his job at the college outside Boston where he had met his affair partner. They would start over where no one knew them.

He applied for jobs, and he got an offer at American University offering less pay and not on a tenure track, but Gwen insisted he take it.

It was a test. If he really loved her, if he was truly sorry and wanted to make the marriage work, he would be willing to take the career hit.

They had been forced to turn to her parents for financial help. Her mom and dad were happy to do it, thrilled to have their grandchildren closer. That it was a bit punitive, the tiniest bit emasculating of Anton, was something Gwen wasn't bothered by.

And Anton agreed.

Gwen searches Aimee's face. Is she a real friend? One who will stick by her and not judge? Everyone will expect her to be sad and heartbroken over Anton's death. And she is. Especially when she thinks of how it will affect the boys. But she's got this anger inside of her that won't go away.

She wishes she could tell Aimee the whole truth. Well, not the *whole* truth. Certainly not what Anton revealed last night. Aimee would never forgive her. She wouldn't understand. Aimee and Scott appear to have an almost perfect marriage, to not just love each other but, shockingly, to *like* each other. Will that make Aimee more sympathetic to what she has been through? Or will Aimee not be able to relate at all?

"Anton cheated. In the past. Three years ago, in Boston."

"Oh Gwen, I'm so sorry," Aimee says. "You never told me."

She shrugs. "I don't like to think about it. We did a lot of work to repair our marriage. It was awful. We moved to D.C. for a fresh start. But lately I'd been having this weird feeling."

"That he might be . . ." Aimee doesn't finish her sentence.

Gwen nods. "That's what the fight was about last night. I threw a coffee mug, it caught him on the side of the head. I swear I wasn't aiming at him." The truth marbled through with lies. Can Aimee tell which is which? "That's the piece of bloody china you found this morning."

"Makes sense," Aimee says, then adds in a bashful tone, "I actually heard you guys fighting last night."

"You did?" Gwen straightens up. "Then maybe you can understand. It's what makes his death so complicated for me. I've been so furious at him lately that I'm having trouble shifting into grief."

"If you don't mind my asking—did he admit to cheating last night? I couldn't hear the words. Just raised voices." Aimee takes a careful sip from her wineglass.

Gwen thinks about this and how much she wants to reveal. She can feel the alcohol loosening her barriers. She has to be careful here. A little bit of truth will go a long way. "No. He denied it, of course, but . . ."

But then he said something so much worse. *Something so terrible, something you would never forgive me for, Aimee.* And Gwen realizes how lucky she is that Anton's secret died with him. That her best friend will never know.

"But what?"

"But I don't know if I bought his act." Gwen proffers a tight smile. Aimee nods and the irony is not lost on Gwen. Her friend may be wondering the very same thing about her. Does Aimee buy her act?

12

Sunday morning means pancakes and bacon. Aimee sits at the counter surrounded by dirty dishes, sipping coffee and nursing a hangover. Scott is upstairs getting the boys into their soccer uniforms. The carpool is arriving soon. Noa is in her room doing Lord knows what, although when Aimee walked by earlier, she could hear her daughter talking to her stuffed animals.

Aimee stayed later last night at Gwen's than she intended to, drinking more wine than normal. But Gwen kept drinking, and she felt obligated to keep up. She knew Gwen would keep drinking, and the thought of her friend downing glass after glass of wine all alone in her house was too depressing. Now her pounding skull and dry mouth are the price she is paying.

The boys clatter through the kitchen on their way to the mudroom to collect cleats and a ball, and just as quickly they are out the door. "Hi, Mom!" they yell and then, "Bye, Mom!"

Moments later, Scott comes in and pours himself the last of the coffee. "Make a new pot?"

Aimee shrugs. She's not satisfied with the answers he gave her yesterday about his little trip to Villain & Saint on Friday night, but isn't sure how to bring it up without sounding like she's hounding him. She would have asked him about it last night, but by the time she returned from Gwen's he was passed out in front of the TV.

"I am going to take that as a yes," he says, taking the pot to the sink to rinse. It's hard to stay annoyed with Scott, he is so sunny and helpful. He never holds a grudge or sulks. She watches her husband as he grinds the coffee and spoons out the grounds into the machine, feeling her irritation be replaced by gratitude. Despite Scott's flaws, he would never do what Anton did. It changes how she thinks of Anton. She understands why Gwen never told her. Would Aimee have wanted to spend so much time with a man she knew was a serial philanderer? Go on vacation with him? The answer is no.

"Are you going to tell me about last night? About Villain & Saint?"

"What more is there to tell?" Scott looks up, startled. "I already told you. I went out for a drink."

Aimee bites her lip, trying to fight her annoyance. "C'mon, Scott, you have to admit it's a really strange coincidence. The one night that you head out for a drink and Anton ends up getting hit by a car in an alley behind that same bar. You're saying that's a total coincidence?"

"What are *you* saying?" he snaps. "I don't know, Aimee. It's not that weird. It's the closest bar to this neighborhood. I'm sure there were other people from East Bethesda that were there. Maybe Anton decided he didn't want to go home, after all. Maybe after I left him at his house he headed to the bar."

"You think he followed you?"

"I didn't say that."

The doorbell rings, cutting their conversation short. When Aimee peers through the peephole, she recognizes the detective from yesterday. Her chest tightens. He said he would come by to talk about the video, but opening the door and letting him into her home feels like a turning point. There's no going back, but she has no choice. She can't not let him in.

"Detective, hi."

"Sorry to disturb you," he says. "Mind if I come in?"

He follows her into the living room as Scott enters from the kitchen. The two men introduce themselves and everyone sits, Aimee and Scott side by side on the sofa and Detective Salazar in an armchair across from them.

"We wanted to thank you for sending that video over, that was very helpful," Salazar says.

"What video?" Scott asks.

"I told you." She flashes a tight smile at Scott. "The doorbell camera? Remember?"

He nods, but a strange expression settles on his face that she can't read.

"You were the one who answered the door that night, is that right, Mr. Crowder?"

"Yes. I was on my way out, anyway."

"And do you mind telling me where you were heading?"

"I was just going out for a drink." He turns to Aimee and nods. "Aimee was in bed, but I'm a bit of a night owl. I thought I would head down to Villain & Saint, have a drink, see if there was any live music."

"Villain & Saint, huh? In the video, you walk down the street with Anton Khoury. Did he join you at the bar?"

"No. I walked him home. He seemed pretty drunk. I left him at his house and then went on."

"Alone?"

Scott nods.

"And how long did you stay at the bar?"

"Maybe an hour? I had one drink and then I came back."

"Were you by yourself?"

"Uhh, no, I met a friend."

Aimee feels her shoulders tighten. This is the first she's heard of a friend. But her instinct tells her not to betray her surprise, and she keeps a placid smile on her face.

"And could you tell me who that friend is?" The detective shoots a quick glance Aimee's way. "Just so we can alibi you and cross you off the list."

"His name's Jon Block. Just a guy from the gym."

Guy from the gym? It takes everything she has not to turn to Scott and scoff. She's never heard of any friend from the gym.

But her loyalty kicks in. They must present a united front to the police. That's what they do, her and Scott, stick together. Scott can explain later, when the detective is gone.

"We'll need his contact info," Detective Salazar says.

"Of course."

"Did Mr. Khoury show up at the bar, later?"

Scott shakes his head. "No. If he came to the bar, I didn't see him."

"What about in the parking lot? Or the alley? Did you see him there?"

"No." Scott's voice is strained. "I told you. The last time I saw him was here, in the neighborhood. I left him at his house."

"So you keep saying, but it is odd, isn't it? That you were the last person seen with Anton Khoury and then you go to a bar, and he ends up in an alley behind that bar, dead."

"Hold on a minute," Aimee says. "Are you accusing Scott of having something to do with Anton's death?"

"It's fine." Scott puts his hand on hers. "He's just doing his job." Scott leans forward, and Aimee can see his muscles tensing and relaxing under his T-shirt.

"It's not that weird," Aimee says, parroting some of what Scott said earlier. "There's one bar within walking distance. It's where Anton would go if he wanted to get a drink and didn't want to drive."

"And how did you get there?" Salazar asks Scott. "Did you drive?"

"No, I walked."

"Did you take the cut-through that runs from the back of your cul-de-sac?"

Scott nods. "It's the fastest way, yes."

"Why don't you tell me what happened when Anton came to the house. Exactly."

"He was drunk. He was bleeding from his temple. I figured he fell and hit his head. He was babbling."

"About what?"

"Oh, I don't know. I wasn't paying attention. I was late, and I wanted to get going. I told him I was meeting someone at Villain & Saint and then I walked him back to his house. I walked him right up to his front door. I assumed he went back inside."

"But you didn't see him go inside?"

Scott shakes his head. "I don't think so. He was kind of hanging out by the door, but like I said, I was late. I took off."

"And that's the last time you saw him."

"Yes. That's the last time I saw Anton Khoury."

"How well did you both know Mr. Khoury?"

Scott and Aimee exchange a glance. "We've known Anton and Gwen for just over a year," Aimee says. "They moved in last summer."

"It's really Aimee who is good friends with Gwen," Scott says. "And with Lisa, who lives down the block. The husbands—me, Marcus, and Anton—all get along but I wouldn't say we're close friends."

Aimee nods. "Our families go on vacations together and stuff like that."

"Has he ever mentioned any problems with anyone? Someone who might have a grudge against him?"

"No, I can't imagine anyone holding a grudge against him," Scott says. "He's a pretty quiet guy. Keeps to himself. He's a writer. I think he mostly works from home."

"And nothing unusual in the neighborhood lately?" Salazar asks. "Nobody lurking around who doesn't belong?"

"No. It's very quiet here. Very safe," Aimee says. "It's a cul-de-sac, so no one who doesn't live here ever goes through here. Except, like, Amazon and DoorDash."

"People from the neighborhood don't come through the cul-de-sac to use the shortcut to get to downtown Bethesda?"

"Sure, I guess. But just locals who live here," she says. "Do you think someone from the neighborhood is involved?"

"We're just asking questions at this point. Can you think of anything else that might be relevant? Anything at all?"

Aimee debates whether she should offer up any of the jigsaw pieces she's picked up in the past day: the fight she overheard last night, where the blood on Anton's head came from, Anton's history of cheating. But she decides it's none of her business. Detective Salazar is a professional. He'll find these things out if they are relevant. It would feel like a betrayal of her friendship with Gwen to mention any of them.

Detective Salazar looks at Scott. "If you could walk me out, give me that name and number of the friend you met. The one from the gym."

His tone is slightly amused, as if he thinks Scott has made it all up. But maybe that's how he talks to people, Aimee thinks, keeping them off guard. She watches as Scott and the detective leave, and goes to the kitchen. As she busies herself with the remaining breakfast dishes, she replays the interview. She's shaken, as much by the fact that her neighbor has been killed as by her husband's behavior. It's off, there's no denying it. She doesn't believe Scott is capable of violence, but he is hiding something.

"So, who's this friend?" she asks as soon as he crosses the threshold into the kitchen.

"Whoa, easy there." He holds up his hands as if he's being robbed. "He's nobody. Just a guy from the gym."

"What did you say his name was?"

"Jon Block."

"How come you never mentioned him before?"

"Aimee. What's going on with you? I'm not allowed to meet a friend from the gym for a drink?"

"Daddy, Daddy, Daddy!" Noa runs in and yanks at Scott's pants. "Can you get the first aid kit down? I'm setting up an animal hospital and I need bandages." Aimee had placed the first aid kit out of Noa's reach for this very reason—she could go through a jumbo pack of Band-Aids in an hour. A look of relief flashes across Scott's face. He's glad, Aimee realizes, to have an excuse to cut the conversation short.

Moments after Scott leaves the room with Noa, his phone pings. Aimee stays still a moment, trying to establish where the sound is coming from. *Ping.* She finds the phone plugged into their charging station on a table by the back door.

Aimee holds it in her palm, torn about what to do.

They have a marriage built on trust. She's not like Gwen, full of suspicions. She's never gone through Scott's things, never read his texts or his emails. But then again, she's never had any reason to doubt him before.

She's dying to read what has just come in but knows that will be crossing a line. She's never been tempted to invade his privacy before. The last thing she wants to do is turn on Scott, but in light of Detective Salazar's questions and Scott's slippery responses, she feels justified.

Aimee turns the phone over in her hand. The home screen has a text from Jon Block. *I've found something. Can you meet me . . .*

The text cuts off and she can't access it because she doesn't know his passcode. She tries their anniversary, her birthday, the twins' and then Noa's birthday, but nothing. She hears his footsteps approaching and drops the phone back on the table, stepping back, pretending to look for something in Max's backpack, which hangs on a nearby peg.

"There it is." Scott picks up his phone. Peering over her shoulder, she watches him read the message.

"Get the first aid kit for Noa?" She watches his face as he reads the texts, searching for any change in his reaction.

He doesn't respond straight away. He's absorbed in what he's reading. Finally, he looks up. "Huh? Yeah. Hey, listen, I think I'm going to head to the gym while the boys are at soccer. That cool with you?"

He doesn't wait for a response but walks away, obviously distracted. Something shifts inside her. She can sense a crack in what she had long taken for granted. No matter what challenges she faced as a mom and a business owner, she always thought her marriage was rock solid.

But Scott is lying to her.

She doesn't know why, but she is going to find out.

13

Gwen stands in the middle of her kitchen and stares at her to-do list.

She can't put it off any longer—it's time to call Anton's father, Henri.

The thought terrifies her. Henri is a taciturn man who had moved back to France after Anton's mother died, retiring to a small town about thirty miles north of Marseille. She and Anton had one awful visit with him in France. It was a few years after the publication of *The Last Cyclamen*, a time when she and the rest of the world thought a follow-up novel was imminent. The month-long trip to the South of France was a chance for the twins, who were small, to spend a good chunk of time with their grandfather, as well as an opportunity for Anton to do some research on his new book. The whole trip went poorly. The crumbling seventeenth-century house that Henri lived in was not child-friendly, and Gwen spent the first two weeks chasing after the boys, barely three at the time, making sure they didn't crack their skulls falling down stone steps or cut themselves on the rusty metal scraps in the overgrown garden. George and Rafi failed to live up to Henri's expectations about how little boys should behave, and Gwen felt judged and embarrassed. Anton abdicated any parental responsibility on the trip, as if being in a foreign country absolved him, spending his days driving around the countryside solo "for his book." His father had never approved of Anton's choices—to study literature instead of something practical, to abandon his Catholic faith, to pursue a career as a writer. Marrying Gwen was just another bad choice. Henri didn't consider his son a serious person.

At the beginning of the third week, Gwen witnessed a blow-out between the two men. The fight in the kitchen started with yelling and hurled insults. It was the sound of broken pottery that sent her scurrying outside with Rafi and George. She took them on a long walk into the village to get treats, only to arrive just as the town's bakery and sweet shop had shut down for their customary two-hour lunch. When she returned to the house be-draggled, Anton had packed their bags. They were leaving im-mediately, he said.

He never told her what had led to the break with his father. He made it seem like it was a long time coming, but not about anything specific.

And now she had to phone Henri and tell him his son was dead.

Ignoring the empty wine bottle and dirty glasses, Gwen makes coffee. She is both sad and grateful that the boys aren't here. It's as if her mother cast a magic spell on her by suggesting she was a mess, and now she has to become one. She takes her coffee into Anton's office and sits at his desk. It is five hours later in France. When is a good time to call and tell a man that his son is dead? Murdered? Isn't there someone else who could do this for her?

She picks up her phone and dials her mother.

"Sweetie, I'm so glad to hear from you."

"How are the kids?" Gwen asks.

"Wonderful. They're at the club with Daddy."

"They have school tomorrow."

"I thought I would drive them home sometime tomorrow. We can break the news to them together. How does that sound? Do you think you are up to that?"

"What about school?"

"Gwen, honey, you're not thinking straight. Their father is dead. They're going to be missing some school."

She feels chagrined. She had heard it was good to keep routines going for children when they experience a trauma, that their whole life shouldn't be disrupted. But maybe she had remembered that wrong. Her mother seems very confident.

"I guess you're right. I'll be here. I'm not going anywhere."

"I don't want to bring the boys back to the house and find you in your pajamas, or drunk. Not that you don't deserve to be both things, sweetie, but we must remember to put on a brave face."

"I need you to call Anton's dad."

"Henri doesn't know yet? Gwen!"

"I couldn't do it yesterday."

"Give me the number, I'll take care of it. I always liked him."

Gwen scrolls through her phone for his number, feeling both relieved and disgusted with herself. As much as she rails against her parents, she has never really grown into a full adult, has she? She depends on them financially. Always has. She didn't have the burden of college loans, and when she entered the working world, they subsidized her meager salary. Would she have been better off if they had told her no? She would have hated them for it at the time, but maybe she wouldn't be where she is now. If she had developed some strength early on, she would have left Anton the first time he cheated on her, before they were even married, with another writer at his MFA program.

"I can't find it," she says. "I must have deleted it by accident."

"You don't have your father-in-law's number?"

"I will find it and text you as soon as I do."

"Don't put this off, Gwen. He needs to be told."

Gwen hangs up, trying to decide where to look for Henri's number. The police still have Anton's phone, but he has to have information on his dad somewhere. She opens a drawer to the right of the desk and finds a jumble of office supplies and a half-empty pack of Camels.

The one below it holds a random assortment of notebooks, magazines, stories ripped out of the newspaper. The detritus of a writer's life, but no signs of information about Henri. She spots a photograph and pulls it out.

Her throat catches when she sees it's a picture of the night they first met, fifteen years ago. A casual selfie taken at a party in New York City. Gwen had been living in the city, churning out press releases for a PR firm in Soho that specialized in luxury brands, when she bumped into a friend from college who was getting her master's in fiction at Columbia. They had been in a creative writing class together, back when Gwen had flirted with the idea of becoming a writer.

But she didn't have the confidence, and her parents insisted that she study something more practical, so she decided on marketing for her major.

Her friend invited her to a party, but Gwen almost didn't go. It wasn't only that the party was all the way uptown in Morningside Heights, at least thirty minutes on the subway from her apartment on a quiet street in Greenwich Village, it was the fear of seeing all these burgeoning writers embarking on a life she wished she could have had. If she only had the courage to say no to her parents. She was talented, but she had no guts.

At the last minute she decided to go and it was a decision that altered the course of her life, because that's where she met Anton. She felt awkward and out of place as soon as she showed up. Almost everyone was from the writing program, along with a few other random Columbia graduate students. She flitted in and out of conversations but was unable to get a toehold in any of them. She felt ashamed and took refuge in the bedroom, where she walked in on a man examining the books on the floor-to-ceiling bookshelf—Anton. They started talking and when it was time to go, he walked her to the 116th Street subway station, but at the last minute they decided they would keep talking and he would walk her to 110th, then 103rd, and so on until they had walked all the way down Broadway to the Village, the conversation never ceasing. They didn't stop talking all the way up the five flights to her small studio apartment. By the time he left two days later, Gwen was in love.

Tears fill her eyes. They were happy once. She yanks open the drawer on her right, searching for a tissue packet.

Instead, she finds an overstuffed manila folder. It's addressed to Henri Khoury in France, and the return address is their old house in Boston, written in Anton's familiar block lettering.

Bingo, she thinks and empties the contents onto the desk. A parcel wrapped in a piece of blue-and-white cloth slides out along with an unmarked white envelope.

As Gwen turns the parcel over in her hand, confused, the cloth falls away, revealing a worn leather journal. Gwen opens it but cannot make out the small, tidy cursive. She recognizes a word here and there and realizes it's all in French. Every page has a date on top; the first page's date is June 1, 1968. She flips to the last page and her stomach lurches when she finds a pencil sketch of a lone flower.

Le dernier cyclamen

The Last Cyclamen. This must be where Anton got the name for his book.

Gwen takes the heavy white envelope in her hand, recognizing it as the expensive stationery she gave to Anton on their first anniversary—the paper anniversary. Inside is one folded sheet, which she takes out and begins to read. It's dated right after they returned from that awful trip to France.

Dear Father,

In France you called me a fraud. A thief.

You said that if Maman were alive she would be aghast to know that her innermost thoughts, her dreams and her fears were published for the world to see.

But I don't see it that way. I see my book as a testament to her strength and courage, a way of honoring what a beautiful writer she was.

You say it's plagiarism, using her words. That she's the one who wrote it and I just slapped my name on it. That I'm profiting from her pain, stealing her glory.

But did you ever consider that she would want that for me? For her suffering to be transformed into my success? Isn't that what every mother wants? For her children to become somebody?

I am somebody, thanks to her journal. I think if Maman were alive she would be thrilled for me. And even if she weren't, she would never do what you have done. She would never cut me out.

I am your only child.

You have two grandchildren who deserve to have you in their lives.

I have enclosed Maman's dairy. I don't need it anymore and I thought you might want it back. I don't regret writing The Last Cyclamen, *but I do regret what has happened to us.*

Always your son, Anton

Gwen drops the letter on the desk, stunned. She opens the journal to a random page and tries to make sense of the words printed in neat script. She took four years of high school French, but she can only make out a few words here or there. When she turns the page, she finds a section that has been underlined in pencil. Did Anton make these marks?

She boots up Anton's computer and opens Google Translate. There are two boxes next to each other—one in which to type in the original text and a second where the translation will appear. She begins to enter the underlined words from the diary. *Aujourd'hui, il faisait une chaleur insupportable. J'ai rencontré J à La Gondola pour le déjeuner. Nos sièges étaient juste au bord de l'eau. Nous naviguerons sur cette mer ensemble, a-t-il dit en me prenant la main.*

Like magic, as soon as she types in a combination of letters that make no sense to her, a series of English words appear in the second box. The words of Anton's mother. It's almost as if she is speaking directly to her from the grave.

Today was unbearably hot. I met J at La Gondola for lunch. Our seats were right by the water. We will sail that sea together, he said, taking my hand.

A chill runs through her. The Gondola restaurant played a large part in *The Last Cyclamen*. It's the setting of several meals at which the main character, a sheltered young woman, is seduced by an older, wealthy man. The Gondola represents the world she desires to be a part of, one of privilege and freedom.

Gwen recalls one *New York Times* review of the book mentioning The Gondola by name as an example of how Anton's book captured the sophistication of Beirut in the 1960s before the civil war broke out.

Gwen turns to Anton's bookshelf and pulls out a leatherbound copy of *The Last Cyclamen*, a gift from her to Anton upon its publication. The pages are gilded, the spine uncracked. It takes her a few moments to find what she is looking for, but about halfway through the book she sees it. Gwen traces the lines with her finger as she reads the now familiar words.

Today was unbearably hot. I met J at La Gondola for lunch. Our seats were right by the water. "We will sail that sea together," he said, taking my hand.

Gwen drops the book in shock. Anton had stolen the words of his dead mother and passed them off as his own. That's what the fight with his father had been about.

He had written this confession to his father, but he couldn't bring himself to send it.

Of course Anton hadn't been able to finish a second book in the past eight years, Gwen thinks with bitterness. He had nothing original to say.

He never did.

14

LAST WINTER BREAK

On the third day in Vermont, Lisa woke up to a miserable blue sky. There had been talk of sleet, which everyone had bemoaned—it would scuttle their skiing plans. But Lisa was secretly praying for it. Maybe they could go into town and do a little shopping. Stowe had some great day spas—a manicure and a massage sounded lovely. But no, the conditions for skiing were perfect.

The day before, she had muddled through a day on the slopes, hating every minute of being out in the bracing cold. She was on the green slopes, the bunny slopes, with toddlers speeding past her. She thought she could at least count on Kai for company, but he had taken to snowboarding and by the late morning had graduated to more difficult courses. Marcus had done a few runs with her and then, clearly bored, left her for more challenging terrain. Lisa had pretended to sprain her ankle so she could spend the rest of the afternoon at the lodge in front of the roaring fire, sipping spiked cocoa and scrolling through Instagram, jealous of neighbors who were spending the break in the Caribbean with white sand and azure waters while she was stuck in the icy wind of northern Vermont.

This morning, she exaggerated her limp as she made her way up the stairs into the kitchen for breakfast. She wasn't going to say anything; she wanted someone to notice. She had learned that from her mother. People were more sympathetic if they were the ones who picked up on your suffering. But no one did. It wasn't until she got up to refill her coffee, limping across the kitchen, that Aimee took note.

"Oh my gosh, are you okay, Lisa?"

"I'm fine. I think I just sprained it a little."

"You better wrap that up tight before you go skiing," Scott said. "I've got some tape if you want."

"Couple of ibuprofen and you'll be fine," Marcus said.

Lisa felt her stomach lurch. Were they going to bully her into skiing on a bad ankle? True, she wasn't really injured, but they didn't know that. She *might* be. It wasn't as if she hadn't taken a tumble or two yesterday, and she very well could have twisted her ankle. She filled her coffee and turned, lurching back to the table, wincing with each step.

"You're probably right. I'll be fine." She bit her lip hard as she eased into her seat.

"Oh no," Aimee said. "You're not skiing on that ankle. You should stay here and rest."

"Maybe we should drop you off at a clinic?" Gwen's words dripped with faux concern. Couldn't anyone else see it besides Lisa? "I mean, what if it's broken?"

"Those clinics are packed during the holidays," Anton said. "You might get stuck there for hours."

"Oh, but better safe than sorry," Gwen said. "I can run you over after breakfast."

Gwen would like that, all right. Park Lisa in some clinic in the sticks for the whole day. It took a little finessing, but Lisa managed to thread the needle between too injured to be expected to go skiing, but not injured enough to require a visit to the clinic. Before they left for the slopes, Gwen asked her if she wouldn't mind just letting Sababa out to pee.

"If it doesn't hurt too much to move, of course."

Lisa happily agreed. So what if Gwen was on to her? She knew if Gwen tried to say anything negative about her to Aimee, she would only make herself look bad. Like a vindictive gossip. Aimee didn't think she was malingering, neither did the guys. Gwen wouldn't find a sympathetic audience with them. They would think Gwen petty for saying anything. The thought filled her with satisfaction and she found herself half wishing that Gwen might say something nasty about her behind her back, just so they would shut her down.

By the time they left, Lisa was so thoroughly playing the part that she found herself limping through the house on her way upstairs, even though she was alone.

On the third floor, she did a quick scan of the bedrooms, curious about what Gwen and Aimee had brought with them. It was always interesting to peek inside other women's beauty routines, the items they found indispensable for their trips. She helped herself to some of Gwen's anti-aging serum, tried on one of her cashmere sweaters, and flipped through her gratitude journal. It was as vanilla and boring as she expected. *So grateful for my boys. So thankful for this family vacation.*

In the top drawer of her bedside table, Lisa found a prescription bottle of Xanax. Lisa pocketed that. She giggled at the thought of Gwen feeling a panic attack coming on and not being able to locate her meds. She'd feel like such an idiot, so sure she had packed it. Lisa would have to remember to place it somewhere in Gwen's house when they got back to Bethesda.

In the afternoon Lisa became bored enough to walk Sababa, who had begun to whimper by the back door. The cold wind whipped at her, stinging her face. The sun would set soon, and everyone would be back. Lisa felt a cloak of melancholy settle around her shoulders as she thought of the energy everyone would bring with them. Having spent a day outside, they'd be full of laughter and stories, and their bonds would be knitted tighter, with her even further on the outside.

She walked around the village, passing an occasional person on snowshoes heading back from the woods. When no one was watching, she didn't have to limp. She had researched minor sprains on the internet, and it seemed that most resolved within twenty-four hours, so by this evening she could drop the act.

Sababa momentarily bounded away from her, pulling the thin

leash from her thickly mittened hand. Lisa called his name and he froze. But when she made a move toward him he ran a few feet farther, to the edge of the dark woods. The sun was almost set now, and she had a flash of panic, realizing that if he took off into the trees she might never find him.

Of course, *she* would be blamed. She could imagine Gwen's face turning a mottled pink as she cried over little lost Sababa. Lisa knew the sympathy would be entirely with Gwen, everyone would turn against her. As much as she'd like Gwen to suffer, she couldn't do that to the dog. He was innocent. She took a step, gingerly, and Sababa cocked his head as if realizing his error. With satisfaction, she put her foot down on his leash so he couldn't run off again.

No, she wasn't going to hurt Sababa to get to Gwen. It was the kind of impulsive mistake she might have made when she was younger. Once, at an office party when she was in her twenties, she had stolen the wallet of a coworker she despised and tossed it in the bathroom trash. Her cubicle was adjacent to this woman, and she enjoyed ripples of satisfaction for days as she listened to the woman's laments about the inconvenience of replacing all her credit cards and her driver's license. But other times her impulsivity had backfired—like when she spotted an ex-boyfriend's new girlfriend's car at the gym and used her house key to make a deep scratch down the driver's side door. She hadn't known there were security cameras in the gym parking lot. The police questioned her. The new girlfriend decided not to press charges, but it had been embarrassing.

That night, after everyone had returned and showered, they all went out to dinner in Stowe. The restaurant was packed with people just like them—upper-middle-class families from Boston, New York, and Washington. The kids got their own table right next to the adults, all six of whom were crammed into a wooden booth. Lisa was squished between Anton and Marcus, while across from her Scott was sandwiched between Aimee and Gwen.

At some point in the evening, after the appetizers but before the main course arrived, when people were on their way to being drunk, Anton asked her about her ankle.

Lisa turned her body away from Marcus, who was regaling everyone with a story about his first run on the black diamond slopes, and focused her full attention on Anton. Feeling the alcohol unhook her inhibitions, Lisa described how the ankle sprain activated an old injury from college when she ran track competitively. He seemed impressed. She saw herself becoming a more interesting person in his eyes. Her telling borrowed details from a movie she once saw about a star athlete who twisted her ankle during a race and had to sit out the track season, and learned some valuable life lessons in the process. As she told this story to Anton as her own, it became real. So real that tears sprang to her eyes, which she wiped away.

"It was a really tough time for me," she said. "But it made me grow up. I needed to move beyond the external validation that being a track star had brought me."

"That's an incredible story. I had no idea you were a competitive athlete."

Panic seized her. What had she done? She knew this was the kind of lie that could easily be checked. She had run track in high school for two seasons, but was hardly a star. She had quit at the beginning of her senior year, bored with the whole thing. "I don't like to talk about it." She lowered her head and looked at him from the corner of her eyes. No one was listening to them. No one had noticed she and Anton had started their own side conversation. "I guess it's something I've tried to put in the past. But the alcohol, and you're so easy to talk to. You're a Sagittarius, right?"

He nodded.

"I remember your birthday was at the beginning of December. That's why we get along so well. I'm an Aquarius. There's this whole poem about us. The Aquarius woman is gentle yet tough, sociable but also a loner. Predictable in her unpredictability."

"Wow. Sounds complicated."

"I'm like an orchid. Beautiful and wild and I need just the right growing conditions." She placed her hand on Anton's and looked him in the eye. "But once you know what I need, I'll bloom for you over and over and over again."

It was a gamble. He could pull his hand away, make a joke, change the subject. But he didn't move his hand. He nodded. "I didn't realize you were so creative. Gwen, Scott, everyone teases me about how long it's taking to finish my second book. They have no idea how hard it is to create something."

"I do. I admire you so much. I loved your first book. I never told you that before because I don't feel qualified to talk about literature." She flashed a coy smile. "But your prose, your images, your language. The book is beautiful." She had bought the book with every intention of reading it when the Khourys first moved onto Nassau Court. It was fun to leave on the coffee table and point out to guests that the author was a good friend. But in truth she had found the writing impenetrable, the language confusing. She wasn't much of a reader.

"Thank you for saying that." Anton smiled. "If a book speaks to you, that makes you qualified. Art is for everyone. Anyone can read a book." His face seemed to open now in a way Lisa hadn't seen before. He really was a very attractive man, in a brooding, serious way. "And I'm glad you told me your story. It's okay to admit you've been hurt. It's okay to be vulnerable." He shot a quick glance at Gwen, who was laughing uproariously at something Scott said. "Some people try to act like superheroes. Never let anyone see that they're human." He took a swig of his drink. "But that just pushes people away."

There was no misunderstanding his meaning. He may have been drunk, but he was insulting his wife. Lisa loved it. Her belly fluttered. Gwen and Anton were not an unbreakable duo.

When he pushed his leg against hers and said *sorry*, she smiled. "Don't apologize," she said, pushing her leg back.

Forget ski accidents, or lost wallets, or missing dogs.

Here's something she could take from Gwen, something she would relish taking.

Anton.

15

Scott comes down the stairs with his bright-green gym bag slung over his shoulder.

"Wait, hold on a minute," Aimee says, getting up from her perch at the kitchen island. "I think we need to talk."

"Now? The boys are still at soccer for another hour, and I promised I'd take them to Norwood Park later. If I don't get to the gym now . . ." He shrugs. "And I haven't been to the gym in three days. I need some exercise." Scott sighs. "Tell you what, I'll make dinner and do the big shopping tonight if you make a list."

"This isn't about the shopping," Aimee says.

"What is it about?"

She's on the spot. She can't blurt out, *I read part of your text, can I read the rest?* Or can she? It's hard for her to figure out her role as adult, wife, and mother sometimes. She was naïve when they married and had kids, thinking that they would naturally divide up the work evenly, and she was surprised when it didn't work out like that. Scott was willing, more so than many of the husbands she saw, to contribute to the daily work of making a household run—but he needed to be told. As if he were her employee. She never wanted to be the CEO of the family. She already ran her own business and managed Tim and the crew.

That's when she began to miss her mother anew. The ache that she thought had subsided years after her death began to throb more urgently when Aimee had her own kids. She longed to turn to her when faced with the challenges of being a wife and mother, and her mother's absence felt like a fresh pain.

Scott should be allowed to go to the gym if he wants. Even using the word *allowed* seems ridiculous. He's a grown man.

But today is different. Anton is dead, murdered, and the police were just here questioning Scott. And now he's running off again. He says it's to the gym but the timing with that text has her on alert. "I feel weird. I want to talk about what the detective was saying. Do you think Anton followed you to Villain & Saint? Can you think of any reason why he would?"

Scott looks at his watch, then at her, as if deciding that he can spare a few minutes. "No. I can't think of any reason he would follow me. I've told you about that night. Several times. I feel terrible about what happened to him. I'm just as freaked out as you are that he was killed outside the same bar that I went to. But I've racked my brain trying to remember anything that could explain what he was doing in the alley. I keep coming up with nothing." He shifts his bag. "I wish I could go back, Aimee. I wish I could go back to Friday night and take the time to listen to him babble. But I was in such a hurry. I feel like an asshole."

"You're not."

"It's just, he was drunk and annoying, and I should have stayed with him but I just wanted to get out of there. I keep going over it in my mind. Why would he follow me?"

He searches her face with his eyes.

"I don't know," she says. "Maybe he didn't. Maybe he was going there for some other reason."

"I hope so. I really do. I don't want to be part of his death in any way, not even tangentially."

"Go to the gym," Aimee says. "We can talk more tonight."

Before the door has clicked shut, however, a plan has formed in her head.

Aimee pulls on her shoes while calling Lisa.

"I have a huge favor," Aimee blurts out. "I have to run out. Noa is here alone, can you—"

"Come over? Of course I can! I'll be there in five minutes. Is everything okay?"

"Everything's fine. But I have to go. Like now." She knew the answer would be yes and feels a little guilty about it. Lisa is always around. Always there. Always willing. As if by making herself needed, people will like her more. But Aimee likes Lisa despite how the scent of neediness clings to her like a cloying perfume. Lisa is insecure, and Aimee feels bad for her. She remembers how vulnerable she was in the years after her mother's death, searching for friendship and kindness. She tries to show that kindness to Lisa even when she comes on too strong.

She is about to hang up when Lisa clears her throat.

"Did I just see the police at your house?"

"Yes. Can we talk later? I'm sorry, I have to get this thing to a client, I'm halfway out the door." She hates lying, but what is she going to say, that she needs to chase after her husband? That she wants to spy on him because she read half of a text message? Aimee hangs up and grabs her coat. From the front door she can see Scott, his gym bag over his shoulder, walking toward the cut-through to downtown Bethesda. She'll have to run to catch up to him.

"Where are you going?"

"Huh?" She turns to see Noa at the top of the stairs. "Oh, sweetie, I have to run out for a minute. Lisa is on her way. You can just keep doing whatever you were doing, and I'll be back before you know it."

"I don't want her to come over. What do you have to take to your client? You don't have anything in your hands."

Amy flinches, startled. "Were you eavesdropping?"

"What's that mean?"

"That's when you listen in on other people's conversations."

"I wasn't. I wasn't trying to. You just talk loud. I heard it, but I wasn't listening."

"Eavesdropping is wrong." It feels absurd to be delivering an ethics lesson as she's leaving to tail her husband.

"So is lying. Lying is wrong. You said so."

Aimee peers out the door. Lisa is coming up the walk, but Scott is out of sight. She has to go now if she hopes to catch him.

Aimee blows Noa a kiss and opens the door. She waves at Lisa as she races to the cut-through. She runs down the alley between two houses. When she emerges on Wisconsin Avenue, her heart sinks. Scott is nowhere to be seen. She's too late. She turns in the direction of his gym, which is on the opposite side of the wide thoroughfare, away from Villain & Saint and the alley where Anton was found. *This was stupid*, she thinks, feeling foolish as she passes shoppers and small groups of teens out for an afternoon of fun. She should be at home with Noa. Or tending to Gwen. But Scott's strange behavior has her playing Nancy Drew.

Aimee stops outside the immense plate glass windows of Tatte, a large café with a twenty-foot ceiling that leans more Parisian atelier than suburban coffee shop. On a whim, she peers inside, and that's when she sees him. Or rather, his gym bag. Its bright green catches her eye. It's stuffed beneath a chair in a corner, and Scott's back is to her. From this far away, she cannot make out who he is with, if anyone at all.

She enters the cavernous restaurant and takes her place in line, her heart beating. A large U-shaped island dominates the center of the room. One side is lined with display cases and two cash registers. The other side has stools for customers to sit on. In the middle, baristas rush around making coffee and tea and fulfilling orders. The clank of cutlery against porcelain echoes loudly off the tiled floor. Aimee keeps her eye on Scott, who is sitting in an adjoining room at one of the small tables pushed against the wall. From her spot in line, she can see his back, but his companion, if he has one, is hidden by an enormous potted fern. When her turn comes, Aimee orders a drip coffee, which they hand to her right away. She wanders around along with

several other customers searching for open seats and finds one
at the counter by the window overlooking the street. When she
angles herself so her back is to the window, she can catch a sliver
of Scott from the corner of her eye, but not much else.

What is the plan here? she asks herself. Perhaps she should just
walk right up to him, act surprised. Tell him she was . . . she was
what? In the neighborhood? Craving a four-dollar coffee? There
is no good reason for her to be here and not at home.

She waits patiently, sipping her coffee.

After about ten minutes, she sees Scott get up and walk out
the door. Quickly, Aimee pops up out of her seat and strides over
to the corner where Scott was sitting. A middle-aged man with
fading blond hair is still sitting at the table.

She doesn't ask to sit down before she does.

The man looks up in surprise. This close she can see he is a
little older than she is, maybe early- to midfifties, but in good
shape. He's dressed casually but looks put together in dark jeans
and a nice shirt, as if he just came from a date. He adjusts his
wire-rimmed glasses and nods at the used coffee cup in front of
him.

"Oh hey, I'm just leaving." He begins to gather his things.

"Actually, can you stay? I don't want the table. It's you I want
to talk to. You're Jon Block, right?"

He freezes, halfway out of his chair. "Uhh, and who are you?"

Aimee pats the table. "Please, sit." She knows that she must
be coming across as mentally unbalanced, and maybe she is after
everything that has happened in the past few days.

But he sits back down.

"I'm Aimee Stern. Scott Crowder's wife."

"Scott Crowder. I see." He cocks his head to one side. "Does
your husband know you're here?"

"No, he doesn't," she says. "I happened to be walking by, and
I saw you guys sitting here. How do you know my husband? It's
not from the gym, is it?"

He gives her a half smile. "Happened to be walking by, huh? You're putting me in a tough spot here."

"Were you with him last night at Villain & Saint?"

Block leans back. "Is that what he told you?"

Aimee flinches. *What a strange response*, she thinks. Block is cool and collected, almost as if he was expecting her.

"It's what he told the *police*," she says, hoping the mention of law enforcement might make him open up. "Please, can you just answer the question? How do you know Scott?"

He frowns. "Why don't you just ask him this?"

The question hangs between them. This isn't how she thought it would go. His confidence unnerves her. She feels like she's on the defensive when he's the one who is sneaking around meeting her husband in secret.

"Well?" he asks.

She doesn't have an answer for why she didn't ask Scott directly. And then it hits her. *Because I'm terrified*, she realizes, *that we might not be as solid as I think.*

"I'm asking you," she says.

He stands up and pulls out a card, tossing it on the table. "You really need to talk to your husband."

He starts to walk away, and she doesn't try to stop him or go after him. Instead, she takes the card he left and turns it over. Above Jon Block's name and contact information, written in small black letters, are the words *Capital Investigators.*

16

NOW

Gwen stands before her immense walk-in closet, unable to move. The Sunday afternoon is almost gone and she's still in the same sweatpants and T-shirt she's been wearing for more than twenty-four hours. Streaked with coffee, stained with tears.

Aimee texted her to come over, and when she didn't respond, Lisa called.

"Come to Aimee's around four, or we're coming to get you."

She knew Lisa wasn't joking, and she didn't want her neighbor to come over and find her like this. So Gwen forced herself to shower. To blow-dry her hair. Even to apply a little makeup—concealer to hide her circles, even darker than usual, some blush and highlighter to bring a little glow to her sallow skin.

She needs her friends. She can't stand being in this house right now with the boys gone. Everywhere she looks, memories of Anton confront her. In the living room, it's the leather club chair he sat in to read his students' work. In the bedroom, his reading glasses perch atop his half-read copy of *Crime and Punishment* on the nightstand. And on so many surfaces, little scraps of paper with unintelligible scrawling. He owned dozens of small notebooks yet often found himself without one, so he would rip off corners of whatever was at hand—bills, the backs of receipts—and jot down flashes of inspiration. Snippets, he called them, but when Gwen read them, they never made any sense to her.

Golden fears
Boy wears blue shirt

Gwen stares at her neatly folded clothes on the shelves, the precisely hung garments. Everything in her custom closet is light in color—cream and oatmeal and beige. This is her signature look—it goes with her blond hair and the image she tries to project. Airy, neutral, sophisticated. It seems ridiculous now to put on these clothes. She wants something dark to match her mood, but she has no black or navy or gray. The best she comes up with is jeans and a taupe sweater that seems to accentuate the purple circles under her eyes that no amount of makeup could conceal.

The distance between her front door and Aimee's is about forty feet, but it feels like miles. Out on the street she feels vulnerable, as if people are watching her from the safety of their homes. Everyone must know by now that Anton was murdered. A few neighbors dropped off flowers, or bags of ready-to-eat food from Balducci's. But there must be talk. Gossip. Leaving the house feels like a mistake, and she hesitates at the bottom of Aimee's walkway. She entertains the thought of turning around, sending a text, but the front door swings open and Aimee is standing there.

"Come in, come in." Aimee ushers her inside. Gwen follows her into the living room, where Lisa is sitting. Lisa springs up and gives her a hug. She smells like vanilla and musk. Aimee leaves the room to make tea while Lisa peppers her with questions about the boys and how long they are staying at Barb's. The more concern Lisa shows, the colder Gwen becomes. She can't help it. There's something about Lisa's warmth and enthusiasm that has always felt forced to Gwen, like an act she's putting on. She's seen Lisa smile enthusiastically, laugh and joke, and then the moment she doesn't think anyone is looking, her face turns to stone. But she has Aimee completely snowed.

Aimee comes back with tea.

"Where is everyone?" Gwen asks.

"Scott took the kids to Norwood," Aimee says. "Even Noa."

"The police came by our house today," Lisa says. "Asked Marcus and me about Friday night. I wish we could have been more helpful. They asked if we had a doorbell camera, which we don't, although now I think we should get one. You have one, Aimee. Did the police ask to see the footage?"

Gwen looks at Aimee, who shifts, visibly uncomfortable. "Yes. I'm sure they're asking everyone."

"Is there anything on it?" Gwen asks.

Aimee looks down at her hands and spins her wedding ring.

"Aimee," Gwen says, the skin on her neck prickling. "What was on it?"

Aimee glances up at her and then looks away. "Well, Anton came to our house Friday night. Late. After I had gone to bed."

"What? You didn't tell me that."

"I didn't have a chance, and honestly, with everything going on, it didn't seem that important."

Gwen's breath catches in her throat. "How could that not be important? You might have been the last person to see him. And you didn't tell me?" The room falls quiet, the only sound the revving of a leaf blower from somewhere nearby. Aimee and Lisa exchange a glance, which infuriates Gwen. She knows that look. She's *given* that look. It happens in trios when one person is acting badly. But how is she acting badly? Her husband was murdered, and her friend is withholding important information. Gwen sinks into herself. She feels more alone with her friends than she did when she was by herself at her house. She doesn't understand how Aimee can't see that she's done something wrong. "You should have told me."

"I am truly sorry," Aimee says. "I didn't mean to hurt you or hold anything back from you."

"We're on your side," Lisa says. "We're not against you."

Gwen brings the steaming tea to her face and inhales. Lisa is the bonus that comes along with friendship with Aimee, whether she wants it or not, and there doesn't seem to be any room for negotiation. If she kept Lisa at arm's length, she could tolerate her, but she has never trusted her. She is one of those women who is always on high alert, looking for slights or insults, or opportunities to compete. At the beginning of the summer when Gwen mentioned that she wanted to enroll the boys in the local swim team, Lisa regaled her with Kai's swimming triumphs. "Just like you, all I wanted was something for him to do in the summer, maybe learn how to swim. One thing leads to another and now two years later, I'm driving all over the place taking him to regionals here, and state finals there. Who would have guessed he would be a champion swimmer!"

"I know you're not against me," Gwen says. "I don't think that. I hate being blindsided by information." She tries to smile and smooth things over. They don't know what she's discovered in Anton's study, and she's not going to tell them. She worries that if she starts talking about that, she might accidentally divulge Anton's other secret. "What did Anton want?"

"I don't know. I didn't talk to him," Aimee says. "Scott was the one who answered the door."

"Well, what did he say to Scott?"

"I don't think anything important. Scott was on his way out to meet a friend for a drink. He said Anton seemed—" She stopped, a guilty look on her face. "Do you really want to talk about this?"

"I need you to stop trying to protect me, stop trying to be so nice, and just tell me," Gwen says. She knows her tone is harsh, her words direct, but she doesn't care at this point.

Aimee nods. "All right. Scott said that Anton seemed really drunk and he walked him back to your place. That's all."

"Where was Scott going for a drink?"

Aimee pauses, unable to meet her eye. "Bethesda."

"Aimee?"

"Fine. Villain & Saint."

Gwen feels like she's been punched in the throat. She gasps for air. Lisa rushes over, taking the tea from her and patting her on the back. Gwen's mind is racing now, galloping off into dark territory. Would Anton have been foolish enough to confront Scott? He was so drunk on Friday, willing to spill his secrets to assuage his conscience. But even he would not have been that stupid. And even if he did talk to Scott, did confess everything, would that be enough reason for Scott to kill him? It's crazy. She's going insane with this train of thought.

"I'm fine now, thanks," Gwen says, pushing Lisa off her. She needs space. Lisa is smothering her.

"You okay? We don't need to talk about this. We don't want to upset you," Lisa says.

"Maybe we should talk about something else," Aimee says.

Gwen examines her friend, her auburn waves pulled into a ponytail, her freckled, makeup-free face, her brows furrowed in concern. Is she really that clueless, or is she hiding something?

"I'm not upset, I just think it's very weird that Scott went to Villain & Saint the same night. Did he see Anton there?"

"No, of course not. He was meeting a friend."

"You're telling me you don't think that's odd?"

Aimee bristles. "It's the nearest bar."

"We all go there," Lisa says. "Everyone in the neighborhood. I know for a fact that Liz and Dave Muhlbaum were at Villain & Saint on Friday night. So was Michelle J." She lets out a little shudder. Of all the Michelles in the neighborhood, Michelle J. is the craziest.

"Yeah, but—" Gwen starts and then stops. If Aimee knew something, she wouldn't be able to hide it. She's the worst card player Gwen has ever met. Every time they play Pitch, she can always tell if Aimee has the jack because she starts wiggling in her seat, smiling. There is no way she is keeping any secrets. But that doesn't mean Scott isn't. "But Anton came here. He came here to talk to Scott. And we're supposed to believe they both ended up at Villain & Saint separately?"

Aimee stiffens. "I don't see where you're going with this. I feel like you're saying that Scott had something to do with Anton's death—"

"I'm not saying that," Gwen says. But isn't she?

"Well, he didn't. For the record."

"Fine."

Aimee forces a laugh. "I mean, this is Scott we're talking about. I think I know my husband."

"Of course you do."

"So then what's your problem, Gwen?"

Aimee glares at her like a cornered cat, challenging her. She's never seen this side of Aimee before. She's not willing to even consider Scott as anything less than perfect. Gwen knows that feeling well. How you can't let even the sliver of a doubt in, or it might crack your whole façade of perfection wide open. She smiles ingratiatingly at Aimee. The ideal friend, the forgiving wife, the selfless mother. Would her role-playing ever end?

A car door slams outside and Aimee stands. "I think Scott's home with the kids," she says.

"I better get going, too," Lisa says, putting her mug down. "I promised to make spaghetti and meatballs."

The three of them are in the foyer getting their shoes on when Aimee snaps her fingers. "Wait, hold on, Lisa. I have something of yours." Aimee disappears and comes back holding a pen.

"What is that?" Lisa looks up from where she is kneeling, adjusting the laces on her sneakers.

"A pen. Apparently Noa, uh, borrowed it from you." Aimee flashes a sheepish smile. "Sorry about that."

"Aimee, isn't she a little old to be engaging in that kind of stuff?" Lisa asks, looking up from her crouching position. "I mean, I know that kids steal, but they grow out of it by her age. It's not normal."

"Oh, leave her alone, it's a freaking pen." Gwen takes the pen from Aimee. It's hefty, not a cheap one. She turns it over and reads the gold lettering: Le Cannu. For a moment she can't breathe. That was the name she couldn't remember. The restaurant with the outrageous bill.

Do you begrudge me a dinner on a work trip?

Lisa takes the pen from Gwen's hand and for a fraction of a second, the two make eye contact.

In that moment, Gwen realizes who her husband's been sleeping with.

17

True to his word, Scott is making dinner, a stir-fry with rice noodles, while Aimee sits on the living room floor with three backpacks, surrounded by crumpled papers, folders, broken pencils, fidget spinners, and other detritus.

"Do you still need this, Benji?" she calls out, holding up a sheet of math problems that has not been written on. "It doesn't look like you even filled it out."

"Nope!" Benji zooms by. "That's so old."

Aimee looks at the sheet. Calling it math might be a stretch. It's number patterns. She's not sure who decided it was a good idea to give first graders homework. She doesn't remember getting homework when she was in first grade, but she may have just blocked it out. Academics weren't her strong suit.

Normally she would be happy to be doing busywork. Watching the recycle pile grow larger usually filled her with a sense of accomplishment. But not tonight. Tonight, her nerves are jangly and she is jumpy. She needs to figure out what she's going to say to Scott. She's been going over various approaches in her mind all day, but nothing seems right. If she confronts him about Jon Block outright, he might shut down, or turn the tables on her, accuse her of spying. She feels justified in what she did, but she doesn't want to derail the conversation. So how to bring it up without putting him on the defensive right away? She hasn't figured that out yet.

You deserve to know.

Anton's drunk rambling barges into her thoughts. What had he meant by that? Maybe he was trying to tell her something about Scott. Maybe he was trying to tell her that her husband had hired a private detective. Then why did he show up here later that night? None of it made sense.

She gets up, her arms filled with papers, and heads to the recycling bin. The kitchen smells like ginger and garlic.

"Dinner in five," Scott says.

After depositing the papers, Aimee goes to the bottom of the stairs. "Dinner!" she calls. "Wash hands!"

As she waits at the bottom of the stairs, her mind wanders back to afternoon tea with Lisa and Gwen. She had been tempted at first to confide in them about what she had learned when she followed Scott, but she is relieved she didn't. Gwen seemed to be losing her grip, not that she blamed her. But for a moment there, this afternoon, it almost felt like Gwen thought Scott had killed Anton. It was crazy. Scott might be hiding something—in fact, it was obvious he was—but the idea that he could murder someone was absurd. Aimee could only imagine how Gwen would have freaked out if she told her Scott had been sneaking around and had hired a private investigator.

She can't shake the feeling that this is all connected, although she can't piece together how. Scott is the only person who can help her do that.

She has to make it through dinner first. At the table, she's too distracted by her thoughts to referee Noa and Benji when they get into a spat over elbow room. Scott tells Noa she can stand as she eats, something Aimee normally prohibits, but Aimee doesn't make a fuss tonight.

She broods about the upcoming confrontation—neither she nor Scott is a fan of difficult conversations. Scott usually makes a joke to avoid discussing anything serious. Just as she learned to avoid speaking of her mother's death with her father, Aimee has learned to tiptoe around topics with Scott. It is the opposite at work. She can be direct, even blunt, with her crew. But the stakes are so much higher with Scott. She wouldn't do anything that would risk her losing him, so she's learned to avoid delicate topics.

They both have the same sore subject—family.

His wasn't a happy one. Like her, he grew up as an only child, but unlike her, he wasn't raised in middle-class comfort with loving parents. His dad died when he was so young that Scott barely remembers him, and his mother wasn't stable. He ended up moving in with his aunt during his senior year of high school.

But those conflict-avoidant skills they both honed to help them get through the traumas of childhood aren't helping them now.

It isn't until after dinner has been eaten, the dishes cleaned, the kids bathed and put to bed, that Aimee has a chance to talk to Scott. He's in the kitchen, taking inventory of the fridge and getting ready for the big shopping of the week.

"Can we talk for a second?" Aimee sits at the counter.

Scott turns his body from the open refrigerator. "Now? I want to get to Giant soon. It's getting late."

"Well, I need five minutes."

"All right." He shuts the fridge and leans against it. "What's up? You okay?"

No, she thinks, *I'm not okay*. She tells herself not to be scared, that his explanation will illuminate everything. She delivers the line she has practiced, one she hopes will allow him to tell the truth without getting too defensive.

"I feel like you are holding something back from me, like something is going on," she says.

Scott scratches his head. "Not sure what you mean."

He's not going to make this easy for her. "Who was that friend that you met? At the bar?"

"I told you. A guy I met at the gym."

This lie stings. Aimee knows she has to push through, but she's never been a pusher. She has no choice.

"I followed you to Tatte."

He straightens up, on alert. "You did what?"

"I followed you, and I saw you meet a man. And then I spoke to him. I met him. He gave me his—"

"Hold on—you followed me to Tatte? And you're just telling me this now?"

"Why did you hire a private investigator, Scott? You need to tell me the truth."

He laughs bitterly. "That's rich coming from you."

"What does that mean?"

"When were you going to tell me that we got the report back from the psychologist about Noa?"

Aimee recoils. "How do you know about that?"

"The psychologist's office called me to schedule the follow-up. They said they wait a week after the report has been emailed so there's time to read it. And it had been a week."

"I was going to tell you. Last week was crazy, and then this whole thing with Anton happened."

"You didn't tell me because you're in denial. You don't want to hear there's anything wrong with her."

Aimee feels like she's got whiplash. Where is this coming from? How is she the one on the defensive all of a sudden? "You're not being fair."

"You didn't want to get her tested, and now you don't want to face what those tests might say."

The words pierce her. "I didn't know you felt that way." She is reeling. She has never seen him angry like this before.

"I have to go to Giant." He goes to the basket where they keep the reusable grocery bags and grabs a few.

She follows him. "But we're not done talking."

"I'm done."

"Scott." she touches his shoulder and he spins around. "Why did you hire a private investigator? Does this have something to do with Anton?"

Genuine surprise spreads across his face. "Anton? No, it has nothing to do with Anton. It's work related. We are running into some intellectual property theft issues."

"It's work related."

"Yes. Work. You know, my job?"

"Why didn't you say anything?"

"It's not something I'm supposed to talk about. We're having some problems with one of our consultants and things are kind of tense right now. Jon Block is helping us out. But we don't exactly want to advertise this. You get that, right? So, I'd appreciate it if you didn't mention it to anyone."

"Who would I mention it to?"

He shrugs. "Anyone. Lisa. Gwen."

"Is your job in trouble? Should I be worried?"

"No. It's going to be fine. It's just a rough patch."

"I wish you had told me. With everything going on, with Anton, and then you being at Villain & Saint—"

"I went to Villain & Saint to meet Jon Block. If Anton followed me there after I left him, I had no idea. I swear. The last time I saw him was on the stoop of his house. And if the police talk to Jon Block, which I'm sure they will, he will say the same thing."

Aimee nods.

"We good? Can I go grocery shopping now?"

Aimee winces at the sarcasm in his voice. "Yeah. We're good."

Scott grabs his keys and heads out the back door. Aimee stands there, as if frozen on the spot. She doesn't feel *good*. It's the first time Scott's ever come close to raising his voice with her, and she still can't decide what exactly he was so upset about. He had a right to be angry that she followed him, but the way he turned it around on her so quickly makes her uneasy. Her head is spinning.

But that isn't the only thing bothering her. It is something she can barely admit to herself.

She doesn't believe her husband is telling the truth.

18

LAST JANUARY

The affair started on an ordinary Tuesday morning, when everyone else on the cul-de-sac was gone.

Everyone except Lisa and Anton.

After watching the school bus leave, Lisa waited at her window with a cup of coffee until she saw Aimee's truck drive away. Moments later, Gwen appeared in a pencil skirt and three-inch heels and teetered to her car with a work bag slung over her shoulder. Lisa knew that she worked in Georgetown on Tuesdays and Thursdays and wouldn't be home until late afternoon.

Her own house was empty. Marcus and Kai were long gone—middle school started earlier than the elementary school. Scott had left a while ago, so besides Paola and her ancient poodle, no one else was home in this little corner of Nassau Court.

It had been two weeks since the ski vacation in Vermont, and if Lisa was going to act, she needed to do it soon, before whatever had transpired between her and Anton evaporated. And something had transpired. It had animated the both of them for the remainder of the trip. Thrilling moments of eye contact from across the room, whispered jokes, although not obvious enough for anyone to notice. They were such a self-absorbed bunch, anyway, Lisa thought, they couldn't even see it happening under their own noses. But Lisa felt it in every fiber of her being. Anton was interested.

It was unsettling to have an awakening of this part of her, which had lain dormant for so long. She had been faithful to Marcus in their fifteen years together. They still had sex dutifully once a week, always in the same position—starting with her on top, ending in doggy-style—at which point Marcus would jump up and head straight to the shower. Their sex life was as routinized and efficient as their grocery shopping on Instacart or the automated payments to their utilities that left their checking account each month.

But Anton made her feel like a teenager again, back when sex was forbidden. How many times had her mother blamed Lisa for ruining her life by being born? Her mother had gotten pregnant right after high school and had married Lisa's father. Both were products of an insular Italian community in Syracuse, where they grew up. The divorce came three years and two more kids later. Then her mother's second marriage and two more kids. But all through Lisa's adolescence and teen years, the specter of teen pregnancy hung over her. With withering looks, her mother would call her a *slut* if her shirt was too tight, a *whore* if she painted her nails red. It only made Lisa more curious about sex, and good at hiding it when she discovered it.

Thinking about Anton tapped into that same teen thrill of sneaking around. On his own, he wasn't that appealing of a man. She wouldn't call him a failed writer, exactly; his one book, so many years ago, was a commercial success. But then nothing. No sequel or anything. There had been talk of a movie, but nothing ever panned out. As for his tenuous position at the university, he wasn't even a full professor. He was good-looking enough, with nice brown eyes and a full mouth, and he was in decent shape.

But what made him sizzle was that he belonged to Gwen. And he was unhappy with her.

Since Vermont, she had established a pattern of taking a glass measuring cup to Anton's on the days Gwen was gone. The first time, she went so far as to pretend she was really there for some sugar for baking. But now when she showed up, waving the empty cup, he smiled and let her in. Still, she carried it with her just in case someone on the street stopped her and asked what she was doing.

So far, when she had been over, they only talked and hung out. But today that would change.

Lisa threw a sweater and pants over her prettiest bra and matching thong—a bright bubblegum-pink lace set that showed off the tan she kept year-round. She was the opposite of Gwen physically—dark where Gwen was pale, voluptuous where Gwen had the figure of a hipless teenage boy. She was counting on the fact that Gwen would never wear anything like this. Her underwear was probably unbleached organic cotton.

Outside, the sky was milky white and the air damp. It was a miserable January day. There was talk of a snowstorm, but that's usually all it was in Washington—talk. Despite the cold and gray, Lisa was as giddy as a little girl on her birthday. She swung her glass measuring cup by her side as she walked toward the house, a little bounce in her step.

She knocked to announce her presence, but then let herself in. Anton always left the door unlocked. Everyone on the cul-de-sac did. She surveyed his shoes lying on their sides in the foyer, Sababa's leash on the floor, and his jacket strewn over the banister. Neither Lisa nor Marcus could tolerate personal belongings left about, and it bugged her to see a grown man being so lazy.

But she bit her tongue.

She wasn't here to lecture Anton on housekeeping.

"Hello? Do you have any sugar by any chance?" she sang out. "I'm baking a cake and we're all out." She giggled. It was preposterous, comical even. She wasn't a baker. She couldn't remember ever using this glass measuring cup, or even where it had come from. She had never understood the point of spending hours destroying the kitchen just to make things that were sold in stores.

"Oh, I think we've got some," Anton called from inside. "Come on in."

She found him in the living room, sitting on the sofa, game console in his hand. Who was Anton? She had never really considered him before Vermont, as she had never really considered

any of the husbands of the women she knew. They were append-
ages to the women, interesting only in what they might reveal
about the women themselves.

Women were infinitely more fascinating.

And what did Anton reveal about Gwen?

That she was willing to put up with a man-child. He taught at
the university on Mondays and Wednesdays but was otherwise
home, theoretically working on his novel. Lisa had once heard
a tipsy Gwen complain that Anton spent hours playing video
games, drinking, and watching porn. It made her think that Gwen's
self-confidence was a façade—she had to have low self-esteem to
put up with behavior like this. A guy like Anton might be fun
to date, he might make a great boyfriend, but he wasn't husband
material, and probably never had been.

Anton went into the kitchen and came back with two mugs of
coffee, stopping at the bar cart to pour some whiskey into each.

They had begun this ritual—drinking hot coffee with just a
splash of whiskey—on her first visit, when she had professed a
deep interest in video games and an eagerness to try playing them.

It was bullshit, of course. But Anton wanted her to want to
play. He was like a child that way, the way so many men were.
Wanting to be watched and cheered on. They were all like that.
Marcus with his cycling. Kai with his soccer.

She had learned this as a young girl, ingratiating herself with
her mother's boyfriends. Big-eyed, attentive, demure. A few ended
up liking her more than they liked her mother, which didn't en-
dear her to her mother at all.

Lisa knew there was no way Gwen was playing video games
with Anton. She didn't need him to tell her that Gwen didn't
approve.

Why would she? Lisa wanted to laugh. She was probably at
her fancy PR firm tweaking some press release. PR was a perfect
job for Gwen, she was so obsessed with her image. Lisa could
tell by looking around the curated house, with its oatmeal-and-

cream palette, that Anton was the one thing that just didn't fit. He must have felt it, too. His slovenliness was an act of rebellion.

Lisa took a seat next to him on the couch, but she could barely make small talk. She was trembling with excitement. Knowing that she was about to take someone else's husband was such an aphrodisiac, it was making her physically jumpy. What was Gwen doing now? Was she managing the Insta of one of her PR clients, touching up that one stray hair, or staring out the window of her office in Georgetown, praying that someone might put her rich, bored housewife self out of her misery? Lisa giggled.

"What's so funny?" Anton cocked her head.

"Oh, I don't know. This. Everything."

"You mean playing video games in the middle of the day when I should be writing?" He smiled, but he looked a little hurt.

"Oh no, not that. Not that at all. I was just thinking of how when I was getting dressed this morning, I was wondering if you'd like what I was wearing." Her heart sped up. This was it. She felt like she might explode.

He looked at her sweater and her jeans. "I like your sweater."

"No, silly, not the sweater."

She put the mug of coffee down and stood up. In one move, one she had practiced in front of the mirror until she got it down pat, Lisa pulled her sweater over her head and tossed it, then wiggled out of her jeans so she was standing before him in only her pink bra and thong. "I mean this." She did a very slow twirl so he could take it in, including the barbed wire heart tattoo she had on her ass. She came back around and stood in front of him, her skin starting to get goose pimples from the cold.

For a millisecond Anton was frozen, and an icy chill went through her. Had she miscalculated? Was she about to be humiliated?

He put the game console down and stood, smiling.

"Oh, I like it," he said. "I like it a lot."

19

NOW

Monday, Gwen moves through the kitchen feeling like a zombie, spent, both emotionally and physically. It's almost two in the afternoon and she hasn't eaten lunch. She needs to eat, keep up her strength, but she has no appetite.

This morning, before Barb showed up with the boys, Gwen had researched how to break the news of death to small children. All the experts agreed to use straightforward, declarative language. No euphemisms. No avoiding the hard truth.

She might have avoided it a little longer if the twins hadn't come into her bedroom as soon as they got home asking where Anton was, asking why they weren't in school on a Monday.

She sat on the bed and motioned for George to sit beside her while Rafi curled up on the floor with Sababa.

There is no easy way to say this. I'm sure you've noticed that Daddy isn't here. There was an accident. Daddy died. He's not coming back.

Nothing she had researched online prepared her for the visceral way her boys responded. Not just tears, but guttural wails, like the kind a wounded animal might make. Rafi buried his face in the dog, refusing to look up, while George crawled into her lap, sobbing. Thank God for Barb. Gwen had started crying, too, and Barb tended to all three of them with soothing tones and cool, damp washcloths.

The boys were still upstairs now, spent from their big emotions and their grief. She left them curled in the king-sized bed she shared with Anton, and turned on *Over the Garden Wall*, a favorite show of theirs.

"That was brutal," Gwen says as Barb enters the kitchen.

"I think it went as well as could be expected. This is just the beginning, Gwendolyn. You have to give them time to process this. You must be their rock."

Gwen feels her shoulders tighten. She's no one's rock, but at least she's making an effort and she'd like some credit for it. This morning, she showered, blow-dried her hair, applied her makeup perfectly, and picked out a nice outfit. She even cleaned the kitchen before Barb showed up with the boys, removing the evidence of a weekend spent drinking and eating junk food. "I think I'm doing a pretty good job, under the circumstances."

"Are you?" Barb arches one eyebrow, a skill that used to both impress and intimidate Gwen when she was a girl. "And that?" Barb gestures to the dining room. "What do you call all that?"

Gwen follows her mother's gaze, seeing with fresh eyes the result of her meltdown last night.

The fury had been so raw when she came home from Aimee's. *Le Cannu.*

Anton was fucking Lisa, right under her nose. And that bitch had pretended to be her friend.

She opened a bottle of wine, blasted Carrie Underwood, and grabbed everything she could find of Anton's and dumped it in the dining room. All his clothing, his toiletries, his record player, and his precious record collection, which ranged from punk bands like Fugazi to 1950s jazz like Miles Davis and Dexter Gordon.

The rest of the night is blurry. She moved through each room of the house as she cried loudly, wineglass in hand, music blaring, searching for evidence of the lying, cheating bastard's crimes.

The cut was deep, deeper than she'd ever experienced. The humiliation of being cheated on once again was bad enough. But Anton screwing her friend magnified it a thousandfold. All those moments she had let her guard down around Lisa, all those times she revealed some vulnerability—Lisa must have been laughing inside. Did they laugh at her together? Did they mock her clue-lessness?

Imagining them together felt like a physical assault. Gwen had been sick last night. She'd thrown up all over the kitchen floor. Sobbing, she'd cleaned up her vomit.

After her righteous anger had dissolved into self-pity, she put the song "Take Me as You Please" on the speakers. It was a song she could ugly cry to. And why shouldn't she? Her life was shat-tered. She was on her own with two small boys. Her husband and one of her closest friends had betrayed her. She had curled up on the sofa with Sababa, taken a Xanax, and closed her eyes as the song repeated until she'd passed out.

"I just . . . I thought I would get started clearing out some stuff." Gwen walks into the dining room to examine last night's handiwork. She doesn't remember dragging Anton's Olivetta Lettera, a robin's-egg blue vintage Italian typewriter, into the room, but she must have, because it was thrown on top of his winter coats on the floor.

Barb gets up and follows Gwen into the dining room. "Looks like someone had themselves a little tantrum. Well, you're en-titled to one. But, honey, this is no way to go about things. We need to get this cleaned up before the boys ask about it." She bends down and picks up the typewriter. "I hope you weren't going to toss this. Did it ever occur to you that George and Rafi might want a few things to remember their father by?"

Gwen feels her face burn. She is as embarrassed at this mo-ment as she was in tenth grade when her mother read her diary and learned Gwen had given a hand job to Skip Blandon after the Christmas party at the club. She's a child again, emotional and immature, disorganized and hopeless.

"What is going on, Gwen?"

"What's going on?" She turns to face her mother, seeking some sign of support or kindness. "My husband was murdered a few days ago." Gwen wipes the tears from her eyes. "Anton was cheating. Okay? He was cheating on me again, and this time it was with someone I know. A neighbor."

Barb inhales sharply. "Not with that gardener woman? With the curly hair?"

"Who, Aimee? No. Not her. It's my other neighbor. The one who was watching the boys, actually. The one who called you."

Gwen can hear her mother's sharp intake of breath. "Are you absolutely sure? Is there the tiniest chance you might be wrong?"

Gwen pulls out a dining room chair and sits. "Maybe." Her mother's question unsettles her. There is the tiniest sliver of a possibility that the Le Cannu pen was actually Anton's, that Marcus borrowed it, and that's how it ended up at Lisa's house. That this whole thing is a giant misunderstanding and she's jumped to a terrible conclusion. "But I think it's true."

Her mother sits in the chair beside her. "Think?"

How can she explain to Barb what her gut is telling her? How Anton's behavior had changed over the past few months, how he seemed happier and less like a caged cat. How he was spending money that he didn't have. How the writing was flowing suddenly. How could she explain the writing she found in his notebooks that was supposedly fiction but was obviously not? Or the pen.

No, on its own, not one of these facts was a smoking gun. But it added up to the truth, and every part of her knew it.

"Sweetie, I think we could both use a drink before we tackle this."

"It's not even two o'clock, Mom."

"Well, it's seven o'clock in Liverpool, and that's where Grammy Ann is from, so let's drink to her."

She stands up. It was the same line she used when Gwen was growing up and she came home from school to see her mother already drinking. Barb comes back with two tumblers filled with a dark liquid and rattling ice cubes.

"What is this?" Gwen asks, taking the glass.

"Jack and Coke. The Jack will dull the pain, the Coke will give you a boost. Now, don't argue. Just drink."

They clink glasses and each takes a long sip. "Now, you may be right about Anton. And that witch of a neighbor. But you need to decide how much you are going to let that affect you going forward. You know what they say—history belongs to the victor. And by dint of still being alive, you're the victor. He may have been the professional writer, but now it's you who gets to write the story. However you behave, whatever you say—to your boys, to the world, to yourself, and yes, even to that awful woman—will become the truth. Take that responsibility very seriously."

"What are you saying?" Gwen asks. "I pretend none of the bad stuff ever happened?"

"I'm saying let it die with him."

Easy for you to say. What Barb doesn't know is that Gwen isn't the victor, not really.

Because that *luscious* woman with *devouring eyes* that Anton wrote about not only exists in real life but lives on the same block.

And Gwen knew her husband. How talkative he got after sex. He liked to smoke a Camel unfiltered and expound on life like the hero of a French art film.

There's no escaping the possibility that in one of those post-coital conversations, Anton had chosen to unburden himself to Lisa, just as he tried to confess to Scott.

And that terrifies Gwen, because the chances are close to nil that the whore will keep her mouth shut.

20

Aimee sticks the shovel into the ground and gives it a satisfying thrust before lifting out another clump of dirt. More like clay, the kind used to make ceramics. The Washington area is notorious for it. Thick, water-logged, and heavy—only certain plants could thrive in this soil unless it was amended. But she's planting one of those clay busters now, a false indigo that will grow four feet tall and just as wide. In the spring and summer, it will explode in loads of tiny purple flowers that attract bees. And the leaves will provide food for several types of butterflies, from wild indigo Duskywings to silver-spotted skippers.

Aimee stops and wipes her brow, sure she's streaking dirt across her forehead. Manual labor usually distracts her, but it isn't cutting it today. Her mind is muddled. She's consumed with thoughts about friendship and all the people whose lives intersected with her own over the years. Her best friend from childhood would be a complete stranger if it weren't for Facebook and Instagram and the yearly exchange of holiday cards. Others have come and gone, too. Friends she really liked, even loved at the time, and swore she would always stay in touch with. They were merely in the right place at the right time.

She thinks of the other moms in the neighborhood like work colleagues. Together, they are all in the business of raising kids and sending them to the local public school. And just like at any job, there are bound to be people you get along with more than others, but you try to be cordial to everyone to make the workplace pleasant.

But she considers Lisa and Gwen real friends. Their bonds are based on mutual affection, not just shared school schedules. So why is she feeling this barrier between Gwen and herself? Yesterday at the house, there was that moment when Gwen seemed to imply that Scott was involved in Anton's death. It was a flash of insight into Gwen's psyche, and it occurred to Aimee that she really didn't know the woman who lived next door to her that well at all. After all, she didn't know that Anton had been a cheater. What else didn't she know about her neighbors?

"You ready?" Tim asks, lugging over the large false indigo.

Together they set it into the hole.

"One down, two to go."

She's eating lunch in her truck when her phone alerts her that thanks to flooding in the cafeteria, school is letting out early. Aimee drives over to pick everyone up. Benji and Max run out, yelling about how they want to go to a friend's house. The other boy's mother, a woman named Janet that Aimee has spoken to a handful of times, stands on the sidewalk and waves. Aimee waves back, sending them on their way. But when she turns back, she sees Michelle J. marching over in her signature OBX baseball cap, her long hair trailing down her back in a scraggly ponytail.

"Hi, Aimee. I hope you don't think this is forward, but we need to talk. I mean, I am just so devastated about what has happened to Anton." She leans against the passenger side of Aimee's truck and peers through the open window.

"Yes, it is terrible." Aimee doesn't want to get caught up in a conversation with Michelle J., whose mood swings are legendary. She once made their beloved mailman, Kenny, cry because he had misdelivered a package from Garnet Hill. Aimee spots Noa amid the crowd, a solitary figure weighed down by an immense backpack, and waves her over.

"Do the police think it was random?" Michelle J. cocks her head to one side. "I'm only asking because I run by Villain & Saint every morning at around five-thirty. It's still dark. But I've always felt safe. I have to run, it's a mental health issue for me. Stopping is not an option. I can't tolerate antidepressants."

"I didn't realize," Aimee says, unsure of how to respond to this confession.

"But is it *safe*? I mean, have you heard anything? Just because you're so close with Gwen, I thought if anyone would know it would be Aimee."

Noa trudges toward the truck, staring at the ground. She inches closer to Michelle J. until the woman finally gets the message and moves back so Noa can climb in. Aimee watches her daughter do so without saying hello or even lifting her head and knows that it's been a bad day. Aimee's heart sinks.

Aimee looks past her daughter to Michelle J. "Wish I could be more help, but I'm afraid I know as much as you do." She starts the engine and Michelle J. jumps back.

"Oh. I thought you'd know more. I'm surprised. Anyway, Michelle P. and Sara think we should send Gwen a fruit basket. What do you think? Would Gwen want a fruit basket?"

"That sounds great," Aimee says as she pulls away, eager to put some distance between her and Michelle J. Drop-off and pickup have never been her favorite. There aren't any other mothers that she knows of at the school who did manual labor for a living and she had felt excluded from certain mom cliques when she first moved here. She was never going to bond over mani-pedi sessions—there was no point; her nails were always a disaster. She always felt a little too unkempt for the working-mom crowd and too harried and career-oriented for the stay-at-home moms. Until she met Lisa, that is. They clicked right away.

Aimee takes one last look at the scene of parents and kids as she drives away. She doesn't see Gwen anywhere, or George or Rafi, and wonders if they went to school today.

"Hey, sweetie. It looks like it's you and me, kid, and you're in luck. Guess where I'm headed to drop off a proposal?"

Noa looks up, a smile spreading across her face. "Cathy's?"

"You got it. I can't stay long, but at least you can have a quick visit with the kittens."

Noa beams, and Aimee is glad to be able to deliver some good news. Fourth grade has been tough so far. *This is a cusp year*, the teacher said during the parent conference. *We don't hold their hands in fourth grade. They need to start taking more responsibility.* The way these kittens have brightened up Noa's days has her reconsidering her ban on a family pet. Maybe a hamster.

When they arrive at Cathy's, Noa dashes out of the car and through the front door. Aimee grabs the manila envelope containing the preliminary sketches and plans she has come up with for Cathy's front yard, and heads to the house.

"You can look at these whenever you get a chance and let me know what you think," Aimee says, handing Cathy the envelope at the door. "I can put you on the schedule for mid-October, which is great for transplanting shrubs."

"Thanks, I look forward to seeing what you've come up with." Cathy adjusts her big glasses that give her an owlish look. "How is your friend doing?"

"As good as can be expected, I guess. In fact, I should probably head back there now. Let's see if I can pry Noa away from those kittens."

"She's welcome to stay for the afternoon. I'm just sitting in the kitchen paying bills. She's no bother when she's here."

Aimee hesitates, but Cathy seems genuine. Besides, Noa is always calmer and in a better mood after spending time here. "If you're sure."

"I'm sure," Cathy says, laughing. "I miss having a classroom full of little people. It's nice having someone else in this big ol' house."

"Well, if that's the case, then either I or Scott will come by in a couple of hours."

* * *

Aimee comes home to an empty house, a rarity. She takes a shower, washing off the day's sweat and grime, and changes into clean sweats. Downstairs, she makes a cup of tea and decides to follow Cathy's lead and pay the bills. She grabs the mail she stuck in her bag a few days earlier and places the stack beside her open laptop on the kitchen island. She's halfway through the stack when she finds a letter from the financial institution where they keep their investments and IRAs. Since both she and Scott are self-employed, they have no work 401(k)s and are entirely responsible for saving for their own retirements. They have set it up so that the money comes out of their checking accounts automatically. Once they've maxed out their yearly IRA contributions, they send money into several mutual funds.

The letter is one sheet of paper, a confirmation for the withdrawal of fifty thousand dollars. At first, Aimee thinks this is the same fifty thousand dollars that Scott mentioned withdrawing earlier. But after double-checking the accounts on her computer, she realizes there have been two fifty-thousand-dollar withdrawals—one from their home mortgage equity account, and one from their mutual funds. One hundred thousand dollars in total, gone.

She feels her stomach lurch. The numbers on the computer screen grow blurry and unreadable. *One hundred thousand dollars.* Aimee stands up, shaken. She paces the kitchen, trying to understand what he could have done with so much money.

Neither she nor Scott had rich parents. She went in state to Towson University and worked summers and during the school year to pay the tuition. Same for Scott. They had saved while renting all through their twenties and early thirties, skipping vacations and not eating out.

East Bethesda seemed out of their budget when house shopping, but they had both fallen in love with the house and the quiet block. The school district was great, and it was close to both Scott's work and to Aimee's client base. It was a financial stretch, but they were confident that they would continue to earn more money in their careers, and so far they'd been right. Aimee had broken six figures with her landscaping company last year, and Scott was doing even better than that.

But she was still money conscious. She still clipped coupons and preferred to pay cash for big purchases like her truck. It was second nature to her. They might have money now, but there was no family fortune to fall back on if things went south.

Sometimes it was a sore point with Gwen and Lisa. They seemed to be under the impression that she could afford the little luxuries—like spa days—that they enjoyed. Gwen didn't exactly advertise that her parents subsidized her and Anton's life but once when Gwen was drunk, she let slip that her parents provided ten thousand dollars a month. As for Lisa and Marcus, he was making close to a million dollars a year as a partner at his lobbying firm.

With trembling hands, Aimee grabs her phone and dials Scott's number.

"Hey, sweetie, what's up?"

"Scott, did you take fifty thousand dollars out of our retirement account?" There's no response, but she can hear street noise in the background, so she knows he is still there. "Scott, you need to answer me."

"How did you find out?"

"Does it matter?" She is practically shouting. "What kind of response is that? Who cares how I found out?"

"Please, calm down. I can explain everything."

"Great. I'm listening."

"Now? I'm outside a Starbucks in Reston. Can we talk tonight?"

"You need to tell me something, Scott. I'm losing it here. What did you do with one hundred thousand dollars?"

"I made a bad financial decision, Aimee."

His words hit her like a blow to the chest. "What does that mean?" she whispers.

"I was scammed."

Aimee struggles to slow her breath and calm down. "Maybe there's a way to get the money back. Have you gone to the police?"

"No. That's why I hired Block. He's going to help me. That's why I was meeting him Saturday night. And Sunday. I was going to come to you once I had all the information I needed."

"I don't understand. Why hire him and not go to the police?"

"That's a good question, and I can't really answer it right now. But I'll answer everything tonight. I promise. I'll lay it all out for you. You're just going to have to trust me."

He hangs up and Aimee stares at the phone. Her whole body is shaking. Trust him? Scott has been keeping secrets, ones that affect her and the kids. Last week she trusted him implicitly, but now she doesn't even know how she's going to get through the rest of the day.

Scott, what have you done?

21

After they had sex for the second time, Lisa and Anton lay in a pile of limbs and throw blankets and pillows on the living room floor, breathless.

Lisa rolled over on her side, propping her head up. "So, am I your first?"

Anton looked at her quizzically.

"I mean, stepping out on Gwen."

He rolled onto his back, looked at the ceiling, and sighed. "No. But I haven't done anything like this in a long time."

Lisa winced. His words hurt. It wasn't jealousy, not exactly. She didn't feel possessive about Anton. But she wanted to be special enough that he had crossed a line just for her. It wasn't a win for her if his marital vows meant nothing to him and he was a serial cheater. She wanted the pain Gwen would feel to be fresh.

She stared at a painting on the wall, an abstract swirl of blue and cream that looked like a first grader could have made, but knowing Gwen, probably cost thousands, and waited for the sick feeling to pass. It felt like a black hole had opened in her soul. The same gnawing emptiness she had felt in college, when Ruth pulled away, made new friends. Lisa had acted rashly then. She had seduced Ruth's boyfriend one night when he stopped by the room, drunk, looking for Ruth, who was out at the movies. Lisa had done it *for* Ruth, to show what an asshole her boyfriend was. It was obvious he would screw anything that moved. And yes, a part of her did it so Ruth could taste the poison she had forced Lisa to drink—abandonment. It was the worst feeling in the world.

What she hadn't foreseen was that Ruth would not just end the friendship but move out of the dorm room they shared. Coming back to the room and seeing Ruth's things gone, her bed stripped, her poster that listed all of Jane Austen's books taken down, had activated something in her.

She'd always been prone to rage-tinged loneliness—like when her father left when she was in preschool, or when her mother doted on her younger brothers while turning her into an unpaid servant, making Lisa iron their school uniforms. It arose when girls didn't invite her to sit with them in the cafeteria, or to come to their parties. It braided itself alongside the shame she felt when the boys she let touch her pretended not to know her when they passed her in the school hallways.

That feeling had soured into something very ugly with Ruth. She had tracked Ruth down in her new dorm room, and, feral with vengeance, had banged on the door, screaming to be let in. The fire she had set outside Ruth's door was small, but it was enough to set off the sprinklers. Ruth had barricaded herself inside and called campus security.

The police, the lawyer, the quiet transfer out of the school. It had all been so humiliating.

If she wanted to succeed this time, she needed to keep her emotions under control. Lisa reached out a hand and laid it on Anton, twirling her fingers through the curls on his chest. "What would Gwen do if she found out?"

Anton let out a low whistle. "I don't even want to think about it. That would be the end. I promised I would never do something like this again, and I kept that promise, I really did."

"Until I came along?"

He turned to face her and smiled. "Until you came along."

A warm feeling spread in her chest, the feeling of being wanted and desired. Was there any better feeling in the world? This man was willing to risk his wife's wrath, his standing in this neighborhood, his relationship with his children, all to be with her. His validation made her as giddy as when she crested the top of the Galaxi rollercoaster for the first time when she was twelve.

"Well then," she said, giggling, "we'll have to be very, very careful, won't we?"

Tuesdays and Thursdays became the highlights of the following weeks. She had long grown tired of listening to her coaching clients complain about their lives and had winnowed down her roster to about a half-dozen people. They paid several hundred dollars a phone session, but she had begun to feel like one of those therapists whose patients never make any improvement year after year. She knew she could get more certifications, segue into corporate coaching—there was real money there—but she couldn't be bothered. Marcus was making so much money now, it was highly demotivating.

Her real passion became getting even with Gwen.

An unexpected side effect of sleeping with Anton was that being around Gwen became more tolerable, fun, even.

Those long games of Pitch, which used to bore Lisa, now thrilled her. Instead of focusing on the cards, her attention was on how she might slip her stockinged foot out of her shoe and rub it up and down Anton's inner thigh without anyone else noticing.

It was a challenge to keep herself from laughing out loud when he shifted in his seat and closed his eyes in ecstasy while everyone else droned on about the card game or neighborhood gossip.

The clandestine aspect was exciting, but the real kick was knowing how it would destroy Gwen. Having an enemy was like drinking from the fountain of youth. Enemies, after all, were a hallmark of childhood. She remembered how classmates would flit from friend to enemy and back again, sometimes the result of a slow cooling, other times suddenly after a nasty cutting remark.

But most adults didn't have enemies, did they? And why not? There was something so clarifying about it. Sure, countries had enemies, and so did characters in books and movies. But not individuals, at least not people like her, not upper-middle-class women who drove BMWs and had their roots done every six weeks.

But it energized her.

She found it easier to fake being nice to Gwen now that she knew intimate details about her life. Anton was terrible at keeping secrets. He told her about Gwen's college battle with bulimia, how she bombed in her creative writing class and was excluded from the social clique of wannabe writers at her college, so she turned to public relations. She made him recount every rejection, hurt, or failure that Gwen had endured, and she held them tight, turning them over in her mind at night in the dark, like little luminescent stones. Knowing Gwen's perfect façade was an act bolstered her own self-worth.

Anton also started telling her about his marriage problems, how Gwen controlled the finances, poring over every purchase, and how a monthly infusion of cash from her parents was what kept the family going.

In the spring, he became incensed about Scott's new grill, which Aimee bought him for Father's Day. At first, Lisa had thought he was joking, but the subject made him furious. Gwen had overridden a grill on safety grounds. *We don't need our own.* He recounted her words to Lisa, mocking her. *You don't even like to cook.*

"Why should Scott get a grill and I don't? He doesn't cook, either. He just wants to flaunt his wealth."

Anton reminded her of a petulant child, a little boy, irrationally angry when someone else received birthday gifts.

She loved when he was like this. Nasty and petty. She enjoyed nourishing his hate toward others. It made her feel as though they were a team, united against the world. Marcus exhausted her with his self-help optimism and positive psychology. The only person Lisa wouldn't let Anton criticize was Aimee. She was off-limits. Sometimes after they had sex in his and Gwen's bed, Lisa would go into the bathroom and lock the door, taking in the luxury of it. A soaking tub, a separate shower, a door that led to an outside deck. She and Marcus had never gotten around to updating their bathroom, which still had the original seafoam-green tiles from the 1930s. Even Gwen's medicine cabinet was Instagram-ready, with dust-free mirrored shelves laden with only a few bespoke glass bottles that Lisa knew cost a fortune.

Lisa could afford these things, that wasn't the issue, but she wouldn't even know where to buy them. Or how to design a bathroom like this. It was no use having the money if you didn't understand how to spend it. Gwen's understated elegance made her feel tacky and loud. Lisa had thought her brown Louis Vuitton tote with the small tan logos was the epitome of chic until she brought it once on a girl's night out and Gwen made some comment. Apparently, in the gospel according to Gwen, one logo was acceptable, but Lisa carrying the bag while wearing a Prada-branded sweater was tacky.

She still burned when she thought of the humiliation.

*   *   *

In April, the entire cul-de-sac and a few adjoining houses had decided to host an Easter egg hunt for all the kids. Even Kai agreed to partake when he heard there were dollar bills stuffed into some of the eggs. There had been some squabbling between Lisa and Gwen about how many eggs to hide. She mentioned to Aimee that Gwen's penchant for organizing things was veering on OCD.

Later in the afternoon, when the eggs had been found and the kids were playing in the street, the parents gathered in lawn chairs to chat and drink. Lisa went inside Scott and Aimee's to use the bathroom. When she emerged from the bathroom into the hallway, she overheard them talking in the kitchen. About *her*.

". . . it's okay if you've outgrown your friendship with Lisa," Scott was saying. "She a bit of a drama queen."

"You think?"

"You know, you three have nicknames in the neighborhood."

Aimee laughed. "You're kidding."

"Jason told me when we were playing tennis a few weeks ago. Some of the other moms call you three Queen, Lean, and Green."

"Am I Green?" she asked.

"Of course. And Gwen, well, she's definitely on the thin side."

"And people think Lisa's a drama queen?"

"She's been known to stir up drama with the other moms, apparently," Scott said. "And the fact that she wore a leopard-print bikini to the pool."

"That's not very nice," Aimee said. "She has a great body. She can wear what she wants."

"And this is why I never told you. Because it's kind of mean."

People were talking about her behind her back. *Drama queen?* Maybe she had stuck up for herself—she was no doormat—but that didn't make her a drama queen. Scott certainly found it amusing. She had no idea that he didn't like her, that he was poisoning Aimee against her.

"Lisa's always been such a good friend to me. We used to be so close," Aimee said. "That's why what she said about Noa was so out of character."

Lisa's heart leapt into her throat. What had she said about Noa to Aimee? She searched her memory for something she could have said that offended her—perhaps she had unintentionally insulted Aimee—but she couldn't pinpoint anything.

"People outgrow friendships," Scott had said. "It's not a crime. If you want to pull back, that's fine by me. I mean, I like Marcus, but I don't need to see him every Friday night."

"Maybe," Aimee said, sounding dubious. "I'll see."

"I just don't like to see you so upset."

"Do you think Noa's an *oddball*?"

"Stop. You know I don't."

So that's what it was. A throwaway comment. She remembered now. Noa had interrupted their coffee together and demanded attention, going on and on about orcas or whales or something, just nonstop reciting all kinds of useless information. It *was* odd. And the way Aimee just indulged her instead of reprimanding her like Lisa longed to. She had made one little off-the-cuff remark when Noa finally left the room. "What a little oddball." She had meant it in an affectionate way.

And Aimee was willing to trash their friendship over that one silly remark? It was Scott's doing. He was going to use that one comment as a wedge to turn Aimee against her. Lisa went back into the bathroom to wait until Scott and Aimee went outside. She clamped her hand over her mouth and let out a silent scream. If they hadn't been right outside the house, she would have smashed the mirror on the medicine cabinet. Scott was trying to come between her and Aimee. What had she ever done to him?

She seethed for the next few days, vacillating between being unable to shake Scott's words from her mind and worrying over whether Aimee was going to dump her. She was sure Aimee would forgive her if Scott wasn't in the way. She entertained various plots of revenge against Scott, but none withstood the light of careful examination. She didn't want to hurt Aimee. She was as much a victim of Scott as Lisa was. The poor thing was being manipulated by that bastard. He was a golden boy, had sailed through life with his smile and jokes and athleticism. But those were the worst bullies of all. Sweet Aimee couldn't see it, but Lisa could. Aimee needed her then more than ever. What it must be like to be married to someone like that, who gaslights you about your own best friend.

When Marcus noticed her sullenness, Lisa told him she had a sinus headache. On the following Friday, she begged off meeting up for dinner with everyone, sending Marcus and Kai without her, claiming her head hurt too much. Alone in the house, she poured a glass of wine and curled up in bed with her laptop. There had to be some way to get back at Scott. Some weakness or past mistake he had made. Maybe an old girlfriend Lisa might activate and bring back into his life. That could cause a nice rift between him and Aimee, which she could exploit.

But the more she looked, the less she found about Scott. He had no social media at all. His company did, but he was only mentioned by name on the website. There wasn't even a picture.

The following day, she stopped by Aimee's just as Scott was leaving. She entered and found her at the kitchen counter, paying bills.

"Oh, hey, did we have plans?" Aimee looked up, confused.

"Oh, no," Lisa had said, holding a wooden spoon aloft. "Just returning this." She'd had Aimee's spoon at her house for weeks, but it was a good excuse to come by and feel out her friend, to try and strengthen their friendship. "I also brought this, for Noa." She held up *The Encyclopedia of Marine Mammals*, which she had found in the bargain section of Barnes and Noble.

"Oh, that is so sweet of you! You shouldn't have."

"I know how into whales and things she is. She'll probably be a famous scientist when she grows up!" Lisa wondered if she was laying it on a bit thick, but she needed Aimee to move past the hurt she had caused her. She would address it directly, the oddball comment, but she didn't want to arouse any suspicion that she had been listening in on her conversation with Scott.

"She is going to love this," Aimee said, taking the book. "That reminds me, I have Kai's soccer shirt. The one Benji borrowed? I washed it. Let me get it for you."

She slid off the seat and went to retrieve the shirt, leaving Lisa alone in the kitchen. Aimee didn't seem angry, Lisa thought as she peered at the paperwork spread out on the counter. Her eyes stopped on a medical form Aimee had been filling out. As she looked over the form, she saw that a field for Scott's social security number had been filled in. This was it. Her opportunity to dig a little deeper. Quickly, she took a picture with her phone. That evening, after Marcus was fast asleep, she slipped open her laptop and searched for a reputable company that did the most thorough background checks. If she was going to do it, she was going to spend the money and do it right.

She found one that promised to deliver: address history, a social security number trace, sex offender search, employment history, and other criminal searches. Lisa entered Scott's personal information and then typed in her credit card.

If there was any dirt in Scott's past, she was going to find it.

22

Barb is downstairs in the kitchen with the boys, serving them dinner, and Gwen is upstairs helping herself to another glass of wine that she smuggled into her bedroom.

This Monday had been torturous. She'd stopped by the morgue to identify Anton's body and had almost collapsed when she saw him stretched out on the cold metal slab. Detective Salazar had been there, had tried to discourage her from leaving the viewing area where she could look at Anton through a window and actually entering the room the body was in. Gwen insisted but quickly regretted it. It had been a mistake to enter the cold, lab-like room that stank of chemicals. When she got close enough to Anton to see the waxy sheen on his skin, the faint bluish tint on his lips, she thought she might be sick, and had to rush out.

Now, back at home, she wants to drink and forget it all. Forget that her husband is lying dead and cold in an industrial room. Forget that she is a widow who will have to raise her boys on her own. Forget that her marriage was built on lies.

But she can't forget that feeling she had when she saw that pen from Le Cannu. At that moment she *knew*, deep in her bones, that Anton was cheating with Lisa. Didn't she? She takes a swig of wine and goes over the little details of the past year, searching for clues. Her mind might be playing tricks on her, but she can't recall a single incident that suggests they were having an affair. Is she in denial? Has she forgotten—or did she never notice—what was right in front of her? Maybe her mind has buried those memories deep inside the recesses of her brain in an ill-conceived effort to protect itself from going mad.

Or maybe her mother's right, and she's concocted the whole thing.

Then again, she thinks as she pours another glass full, her mother hasn't read Anton's latest *fiction*. Gwen picks up her phone. Every moment of their lives is documented on these things—doctor's appointments, bills, photos, receipts. They are digital time capsules. If there is any proof to be found, it will be on the phone. She wishes she had Anton's, but the police still have it.

Gwen scrolls through her phone, not entirely sure what she is searching for. She squeezes her eyes shut, trying to remember when exactly Anton went to that writer's conference in Tampa. Sometime in June, maybe July? She checks her phone's calendar and finds the dates. What else was going on that weekend? She opens her Instagram and scrolls all the way back to the beginning of the summer, cross-checking the dates with texts and the photos she's posted.

A photo of her and Aimee and all the kids at Brookside Gardens jogs her memory. They were there for Wings of Fancy, the butterfly exhibit. She looks at a photo of Noa and Benji, grinning, butterflies alighting on their arms, shoulders, heads. Lisa was out of town that weekend, and Gwen remembers her saying they should go without her because Kai wouldn't want to go, anyway.

Out of town. *Because she was with Anton.*

Gwen gulps down more wine and stands up. Her mother's words in her ears: *let it die with him.*

The advice seemed sensible a few hours earlier. And maybe a different woman would be able to follow it. Let her husband's dirty secrets be buried with him.

There is no way she can let this go. It is like asking a person who's been set on fire to stand still and be consumed. She would thrash for her life. She needs to know the truth, to confront Lisa in person. Otherwise, she will be stranded between grief and rage forever. Hatred would be easier to deal with. Purer and brighter, it could be a source of energy, whereas grief is damp and depleting.

Or maybe she just wants to hate Anton because that will make it easier to deal with his death.

Gwen reaches for the bottle and finds it empty. She grabs her phone and walks downstairs. Her mother is on the couch in the living room, the boys on the floor near the coffee table where the board game Sorry! is set up.

"I'm winning," George says.

"That's great, honey." Gwen walks over and stands over them, but no one invites her to join. She's become an outsider in her own family.

"I better take the dog out before it gets too late." She is careful to articulate each of her words. She doesn't want her boys or her mom to think she is drunk. Both her parents are heavy drinkers—cocktails before dinner, nightcaps, Bloody Marys at the club on the weekend. But somehow it never seems to slow them down. Not being able to hold your liquor is a sign of moral weakness to them, as though if you really put your mind to it you ought to be able to drink half a bottle of gin and still win at Bridge.

But I'm a grieving widow. I should be allowed to fall apart.

"Sounds good," Barb says, without looking up. "One, two, three—sorry!" Barb returns one of Rafi's pieces to his home base.

"That's not fair!" Rafi cries.

Gwen latches Sababa's leash and steps outside. The cool air invigorates her. She's been cooped up all day, since yesterday, actually, breathing in the stale air of her home. If it weren't for Sababa, she might not ever venture outside. She walks around the edge of the cul-de-sac, allowing Sababa the full length of the leash so he can sniff the curb and wander a little way up onto the lawns of her neighbors. Fall comes late to Washington, and her Argentinian neighbor still has tomatoes ripening on six-foot-tall vines in her front yard. The whole thing seems like an exercise in futility to Gwen. Could a half-dozen tomatoes really be worth all the work it takes to grow them?

Negative thoughts. They are coming fast and furious now. Anton's death has opened the floodgates. The low-lying river of depression has threatened to swamp her before in life, most notably in college, when she had what might be called a breakdown and had to leave school for a semester to enter an eating disorder program. She can feel that pain starting to swell within her again. She needs something to focus on.

Gwen is at the end of the street now, where Nassau Court meets Barstow Road, and the lights are all blazing at Lisa and Marcus's house. Without hesitation, Gwen strides up the walk, Sababa trotting beside her, and rings the bell.

Marcus answers in sweatpants and a Duke T-shirt. "Hey, Gwen. It's good to see you. Come on in." He steps back to allow her through, but she doesn't move.

"No, no, I can't. I just want to ask Lisa something."

"You sure?" He frowns. Marcus has always struck her as a very straightforward guy, one of those men who ascribes to a work-hard, play-hard ethos. Gwen has never really understood what bonded Lisa and Marcus, and now she looks at him with new-found pity. He clearly has no idea his wife was cheating on him while he was hard at work, or away on one of his cycling trips.

"I'm sure. But thanks."

"Can I give you a hug?"

She nods, stepping forward and allowing him to hug her. He smells nice, like lemon and cedar, and the thought occurs to her that she is hugging the husband of the woman who was sleeping with her own husband. Could she have had sex with Marcus? She shudders at the thought, and he releases her.

"I'll go get her."

Gwen stands on the step with Sababa, listening to the sounds of a typical suburban household. The TV going, Marcus calling for Lisa, Kai's laughter ringing through the house.

Lisa shows up, wiping her hands on the sides of her yoga pants. Her long black hair falls in thick waves past her shoulders. She's an attractive woman, Gwen cannot deny it, although she finds Lisa's style a little vulgar. The low-cut tops, the year-round tan, the long nails.

"Hey, Gwen," Lisa says. "Come on in."

"No, I'm not coming in."

The smile on Lisa's face disappears. "Is everything okay? You seem upset."

"The pen," Gwen says. "From the restaurant. Where did you get it?"

"What?" Lisa blinks but doesn't break eye contact, and in that moment Gwen knows for sure. The certainty is a hot coal in the center of her chest.

"How long?" Gwen asks.

"I'm sorry. I don't follow."

"How long were you fucking my husband?"

Lisa winces at the word. She steps outside and shuts the door behind her. "Keep your voice down."

"I will not." Gwen steps back. "Why should I?"

"You're making a scene. It's embarrassing." Lisa crosses her arms. "For you, I mean."

"You afraid the neighbors might hear?"

"You're making a mistake," Lisa says. "Anton and I were just good friends. We happened to be in Tampa at the same time, and yes, we had dinner—"

"I know about the tattoo." It is a long shot. Anton could have made up the part in his book about the ass tattoo. Or could he? It was turning out that he couldn't make up a damn thing. But Gwen can tell by the look of horror on Lisa's face she nailed it.

"He told you about that? I was drunk, I shouldn't have said anything to him about my tattoo."

"Don't lie to me, Lisa."

"You sound paranoid, Gwen. The stress of losing Anton must

be getting to you. You're all alone, with two young boys to raise. You're in your early forties, no real job, no prospects, your looks fading. It must be awful. Terrifying."

Marcus opens the door, a cautious smile on his face. "Hey, ladies, everything all right out here?"

Lisa twists her body to face Marcus. "Gwen here is a little, shall we say, upset." Lisa turns back to Gwen and gives her a pitying look. "She's come here to accuse me of having an affair with Anton."

"What?" Marcus takes a few steps until he is standing beside Lisa. "Gwen, is that true?"

"Yes, because she did. I know she did," Gwen says. "She slept with Anton. I have proof."

"What proof?" Marcus asks, the picture of patience. He shoots a quick glance at Lisa. It's all a joke to him. He's in denial. She wants to scream. Instead, Gwen inhales and tries to steady her voice.

"I have the pen, for starters."

"The pen?" A smile teases his lips.

Lisa places her hand on her husband's forearm. "Remember how I told you I bumped into Anton in Tampa? I took home a pen from the restaurant. Gwen seems to think that's evidence of something."

"And I know about the tattoo."

Lisa leans into Marcus as if having this whole conversation is exhausting. "It's true I blabbed to Anton about my tattoo." She sighs. "So that's why she thinks we were, um, *sleeping together*."

Those last two words hang in the air for a moment. Gwen feels like she is going mad. She is speechless, her mind frozen. Somehow Lisa has both admitted to the facts and denied them at the same time. Marcus believes her every lie. He has no inkling that Lisa is manipulating the facts. But how can she tell him without sounding crazy?

"Gwen, why don't we take you home?" Marcus takes a step forward. "You're not wearing any shoes."

Gwen looks down, wobbling a little. It's true. She's barefoot. How did that happen? She knows she was drinking, but she is sure she put on her shoes before she left.

"I don't need you to take me home. I was going, anyway." She looks up at their pitying faces and witnesses the tectonic shift. They think she's crazy, out here in the street, barefoot and throwing around wild accusations. But she knows.

Gwen pivots, yanking at Sababa's leash. "C'mon," she says loudly so Marcus and Lisa can hear her. "Aimee will believe me."

She can hear the sound of footsteps coming up behind her. "Gwen, where do you think you're going?" Lisa's voice is sharp now.

Gwen keeps walking. "I'm going to Aimee's, and you can't stop me. I'm going to tell her everything."

Lisa grabs her arm, halting her. Gwen stumbles but catches herself before she falls. "Let go of me. I'm going to tell her you were screwing my husband, right under our noses." She glares at Lisa, inches from her face as she says this. "We'll see what she thinks of you then."

23

Aimee has just put the chicken in the oven when Scott comes in the front door. Benji and Max run up to him and give him big hugs as he hangs up his coat. He holds up a bag.

"Stopped by the bakery on my way home and bought some black-and-white cookies."

Aimee takes the bag from him and sees there is an elephant ear inside for her. His attempt to butter her up. But it will take a lot more than her favorite pastries to assuage her. She wants answers.

Aimee sets the timer for twenty-five minutes and checks on the potatoes. She wanted to serve a real dinner tonight, the whole family sitting down together. Since Anton's death, they've been grabbing what they can eat, ordering takeout, and eating frozen food. If she is being honest, she and Scott have let family mealtime slip a little over the past few months.

But getting through dinner will be challenging when what she really wants to do is grab Scott by his shirt and drag him into the next room to yell at him. She is torn between grilling her husband in fury and playing nice, enjoying a pleasant family meal. A part of her worries this might be their last one for a while. She is more than a little afraid that what he is going to tell her will change the way she sees him. And she's not ready to say goodbye to the version of Scott she's been in love with for so long.

"Smells good." He comes up beside her. "Can I help? How about a glass of wine?"

"Sure," Aimee says, watching him take a bottle from the

fridge and open it. He's on his best behavior. Not the distracted, overworked Scott of the past few months, but her old Scott. Cheery and easygoing. The Scott she met and fell in love with at a co-ed kickball league on the National Mall. A friend from college begged her to come bolster the number of women on the team—they needed a certain threshold to play in the league. Afterward, they all went to the Big Hunt in Dupont Circle. She and Scott were friends first. It wasn't until he helped her move out of a group house on Q Street and into an apartment in Mount Pleasant that he confessed his feelings for her. She thought he was just being nice, and he thought it was funny that she hadn't picked up on his signals. That was almost fifteen years ago.

Aimee accepts a glass.

"To us," Scott says, holding up his.

"To the truth." Aimee clinks her glass against his and takes a sip. "I'm looking forward to hearing it. All of it."

"I deserve that. I've been holding back. But tonight I am going to tell you everything. I swear. As soon as the kids are in bed, I will explain it all. Jon Block. The money. You can ask me anything. I promise."

She nods. "All right."

"I want to make this right with us. I know I haven't been honest with you. I told myself I was trying to protect you, but the truth is that I was ashamed."

"Why? What have you done to be ashamed of?"

He smiles sadly. "Can we wait until tonight? Have a nice dinner with the kids at least? Where is Noa, by the way?"

"Oh, shoot." Aimee puts her glass down. "She's at Cathy's. I'm supposed to grab her. Listen, if the oven beeps while I'm out, take the chicken out, okay?" She goes to the mudroom for her jacket and keys. As she walks through the dining room to the front hall, she sees Scott peering out the window.

"You better come see this," he says. "You're not going to believe it."

Aimee rushes to the window, where it takes her a second to make out Gwen and Lisa tussling on her walkway.

"Aimee!" Gwen yells up at the house. "Aimee!"

Aimee goes to the front door and opens it. The two women stop moving and look up at her. Aimee steps outside. "What is going on? Did something happen?"

Lisa steps forward. "Gwen has had a little too much to drink. I'm trying to get her home. She forgot her shoes."

Aimee looks down and, sure enough, Gwen is barefoot. Her chest tightens. Poor Gwen. She's falling apart before everyone's eyes. Scott comes out on the porch. "How about I grab Noa while you deal with this?"

"Thank you," Aimee says. "I'll text you the address. Just head out River Road toward Potomac."

They all watch Scott get in his car and drive away. Aimee texts him Cathy's address and then approaches Gwen, who won't make eye contact.

"Honey, you okay?" She reaches out and touches Gwen's arm. "Do you want to come inside? Your feet must be freezing."

"Gwen is very upset," Lisa says. "I think I should just take her home."

"Don't." Gwen whips her head around to face Lisa. "You don't get to speak for me." She turns back to Aimee. "Anton was cheating on me. With Lisa. They were sleeping together."

Aimee winces, as much from the words as the vitriol in her friend's voice. "No, that can't be right." She peers past Gwen to Lisa. "Lisa, is that true?"

"Of course not." Lisa shakes her head and sighs. "She's jumped to some crazy conclusions. Talking about some pen?"

Aimee nods, not quite sure what to believe. "Okay, I'll get her home. Thanks, Lisa."

Aimee pulls Gwen closer. "She was fucking my husband," she says.

Startled, Aimee shushes her. "Let's try and keep our voices

down, huh?" She shoots Lisa a look of sympathy. "I better take it from here."

But Lisa doesn't walk away. She steps a bit closer. "Maybe I should come with you. So I can explain."

"Not now, Lisa. Maybe later."

"When? She's only going to tell you her side. She's going to tell you lies."

"There are no sides. Gwen needs my help right now. We can talk later."

Aimee takes a shivering Gwen inside and puts her on the couch, wrapping a blanket around her feet and bringing her a box of tissues. Sababa, once unleashed, runs off to explore the house. She knows he's found the boys' room when Max and Benji erupt in squeals of laughter.

"I am so sorry." Gwen wipes at the tears that are coming from her eyes.

"You want to tell me what's going on? What were you doing in the street?"

"I went to Lisa's to confront her."

Aimee nods. "And what makes you think Anton and Lisa were having an affair?"

Aimee shrugs. "A lot of little things. That pen that Noa took from Lisa's. Anton went to that restaurant in Tampa last year. Le Cannu."

Aimee chews her lower lip for a second, measuring her words. "Is there anything else?"

"Yes, there's more. I don't feel like getting into it." She puts the tissues down and looks straight at Aimee. Her friend, normally so pulled together, is almost unrecognizable. Her skin blotchy, her eyes red and swollen. "You believe me, right? I feel like I'm losing my mind."

The oven lets out three short beeps. Aimee jumps up, grateful to have an excuse to avoid answering the question. "Stay here. I need to take out the chicken."

Aimee takes the chicken out of the oven and lines it up on the counter, cafeteria-style, next to the potatoes and broccoli. She calls Benji and Max, oversees them washing their hands, picks off a little chicken for Sababa, and then sets the boys up in the family room in front of the TV.

She makes two more plates and carries them back to where Gwen is curled up on the sofa like a pill bug.

"Gwen, honey, I have dinner." Aimee puts the two plates on the coffee table and kneels by her friend, stroking her hair.

"I'm not hungry," Gwen mumbles.

"You have to eat. You have to keep your strength up. Where are the boys?"

"My mom's over there. She's watching them."

Aimee sighs with relief. The boys are being looked after, at least.

After some prodding, she convinces Gwen to sit up and take a few small bites of chicken and potatoes. The bites are minuscule, not nearly enough for a grown woman to live on and no match for the alcohol she's obviously been imbibing. She's in much worse condition than Aimee realized. A wave of guilt hits her. It feels like watching a drowning friend from the safety of the shore. Only she can't dive in and save her.

"Do you mind if I close my eyes for just a few minutes?" Gwen fluffs a pillow and places it under her head.

"Of course." Aimee leaves her on the sofa and takes the opportunity to check on the half-dozen New England Asters that are in pots resting in a shady spot on the side of her house. She's going to plant them at a client's in a few days, but with the warm weather she needs to make sure they don't dry out before then.

When she's done watering the Asters, she comes inside the back just as the front door opens, and Noa yells, "Mom! I'm hungry!"

Aimee lets out a breath she didn't realize she was holding. Thank God Scott is back. He's not going to believe what happened with

Gwen and Lisa in the street. "Dinner is in the kitchen," Aimee calls out as she walks toward the foyer. "Wash hands."

But as Aimee enters the foyer, the person walking through the front door is not Scott. It's Cathy.

Aimee stops short. "Cathy. Hi. What are you doing here?"

"I'm so sorry to show up like this. I called." Cathy looks sharp in a burgundy crushed velvet blazer and bright lipstick.

Aimee looks at her phone, and sure enough she has a missed call from ten minutes ago. "Oh, I was distracted with something, and I didn't hear the phone."

"I have dinner plans tonight. I hope you don't mind my dropping Noa." She smiles apologetically. "I couldn't wait any longer or I'd be late."

"I understand, of course. But what about Scott?"

Cathy's eyes widen behind her thick black glasses. "Beats me. I waited and waited, but your husband never showed up."

24

THIS PAST SPRING

Digging up dirt on Scott took a little work, but Lisa had always enjoyed a good project. It helped distract her from unpleasant thoughts, like how unsatisfying her home life had become. Sometime in the past few months, Kai seemed to have shifted his affection from her to Marcus. Where he was once a mama's boy, now he would barely let her touch him, much less hug or kiss him. All he could talk about was sports, and all he seemed to want to do was hang out with his friends, or in his room with the door shut. She had heard this was a phase that boys went through, and that they came back around toward the end of high school, but it hurt. He used to want to tell her everything about his day, and now sometimes he could barely bring himself to grunt at her.

Her relationship with Marcus was no better. Having just made partner at his lobbying firm, he was riding a professional high, but it meant even less time for her. Sure, there was more money, more prestige, private boxes when they went to see the Nationals play baseball, that sort of thing. But she couldn't help but feel his success diminished her. She was an appendage to him now, a vestigial one, at that. They hired people to clean, to tutor Kai in math, to tend the yard, to shop for their groceries. How essential was she?

To Anton, she was essential. He said he could barely function on the days when he didn't see her. She didn't love him, but she was addicted to the surreptitious nature of their affair, to the secrecy, the thrill of sneaking around. It injected a much-needed boost of adrenaline into her boring suburban days that seemed to meld into one another. She pondered how he might help her get even with Scott. Just remembering those cruel words of Scott's, how casually he encouraged Aimee to pull back from their friendship, set her pulse racing.

The background check she paid for hadn't offered much of interest upon her initial reading. But when she re-read it, a detail jumped out at her. The first time Scott's social security number had ever been used was twenty-eight years ago, in a small town in Northern California. Her interest was piqued.

Because Scott said he grew up in New Mexico.

And according to her math, he would have been around eighteen when he used this social security number to get a job.

A little sleuthing around the internet gave Lisa a pretty good idea about this small town, which had emerged as a logging hub in the early twentieth century but had since fallen on hard times. It was a little too far north, past Sonoma and Napa Valleys, to make it a weekend destination for wealthy tourists from San Francisco. It lay right in the middle of what was known as the Emerald Triangle, a vast area in Northern California famous for its cannabis production—both legal and illegal.

What was Scott doing up there when he was eighteen?

A few days later, when all three families were together, she floated the idea of taking a trip to wine country.

"Wouldn't that be great, Marcus?" she asked in front of everyone. "I've never been to Northern California. I mean, not past San Francisco. Have you?" She turned to Aimee when she asked this.

Aimee shook her head. "Never been west of the Mississippi, but I'd love to go. Maybe when the kids are older."

"How about you, Scott?" Lisa asked.

"Have I ever been west of the Mississippi?" He smiled. "Well, I grew up in New Mexico, so that's a yes." He winked at her and took a swig of his beer. It was a non-answer. Lisa pushed a little.

"What about Northern California? Any interest in seeing

wine country, or going even farther up the coast, maybe see the redwoods? It's supposed to be beautiful up there."

This was the moment when he could say, *Oh, I've been there. I worked up there one summer.* Or some other plausible explanation.

"Love to. One day I'd like to drive all the way up the coast from L.A. to San Francisco and then up to Eureka. Maybe even keep going to Crater Lake in Oregon." He turned to Aimee. "One day we'll do that together."

"You never visited California playing baseball?" Aimee asked Scott. She turned to everyone. "Scott started at third base on his high school varsity team." She beamed at him.

"Nope. Never traveled that far. We drove all over the state, and we did end up in Arizona more than a few times, but not California."

The conversation moved on to road trips, to must-see national parks, and the difficulties of traveling with children. But Lisa zoned out. All she could think about was that Scott was lying. He had been to California, all right.

She could barely contain her impatience waiting for Marcus and Kai to leave the house the following Monday morning. She had cleared her schedule, switching her appointments around so she would have the whole day to spend online if needed.

She settled into her desk chair with a can of Yerba Mate and fired up her computer. On the desk was an 8 × 10 photo of her and Marcus standing with Aimee and Scott at Tikki Night at the school a few years ago. They had smiles on their faces, leis around their necks, and a glossy sheen, thanks to hours spent dancing. Lisa had gone to Michaels and bought an unfinished wooden frame, which she had painted and glued letters to at the bottom. *#SLAM TIME!*

She turned the photo facedown so Scott wasn't staring at her. SLAM was over. Gwen had ruined it. There was no going back. She began googling and it didn't take long to find what she was looking for.

The tiny newspaper story was written the same year Scott was in California. She leaned forward in her chair, as if getting closer to her computer screen might bring her closer to the truth about Scott. There was something here, all right. But what was it? The story was buried in the middle of the Metro section of the *Redwood Independent*, a local paper that had closed in 2010, but lucky for her, had been archived online.

AUTHORITIES SEARCH FOR MISSING STUDENT ATHLETES the headline read.

Police are asking anyone who knows the whereabouts of Michael Finch, 18, and Dexter Kohl, 18, to contact authorities immediately. Both young men are seniors at Mad River Regional High School, where Finch and Kohl were co-captains on the school's regional championship-winning baseball team. They were last seen together on Friday, Sept. 20, parking at a trailhead in Mad River, embarking on a three-day backpacking trip. Anyone with information is asked to call the authorities.

Lisa sat back in her seat and re-read the article twice. The mention of baseball convinced her that Scott was connected to this story somehow. She wasn't sure what it all meant, but she had a feeling it was going to be good news for her, and very bad for Scott.

25

Sometimes husbands don't come home for the night.

Aimee stares at the phone. Did the 9–1–1 dispatcher really just say that to her? The woman didn't say it in a cruel way—there was no mocking undertone, no sneer in her voice. She was gentle, as if she had heard it all and was trying to reassure Aimee.

"He's been gone what, four hours?" the dispatcher asks.

"I know that doesn't seem like a long time to you, but trust me, I know my husband. He's not answering his phone." Aimee is pacing the kitchen as she says this. She was able to keep it together while getting all three kids to bed, but now, in the empty, quiet house, her anxiety has taken hold. "He could be hurt somewhere, his car in a ditch."

"And you've called all the local hospitals?"

"Yes, I told you that already." She catches herself. She doesn't want to take out her frustration on this woman, who is only doing her job. "Sorry. I know you're trying to help. But he was supposed to pick up our daughter. He wouldn't just not show up."

"Look, we can fill out a missing persons report if you'd like."

"I would, yes." Aimee answers a barrage of questions. Name: Scott Crowder. Height: six-one. Hair: brown. Eyes: brown. No distinguishing scars or tattoos.

"And when exactly did you see him last?"

"He drove off around six P.M." Aimee looks at the mess in her kitchen from dinner. It already feels like he's been gone for ages.

"Does your husband suffer from any mental health issues, meaning, are you concerned he may cause harm to himself?"

"What? No. Absolutely not."

"What about medical conditions—epilepsy, diabetes, heart condition?"

"No. He's very healthy."

The woman takes down the make and model of Scott's car, along with the license plate. "I will file this and we will let you know if anything hits on his car," she says. "Feel free to call our missing persons department tomorrow to follow up."

"Thank you. I really appreciate it."

"Listen, most people who are reported missing show up on their own."

Aimee hangs up and gets to work cleaning the kitchen. A week ago, she was preoccupied with the stress of daily life— ordering plants, making payroll, arranging checkups for the twins, and Noa's psychological report. Now all she can think about is what has happened to Scott, and whether his not coming home is connected to the money he said he was scammed out of. He was going to answer all her questions tonight, tell her everything, and then—poof—he's gone.

Sleep doesn't come easily. Aimee wakes at the slightest sound, thinking it might be Scott coming home, but it never is. When her alarm goes off in the morning, she sighs. At least the long night is over. She puts her hand on Scott's side of the bed, as if she can divine some information about what has happened to him by laying her palm flat on the mattress. But no answers come to her. Scott is missing and she has no idea why.

She goes downstairs with the faintest flutter of hope that she will find him in the kitchen, but he's not there. Scott never came home. He didn't sneak into the house in the middle of the night under the cover of darkness and crash on the sofa. She checks her phone. Nothing. No text. No voicemail.

Panic swells within her anew. She is surer than ever that something has happened. Scott would never put her through this kind of worry. She doesn't have time to dwell on those thoughts;

she can hear the kids are up. The morning is a blur. When Noa asks where Dad is, Aimee tells her he had to leave early for work. Noa accepts this answer without question. And why not? It's been the case so many times before. Aimee wishes it were true, that Scott had come home late and left for work early. As soon as the kids leave for school, she will call the police again.

She walks the three kids to the bus stop, her thoughts far away from their chatter. Noa finds a spot under a tree, takes out her Warrior Cats book, and begins reading. The boys run off to find their friends and Aimee steps back from the crowd slightly so that she is close enough to keep an eye on things, but just far enough away to discourage anyone from talking to her. She takes out her phone to check her email. Several consultation requests from new clients have come in, and she needs to respond. She likes to get back to people within twenty-four hours, but with everything going on in the past few days, she hasn't had a chance.

"Aimee? Yoo-hoo, Aimee!" Gabby from around the corner rushes up, her son dawdling behind. "I'm so glad I caught up with you."

Aimee feels her body tense up. She normally enjoys Gabby's company at the bus stop. But this morning the thought of dealing with the woman's high-octane energy exhausts her. In addition to working as a fundraiser at the headquarters for the American Cancer Society in D.C., Gabby runs the school's PTA Listserv, organizes the twice-yearly neighborhood yard sales, and coaches girls' soccer.

"Hey, Gabby."

"Aimee, oh my gosh, how awful. I am devastated." She looks around to make sure her child is not in earshot, and when she spots him a few yards away with a cluster of boys, she turns back. "Anton killed," she stage-whispers, "right here in our own neighborhood. Who would do such a thing? What is this world coming to? Gwen, you, those poor kids. What can I do? How can I help? Say the word."

"I don't think there's anything we can really do right now except cooperate with the police."

"The police, of course. I've been meaning to ask you. Have the police arrested anyone? I keep looking online and there's nothing. It must be someone from D.C., or farther out in the county. There's more and more of that, you know, outsiders coming into Bethesda to rob people and commit, you know . . ."

"I haven't heard that it was a robbery."

"Homicide," Gabby mouths silently and then nods at Aimee. "I haven't had a good night's sleep since it happened. And I know I'm not the only one."

Aimee makes a noncommittal grunt. She has no patience for this, not today, not while Scott is still unaccounted for. She wants to shake Gabby's shoulders and scream *I don't care if you can't sleep. My husband is missing.*

"You're so close with the Khourys," Gabby says. "And we all feel terrible for Gwen. But at the same time, we're victims, too, in our own way. We all feel very unsafe right now. I was talking with a few other moms, and we need some answers. We're thinking of asking a Montgomery County police officer to come and give a talk about safety. What do you think?"

Aimee narrows her eyes. "About which part?"

"Should we invite Gwen? Is that rude? I don't want her to feel excluded, but at the same time, I'm sure she has a lot on her plate."

Aimee laughs before she can stop herself. "I'm sorry. I didn't mean to laugh."

"This isn't funny, Aimee. A man was killed. In East Bethesda, no less."

"No, you're right. It's not funny." Aimee glances at Gwen's house, wondering if she's home. Her car is out front. After she calls the police about Scott, she vows to check on her later. "I think giving Gwen a wide berth on your public safety campaign is probably a good idea right now. I don't think that's going to help her heal."

"I do want to help her. Really. I could organize a meal delivery train, you know, do dinners on different nights."

"Now that I think would be nice," Aimee says, feeling a bit guilty for her impatience. But she needs to see the kids off and get back to the house. "I'm sure she'd really appreciate it. I should have thought of it myself."

"Oh, I'm sure you have a lot on your plate."

You have no idea, Aimee thinks. The bus pulls up, and all the kids pile on board.

"Do her kids have food allergies or preferences? Is gluten okay? What about dairy?"

"Who cares, Gabby? I'm sure anything you make is fine. Don't overthink it." Allergies and food preferences seem so petty compared to what she and Gwen are dealing with. A dead husband. A missing one.

Gabby stares at her in shock.

Aimee backs away, offering an apologetic smile, and then turns and speed walks back to her house. Inside, she pours a large mug of coffee and picks up her phone. She is afraid of being dismissed, of appearing hysterical. Instead of calling the police she decides to re-call all the hospitals first. But there are no patients named Scott Crowder at Sibley, at Suburban, or at any of the other local hospitals.

Sometimes husbands don't come home.

But not hers. Not Scott. Scott always comes home. She can count on one hand the nights they've slept apart. Occasionally Scott travels for work, but not more than a few times a year. Maybe some husbands take off, but not Scott.

Finally, she calls the police.

As soon as she explains to the sergeant on the line why she is calling, she feels like she's been plunged into Kafka-esque nightmare, restating the same information as last night and in return receiving the identical responses. *No, he's not at any of the hospitals. No, he doesn't have a history of mental illness.* The sergeant

YOU DESERVE TO KNOW   167

checks the car's license plate number against traffic accidents in
the area, but there's no match.

"Sometimes people need to get away from their families for a
day or two. They usually turn up," the sergeant says. "Has there
been any tension in his life recently? A fight?"

"No, nothing like that," Aimee says. But there has been tension, hasn't there? One hundred thousand dollars' worth of tension. Not to mention Anton's murder. The police were poking
around, asking Scott questions. You could definitely call that
tension. Yet if she mentions the missing money to the police,
she knows how it will look. Like he took off. They'll never take
it seriously that he might be hurt somewhere. They'll chalk his
disappearance up to marital strife. She gets off the phone and
immediately texts Tim that she won't be able to meet him today at a job site. He texts back saying he will handle it, and she
feels some relief knowing at least one thing in her life is under
control.

Alone in the house, the panic builds within her until her heart
is beating so fast she thinks she might pass out. She can't do this
all alone, but she doesn't want to burden anyone else. Besides,
what help could anyone else offer her? She hunts down the business card left by the detective who visited them.

"Hello, Detective Salazar? This is Aimee Stern. Scott
Crowder's wife? I need your help. Scott is missing."

It takes him less than twenty minutes to pull up in his sedan.
Aimee notes with some irony that seeing this same car outside
Gwen's house on Saturday morning was the first sign that something was amiss on Nassau Court. Back then, she considered for
a brief moment that Gwen and Anton had been in some kind of
domestic fight. Is that what other neighbors will think now, of
her and Scott? She opens the front door and greets the detective.

"Let's start at the beginning," he says once they are both
seated in the living room. "You say your husband left the house
to pick up your daughter?"

Aimee leans forward, desperate for help. "Yes. Around six-fifteen. Noa, that's my daughter, was visiting a family friend in Potomac." She stops herself. "She's a client of mine, I run a landscape design business, but she's become a friend."

"And what's this woman's name and address?"

Aimee reels off Cathy's address, which she knows by heart. "But he never showed up."

"When did you realize he was missing?"

"Around seven-thirty maybe? Cathy brought Noa home and said Scott had never shown up. And his phone had been turned off, because when I called, it went straight to voicemail."

Salazar pulls at his chin. "Six-fifteen to seven-thirty. That's an hour and fifteen minutes. You didn't become concerned that it was taking so long to get to Potomac and back?"

Aimee straightens up, rebuked. "I was preoccupied with something here. Otherwise, I would have noticed."

"I see. And you haven't heard from him? No texts or phone calls."

"No," Aimee says. "Like I said, his phone is off."

"We can try to track it. Has your husband ever done anything like this before? Stayed out late, maybe had a few too many, slept at a friend's?"

"No, nothing like that. He's not like that. He's a good man. He's a good father. He would never not contact me and leave me worrying like this. That's how I know something is wrong." She searches the detective's face for some sign of understanding but sees none. "We have twins, and a girl. Neither of us would just leave the other with the kids."

He lets out a low whistle. "Wow, three kids. That's a lot." He gives her a sympathetic shrug. "I've got a newborn at home, and sometimes just the one feels like more than I can handle."

Aimee bristles. "You're not getting it. Something's happened. I know it."

"What about Anton Khoury? What was your husband's relationship with him?"

Aimee blinks, startled. "Anton? What does he have to do with this?"

"How often did the two of them spend time alone?"

"Basically never. Not that I know of. It was always as part of a larger group or sometimes just us four. Me and Scott. Anton and Gwen."

"How did Scott react to Anton's death?"

Stunned, Aimee stands. "I'm not comfortable where this is going. My husband is missing. He might be hurt somewhere, and you're asking me all these questions about Anton Khoury."

The detective stands as well. "You have street parking, right? No garage?"

"What does that have to do with—"

"You said you were asleep when Scott went out. That you didn't hear him leave. If Scott did drive to Villain & Saint on Saturday, there would be no garage door opening to alert you."

"We have a doorbell camera, remember?" she asks. "It would be on the video I sent you."

"Ah, the video." He gets up and walks to the front window, peering out. "It cuts off at the hedge. If your truck is parked right in front, as it is now, Scott would have to park past the hedge. And if that were the case, the camera wouldn't catch him driving away."

Aimee feels like she's been slapped. She invited Salazar here to help her find Scott, and now he's twisting everything around, talking about the night Anton died. "I don't understand. Why do you keep implying that Scott is involved in Anton's death?" Her voice has risen to a sharp shrill, but she can't stop it. She is on the edge of hysteria. "He explained it to you! Anton came here drunk and he took him home. You talked to his friend from the bar, right? He must have told you that Anton wasn't there.

So why do you keep coming back to that? Is there something you're not telling me?"

He turns back from the window, giving her a long, hard look. He's evaluating her. "I'm not at liberty to discuss the details of this case with you," he says. "But if your husband should contact you, you need to tell him we want to speak with him immediately."

26

Tuesday morning and Gwen is up early, awakened by a panic dream and unable to drift back to sleep. Down in the kitchen she notices movement through the window and peers out. A familiar sedan pulls up in front of Aimee's house, and Detective Salazar gets out.

Her stomach does a little flip. What could he want with Aimee and Scott? She remembers what Aimee said the other day, that Scott had gone to Villain & Saint. Yes, it was the closest bar to where they lived and Anton could have been going there to have a drink.

But she feared it wasn't just a coincidence.

She's scared Anton went after Scott, went to confess everything.

She wonders what the detective is saying inside that house. She'd love to be a fly on the wall.

"It's quiet down here. I suppose the boys are still sleeping." Barb opens the fridge and begins taking out eggs. She holds up a bottle of maple syrup. "Thought I'd make breakfast. Pancakes? French toast?"

"Pancakes are good."

"The boys were up very late last night. Too late. We don't want them to get into an unhealthy sleep schedule. Just because they aren't going to school doesn't mean they shouldn't have a routine."

"It's fine. It's not even nine o'clock in the morning. And they only found out yesterday that their dad is gone. I think they're allowed to sleep in."

"Have you called the school? Told them the boys will be out for the week?"

Gwen winces. "No, but I will."

"I can do that, right after I make breakfast. Have you thought about the funeral?"

"Mom, I haven't had coffee yet."

"I'm putting on a pot as I speak," Barb says. "This isn't one of those things you can put off. Arrangements need to be made." Barb works as she talks, efficient, although the tremble in her hands gives her away. Gwen wonders whether she'll turn into her mother, especially if she keeps drinking. Brittle and strong, yet trembling and fragile. "When will the police release the body?"

"I told you," Gwen says. "When the investigation is done." Whatever energy she had drains right out of her by the rat-a-tat of questions from her mother's mouth.

"What am I supposed to tell people?"

"Whatever you want."

"Gwen, you're not being any help." Barb turns, hands on her hips. "This helpless little girl act will not get you very far. With your permission, I'd like to contact the police myself. Someone has to take charge here. Did you find Anton's life insurance? Have you filed a claim yet?"

"I can't, Mom. I don't have the death certificate yet." She had forgotten about the life insurance. A two-million-dollar policy her parents insisted he take out when the boys were born.

"Well, why not?"

And around and around they go, discussing the logistics of death as Barb cracks eggs into a bowl and whisks them. Gwen feels herself fading. She wants it all to be over. Not just this conversation, but this whole section of her life. She wants to fast-forward to the next part, whatever it may be. Whether it is here in this cul-de-sac in Bethesda, Maryland, or in an entirely different state. She doesn't know how she'll get through these next few days, weeks, months. The last time she felt this way was after the boys were born. The dense, timeless haze of postpartum depression. She went on Zoloft and stayed on it for more than a year, until the good it was doing was outweighed by the twenty pounds she had packed on. Should she see a doctor? Ask for some pills to get through this?

At least she has Aimee. She thinks of how Aimee tended to her last night, even in her barefoot, drunken state. Aimee is more of a sister to her than her own sister, whose only contact since Anton's death has been a text, followed by a stock image of a wreath of flowers with *Sorry for your loss* written in script. It took Gwen five seconds to pull up the same GIF on her phone. Unbelievable.

Through the kitchen window she spots Detective Salazar leave Aimee's house. She adjusts the curtains so she can watch him.

"What is it?" Barb asks. "What are you looking at?"

Gwen doesn't answer. She expects him to get into his car, but to her dismay, he begins to walk up her path. When the doorbell rings, Gwen jumps.

"Someone is at the door," Barb says. "I'll handle it."

Gwen stops at the entrance of the dining room and hides behind the wall so she can overhear the conversation.

"Detective Salazar, ma'am. From the Montgomery County Police. I was wondering if Mrs. Khoury was home."

"Gwen? She's my daughter. And yes, she's in the kitchen. Please come in, Detective," Barb says. "Have a seat and I'll get her. May I bring you some coffee? Tea?"

"Just a water, please."

"Certainly." Barb has gone into full hostess mode. Her voice always turns melodious when talking to men. Gwen stiffens when she hears her mother's footsteps approaching.

"There you are," Barb says, stopping at the entrance to the kitchen. "There's a detective here to see you. I'm getting him some water. Why don't you go out, and I'll bring you a glass, too."

Gwen feels like her limbs are made of lead as she drags her-self into the living room. Nothing good can come of this visit. She takes a seat across from Salazar, giving him a little nod. Today his tie is a deep forest green, his dress shirt steel gray. She can see him in the morning, carefully choosing his clothing. He must think it reinforces his image as detail-oriented and meticu-lous. And he's right. So few men are like that these days. Anton could go days in sweatpants or ill-fitting jeans, T-shirts with the names of his favorite bands, looking more like an overgrown teenager than an esteemed author. Gwen picks a golden hair of Sababa's off her pants.

The detective jerks his head toward the dining room, where her mother has been hard at work organizing all of Anton's things. What was chaos is now organized into neat piles and half-filled cardboard boxes.

"Looks like you've been busy, Mrs. Khoury," he says.

"Yes, well, I'm not sleeping. I sort of don't know what to do with myself."

"So you're packing up all your husband's things?"

"Not exactly," she says, more sharply than she means to. But that is what she is doing. She wants every trace of that man out of her house. Out of her life. She glances at the detective's face. What must he think of a widow who empties the house of her husband's belongings only a few days after he is murdered? "I'm sorry, but why did you come here? Do you have any news?" she asks. "Any suspects?"

"Were you aware that your husband was having an affair?"

The question is so abrupt and unexpected that Gwen recoils. Before she can answer, Barb bustles in with a tray and puts it on the table. "Here we go, two waters. I brought some of these little hazelnut cookies, too, in case you two were hungry. If you need anything else, I'm happy to get it." She takes a seat next to Gwen.

"Mrs. Khoury?" the detective asks.

Gwen sputters, unable to find the words to respond. "Yes. I mean, no."

"Which is it, yes or no?"

"I didn't know before he died. But since his death I have learned that Anton was seeing someone."

Barb reaches out and squeezes Gwen's hand. "Is this an entirely necessary line of questioning?" her mother asks.

"I'm afraid it is, Mrs. . . . ?"

"Buckley. Barbara Buckley." Barb gives Gwen's hand a tight squeeze. "My daughter has been through a lot, Detective. I don't want to see her upset needlessly."

"I assure you I have no intent of upsetting her needlessly. Unfortunately, this is a murder investigation, and we have to ask these difficult questions." He reaches for one of the two glasses and takes a big sip. "It's been my experience that the best way to approach sensitive topics like these is to be honest and straightforward from the beginning. Now, Mrs. Khoury, do you mind sharing how you learned he was seeing someone?"

"I can't explain it. Just little things." Gwen stares at her knees as she speaks. One of the cruelest aspects of infidelity is that the wronged party often ends up feeling ashamed. As if she were deficient in some way, and Anton's betrayal was a reflection of her worth. That was part of the work she had done in therapy three years ago, to realize the cheating was about *him* and not *her*. And yet, here she is in the same position again, back to square one, shame building inside her like steam in a pressure cooker. "It's happened in the past. I just know."

"This may be difficult to hear, but we also found evidence of an affair," he says. "Do you have any idea of the identity of the person he was involved with?"

Gwen removes her hand from under her mother's and reaches for the other glass of water just to have something to do. The silence in the room feels oppressive. Does he know who Anton was cheating with, and he's testing her? She regrets confronting Lisa.

She was drunk, not thinking straight. If it gets out that Anton was screwing her neighbor, her friend, she'll have to move. She can't stand the thought of being the object of gossip and pity. What would chatty Gabby say? Or crazy Michelle J.? And a tiny part of her wonders, what if she's got it all wrong? What if Lisa did just bump into him, and he was actually sleeping with someone else entirely?

And then there's the question of what Anton told her he had been up to.

Sending the police after the *other woman* increased the likelihood that all of his secrets would be revealed. This feels like chess, and she was never very good at chess. She could remember all the pieces and where they went, and that the rook did this and the bishop did that. But she was never very good at imagining the steps that would follow next. Strategy, that's what people called it. She wasn't one for strategy, and what is her strategy here? To tell the truth? To play dumb? To outright lie? Is there another choice? A coughing fit perhaps, or breaking into hysterics?

"Mrs. Khoury, are you aware of the identity?"

"I'm not sure, but I have my suspicions. A neighbor of ours. Lisa Greco-King. I considered her a good friend. At least I did, before."

"You must have been very upset to learn that your husband was sleeping with a good friend of yours," he says. "Your families are close. You've even been on vacation together, haven't you?"

She gasps. He knew all along and was testing her. She feels vindicated—she was right to have accused Lisa. But that sense of vindication is overpowered by a wave of humiliation. Anton couldn't even be bothered to leave their street to find someone to cheat with. Lazy bastard.

"We found messages on his phone," the detective says.

"Where? I check his texts." The words slip out before she realizes what she's saying. *The jealous wife, the insecure nag.*

"He had WhatsApp on his phone. We found it hidden inside another folder."

Gwen sinks back into the sofa, wishing the cushions could swallow her up. He must think her a fool. No, he sees deception every day. She's just another clueless woman with a cheating husband. She had checked his messages—it was part of the condition of taking him back. But he was determined to cheat on her, so he found a way. She couldn't watch his every move.

"Where were you Friday night?" the detective asks.

This question shakes her out of her thoughts. "Me? What do you mean? Here with the kids."

"After your husband left, did you follow him in your car?"

Gwen coughs out a broken laugh. "Follow Anton? No. Of course not."

"Did you drive to Villain & Saint, hoping to intercept him, catch him there?"

"What? No."

"Did you have an argument with your husband that evening?"

"Why are you asking—"

"Neighbors overheard arguing. Raised voices."

"What neighbors?" Surely not Aimee. She would never talk to the police about her, would she? Maybe it was Paola, who lived on the other side.

"Your husband had a gash on his head. Did he get that during your fight?"

"No, he slipped. He hit his head. He stormed out."

"All right, I think that's quite enough." Barb stands up. "Maybe it's time for you to go."

"Not quite," says Detective Salazar, standing as well. He pulls out a piece of paper. "We have a warrant to search the house. And your car."

27

After seeing the detective out, Aimee retreats to her kitchen and begins to load the breakfast dishes into the dishwasher. She tries to process what Salazar told her. There can be no mistaking his meaning: he thinks that Scott is involved in Anton's death. And now that Scott is missing, it's becoming harder for her to maintain her faith in him. She wants to. She wants to give him the benefit of the doubt, to believe everything can be explained away, but it's nearly impossible to keep her thoughts from racing to the worst possible conclusion.

That Scott has fled.

Jittery and distracted, she goes upstairs to strip the beds. She keeps Tuesday mornings free for laundry and maintenance of her business website—updating seasonal sales, spotlighting different plants each week. This week she'll put up a picture of a New York ironweed, a native plant with purple flowers that bloom in early fall and can grow as tall as seven feet. She'll reach out to her dad and see how many ironweeds he has in stock, because if she puts it on her website, people will ask for it. It always works like that—people like to buy plants when they are in bloom.

Life has to go on, even if Scott isn't here. She can't just sit here in the house and wait for something to happen. She's always been a doer. She made it through the grief of losing her mother by throwing herself into activity. She played softball and soccer and worked at her dad's nursery. Later, in college, whenever she felt the darkness rise in her, she would go to the gym or for a run. She needs to be physically exhausted by the end of the day to be able to sleep. Exercise is her antidepressant and sleep aid rolled into one.

In the boys' room, she quickly strips the sheets. Finding several socks and shorts on the floor, she tosses them into a laundry basket. As she remakes the beds, she wonders if she should have said something to Salazar about the one hundred thousand dollars. She didn't want to make it look like Scott took the money and ran—Aimee is sure this can't be what happened. He was going to tell her everything last night; he was going to explain it all. And she still believes him.

Even if he never came home.

The only possible answer is that he *can't* get home. But why that would be eludes her. He could be injured. Perhaps his car crashed and he's on the side of the road, but that seems farfetched. They don't live in a rural area. The road he would have driven on to get to Cathy's was well-traveled and someone would have spotted his car had it crashed. That leaves the disturbing possibility that someone is keeping him from coming home.

But who? It has to be connected to the money. Maybe Scott had gotten mixed up with the wrong people. She knows how hard it can be to run your own business. Not just from her personal experience, but from watching her dad. There was a late, hard freeze her sophomore year in college, stunting and killing many of the plants the nursery grew. He couldn't meet buyer expectations and had to take out a second mortgage on the house to keep the business going. He told her all of this years later, when she was going through a rough patch and he offered her a loan. He said that when his business almost failed, he had been tempted to borrow money from moneylenders. *People who don't play around if you can't pay them back. Don't ever do that. Come to me.* It was the most honest and most vulnerable thing he ever told her.

Noa's room is more chaotic, even though she's older and

everyone says that girls are neater. Not in Noa's case. Clothes are strewn everywhere, and Noa has pulled the pillowcase off her pillow and used it to store My Little Pony figurines. As Aimee straightens up, she wonders if Scott might have become mixed up with shady people. Was he paying someone back, someone he had borrowed money from? She knew how much was riding on this software launch. He took a buyout from a biotech company a few years back, and instead of looking for new employment, he put together a team to pursue this dream. Was some of that funding less than legit? No, it's impossible. She has ridden with Scott when they drove all the way back to the grocery store to pay for the case of La Croix that they had forgotten to pay for. He is honest to a fault, a rule follower.

She's tucking a fresh sheet into Noa's mattress when she spots something under the bed. It's a shoebox, and her stomach clenches at the jangling noise it makes as she drags it out. She pulls off the lid and is saddened but not surprised to see a collection of items she knows don't belong to Noa.

"Damn." She picks up a small jade heart, trying to remember where she might have seen it, and she realizes it was in a bowl in Cathy's kitchen with several other stone hearts. She carries the shoebox into her bedroom. She'll talk to Noa about it later, try to establish where everything came from and how to get it all back to the rightful owners. Suddenly, exhaustion hits her. She sits on the edge of her bed and bursts into tears. It's all too much, worrying about Scott, about Noa, trying to keep it together when she has no idea what's going on. After letting herself really cry for several minutes, she goes into the bathroom to wash her face.

In the mirror she stares at the puffy bags beneath her eyes and scowls. "You can handle this," she tells herself. She won't be a victim. She won't sit around here feeling sorry for herself.

Aimee heads down to the mudroom and digs through the pockets of the jacket she was wearing on Sunday when she fol-

lowed Scott to the coffee shop. She finds Jon Block's card and
dials his number.

"This is Aimee Stern, Scott Crowder's wife," she says when
he answers with a gruff hello. "We met at Tatte the other day."

"Listen," he says tersely. "Like I told you before, I really shouldn't
be talking to—"

"Wait, don't hang up. Scott is missing; he didn't come home
last night." The words come rushing out. "I need your help."

He exhales loudly. "Fine. I'm only going to be in my office for
another twenty minutes. If you make it here in time, great. If
not . . ." He doesn't finish the sentence.

"I'll make it."

Aimee rushes out the door, and as soon as she does, she sees
Lisa come out of her house and start walking over. She must
have been watching at the window, waiting for Aimee to leave.

"Aimee!" Lisa calls and waves. "Hold on."

"Not now," Aimee yells back as she climbs into her truck. She
guns it, driving past a stunned Lisa and almost hitting a marked
police car that is turning onto their street. She watches in her
rearview mirror as it pulls up between her and Gwen's houses.
A lump forms in her throat. What could it be doing there? She
wonders if they are coming to her house with news about Scott,
or if they are going to Gwen's. At the next light, she pauses
when it turns green, debating whether she should go back to see.
Instead, she calls Lisa.

"Hey, sorry I ran off like that," she says by way of a greeting.

"That's okay. Is everything all right?"

"Not exactly. Scott didn't come home last night. He's missing."

"Missing? Oh my gosh, Aimee. That's terrible. Did you check
the hospitals?"

"Yes, several times. But I had to run out to meet someone, and
as I was leaving I saw a police car pull onto our block. Can you

do me a favor and see if they are going to my house? I thought maybe they had some news and were coming to tell me."

"You got it. I am walking out the door now." Aimee hears the creak of the door opening and then a screen door slam shut. "Let's see. Nope, they're not at your house. There are two officers on Gwen's front stoop."

Aimee lets out a deep breath. The worst has not come to pass. No one has come to her house to tell her they've found Scott somewhere hurt, or dead.

"What do you think is going on?" Lisa asks.

"I have no idea," Aimee says as she pulls into a strip mall with a laundromat and a Korean grocer. This is the address of Jon Block's office, but she doesn't see anything that looks promising. Aimee takes Lisa off speaker, cuts the engine, and holds the phone to her ear as she gets out. "I have to go, Lisa."

"Wait, I still want to talk to you about last night," Lisa says. "I hope you know what Gwen was saying wasn't true. Sleep with Anton? I mean, you know I would never, ever do anything like that. I'm not that kind of person. You know me, Aimee. I just wouldn't do that."

"Of course, right." But Aimee isn't paying attention to what Lisa is saying as she walks past the laundromat. She stops in front of a nondescript office. There's no sign, and when she peers in the darkened window, it looks like an empty waiting room. But this is the right address. "Gotta go. I'll call later."

Aimee hangs up and pulls open the glass door, a little bell attached to the top tinkling as she does. The small room is empty except for two plastic chairs and a table with a *People* magazine on it from 2019 featuring a celebrity she doesn't recognize. HOW I LEARNED TO LOVE MYSELF, the headline reads. She's not sure if she should sit and wait or approach the only other door in the room. She looks at her phone. Eleven minutes until Block said he was leaving. She knocks on the door.

"Come in," someone calls. The door opens into another small room, only this one is crowded with furniture. Block sits behind a desk crowded with piles of paper and two monitors. Several beige metal filing cabinets line the wall, and stacks of bankers' boxes fill the room.

He looks at his watch. "You have ten minutes."

"Eleven," Aimee says. "You have to help me. You have to tell me what's going on. Why Scott hired you."

Block scowls. He leans back in his chair, grabbing a neon-pink stress ball and squeezing it over his head. "What did he tell you?"

"He told me that he hired you to help him because he had been scammed. For a lot of money." She takes a deep breath. "One hundred thousand dollars. At first he told me that it was a business expense, but then he admitted that wasn't the truth. He was going to come clean last night and explain everything, but he never came home. I'm worried that this is all connected. And now the police are asking me about Anton's death."

"Anton?" He frowns.

"Anton Khoury. My neighbor. He was killed last Friday night. Just tell me, is Scott involved in some shady business scheme?"

"No. Not exactly." His words are deliberate and slow.

Aimee tightens and releases her jaw. She's dealt with difficult men before. Suppliers who want to stiff her, a crew member who was caught stealing from a job. "My husband's life may be in danger. And if something happens to him, I'm going to hold you responsible. Now I'm going to ask again, why did Scott hire you?"

Block smirks at her, his nostrils flaring. She can tell he doesn't like her tone. Aimee holds up her phone. "I've got a detective on speed dial. Detective Salazar? I'd rather hear from you what's going on, but if the only way to get you to tell me is to call the cops, I'll do it."

"Fine," Block says in a tone that tells her things aren't fine at all. He shoots the pink stress ball toward a small plastic hoop on the wall and misses. "Your husband hired me to find out who was blackmailing him."

28

THIS PAST SPRING

Authorities Search for Missing Student Athletes.
Lisa couldn't shake the headline from her thoughts over the next few days. When she had time, she searched for more information about Michael Finch and Dexter Kohl but came up with nothing.

What she did discover was that Humboldt County was so infamous for its high number of missing persons, it had acquired the nickname The Black Hole. It held the dubious distinction of having the highest per-capita missing-persons rate in California.

About a week later, on a Monday, she dropped Kai off at school after a dentist appointment and returned home, where instead of doing admin work for her coaching business, she fell down a rabbit hole of online research. She learned that growers had been cultivating marijuana in Humboldt since the 1960s, and growing was considered a way of life, woven into the culture and texture of the community. Before pot was legalized, the region attracted so many growers because it was remote and inaccessible to law enforcement.

"I believe that everyone living here is either directly or indirectly related to the marijuana industry," one local told a reporter.

But even though pot was legal now, the area still struggled with high crime rates and boasted one of the highest homicide rates in California.

Lisa got out of her chair, energized by the news. She had spent hours online, and Kai was almost home. She was so revved up that she went downstairs to make him a snack plate.

Her intuition told her that the disappearance of these two guys—Michael Finch and Dexter Kohl—was somehow related to drugs. And that Scott's being in the area at the same time was no coincidence. After all, they were high school baseball players just like him. Maybe he had been involved with drugs, but had closed that chapter of his life and didn't want to look back, so he pretended he had never been in California. Maybe they were his friends, and their disappearance had traumatized him, and that's why he wouldn't talk about California.

But over the next few days, the more Lisa mulled over the few facts she did know—these two baseball players missing, Scott's social security number being used in the area at the same time—the more convinced she became that something nefarious was going on.

It was a rainy spring morning when, on a whim, she put in a call to the high school both boys had attended. She wasn't optimistic; it seemed like a long shot. When her call went to voicemail, she improvised, leaving a garbled message about being a podcaster who covered missing persons cases.

After a few days, she all but abandoned hope anyone might call her back, but to her surprise, a return call came at the end of the week. It was a typical Friday in late May. The suburbs of D.C. were in full bloom, and the neighborhood was filled with flowering white-and-pink dogwoods and the last of the azaleas. Kai had spring fever and was counting the days until school ended and summer began. Lisa was with the whole gang, having the first barbecue of the season in Gwen's backyard, when her phone rang. Normally she would let unknown callers go to voicemail, but this time she took it.

"This is Arlette Fagin, secretary at Mad River Regional High School," a woman said. "Sorry it took a few days to call back. Things are busy here with graduation."

"That's quite all right, I appreciate your calling." Lisa stood up and walked briskly inside Gwen's house in search of privacy.

She locked herself in the downstairs bathroom. "Thank you for calling back."

"How can I be of service?"

"As I said in my message, my name is Lisa Greco-King and I have a podcast about unsolved crimes and missing persons. Are you a true-crime fan, Ms. Fagin?" Her tone was steady, and she knew she projected confidence. She would give this Fagin woman no reason to doubt her.

"I can't say that I am. And if this is another one of those documentaries about Humboldt County and the drug trade, I'm sorry, but I cannot help you."

"Oh, no, no. Not at all," Lisa said, quickly backtracking. She'd have to take another tack. "Not in the slightest."

"Good. We've had enough so-called journalists coming here and painting our county as a lawless safe haven for criminals."

"I have no intention of doing that." Lisa peered through the wooden blinds to the backyard to make sure no one was looking for her. Gwen had custom black wood blinds on both the bathroom windows to match the room's crisp black-and-white theme. It was as if she were allergic to color. "I was interested in a very specific case of two boys who graduated from Mad River and went missing about twenty-eight years ago. I think I might have a lead on one of them, but I'm not one hundred percent sure."

"Oh. Well, that is different."

"I'm sure their families would love to know if they are okay. Do the names Michael Finch and Dexter Kohl ring a bell?"

"I can't say they do, but I've only been here seven years."

"My problem is I can't find a picture of either boy anywhere. That's where I thought you might be able to help. Is there any chance you have yearbooks that go back twenty-eight years ago?"

"Sure, we've got yearbooks that go back to when the school opened in 1935. Why don't you give me those names and the year you think they graduated, and I'll see what I can find."

Lisa gives her the information and adds, "I think they both played baseball, if that's any help."

"Well, if they went to Mad River, they'll be in the yearbook."

Arlette agreed to send over a photograph if she found anything, and they said their goodbyes. Lisa's heart was pounding. She could hardly believe how easy this was, and how fun. What passed for fun in your forties was anything that pulled you out of your pathetic daily grind. She had heard other moms use the word to describe Target shopping sprees or half-marathons. What bullshit. Fun was clubbing until three A.M. and doing so much coke that you headed to an after-party and stayed up until the sun went down the next night. Fun was jetting off to Puerto Rico with a married guy you had met at a bar only the week before.

And fun was digging up dirt on the arrogant jerk your best friend married, the one who thought he was perfect. The one who pointed out when one of her eyelash extensions started falling off. "What's wrong with your eye?" Scott had asked with faux concern, in front of everyone no less, as if he didn't know. The one who told her to *calm down* when he came out and found her confronting an Amazon driver who had parked her in. Scott had actually apologized to the driver. *Sorry about that, man.*

She flushed the toilet and ran the sink for a few seconds in case someone was in the hall. No one was when she stepped out of the bathroom, and she returned to the table outside, her whole body quivering with excitement. Her senses heightened, she found it torture sitting silently while everyone else, completely oblivious, enjoyed their ice cream. She wanted to shout across to Scott, *I know! I know you were involved in something! I'm hot on your trail.* Imagining the look on his face, she could not help but smirk.

It wasn't even an hour later when her phone pinged.

Arlette Fagin had come through.

Lisa opened her texts. Even though the photo was only thumbnail size, Lisa could tell it was a team picture, the kind ubiquitous in high school yearbooks. Clicking on it, she enlarged it and could see it was of the Mad River varsity baseball team. The boys' names were listed underneath, and she had no trouble locating both Dexter Kohl and Michael Finch. Under the table, her fingers trembled as she pinched the screen, enlarging the faces of the boys. It was risky doing this here where someone might see, but the need to know was like a physical itch that had to be scratched. The voices around her, discussing the upcoming group vacation in the Outer Banks, faded as she homed in on a tall guy in the back row of the photo with a square jaw and an easy smile.

Lisa gasped.

"What is it?" Aimee asked.

"Huh?" Lisa looked up. "Oh, the house, it sounds amazing."

"It also has a private pool," Gwen said. "A small one, but still."

Lisa turned to look across the table at Scott, sipping his beer, oblivious to the fact that she had found him out. The deliciousness of it all thrilled her and she squirmed in her seat, filled with newfound energy. She held his fate in her hands, literally on her phone, and he was clueless.

He gave her the same easy smile he had displayed in his high school baseball team photo twenty-eight years earlier, and she grinned in return.

Hello, Michael Finch.

29

NOW

"Blackmail him?" Aimee searches Jon Block's face for a sign that this might be a joke. But he's not smiling, just glaring at her. "I don't believe you."

Block stands up and glances at his watch. "Time's up. I have to go."

"No, no way. You're not leaving until you explain what you mean. You expect me to believe someone was blackmailing Scott?" She shakes her head. It's ludicrous. Blackmail. For what? Her Scott, who won't even make an illegal U-turn. Who's dedicated his life to creating software that will help diabetics because his mother died of the disease. It doesn't add up. "You need to tell me why. What did he do?"

"I don't *need* to tell you anything," Block huffs as he grabs his jacket from the back of his chair and puts it on. "You're not my client. Now, do I feel sorry for you? Yeah, you're in the dark, but it's not my problem you don't know what's going on in your husband's life. If you'll excuse me, I have to be somewhere."

As he comes out from behind his desk, Aimee grabs his arm before she realizes what she's doing. "Please. My husband could be in danger. If you know anything that could help find him, you have to tell me."

Block stares at her hand as she slowly removes it. He's a big guy—he's got half a foot and about sixty pounds on her.

"Look, maybe he is in danger, but remember Occam's razor." He has a smug look on his face, like the kid in the class who has all the answers.

"Excuse me?" Aimee asks.

"When there are competing theories, the simplest one is most likely to be true."

"I know what Occam's razor is," she says, "but what do you mean? What's the simplest theory?"

"The pressure was too much and he left." He offers her a wry smile. "It's much more likely that he left of his own volition."

"I don't believe that." Aimee shakes her head. "Scott would never leave us. We have three kids."

"You think husbands don't walk away from their wives and kids every damn day? Believe me, I see it all the time. Throw in the kind of pressures he was under—if you ask me, it's the most likely scenario."

I didn't ask you, she wants to snap. But she did ask.

"You have to tell me what this is all about. I need to know."

"I really can't." He holds up his hands in exasperation.

"I'll go to the police. I'll send them straight to your doorstep."

"Suit yourself. It's all confidential without a court order." He lets out a long sigh. "Look, to be honest, going to the police is not a bad idea. Same thing I told your husband to do from the beginning, but he refused. But remember, some things are a secret for a reason."

"What does that mean?"

"You're going to open Pandora's box with this," he says. "Once the truth is out, you won't be able to unknow it."

"You don't get it. I want the truth."

He shakes his head. "It never ceases to amaze me. People can be married and sleep together in the same bed for decades and have no idea who the other person is."

His words sting her. She knows who Scott is. "Please," she tries one last time. "If you won't tell me why he was being blackmailed, can you at least tell me if you know who was doing it?"

"I can tell you that he was contacted over the past few months by someone demanding money."

"And did you learn anything about who was contacting him?"

Block looks down at his hands, adjusting a fat gold ring on his right pinky. "Whoever it was, they communicated with your husband via WhatsApp. It's encrypted, so it is practically impossible to trace." He looks up at her, his eyes sparkling. "But the initial contact, the one in which the blackmailer sent instructions on how they would communicate, that's a different story. That was sent in an email." He grins, clearly proud of himself. "And that I was able to trace."

"And? Whose email was it?" Her pulse quickens.

"It was a dummy account. Wasn't used before or after. Probably created just for that purpose."

Aimee feels her shoulders slump. This is what her dad called a shaggy dog story, all build-up and no payoff. "So you have no idea who sent it."

"No, I have no idea *who* sent it." He shakes his head, but his grin only widens. "But I do have an idea from *where* it was sent. Whoever wrote the email was not very careful on that front."

"Okay, and where was it sent from?"

"A library," Block says. "On the campus of American University."

30

Gwen sits at the kitchen counter, filling out the paperwork from the insurance company when she hears someone ring the bell. She peers through the peephole to make sure it isn't a reporter and sees Aimee. Relieved, she opens the door, only to have Aimee push past her into the foyer.

"Did you know?"

"Know what?" Gwen asks, taken aback by Aimee's brusqueness. She closes the door and leans against it.

"Don't lie to me. Don't protect him. Tell me." The ice in Aimee's voice scares her. She's never seen her friend angry before. "Were you in on this, too?"

"Was I what?"

"The whole drive over here, I kept thinking that if Gwen knew, she would tell me. We're such good friends. She wouldn't be able to keep this from me, would she?" Aimee lets out a short, harsh laugh. "Come to my house, eat my food, hang out with my family—she couldn't pull off that kind of duplicity."

Before Gwen can say anything, Barb enters the foyer, wearing navy slacks, a pale-blue crewneck sweater, and her signature double string of pearls. She looks like she's heading out to an afternoon at the museum with her gardening club.

"Hello, I'm Barb Buckley." Barb walks toward them, her hand extended. "Gwendolyn's mother."

Aimee's posture softens, and she uncrosses her arms to shake hands with Barb. "Oh, hi. I've heard a lot about you. It's nice to meet you. I'm Aimee. I live next door."

"I know all about you." Barb snaps her fingers. "You're the landscaper. Boy, would I like to pick your brain. I have a black lace elderberry that isn't black. Do you have any idea why?"

"Mom, please," Gwen says. "We're kind of in the middle of something."

Barb laughs. "That was probably rude of me. You must get sick of folks pestering you with their plant questions."

Aimee smiles stiffly. Gwen sees her struggling to overcome her anger long enough to answer politely. "Maybe it's not getting enough sun. To get that dark, black color, elderberry needs full sun."

"Well, aren't you clever," Barb says. "It is in a pretty shady spot. I'll move it before the winter comes. Well, I'm off to the mall with the boys. They'll both need suits." Barb looks directly at Aimee. "For Anton's funeral. Those poor boys, they've been through so much. We don't want them to suffer any more than they have."

Aimee shrinks back under Barb's gaze.

"Thank you, Mom," Gwen says.

"Of course. We must all put the interests of those two boys first right now. I'm sure you two ladies would agree."

A low throbbing starts at the base of Gwen's skull. A headache is imminent. She waits for her mother and the kids to leave, wondering how much she overheard of what Aimee was saying. The message her mother delivered was clear—do whatever it takes to protect Anton's legacy. Barb would say it was for Rafi and George, but Gwen knows that isn't the whole story. Becoming the subject of gossip and curiosity among her country club set would be Barb's idea of hell.

Once Barb and the boys are out the door, Gwen turns to Aimee. "Do you want some coffee? I'm getting a headache and some caffeine might help."

"No. I didn't come here for coffee."

"Well, I need some." Gwen heads to the kitchen, Aimee right behind her, and sticks a mug under the Nespresso machine. "You sure you don't want some?" She turns to see Aimee standing there, glaring at her.

"Forget the damn coffee, Gwen. I need to know what's going on. Last Friday night, when Anton got so drunk, and he came to me in the laundry room? Remember? He said *you deserve to know*. At the time, I had no idea what he was talking about. Because I had no context, no clues. And I thought maybe it was just Anton being drunk and rambling."

"He was drunk." Gwen nods. "Very."

"I want you to think about our friendship," Aimee says. "It's only been one year, but what did we both say? That we knew immediately we were destined to be friends. That we just clicked. That we were so lucky to have found each other. And how hard it was in your thirties, in your forties, to make real friends. Now look me in the eye, Gwen, please."

Gwen raises her head and looks at Aimee. Aimee's freckled face is red with anger, her brown eyes narrowed.

"I just found out that someone was blackmailing Scott, and that they communicated via email sent from a library at American University," Aimee says, her gaze unwavering. "Where Anton worked. I think the person blackmailing Scott was Anton." She pauses a beat. "Gwen, am I right?"

The question is an arrow that shoots straight through Gwen, nailing her to the wall. She can't move, can't breathe, can't look away from Aimee's face. In her silence, her stillness, Gwen's complicity is laid bare. If she imagined that she might be able to lie to Aimee, to pretend she didn't know, she had only been fooling herself. Now that the time has come, she is defenseless against her friend's plea for the truth.

"Yeah, it was Anton." The whispered words barely register to her own ears, but they're loud enough for Aimee to hear.

"And you knew." Aimee's voice is low and measured. "You knew and you didn't tell me."

"Please! Let me explain!"

"Yeah, you're going to explain." She laughs, abrupt and unkind. "Right before I call the police. But I will give you one chance as my friend to tell me your side."

What can she say? There's no side. Just the awful unvarnished facts. That Anton told her everything the other night during their fierce argument, and she did nothing about it. "I'm so sorry. You have to believe me. I had no idea what he was up to, I swear, Aimee. Not until Friday night."

"Is that what you were fighting about?"

Gwen nods. "Yes."

"What did he say? Exactly."

"He was upset. Really upset." Gwen closes her eyes, forcing herself to remember that night. "I had put the kids to bed. Anton stayed downstairs and kept drinking. By the time I got downstairs he was very drunk. He left out the back with Sababa to walk him, and I followed him out. I confronted him."

"About what? If you didn't know he was blackmailing Scott, what did you confront him about?"

"I knew something was up. I thought that he had started cheating on me again. My mind just jumped to that conclusion. I had no idea what he had really been up to, Aimee, I swear."

"But what did he say?" Aimee presses on, louder. "What words did he use?"

"He said he had done something really stupid. He said he had fucked up."

"Meaning what?"

"He was worried . . . he was in a panic. He was almost frantic. He said he had to warn you."

"Warn me about what?" she asks through gritted teeth.

Gwen shrinks before Aimee's ferocity. She will have to say it out loud. Ever since Friday night when Anton told her what he had been doing, Gwen has known that this moment would come, but it's so much harder than she ever imagined.

"About Noa," she says softly.

"Noa?" Aimee's voice catches. "Gwen, what does Noa have to do with any of this?"

"I don't know all the details. I was upset. We were yelling at each other." Gwen feels sick. She shouldn't have to do this. It wasn't her fault. This is Anton, that bastard, ruining her life, even from death. "He told me he needed money. That I had emasculated him, if you can believe that. He said I cut his balls off. How could he be expected to live like this? It wasn't his fault, he said. It got out of control—"

Aimee slaps her hand down on the granite. "Gwen! What does this have to do with Noa?"

"He said he had been blackmailing Scott," Gwen says, the words tumbling out. "That he had some dirt on him. And no, he didn't say what it was, and I didn't ask. I was so shocked. I was so angry. I threw a coffee mug at him. It hit him in the head. I thought I cleaned up all the pieces, but that's what you stepped on. Remember? On Saturday?"

"I don't care about the damn coffee mug!" Aimee steps closer, just inches from Gwen, and for a moment Gwen wonders if her friend is going to hurt her. Aimee may be small, but she's strong from so much physical labor. "You're going to explain what this has to do with Noa."

"Anton said somehow the thing with Scott had gotten out of control. He said it was connected with that woman, that client of yours," Gwen says. "You know, the one with the kittens?"

"Kittens?" Aimee stumbles back. "You mean Cathy? How is she involved?"

"I don't know, I swear."

"Goddamnit, Gwen. We're talking about my daughter. What did Anton say?"

"He didn't tell me the connection. All he said was . . ."

"Was what?"

"He was worried that Noa had been going over there." Gwen paused and looked away for a moment, then in a lowered voice she said: "That she might be in danger."

31

Danger.

The word hangs in the air between them. Aimee looks at the woman in front of her. She thought she knew Gwen. How as a girl she had wanted to be a writer, but realized she didn't have the temperament and settled for public relations. That her favorite flowers are orchids. That she likes pale-pink nail polish from Olive and June, and Bellinis with fresh peach slices, and rewatches *Sex and the City* whenever she's sick. That her first concert was Hootie & the Blowfish in 1995, but she told Anton it was Mazzy Star to seem cooler. That she grew up lonely and counted her horse, Shadow, as her best friend. That she won't let any non-organic food in the house yet keeps a stash of Cokes hidden in the pantry.

But what did it all add up to? If Gwen could keep a secret like this, Aimee realizes that she doesn't know this woman at all.

"He said that Noa might be in danger? Why?"

Gwen shrugs sheepishly. "He didn't say, exactly."

"Cathy's a retired teacher, she's in her sixties, in what way is she dangerous?"

"I don't know, I swear! It had something to do with Scott's past."

Aimee blanches. "His past? What about his past?"

"Aimee, if I knew I would tell you. Anton was upset. Drunk. He said she was dangerous. That Scott needed to know. That Noa might be in danger."

"And you said nothing to me?" Heat erupts across Aimee's

skin, like an instant sunburn. A mother's rage at the thought of her vulnerable child in harm's way.

"Friday night was the first I knew about any of it," Gwen says, tears wetting her eyes. "You have to believe me."

Gwen's theatrics leave Aimee cold. If anything, her display of emotion makes Aimee angrier. How dare Gwen break down, feel sorry for herself. She endangered a *child*. "But on Saturday, and on Monday, Noa went back there," Aimee says.

"I didn't know that! Anton was murdered on Friday night! I've been out of my mind. You have to believe me."

Aimee takes a step back from Gwen, astonished at her attempts to make herself the victim. "This is not about you right now. This is about my daughter. You want me to believe that at no point in the past few days, with the police questioning you about that night, at no point did it occur to you to tell me that Anton warned you about Cathy?"

"You're being unfair. You know how distraught I've been. You don't know what I'm going through. I can barely remember the most basic things, like brushing my teeth. I'm sorry I didn't tell you about Noa, about that woman, but I have been struggling just to function." Gwen's voice has taken on a wheedling tone. "Not to mention that I learned Anton was sleeping with Lisa."

"Lisa? I don't want to talk about Lisa. I want to know how Cathy is connected to Scott. What did he mean, she was someone from his past?"

Gwen shrugs. "He didn't say."

Hot, sweaty, dizzy with anger, Aimee pivots and walks back into the living room.

"Where are you going?" Gwen calls after her.

"To Cathy's. I'm going to confront her. If you won't tell me then I'll find out for myself what's going on." Aimee yanks the door open.

"Is that a good idea?" Gwen asks. "She could be dangerous."

Aimee chokes down a laugh. An image of the older woman

pushing her glasses up the bridge of her nose springs to mind. "I think I can handle Cathy."

Aimee storms outside, adrenaline pushing her forward. She gets in her truck and slams the door. Gwen runs out after her, Sababa right behind her with his leash in his mouth. Aimee starts the engine at the same time Gwen yanks open the passenger-side door and climbs inside as the dog jumps in, as well.

"What the hell are you doing?" Aimee asks.

"I'm coming with you."

She takes a good look at Gwen. Her two-hundred-dollar jeans have a coffee stain on the knee, and there's a small hole in the sleeve of the short-sleeve cream sweater she is wearing. Her face is blotchy from crying, a bit of eye makeup smudged. She's crumbling; her veneer as fake as her friendship. "No. You're not coming with me."

Gwen clicks her seatbelt. "I know you hate me right now, and I don't blame you, but I can't let you do this alone. So, if you want to go to Cathy's house, you're going to have to take me with you."

"I don't need your help, Gwen. No offense, but you've done enough damage. I'm perfectly capable of talking to Cathy by myself."

Gwen doesn't respond, but pulls the dog onto her lap.

"Fine. Have it your way," Aimee says and yanks the steering wheel hard to the left as she stomps on the gas, forcing the truck into a screeching hard turn and slamming Gwen against the door.

They drive in silence toward Cathy's house. All she can think of is Noa, her daughter who thinks everyone is a friend and doesn't understand why people are mean to each other. Who believes what others tell her, even when it hurts her. Like the time three of her former friends told her there was a wounded puppy in the woods behind the school, and Noa wandered off to find it during recess and missed the bell to return. She got in trouble for not coming in on time but remained convinced for days that there was a puppy in the woods that needed her help. Aimee reminds herself that Noa is safe, unhurt. Cathy hasn't harmed her in any obvious way. But what about in less obvious ways? What really went on at Cathy's house?

At Huntington Parkway, she swings a quick left off Old Georgetown as a car zooms toward her.

"That was kind of close," Gwen says, as the other driver honks at them.

Aimee slows down a little over the speed bumps. She has to get her emotions under control. If she wants Cathy to tell her the truth, she can't come in with guns blazing. She needs to play nice. Cathy will respond to nice. But Aimee doesn't feel very nice right now.

"I don't know if this is such a good idea," Gwen says. "Just showing up like this."

"Why are you trying to talk me out of this? You're the one who told me that she was connected to Scott's past, that Noa might be in danger with her. Are you sending me on a wild goose chase?"

"No, I swear."

"If there's any chance that Cathy might know something that could help me find Scott, I want to talk to her. I'd think you'd want to, as well. She might know something about Anton's death."

"I want to know the truth just as much as you do. I just don't think we should barge in like this."

"Next time we can send engraved invitations."

As the familiar house comes into view, Aimee's heart begins to pound. She shoots a hard side glance at Gwen, in no mood for debate. She doesn't want to be talked out of this. There have been a few times in her life when, deep in her soul, she *knew* things.

Like how she knew when her mom went into the hospital that it wasn't going to be all right. She knew when she hugged her and kissed her that last time and everyone promised she would be fine after she got some rest, she knew in her gut it wasn't true. *Mom will be fine*, her father had said. *She only broke a hip. People break bones all the time.*

He had made it seem routine, but Aimee knew it was anything but. Her mom's bones had been hollowed and made weak by the cancer medications she was on. Once she was in a hospital bed, unbeknownst to everyone, an undetected blood clot loosened and began traveling from her leg. Aimee didn't know about the blood clot, of course, but she sensed things were not right.

She begged her dad to let her spend the night. She offered to sleep on the floor. But her father insisted she go home. Her mother died that night of a pulmonary embolism.

It's taken years for Aimee to learn how to speak up when that little gut instinct kicks in. But she's not a child anymore. She doesn't need anyone's permission. Outside Cathy's, she puts the car in park and turns to Gwen.

"I didn't ask you to come here. If you're not comfortable, call an Uber and go home." Aimee gets out, astounded at her own directness, slams the door, and stomps up the front steps. She is grateful she is wearing her heavy work boots and pants, that she has a sharp knife inside her jacket's left pocket. Not that she anticipates using a weapon on Cathy. But she doesn't feel vulnerable. She feels infused with some kind of superpower. She bangs on the front door.

As she waits on the porch she looks around and notices what she didn't see before. A sleek blue BMW at the far end of the driveway, about ten feet in front of the old barn. Not Cathy's usual green Subaru.

Gwen appears beside her, holding one end of Sababa's leash. The dog, nose to the floorboards of the porch, sniffs loudly.

"What is it?" Gwen asks. "What are you looking at?"

"That car. I've never seen it here before."

"Maybe she has company. Do you want to leave? It's not too late."

Just then the front door swings open, and a woman in her midfifties with a choppy dyed-red bob answers. "Hello, may I help you?" She looks at the two women and the dog with obvious confusion.

Aimee pulls back, startled. "Hi, is Cathy home?"

The woman's penciled-in eyebrows arch in surprise. She's dressed in a style that reminds Aimee of Cathy—a flowy gray silk top, black skirt, and chunky acrylic necklace. Aimee wonders if she is a friend or coworker of Cathy's.

"Cathy?" The woman shakes her head. "There's no Cathy here."

"Cathy Stocker," Aimee says with more urgency. "She lives here."

"Oh, Catherine Stocker." She nods in recognition. "Of course, Catherine, my cat sitter. But she no longer works for me. And I can assure you she has never lived here."

32

THIS PAST SPRING

The news that Michael Finch and Scott Crowder were the same person was a hard secret to keep.

But Lisa had no one with whom to share this juicy little tidbit of knowledge. Twice, in the days after her phone conversation with Arlette Fagin from Mad River High School, she almost blurted it out. Once when she and Marcus were watching a movie on their couch the following Saturday, and then a few days later while on a call with a client. The woman was a stay-at-home mom struggling with whether to go back to work or not. She had been a frustrating client for Lisa because she never took any of her advice, never did any of the homework Lisa assigned, hadn't even taken the Myers-Briggs personality test Lisa had emailed her, although Lisa was sure the woman was an INFP. She was a classic Pisces—spiritual and artistic but bad with setting boundaries. Lisa had been talking to her about gut instinct, one of her favorite topics. She was trying to come up with a recent example of following her intuition and found herself almost telling this woman about her hunt for the truth about Scott. She managed to steer the conversation away at the last minute, but she surprised herself with how tempted she had been to spill every detail.

She knew she couldn't share what she'd learned about Scott, not even to a client who didn't know the players, and not even if she changed the names. All she knew at this point was she possessed incendiary information, even if she wasn't sure why. Her research on Michael Finch was fruitless. He did not exist. Rather, many Michael Finches existed—a screenwriter, a makeup artist, a YouTuber, a constitutional lawyer—but not her Michael Finch. She had better luck with Dexter Kohl. She found his name and a picture of a goofy-looking teen with long curly hair and sleepy eyes on a Humboldt County website for missing persons. There were dozens of people listed—men and women of all ages. But Michael Finch wasn't one of them. She suspected that Dexter being listed and not Michael indicated something important.

The following Wednesday, Lisa was in the snack section of Whole Foods loading up on chips and kettle corn for Kai when her phone rang. She recognized the area code, 707, as belonging to Humboldt County, the same area code Arlette Fagin had called from.

"Hello," she answered.

"Is this Lisa Greco-King?"

"Yes, it is." She could barely hear the woman over the din of the supermarket.

"I got your number from Arlette Fagin. At the high school?" The woman's voice was weak, and she coughed a few times before continuing. "We have a friend in common, and Arlette told him about your interest in the case of the two boys that went missing twenty-eight years ago. I hope it's all right that I'm calling you."

"Of course." Lisa stepped away from her full cart, leaving it in the snack aisle, and walked right out of the store. She could barely hear the woman, so she headed to her car for privacy and quiet.

"She said you were looking into the disappearance?" The woman sounded hopeful but hesitant. "And that you may have found one of the boys?"

"Well, I'm not a hundred percent sure," Lisa said, closing the car door. "But I have a lead. Do you mind my asking who you are, and how you are connected to this case?"

There was enough of a pause that Lisa thought they might have been cut off. But then the woman spoke.

"I'm Dexter Kohl's mother."

The words hit Lisa hard. In all her plotting against Scott, she never really thought about the two boys who had gone missing in California and the pain their families might have experienced, or still be going through. What she was doing had broader implications. This woman was looking for her son and, because of Lisa's snooping, thought she might have a lead. But instead of making Lisa cautious, the thought of being at the center of this drama excited her. She might be the one to help this woman answer a decades-old mystery. *Hero* might be too strong a word, but Lisa imagined the gratitude this woman would bestow upon her if she accomplished what law enforcement had failed to do for twenty-eight years. "I am afraid I don't have any information about your son. I don't know what Arlette told you, but it's the other boy, Michael Finch, that I might have some information about."

"Oh, she told me that. I need to find Michael. He knows where Dexter is." The woman coughed again. "Sorry, I have the emphysema. I don't know how much longer I have, and I want to see justice done. I need to talk to Michael. I believe he knows where Dex is at. You see, my son isn't missing, not really."

"I'm sorry?"

"I think Dex is dead, buried somewhere up on that mountain. And I think Michael Finch killed him."

Lisa sank back in her leather seat as it all clicked into place. She felt a euphoria, the kind she hadn't felt since she went skydiving for her twenty-first birthday. The high from having jumped out of a plane and floated among the clouds had lasted days. That same rush filled her now. Scott Crowder—who everyone thought was an upstanding family man, biotech entrepreneur, soccer coach, and all-around great guy—was a fraud. A criminal. A killer.

And she alone had the power to expose him. He could change his name, finesse his history, but he couldn't outrun his past. She was the one calling the shots now. "Please, tell me everything."

Lisa sat in her car and listened to the woman lay out her story. In the fall of their senior year, the boys had embarked on a weekend camping trip. Both were experienced hikers, but the day they were supposed to return, neither came home. Their car was found at the base of the trail, but no trace of the boys. A few weeks later, a hunter found a bloody shirt a few miles from the trailhead. The blood belonged to Dexter. But there were no bodies. They had simply vanished.

Only, the woman said, a few months after the boys disappeared, she saw Michael Finch. She was sure of it.

"It was the end of the year. Often, I would go up to where Dex and Michael had set up camp and leave flowers. Sometimes I would go up and search the ground as if I might find something the police had overlooked. Then one day—it was cold, I remember, snow was on the ground—I saw Michael. I called his name and he ran. I tried to go after him but I lost him."

"Did you go to the police?"

"They were of no help. They thought I was seeing things, a grief-stricken mother. They went through the motions, talking to his mom, that lowlife boyfriend of hers, his friends. They never turned up anything. But I intend to find the truth, even if that means upsetting a few apple carts."

"I am so sorry for your loss," Lisa said. "I think that I can be of some help in finding justice for you."

33

Aimee stares at the woman standing in the doorway of what she had thought was Cathy's house. Cathy doesn't live here. It was all a lie. Bile rises in her throat. She feels like she might be sick. What has she done?

"Can we come inside?" Gwen says from behind her. She feels Gwen's hand at the small of her back, gently nudging her forward. "We need your help," Gwen continues, "and my friend here has had a really big shock. She needs water."

"But I don't know you—" the woman starts.

"I'm Gwen Khoury, this is Aimee Stern, and I'm afraid your cat sitter might be mixed up in something pretty serious."

Aimee watches the woman's face soften as she absorbs this information. She's nodding slowly, but she doesn't look convinced. Gwen keeps talking. "We'd really like to speak with you first, see if we can sort all of this out. But if not, I'm afraid we'll have to call the police."

"The police? Goodness. What is this about?"

"Can we come inside?"

"I suppose it'd be all right." The woman steps back.

Aimee knows that it's Gwen's fortitude right now, both physical and emotional, that she is drawing on to keep going. Gwen's hand on her back, her bodily warmth, is transferring strength into her own body, without which she feels like she might collapse.

"But the dog has to stay outside," the woman says.

Gwen ties Sababa to the porch railing, and she and Aimee follow the woman inside. Aimee has been in the house several times, but now she sees it with fresh eyes. The bohemian decorations, such as wooden masks and small sculptures, had once suggested Cathy was a sophisticated world traveler. Now it strikes Aimee that she had made a series of assumptions about Cathy based solely on these superficial clues. The decor, the NPR playing in the background, the Subaru in the driveway. She had assumed Cathy was a certain kind of woman—educated, wealthy. But maybe none of it was true. She doesn't know the first thing about Cathy. Well, she knows one thing. Cathy lost a son, or at least claimed she did.

"My name is Jean Brewster," the woman says, sitting on the edge of a wingback chair across from Aimee and pushing a lock of orange hair behind an ear. "And I have lived in this house for twelve years. Now, what is this about my cat sitter?"

"May I get a glass of water for my friend?" Gwen asks.

"The kitchen is right through that door." Jean nods and Gwen disappears. A few moments later Aimee hears the faucet running in the kitchen. Jean sits across from her, her shoulders square, her head held high as if she were testifying in court. Aimee recognizes the gray silk blouse the woman is wearing—she's seen it on Cathy.

As she examines Jean more closely, she realizes she's also seen Cathy wearing the clear, acrylic necklace around Jean's neck. Now Aimee wonders about Cathy's signature chunky black glasses. Maybe they weren't even real glasses, simply part of the act.

Gwen returns with a glass of water and hands it to Aimee, who takes a long sip. Her throat is dry, and she struggles to find her voice. "Ms. Brewster—"

"Jean, please."

"All right, Jean, like my friend said, my name is Aimee Stern and I am a landscape designer. I was hired by a woman, she told me her name was Cathy Stocker. She gave me this address and when I showed up, she said she wanted me to replace the azaleas with native plants—"

"My azaleas!" Jean puts her hand to her chest.

"I didn't do it, of course." Aimee gestures to the window, annoyed at the interruption. "The azaleas are still here. She never wanted to get started on the project. She kept delaying. At the time, I thought she was lonely and was really looking for a friend. But now I think it was a ruse. Now I think what she wanted . . ."

Aimee's voice trails off. What does she think Cathy wanted? She still has no idea.

"Now we think there may be something more sinister at play." Gwen leans forward. "May I ask, how did you come to hire Cathy as a cat sitter?"

"There's a site for pet sitters." Jean is soft-spoken and deliberate, and clearly uncomfortable with conflict. She has the air of a librarian who prefers books to people. "I have a cat, and she's fine on her own. But she became pregnant and gave birth. Three adorable kittens. I work as an educational consultant and I have to travel a lot. I knew I would be gone a lot this month, for weeks at a time, actually, and I wanted someone who could come in and look after Zelda, that's my cat, and the kittens."

"And that's how you met Cathy?" Gwen asks. "Did she have references?"

Jean purses her lips together, as if she might stop the ugly truth from tumbling out.

"Jean?"

"Well, no, not references, exactly." She hangs her head a moment. "But I met her, and I liked her right away. She's a retiree, a former teacher, she moved here to be closer to her son and grandchildren."

"Is that what she told you?" Aimee asks. "Because she told me her son died years ago."

"Well, that's what she said. And I just liked her. I felt more comfortable with an older woman. I knew she'd be responsible. No drugs, no drinking. Some of these other applicants . . ." She clucks her tongue. "One girl with blue hair, another who couldn't be bothered to take out his earbuds the entire time he was here. One reeked of pot. I couldn't trust them with the house. Cathy seemed trustworthy. I remember when she came for the interview, I just liked her. We drank Earl Grey together, and it turns out that we both love Ann Tyler. You know, the writer?"

"Where did she say she lived?" Gwen asks.

Jean waves her hand in the air as if this is irrelevant. "Somewhere in Rockville. Maybe Silver Spring? I honestly don't know."

"And that's it?" Aimee asks. "You give the keys to your house to a complete stranger because she likes Earl Grey tea and Ann Tyler?"

Jean recoils. "I beg your pardon?"

"That's so irresponsible," Aimee says. "You didn't even know her." It hits her that those were the same words Lisa shouted at her last Friday at dinner. Lisa had been right. Aimee had made a terrible mistake. She had allowed her daughter to spend time with a complete stranger, just as Jean Brewster had allowed one into her home. They were both taken in by Cathy's gentleness, duped into thinking that an older white woman in chunky glasses who drank tea could not be a threat.

Outside, Sababa barks, once, then again, then a series of short ones like the staccato of a machine gun.

"My friend's husband is missing," Gwen says. "This Cathy woman might know where he is. Do you have any idea where she might be? How did you pay her?"

"Through Venmo. I can give you her email if it helps."

Sababa lets off another round of barking.

Gwen turns to Aimee. "You stay here and get the Venmo information. I'm going to go check on Sababa."

Aimee waits on the sofa, leg shaking with impatience, as Jean fumbles with her phone. A wave of nausea washes over her. She's trapped inside a maze, and every way she can turn seems like a dead end. When she needed her wits the most, she froze. But

Gwen stepped in. She feels so confused, furious at her friend for her betrayal, yet grateful that she is here now.

Jean looks up from her phone. "I don't know if this will be of much help, but I also have a picture of her. I remember now that she was not very happy when I took it, but I told her I like to have photos of all my contacts, so when I get calls at work I know straight away who it's from."

"That could be helpful." She tells Jean her number and waits for her to text over the photo and a screenshot of Cathy's Venmo account. When they both appear on her phone, Aimee examines them but finds nothing helpful. The photo Jean took of Cathy sitting on the floor holding a black-and-white kitten only confirms that there is nothing scary or sinister about her.

"Thank you for your help." Aimee stands. "You should know I will be going to the police, and they might come by to ask you some questions. It looks like Cathy Stocker fooled us both."

Jean walks her out to the front porch, but there is no sight of Gwen or the dog.

"Where did they go?" Aimee asks. She walks around the porch to the side of the house, where she spots Gwen standing below them next to the BMW, a strange look on her face.

"What is it?" Aimee calls from up on the porch.

"Sababa got loose and got into that barn," Gwen says.

Aimee follows her gaze, and sure enough, she can hear the dog scratching. Aimee starts toward the staircase, a sense of dread growing in her.

"He must have found a gap where the door hasn't fully shut," Gwen says. "But can't get out now."

"An animal might have gotten in there," Jean offers. "That happens a lot. I had a raccoon family take up residence there last year."

"The ground is really muddy, and I'm wearing slippers," Gwen says, looking down at her feet. "Jean, do you have boots I can borrow?

Aimee is already halfway down the wide steps, her heart thumping wildly. "What's in the barn?" she calls to Jean. "Besides possibly raccoons?"

"Nothing. I don't use it. You have to manually heave that door open. It's very heavy."

"Then why are there tire tracks going up to it?" Gwen asks.

"That's impossible," Jean says. "No one uses that barn. It's not structurally sound."

Aimee stops short next to where Gwen is standing and looks down. Gwen is right: in the mud leading to the barn are two lines of fresh tire tracks.

Her chest seizes. She knows what she has to do. She slogs through the thick, sticky mud to the barn door. She puts her shoulder against the immense wooden door and heaves, but it barely moves. The frustration swells in her. She has to get inside. She straightens up, trying to get her footing in the slippery mud, and then leans against the door once more. This time, she senses Gwen behind her, pushing as well. For a few seconds, nothing happens, and then the door begins to slide open with a low rumble. Once it's open, Aimee straightens up, breathing heavily, nerves jangly. She takes a tentative step inside the large space, her eyes adjusting to the dim light. Dust mites dance in the air, and Sababa runs out, yapping, happy to be free.

And parked in the middle of the barn is Scott's car.

34

Gwen stays at the entrance to the barn while Aimee runs to the car, flinging the doors open.

"Scott! Scott!" she cries, going from one side to the other.

The air is musty and dank, smelling of mildew and mice. The only things in the barn besides the black SUV are some rusty-looking gardening tools hanging from hooks on the wall. At Gwen's side, Sababa whimpers. "It's okay, boy," she says, bending to rub his head, but she knows it is anything but.

Aimee emerges from the back seat of the car, tears in her eyes. "Nothing."

"Let me check the trunk." Gwen opens the back, but it is empty except for a few reusable grocery bags and a soccer ball.

"I'm so sorry, Aimee," Gwen says, shutting it again. She didn't expect to find Scott in the trunk, but she is desperate to help somehow.

Aimee crumples to the barn floor, her back against the tire of the car, and hangs her head. Her long waves hang like a curtain, hiding her face, but Gwen can hear her crying. Gwen is taken off guard. Aimee never loses it. Gwen crouches beside her. "Aimee, it's okay, we'll find him. This is good."

"Good?" Aimee looks up, tears streaking her face. "How is this good?"

"Because it means he was here. This will give the police something to work with. I'll call them now."

As Gwen stands up and dials the number, it hits her that she would not have reacted this way if Anton went missing. She didn't even burst into tears when she learned he had been murdered.

She is oddly jealous of Aimee for being in so much pain, because it reflects how much she loves Scott. She's forgotten what that feels like. Not to love someone, because she loves her boys more than anything in the world. But to be *in* love.

After Gwen calls the police, she and Jean take Aimee back inside.

"I had no idea the car was there," Jean whispers as they settle Aimee onto the couch.

"No one's blaming you, Jean," Gwen tells her. "Can you watch Aimee for a minute? I need to ask someone to pick up her kids from school." Gwen considers reaching out to Barb, but decides against it. Too complicated to explain everything to her mother. That leaves Lisa. She's loath to contact her but texts her for Aimee's sake. Lisa responds right away that it won't be a problem.

Is everything all right with Gwen? Is this about Scott?

She's fine. Will fill you in later.

Gwen purposely did not write *I* will fill you in later. Someone will, but it won't be her. If she had her way, she'd never speak to Lisa again. She may have Marcus fooled, but Gwen knows the truth about her and Anton. Gwen returns to Aimee's side to wait for the police. Finally, two officers show up, and Jean takes one of them out to the barn while the other comes into the house. Officer Tom Nguyen looks like he graduated from high school last year, but despite his baby face, he seems to grasp the severity of the situation right away.

Gwen is happy to take control, knowing Aimee is too distraught to do much talking. She relays the story—how Cathy Stocker pretended to live here but was really the cat sitter, that Scott never came home last night, and how they found his car in Jean's barn. This is her role to play right now, but she also hopes it will win back some of Aimee's trust. She needs Aimee and can't bear the idea of losing her friendship.

"Where can he be?" Aimee asks of no one in particular. "I don't get it. He can't have just disappeared."

"That's what we're here to find out," Officer Nguyen says.

"Has he been kidnapped?"

"We don't know that. Let's not jump to any conclusions," he says. "Let's talk about Cathy Stocker. Do you have any other information about her? Even if it seems irrelevant? Did she mention friends?"

"I don't know anything more than what she's told you," Aimee says.

"Did your husband ever meet her?"

"No, never. He never had a reason to."

"But there may be a connection between them," Gwen says, cautiously. "We just learned, today, that someone had been blackmailing him. And that this Cathy woman may have been involved."

Officer Nguyen, who has been standing the whole time, takes a seat near Aimee. "Is this true? That your husband was being blackmailed?" He waits a moment for her to respond. Gwen nods. "That's a pretty important detail to leave out."

"We didn't leave it out," Aimee says. "I know it's important. That's why we're telling you now."

"What was he being blackmailed for?"

"I don't know. I just found out today from a private investigator he hired to look into it."

"Why didn't you call the police when you found this out?" Nguyen asks. "What made you decide to come here?"

"I don't know." Aimee looks at her hands. Gwen's heart aches for Aimee. It was a dumb thing to do, and it looks even worse now. But Aimee was so upset earlier.

"Do you think that it was Cathy Stocker who was blackmailing your husband?" he asks.

Aimee looks up at Gwen as if for approval. Gwen nods. She has no choice. They have to come clean if there's any chance of finding Scott.

"No, it wasn't Cathy," Gwen says. "It was my husband. His name is Anton Khoury, and he was murdered Friday night."

The officer stares at Gwen for a moment before standing. "Excuse me, I need to make a phone call."

He leaves the room for about ten minutes, during which Gwen can hear his voice low as he talks on the phone. She wonders what he is saying. The whole story is so crazy. Finally, he returns and tells them they can go home.

"I've got everything I need from you right now. But a detective will come by your residences later to talk to you both," he says. "Oh, and I need a current photo of your husband, if you have one."

When Aimee doesn't respond right away, Gwen pulls up a photo of Scott and texts it to him. She has plenty to choose from over the past year of shared meals and vacations. Once they are free to go, she takes Aimee outside.

"Do you want me to drive?" Gwen asks.

Aimee shakes her head. "I'm fine, really."

The ride home is awkward and silent. Gwen pulls her cold, damp feet out of the muddy slippers and tucks them under her. She'll toss the ruined slippers when she gets home, give Sababa and then herself a long shower. Barb can take care of everything else. Gwen wants to ask Aimee how she's feeling, but she's afraid that her friend might take out all of the day's frustration on her. Aimee is giving off *don't-talk-to-me* vibes, and Gwen wants to respect that. Her mind is cluttered with everything she has learned today and she doesn't have the bandwidth to sort it out. Like the fact that Anton knew about Cathy. She feels the weight of his guilt pressing down on her. She wasn't the one blackmailing Scott, but as Anton's wife, she feels somehow responsible.

She wishes she could reach across the gulf that has opened between her and Aimee, that they could curl up on a couch with a bottle of wine and talk about it all. Together, they have a better chance of figuring things out. But Aimee is shutting her out.

When the truck pulls up in front of Aimee's house, Gwen snaps out of her thoughts.

"I have to go to Lisa's and pick up the kids," Aimee says, getting out.

Gwen slips her feet back into her wet slippers and grabs Sababa's leash. The late afternoon sun is hidden behind thick white clouds, and the air is heavy with impending rain. "Let me know if I can do anything to help," Gwen says to Aimee as she locks the truck.

"Thanks," Aimee says from across the hood.

"Maybe you should ask Lisa about Cathy."

Aimee frowns. "Lisa? You think she knows something about Cathy?"

"Well, she did freak out when you said Noa was going over there."

Aimee looks off in the distance. "That is true."

"And if she was sleeping with Anton, maybe he told her something."

"Gwen, we don't know that."

"You don't believe me?"

"I don't know what to believe," Aimee says, irritated. "And I have enough on my plate right now."

"Of course. You never want to think badly of anyone." Gwen turns to her house, pulling Sababa, who has found something dead on the asphalt to smell, behind her. What she really wants to say is, *You always wanted to see the best in her, but Lisa is a psycho, and your husband, he has some serious skeletons in his closet. And maybe it's time you grew up and faced facts.* But right now Gwen feels like Aimee is the only friend she has in the world, and she doesn't want to lose her, so Gwen forces herself to smile. "And that's one of the things I really love about you, Aimee. Just be careful who you believe."

35

Marcus answers the door wearing an apron and envelopes Aimee in a hug. "You doing okay?" He pulls back to look at her face. "Any word on Scott?"

Aimee shakes her head. "No. But we found his car. I'll tell you about it inside."

"Gwen all right?" Marcus asks, nodding across the cul-de-sac to where Gwen is still standing on the front stoop of her house.

Aimee turns to watch Gwen disappear inside. "Not exactly."

Aimee follows Marcus into the brightly lit kitchen, where she is greeted by smells of garlic and butter.

"Shrimp and rice," Marcus says. "I've made plenty if you want to take some home for the kids."

"You're sweet," she says, suddenly exhausted. She hasn't thought about dinner and is tempted by Marcus's offer, but she doesn't want to impose. "I don't want to be any bother."

"It's no bother." He pulls out a large Tupperware from a cabinet and begins scooping from a sheet pan. "I always make twice as much as we need, so we'll have leftovers. Now tell me, what's going on? Lisa said Scott was missing."

She tells him an abbreviated version of the story—how Scott didn't come home and how her client didn't really live at the house that she claimed to. Aimee leaves out the part about Anton blackmailing Scott, out of a sense of protectiveness for Scott. Whatever Scott has done, she wants to hear his side of the story before she passes judgment. She knows other people will jump to the worst possible conclusion, even friends like Marcus.

"I wonder what's up with this Cathy woman," he says. "Do you think Scott is in some kind of danger?"

"I have no idea. I just hope the police can find him soon." She looks at her watch. "I better give the kids a heads-up that it's time to go. You know it takes them a while to transition."

"I'll do it," Marcus says. He walks to the basement door, puts two fingers in his mouth, and lets out a shrill whistle. "Benji? Max? Your mom's here."

Cries of disappointment come up from the basement.

"This is a five-minute warning," Marcus calls back and shuts the door.

"The whistle's a pretty good trick," Aimee says.

"My mom had an iron triangle she'd ring, and me and my brothers could hear that thing even if we were all the way down at the park." He opens the fridge and pulls out lettuce and carrots. "I only get to cook dinner on days I work from home. I love to cook. In another life, I'm running my own restaurant."

"Lucky for Lisa," Aimee says dryly. Mentally exhausted, she doesn't want to chitchat. She only wants to go home. "Is Noa down there, too?"

"She's in my office, curled up with a book. My sister passed along my nephew's Magic Treehouse collection when he outgrew them, and Noa found them."

"That's sweet," Aimee says. "Is Lisa out?"

"Pilates." Marcus takes a large knife and chops the head of lettuce. "She came here the other night, you know, Gwen did, pretty drunk. Making all kinds of crazy accusations."

"Yeah, I'm aware."

"And you know what about?" Marcus stops chopping and looks at Aimee, one eyebrow raised.

"Yeah." Aimee nods.

"I wish she would just calm down and talk to us," he says. "I think Anton's death is affecting her. I mean, not just in the obvious ways." He tosses the chopped lettuce into a wooden bowl and grabs the carrots. "If she had come and talked to me, I could have told her that Lisa and Anton bumped into each other in Tampa."

"You knew about that?"

"Sure. Lisa told me as soon as she got back. They went out to some restaurant and got drunk, had fun. Anton was at some conference. She said there were some other writers there, too."

"I think Gwen might be losing it a bit," Aimee says, picking her words carefully. She doesn't want to go into all the details about the secrets Gwen's been keeping from her. Some of her earlier anger has subsided a bit. She's not sure how she feels about Gwen right now. "It's the stress of Anton's death. Not just a death, but murder."

* * *

On the way home to her house, the boys run ahead but Noa stays by her side. Aimee adjusts the warm Tupperware in her arms, thinking about what Marcus said. She doesn't know what to believe. It seems crazy that Lisa and Anton might have been having an affair, yet Gwen was so sure. And Gwen was right about one thing—it was odd how upset Lisa got when she heard Noa had been spending time at Cathy's. But it is impossible to figure out if that was just Lisa being Lisa, or if she might have known what Anton was up to. Aimee would need to ask her in person, to gauge her reaction, in order to know the truth.

"Mommy, Kai said that George and Rafi's dad was murdered. But you said he died in a car accident." Her tone is slightly accusatory.

"Well, he was hit by a car. That's what I said."

"Kai said there's a killer on the loose."

"He said what?" Aimee stops short.

"He said I should put a chair in front of my door so the killer doesn't get in. But I think he was trying to scare me."

"He shouldn't have said that," Aimee says. "I'll say something to Lisa."

"No! Don't. Please, don't say anything. Promise?"

Aimee sighs and continues walking. "Fine, I won't. But I don't want you to worry. No one is coming to hurt you. Did he tell the boys the same thing?"

Noa shakes her head. "No, just me. But was it an accident? Or was it on purpose?"

The boys have gone ahead inside the house and left the front door open. Aimee pauses on the stoop, unsure of what to say. Adults are supposed to have all the answers, but she has none. "We're not sure. The police are trying to figure that out now. But I don't want you to worry. You're safe. Okay?"

Noa nods and then steps into the dark house. Aimee follows, moving from room to room and flipping on all the lights. In the kitchen, she cuts up some carrot sticks and apple slices, spoons the shrimp and rice onto plates, and calls everyone to dinner.

"Since Daddy's not here, can we watch something with dinner?" Noa asks.

The boys instantly chime in, arguing about what show to watch. Aimee relents. She has little energy to enforce screen limits tonight. The kids grab their plates and drinks and head to the family room. Aimee sits at the kitchen table alone, staring out into the blackness of the backyard. The floodlights in Gwen's yard go on and then off. Maybe she was letting Sababa out. Maybe it was a fox that activated the motion sensors. The distance to Gwen's house is about thirty feet, but it feels a million miles away. How strange that they are each going through the suburban dinnertime ritual while both their husbands are gone.

Missing. Not gone. Scott will come back.

After dinner the kids drop their dishes in the sink and rush upstairs. Normally, she and Scott do the dishes together. Tidying up the kitchen is their chance to catch up at the end of the day. She thinks of his car, sitting in that barn. How did it get in there? Did he drive it in himself? Was he forced to? The not knowing is unbearable. She's prioritized stability her whole life, and now she has to accept that she may not really know the person she thought she could count on.

Jon Block's words come back to mock her.

It never ceases to amaze me. People can be married and sleep together in the same bed for decades and have no idea who the other person is.

Aimee goes upstairs and starts looking through Scott's drawers. She is not searching for anything in particular, but hopes that some object might trigger a buried memory, activate some dormant knowledge. But Scott has no secrets in his sock drawer or tucked under his neatly folded sweaters. In his bedside table she finds a stack of cards from his recent birthday. One from her, homemade ones from the kids, and one in a yellow envelope, return address North Carolina, where his Aunt Kay lives. Aimee opens the card and reads it. It's a standard Hallmark card—his aunt has signed her name and that's all. She's the only family Scott has left, a fact that now strikes her as meaningful. With her three stepbrothers, her dad, and Deb, Aimee has people. Holidays are always spent up in Baltimore, and since she married Scott, he has always gone along, happy to be part of a big boisterous family. She loved having him with her at these gatherings. He got along with everyone and, in an odd way, he made her feel like she belonged in her own family. But now she wonders about Aunt Kay.

Aimee glances at the clock; it's only just after nine. Not too late to call. Not when it's something important like this.

She's nervous calling. She's never had reason to pick up the phone and dial Scott's aunt before. She only has the number in her phone because they were traveling through North Carolina a few years ago, and they stopped by and had a quick lunch with her.

Aunt Kay answers right away. They chat for a few minutes and

Aimee is reminded that, despite how bright Kay is, she's a mathematics instructor at a local community college, and she lacks many social graces.

"I'm actually calling because I have some difficult news."

"I hope you don't need money," Kay says. "I don't have any. In fact, I've taken in a boarder."

"No, we don't need money. It's about Scott."

"He's not in trouble again, is he?"

Aimee's heart gallops. "What do you mean, again?"

"Never mind, hurry up and tell me what you want. I have papers to grade."

"Scott's missing, Aunt Kay. The police are looking for him. I'm very worried about him." She pauses, but Kay says nothing. "I think he was being blackmailed. Do you have any idea what that might be about?"

"I don't want any trouble." Aimee can hear papers shuffling in the background.

"Of course not," Aimee says. "Neither do I." What did Kay mean by that? It didn't sound like simply the skittishness of an older woman who was used to a solitary life. There was an edge to her voice. Where was her concern for her nephew?

"I was happy to take him and help him finish high school, get him on his feet. I gave him a roof over his head and food to eat."

"I know you did. And he was always very grateful."

"But that's the end of it for me. I'm not getting mixed up in anything. I wish you good luck, but I can't be of any help. Please don't call here again."

Aimee gasps, unable to control her surprise. "Aunt Kay, you can't mean that."

"I do. And if I were you, I'd get myself a good lawyer."

36

THIS PAST SPRING

The question Lisa couldn't get out of her mind was—what did Aimee know?

There was no way she could ask her friend directly if she was aware that her husband was a murderer and a fugitive. That wasn't the kind of thing you dropped into the middle of a conversation about which summer camps still had openings for August.

But Lisa knew that she had to figure out what Aimee knew about Scott's past. If this was Aimee's secret, too, if she had committed to protecting Scott, well, then Lisa would help her by keeping his secret, as well. It would bond them together even more tightly. Nothing would ever be able to come between her and Aimee. But if Aimee didn't know, then Lisa was faced with a decision. Doing nothing wasn't an option. What was the point of carrying around a stick of dynamite if you never used it?

Memorial Day was a scorcher, and the neighborhood pool club's potluck was packed with families. Armed with a quart of potato salad from Giant, Lisa headed down to the pool with Marcus and Kai. Gwen had shown up right when the pool opened and placed sky-blue-and-white-striped Turkish towels on half a dozen chaises, as well as commandeered one of the few glass-topped tables with an umbrella.

Tasked with guarding the chairs, Lisa took a seat at the table with Aimee while everyone else went to stand in a long, snaking line for the buffet.

Lisa pulled out a bottle of tanning oil and began rubbing it onto her shoulders. She didn't burn, thanks to her Mediterranean heritage, and she never felt better than when she was bronzed by the sun. Across from her, Aimee sat in the shade of the umbrella and applied a thick white goo on her freckled skin. Lisa had thought for a long time how she might approach the topic of Scott's history with Aimee to discern if she knew anything. She didn't want to appear nosy or suspicious, just curious in a friendly way. Striking just the right balance would be key. She did believe that Aimee didn't know Scott used to live in California—the discussion about visiting the area a while back established that—but that didn't preclude her knowing Scott was running from something, did it?

"Besides the Outer Banks, you guys have any big plans for the summer?" Lisa asked.

Aimee put on a giant straw sun hat. "Nope. Just the usual. We'll take a week and go stay with my dad and Deb."

Lisa nodded. She knew Aimee's dad and stepmom ran a nursery just outside Baltimore and had a house close enough to the Chesapeake Bay that Aimee had grown up kayaking and boating. Whenever Aimee talked about her childhood, or going back home to visit, Lisa felt a pang of jealousy. She had no home to go to. She had stopped speaking to her mother a few years after college over an incident with some bearer bonds. Lisa had found the bonds in a box in the back of the linen closet and cashed them in to pay for furniture, a cell phone, and professional clothing for her first real office job. It was an impulsive and stupid mistake, but when her mother found out, she didn't see it that way. She threatened to go to the police. Lisa had no choice but to cut her out of her life. She left Syracuse for Washington and never looked back.

"Sounds beautiful up there," she says.

"You should come sometime. It's so nice and relaxing. You can spend the day on the water, and you can also get into Baltimore pretty easily. Go to the aquarium, Fells Point. It's fun."

"I'd like that." Lisa meant it. The trouble was going anywhere

in the summer with all of Kai's sports camps. Even taking one
week for the Outer Banks meant him missing out on a week of
club soccer.

"What about Scott's family?" Lisa asked. "Do you ever get
down to North Carolina to visit his aunt?"

Aimee shook her head. "Not really. She lives in a small apartment. The last time we visited was a few years ago when the boys
were still toddlers. Aunt Kay is kind of a strange woman."

"Have you been out to New Mexico, where Scott grew up?
You must be curious what his childhood was like."

Aimee's face was unreadable, hidden behind her glasses and
under that big hat. "I'd like to," she says cautiously. "But Scott's
not that interested. He's not really the nostalgic type. I love going
back to the same restaurants and hangouts from my childhood.
I guess it also helps keep me connected to my mother. She grew
up in the same town I did, and she's buried there along with my
grandparents. So I like to go back and revisit history. But Scott?
Not so much."

Lisa tries to decipher this answer. She senses some tension in
Aimee's voice—but whether it was from hiding a secret or jus-
tifying her husband's odd detachment from his past, Lisa could
not be sure.

Out of the corner of her eye she sees Rafi, George, and one
of Aimee's boys—maybe Max?—hustling over, holding plates
laden with food. She's running out of time. Panicking, she blurts
out the first thing she can think of.

"Do you ever go through Scott's old yearbooks? I've looked
at Marcus's and they are hysterical. He had this fade haircut in
ninth grade, I swear it was almost as high as that guy's from Kid
'n Play." She's rambling, but it's a Hail Mary. "Did Scott have
any funny haircuts in high school?"

Aimee takes her sunglasses off and shakes her head. "He probably did, but I've never seen pictures from when he was a kid. I
don't think he kept his yearbooks from high school. A lot of that

kind of stuff got lost when his mom died and he moved from New Mexico to North Carolina to live with Kay." Aimee grins. "Hey, Benji, where's Max?"

The conversation was over. Lisa's heart was racing and she was sweating. She fussed over Rafi and George to burn off some of her nervous energy, helping them open their juice boxes, getting them napkins.

Aimee doesn't know.

There was no way. She could see how Scott had easily duped her. A childhood in New Mexico, his last year of high school in North Carolina. But what about the in-between? That year, or years—she didn't know how long—during which he was most certainly in Humboldt County, California. He had conveniently excised that little detour from his life, and Aimee was none the wiser.

When everyone returned to the table with their food, Lisa and Aimee took their place in the now much shorter line. Lisa was amazed that someone could be so oblivious about their own husband. She knew everything there was to know about Marcus, down to the names of his ex-girlfriends and where they lived now.

Lisa couldn't sleep that night. She was never a good sleeper; it's why she had a prescription for Ambien. Usually one knocked her right out, but not tonight. She lay in bed in a pre-sleep haze until the flash of an epiphany jolted her awake.

Aimee was in an abusive relationship.

She didn't know it, of course. She had been duped by Scott— they all had. His charming act, his easy smile. But Aimee was living with a lying, conniving murderer.

But how could she alert her friend to the danger she was in without alienating her? She knew how it would go. Lisa rolled over on her side. When she'd seduced Ruth's boyfriend in college to show her what a useless jerk he was, Ruth blamed *her*. No, she wouldn't make that mistake again. Female friendship was so puzzling to her. It wasn't enough to love her friends completely, to have their best interests at heart, she had to *manage* the way she loved them.

She did love Aimee. Needed her.

And Aimee was in danger.

She thought about how she might reach out to the authorities in California. Let them know that Scott-slash-Michael was here. But she thought she knew what Aimee's reaction might be. If her husband was arrested and her family torn apart, Aimee would blame Lisa. A classic case of shooting the messenger.

There had to be another way, a way to arouse suspicion and drive a wedge between them. The goal was to make Aimee feel so betrayed, so hurt, that she would never forgive Scott, that she would turn to her loyal friend Lisa for succor and support.

It wasn't going to be pretty, Lisa thought, but it was for Aimee's own good.

37

This Wednesday morning is running smoothly, a rarity for Aimee. The kids are up, fed, and she still has fifteen minutes before she has to hustle them out the door to the bus stop. She's exhausted, her body on autopilot after another sleepless night. She lies in bed, replaying the conversation with Aunt Kay—her admonition to get a lawyer, how she had reacted when Aimee told her that Scott was being blackmailed. She wasn't shocked. She wasn't outraged. What had she said—*He's not in trouble again, is he?*

She's loading the dishwasher—because even when your husband goes missing, life marches brutally on—when her phone rings. Aimee lunges at it, desperate for news about Scott, but sees it's only her dad calling, not the police.

"I was calling about those oak leaf hydrangeas. They're root-pruned and ready to be picked up if you want to send one of the guys out tomorrow. Looks like good weather, a little cooler with a chance of some rain in the evening."

"The weather sounds perfect. I'll call Tim."

"How are things?"

"Fine," she says without hesitation. It's a reflex of hers to keep any problems from her father. "Actually, things are not fine. Something terrible has happened, Dad." She recounts what's going on without going into too much detail, sticking to the fact that Scott is missing and that the police are involved. "And yesterday I found Scott's car, but we haven't found him yet." Her voice hitches. "I'm so scared and worried. I'm not sleeping."

"Oh, honey. That is a lot to deal with." He clears his throat.

"I'm sure the police will find him. They're very good at this sort of thing. You'll see. There'll be a logical explanation."

She waits for something else, some sign of emotional life in him. She feels as if they are on opposite sides of a great lake, shouting across a vast distance. She longs to be closer to him. She needs him now the way she needed him when her mother died. She wants him to reassure her the way only a father can. *He'll show up. He loves you so much.* The silence is deafening.

"Yeah, I'm sure you're right," she says finally, just to keep the conversation moving.

"And how about the kids? How are they handling this?"

"They think he's on a business trip. I don't want to scare them until we know more."

"Well, that sounds smart. Why don't you all come up to the house this weekend? At least you won't be alone," he says. "Your brothers will be here, too. Deb's making chili. You should be with family at a time like this."

"Maybe," Aimee says.

"Did I tell you your brother and I installed a zip line in the backyard? I bet the kids would love it."

"I bet they would, Dad." A heavy sadness settles on her shoulders. The doorbell rings. "I better go. There's someone at the door."

"Sure. Oh, Aimee, one more thing."

"Yeah?" she asks, her voice rising on a hopeful note.

"I threw in a maple leaf viburnum. I know you didn't ask for it, but it's a beautiful specimen. A real four-season winner. If you can't find a client that wants it, you should keep it."

"I will. Thanks."

Aimee hangs up and squeezes back the tears that are threatening to flood her eyes. She knows his love for her is in there somewhere. He's just never been one to express it with words. But taking the time to select the perfect viburnum specimen and put it aside is his way of telling her he is thinking of her. Aimee just wishes he could say it out loud.

The doorbell rings again. "Coming," she calls as she walks to the front door.

"Who is it?" Noa pops out of her bedroom and takes a perch on the stairs.

"I don't know. You all set for school?" Noa nods and Aimee turns away from her daughter so she can wipe at her eyes. She doesn't want Noa to see her upset. "Let's find out." She opens the door to see Detective Salazar standing there.

"Oh, hi. Good morning."

"Didn't Officer Nguyen mention I would be coming by?"

"I guess he did, but I didn't realize it would be this early."

"I wanted to catch everyone before work, school, you know."

"Please, come in." Aimee steps back to allow him room to enter the foyer. "We can go in the kitchen to talk privately." She jerks her head toward Noa on the stairs.

As Detective Salazar steps inside, he touches two fingers to his brow in a salute to Noa. "Morning, young lady."

Noa stares, wide-eyed.

Salazar turns back to Aimee. "Actually, it's your daughter I'd like to have a quick word with, if you don't mind."

At the sound of the word *daughter*, Aimee's stomach does a flip. She steps back a few feet into the dining room and motions the detective in. He follows her into the darkened room. "I would do anything to help you guys find Scott," she whispers. "But my kids think he's on a trip, and I'd like to keep it that way."

"Of course. I won't say anything," Salazar says. "We just want to ask her about the time she spent with the Stocker lady. Maybe she saw something, or heard something?"

"I've already asked her that. Several times. She doesn't remember anything being off or scary or strange."

"Well, if it's all right with you, I'd like to ask her myself."

Aimee sighs. "I guess so, but you have to keep it short. I don't want them to miss the bus."

He nods and they re-enter the foyer. Noa is still sitting in the same spot. Aimee wishes she could answer Salazar's questions for her. Noa is so sensitive that many of the things her peers love—roller coasters, action movies—often cause panic attacks and nightmares. Aimee has all but given up on Noa sleeping over at a friend's house, a ritual she remembers loving as a child. It was one of the reasons she had felt safe leaving her with Cathy. She had believed the woman to be a former teacher, and she certainly had the demeanor of one. But who knows if any of that is true.

Aimee smiles up at Noa. "What do you think, honey? Can you come down and answer a few questions for this nice man?"

She has no idea why she said that—*nice man*. Nothing about Detective Salazar suggests he is nice. Tough, yes, slightly sinister in his dark shirt and suit, his thick black hair pulled off his face and kept miraculously in place by what Aimee guesses is a significant amount of gel, but nice? She doesn't need him to be nice, however, just good at his job.

Noa narrows her eyes but doesn't move. The girl grips the balusters of the staircase with two hands and presses her face against them like a prisoner in an old-time movie.

"You know," Detective Salazar says to Noa, "we can talk right here. That's fine. I'm a police detective. You can call me Jay if you want. I just wanted to ask a couple of questions. Do you think that'll be okay?"

"I guess," Noa says, shifting her eyes to Aimee without moving her face. "When is Daddy coming back?"

"I told you, Daddy had to go on a business trip." Had Noa somehow picked up on the tension and realized that her father was missing? Or is she just a little girl who misses her dad?

The detective leans against the wall. "I'm actually here to ask you about your friend Cathy, is that all right?" He waits for Noa to nod before he continues. "Do you remember a few days ago when you were at Cathy's house to see the kittens? And she drove you home?"

Noa nods. "Yes. I remember."

"Well, I wanted to know if you remembered anybody coming to her house that day, even if they didn't come inside. A car pulling up. Or Cathy going to the door to talk to someone?"

"No."

"You sure? Did she go outside at some point?"

Noa scoffs. "How can I see if she went outside if I'm with the kittens?" She looks at Aimee. "The kittens are upstairs in the back room, which is the quiet room. They sleep in the closet."

"Makes sense," the detective says. "Did Cathy do anything different that day? Anything kind of strange or weird?

"Like what?"

"I don't know, anything at all."

"Why are you asking about Cathy?" Noa turns to Aimee. "Is Cathy in trouble? Is she going to be arrested?"

"No, not at all," Aimee says, stepping closer. "But we need to find Cathy. That's all."

"Is she missing?" Noa's voice is high, tinged with panic.

"No, not missing," Salazar says. "She went on a trip, and we don't know where. And we need to tell her something."

"Something about the kittens?"

He smiles. "Exactly."

"What do you need to tell her?"

"Well, see, someone wants to adopt one," he says. "A really nice lady, but she needs to know right away. So we're trying to find where Cathy might have gone to on her trip. So we can ask her."

"Because when Cathy comes back, it might be too late?" Noa asks.

"That's right."

Noa puts a finger on her chin and says, "Hmmm," the way a cartoon character might. Aimee feels a pang of guilt. All this lying doesn't sit well with her. She knows it's in Noa's best interest, but she's sick of lies.

"Maybe she went to Texas?" Noa suggests.

"Why would she go to Texas?" Salazar asks, his hawkish face eager.

"I don't know." Noa shrugs. "Did you know that Texas is the second largest state in the country? Alaska is two-and-a-half times bigger."

The detective's shoulders slump, disappointed. "That's pretty cool. All right, Noa. You've been a big help."

Noa straightens up, beaming.

"You go on up, honey," Aimee says. "And tell your brothers they have two minutes to get downstairs. We're not missing that bus."

Noa nods and scurries up the stairs.

Aimee turns to the detective. "I'm sorry she wasn't of more help. I was hoping she knew something."

"Maybe something will come to her later," he says. "Mrs. Crowder—"

"Stern. I kept my last name."

"Ms. Stern, if you have any idea of where your husband has fled to, now would be a good time to tell me. You may think you are protecting him, but the longer this goes on, the more dangerous it becomes for everybody."

At first, she thinks she must have misunderstood him, but the cold look in his eyes tells her otherwise. "You think I'm part of this? I'm the one who called you yesterday morning, remember?"

"We know your husband was being blackmailed by Anton Khoury—"

"Yeah, you know because I told you."

"And we found corroborating evidence on his laptop. And we know that Mr. Khoury came here Friday night to talk to your husband, and they walked down your walkway together."

"Scott explained that. Anton was drunk. He was taking him home."

"And your husband admits to being at the scene where Mr. Khoury was killed. And then a few days later, he's on the run."

"He's not on the run! Something's happened to him. Cathy Stocker has done something to him." Her voice is strident but it belies the doubt that has crept into her thoughts. What if Scott is involved with Anton's death? Being blackmailed is a motive, after all. She won't believe the worst about Scott. Not until she has proof. Until then she will hold on to the shred of hope that her husband is innocent. She yanks open the front door, indicating it's time for him to leave. "Maybe you should go do your job and find them."

"Maybe she has done something to him." Salazar pushes open the screen door. "Or maybe she's helping him."

38

NOW

Gwen stumbles into the kitchen, wiping the sleep from her eyes. Her head feels as if it's been stuffed with cotton, a logy feeling she gets when she takes a Xanax with her nightly glass of wine. The combo helps her sleep, but the next day is brutal. A strong cup of coffee will slice through the fog.

"There you are," Barb says, coming up from the basement with a basket of folded laundry. Gwen almost does a double take. She can't remember ever seeing her mother hauling a laundry basket before. At her own house, Barb has always employed a housekeeper. She wonders what it is about Anton's death that has brought out the domestic goddess in Barb. Her mother was always competitive with her, and this feels like another chance for Barb to win.

"Coffee's made," Barb says. "You look like you could use it. And I'll get you some Tylenol."

Gwen looks at the black-and-white clock on the wall. It's the kind where the numbers flip, and that also shows the date, with such large letters and numerals it can be read from across the room. It had been her grandmother's, who suffered from terrible eyesight, and when she died it was the only thing in her flowery, overstuffed house that Gwen wanted. "It's almost ten. I can't believe I slept that much."

"Hmm," her mother says noncommittally.

"Where are the boys?"

"A very nice neighbor of yours, Katie something, came by this morning and took the boys for a while." Her mother puts two Tylenol tablets and a glass of water in front of her.

"Katie O'Brien," Gwen says before popping the Tylenol in her mouth. "Her son goes to Holy Cross."

"He seemed like a very well-behaved young man. Called me ma'am. Apparently, her boy's school was closed, and the two were headed off to a trampoline park. She asked if she could take the boys with her and I said yes."

"A trampoline park? And they wanted to go?"

"They certainly did. At least George did. I encouraged them. They needed to get out of this house. Especially Rafi, I'm worried he's becoming depressed. And seeing you mope around here isn't going to help."

"Sorry I can't be more chipper."

Barb frowns. "I'm going to put away this laundry. Why don't you eat something?"

Gwen's own laziness would have horrified her last week. Gwen prided herself on being the first one up in the house, showered, dressed, makeup on, and ready to face the day before anyone else. She wanted her boys to look back on their childhood and remember their mother as full of vitality, so different from her own childhood, when Barb would sleep in and the housekeeper would see her off to school. Gwen does have a cleaning company come in twice a month, but other than that, she cleans and cooks most of the family's meals. And it isn't because she bought into some 1950s version of marriage, it's because these acts of domesticity feel like professions of love. Or they did.

It takes all of Gwen's energy to drag herself off the counter stool, get a mug, and pour herself some coffee. The woman who bought this house last year is gone. That version of Gwen found antique hooks in a small Kensington antique shop and installed them at kid's-eye height after she had read in an article that little kids were more likely to pick up after themselves if there were hooks to hang things on.

The old Gwen was convinced that having a perfect family was

still attainable. That the right house, the right neighborhood would somehow compensate for the rot in her marriage.

That Gwen is gone, and never coming back. Problem is, she's not sure what the new Gwen is going to look like.

Gwen takes the coffee and a protein bar into the living room and sits next to Sababa on the sofa. For a year, ever since they moved in, the dog was not allowed on the couch, but after Anton's death, he's taken up permanent residence there.

Her mother's low heels *click-clack* into the room. She doesn't buy into Gwen's concept of a no-shoes house. *Really, Gwen, grow up* had been her exact words the first time Gwen told her that they didn't wear shoes in the house.

Barb sits beside her. "Sweetie, I have some updates to share with you."

"Great." Is it her imagination or is her mother relishing this whole nightmare?

"First, I spoke to a very pleasant man about retrieving Anton's body. The question is, have you picked a funeral home? And do you want a burial or cremation? Did Anton discuss that with you?"

"He wanted to be cremated."

"All right, then. Do you have a preference for a particular funeral home?"

Gwen can't help but laugh. "No, I don't have a favorite funeral home."

"Gwendolyn, I am trying to help. I'd appreciate a civil tone. We still need to talk about where to have the funeral. The obvious choice is a funeral home. My D.C. friends recommend a place called Gawler's. They'll try to sell me the whole package, and I think it's a good idea. They'll handle everything, and since you and Anton didn't attend church, well . . ." Her voice trails off. She doesn't need to finish the sentence, the judgment is clear. Her and Anton's lack of a religious life was another mark against them. "I think a funeral home is the best idea."

"I guess you're right. Do we have to decide now? Like, this minute?"

"I'm afraid life marches on. And the boys need a funeral, honey."

"You know there's an open homicide investigation going on right now, don't you?"

"All the more reason to focus on the person Anton was. The community will want to come together to say goodbye. Whatever marital issues you and Anton were working through—"

"Marital issues? Mom, he was screwing my friend."

"Honestly, this generation." She throws up her hands and looks around the room as if she is on a talk show trying to connect to a studio audience. "They think they're the first to discover their husbands have gotten a little too friendly with one of the other wives. This has been going on since time immemorial—"

"Have those same husbands also been blackmailing their best friends? Has that also been going on since time immemorial?"

"What in God's creation are you going on about?"

"Forget it, Mom."

"Listen, honey. Time for some tough love. Life is hard. What made you think you'd be exempt? Do you live in a refugee camp? No. Have you had to bury your children? No." Barb answers her own questions without pausing for a beat. "We all have to grow up and do what's expected of us. Even in times of grief. Especially in times of grief. There's a right way and a wrong way to handle yourself. Because it's more than just you, it's those two boys. How you handle this will have a huge effect on how they process it. Just because you are angry at Anton, and rightfully so, doesn't give you the right to poison their memories of their father. These boys need to remember the dad who loved them, who was there for them, not the failed husband or weak man that you think he was—"

"That he *definitely* was. Not that I *think* he is!" Gwen sniffs. "By the way, worst pep talk ever."

"Listen, I'm going to head over to Gawler's and talk to someone. I want to do it before the boys get home. How about you take a shower, and then take a little time today to sort through everything." She gestures toward the piles. "Just make piles and I will deal with it. What needs to be donated, what's trash, and which things you want to save in bins. We have plenty of room at our house."

"What things of Anton's would I want to save?"

"Oh, things the boys might want when they're older, but maybe you don't want to have around in the meantime."

Barb pats Gwen on the knee and stands up. "You can do this, Gwen. We're not going to have a repeat of college. Not on my watch."

Gwen goes upstairs to take a shower, praying that when she is done her mother will be gone. Barb had to bring up college and the half year Gwen spent in an outpatient program for disordered eating. Her mother might offer to help, but there would always be strings attached, and she'd never let you forget your weaknesses.

After her shower, Gwen puts on a pair of petal-pink leggings and a beige sweatshirt, twists her hair into a knot, and clips it to the top of her head. She does feel better when she's clean and in cute clothes. Maybe even ready to tackle the piles of Anton's things.

One of Anton's favorite T-shirts sits on top of a tall stack of clothing. She picks it up and shakes it out. It's from the Pixies reunion tour in 2004, an old favorite, worn thin from use. Gwen brings it to her face and inhales. Even though it is clean, she can smell Anton mixed in with the scent of the detergent. Some musky odor that is all his own has found its way into the fibers of the shirt. The tears come as memories break through the walls she has built around them. She squeezes her eyes shut and sees the two of them on their honeymoon in Paris, stopping halfway across the Pont des Arts to add a padlock with their initials to the wall of lovers' locks. "I love Gwendolyn!" Anton shouted, hurling the key into the Seine. She throws the T-shirt back onto the table, not ready to part with it. It lands atop one of the heavy pewter candlesticks she's never liked. She picks up the candlestick. It weighs at least a few pounds. Their tenth anniversary was supposed to mark a rebirth of their marriage. What a joke. She tosses the two sticks into the box marked *donate*, where they make a satisfying thud.

Next to the clothing is an open box filled with notebooks. She flips through the top one and stops on a page filled with sentences and sentence fragments, all in quotes.

"mornings are the worst"

"wakes up and for a fraction of a second, I don't remember my baby is gone. And then it all comes back. He went up the mountain and he didn't come back."

"I'll never stop looking for answers"

"somebody knows something"

"I feel it in my bones, my son is dead. He's gone"

Gwen sucks in her breath. She flips to the front of the notebook. On the first page, written in Anton's neat block lettering is: *INTERVIEWS WITH CATHY STOCKER.*

Gwen sinks to the floor, the notebook open in her lap. She turns to the first page and begins to read.

39

THIS PAST SUMMER

After Anton signed the credit card bill, Lisa took the pen, enjoying the heft of it in her hand. The name of the restaurant was written in gold on the side. Le Cannu. She slipped it into her bag, a souvenir of this night. The night Anton took the bait.

It had taken two weeks to get here. One day, in bed, she had been talking about how nice it would be if the two of them could take a trip. She enjoyed bringing up money because she knew it was a sore spot with him.

"With what money? I have one credit card and Gwen watches my purchases like a hawk."

"Are you serious?" Lisa had feigned outrage. "That's horrible. No one can live like that."

"Last summer she saw a charge she didn't recognize and made me produce a receipt. For headphones! When I told her I was planning to go to a writers' conference, she checked online to see if it really existed. She actually checked! To see if I was on a panel, like I said I was."

"Are you allowed to go?"

He had laughed bitterly. "*Allowed. Allowed.* Like I'm a fucking child."

"What if I went, too?" She had propped herself up on one elbow, letting the sheet slip from her body, exposing her naked breasts. "Got a hotel nearby? A different one from where you are staying for the conference. You could come to my hotel and that way no one would see you or recognize you. We could have a couple of days to ourselves. Long, lazy nights."

"I'd love to. Believe me, that sounds amazing. But could you do that? What would you tell Marcus?"

She had rolled her eyes. "Marcus wouldn't even notice. I'll tell him it's some coaching retreat or something. We'll be able to go out to a romantic dinner . . ." She had walked her fingers across his chest.

"I wish I could pay. I wish I could be the one to take you to dinner, buy you gifts, champagne." He had rolled onto his back, pulling a pale-pink throw pillow from behind his head and tossing it across the room. "I hate this pillow. This comforter. This room. Nothing about this house, not one thing, feels like mine. Besides my leather club chair, I didn't pick out one piece of furniture in this house."

"I wish we could run away, just us two," Lisa had said.

"Me, too. Go somewhere, start over."

"What's stopping us?"

"Money. I have none."

"What about this house?"

"Her parents bought it. It's in a trust. The BMW and the Lexus, too." He had rolled toward her. "Gwen and me were never right. I should have listened to my gut instinct. I cheated on her, you know, when we were first engaged. It was my pathetic way of trying to break it off. I thought she'd dump me for sure. But no, she treated it like a bump in the road, and kept that wedding train on track. Nothing was going to interfere with her plans."

"She's so manipulative," Lisa had said. Anton had begun to annoy her recently. He was so needy and his self-pity was boundless. But she was careful not to let her feelings show. She knew how to handle him, to tell him what he wanted to hear. "Is that all I am? An escape plan?"

"No." He had cupped her face. "You make me feel alive. I love you, Lisa." He had leaned in for a long kiss. After they had made love again, she had returned to the subject. "What would it take for us to run away? To start over? Cash-wise?"

"Realistically? I think a hundred thousand to get us on our feet. A former teacher of mine emailed me about an opening for a writing professor job at a college in Minnesota. It would be a full-tenured position, decent salary, not a ton of money, but it's cheaper there. I wanted to apply, but there's no way Gwen would ever consider moving to Minnesota."

"I would," Lisa lied. She hated the cold, and she had no intention of leaving Marcus. Ever. When Anton talked of them leaving their spouses and running away together, she would encourage him. It was flattering, but she didn't mean it. Marcus earned in one month what Anton made in a year, and unlike Gwen, he gave her free rein.

"You would?"

"Of course. To be with you. Between what you make and what I earn, plus what I'd get in the divorce from Marcus, we could live very comfortably."

"But where am I going to get a hundred thousand dollars?"

"I might have an idea, but . . ." She had paused, looking down shyly and letting out a little laugh. Inside, she was roiling with anticipation, but she had to stay cool. She didn't want to scare him off. "No, you wouldn't go for it."

"Try me."

Two weeks later they were in Tampa, finishing dinner at Le Cannu. So far on their trip to Tampa they hadn't discussed what she had told him that night back in Bethesda. She had given him the broad outlines—that Scott was really Michael Finch and he was wanted in California. That keeping that quiet might be worth a lot of money to him. But that was it; she hadn't wanted to push too hard. The impetus had to come from him.

"Won't Gwen notice?" Lisa asked once their server had taken away the signed check. "When she sees this on the credit card bill?"

"I'll tell her it was a work dinner with colleagues," Anton said.

"I don't know how you live like that. Being watched, being micromanaged."

He reached for her hand and squeezed. "It's not forever. Anyway," he said, pulling his hand free and taking the last bite of the crème brûlée they were sharing, "even Gwen can't object to my eating a meal with other adults."

They walked out of the restaurant, well-fed, drunk, and happy. They locked arms and headed down to the boardwalk so they could stroll along the beach. Lisa leaned into Anton.

"This feels so right," she said.

"I think this is how it's supposed to be," Anton said. "It's just that when you're young, before you get married, you have no clue what marriage is going to be like. You have no idea what qualities to look for in a life partner."

"So why did you ask Gwen to marry you?"

He laughed. "Who said I asked? She wanted marriage, and I didn't see why not. We had been together since right after college, all through our twenties. She took care of me. I was writing, and she supported us, made sure the rent was paid, that there was food. I mean, she made my early success possible. I thought we were well-matched; she was creative, too, but in a different way. But now I realize she had been *mothering* me."

He said this as if taking care of someone was a high crime.

"You mean *smothering* you," she said, and they both laughed.

"It's true. She never allowed me to grow into a man. She was infantilizing me so she could control me."

"That's terrible," Lisa cooed. "So selfish."

"It is," he said. "It really is. She liked that I couldn't cook, or that I didn't know how to do laundry. She'd complain, yeah, but it made her feel needed. She used to say that if it weren't for her I'd never see a dentist or a doctor, and it's true, but she cultivated that dependency. Because if I was allowed to really step up, to become independent, it might threaten her dominance. If

I didn't *need* her anymore, I might leave her. She became even more insecure when *The Last Cyclamen* took off. She insisted on going with me everywhere, to every appearance, every book signing. She was terrified that my success would make me realize I didn't need her anymore. Because she knew, deep down, that she wasn't enough."

The words thrilled Lisa to her core. She could never get enough of this kind of talk. When he trash-talked Gwen, it more than made up for his immaturity and self-absorption. She tilted her head. "In what way wasn't she enough?" Lisa asked, looking up at him.

"She's just not a sensual person. She's nothing like you. She won't even make love with the lights on. Has to be pitch-black."

He held her gaze for a moment, and the warmth exploded inside her. How she wished she could somehow secretly tape these conversations and show them to Gwen! But it had to be enough for now that Lisa knew.

"Not that she isn't a good mother," Anton conceded.

"She's wonderful."

"And very organized and efficient."

"Responsible."

"But a wife? A lover?" He shook his head. They took off their shoes at the top of a set of stairs that descended to the beach. Barefoot, they walked hand in hand, drunk not only on alcohol but on an exhilarating feeling of freedom. They had done what so many middle-aged people dreamed of, if only for a weekend— broken free of their roles. They weren't young again, they were ageless. They existed outside of their contexts and so anything was possible. Later that night, after they'd had sex in Lisa's hotel room, it was Anton who brought up approaching Scott for money.

"We'll start small, maybe fifty thousand?"

Lisa almost choked. "That's starting small?"

"You know how much Scott makes each year? He owns his

own company! What's the point of doing this if we go lower? We only get a few bites at the apple, maybe only one. I estimate to start a new life, we'll need two hundred."

He had said one hundred before. He was getting greedy. But Lisa wasn't about to rein him in.

40

NOW

After Detective Salazar leaves, Aimee packs the kids' lunches. It's only Wednesday, but this has been the longest week of her life. It feels like forever since Scott's been gone. His absence feels like a dull ache, the kind of bone-deep hurt that makes the smallest act feel like a chore. She just wants him back safe. Whatever trouble he has gotten himself into, she will help him find his way out. She stuffs the boys' lunch boxes into their backpacks, but there's no room in Noa's, thanks to all the wrappers and papers in there. If Aimee skips even one day of cleaning out her daughter's backpack, this is what happens.

She empties the contents onto the kitchen counter, wipes out the inside with a wet cloth, and begins reloading it. In go her folders, her pencil pouch, her latest Warrior Cats book. Aimee picks up a small box wrapped in rubber bands. She's never seen it before. She undoes the rubber bands, a sinking feeling in her stomach. Inside the box is a small brass key. In the chaos of the previous day, she forgot all about Noa's box of purloined goodies, but here was a stark reminder.

Ignoring the problem is not going to make it disappear.

Holding the key in her hand, Aimee goes to the bottom of the stairs. "Noa? Noa, come down here, please."

Noa races down the stairs. "What? Am I in trouble?"

Aimee opens her hand to reveal the key in her palm. "Can you explain how this got into your backpack?"

Noa's gaze drops to her feet. "I was going to tell you," she mumbles. "I found it."

"At Cathy's house?"

Noa nods.

"Honey, I found your box. Under your bed? You've taken a lot of things from Cathy's house, haven't you?"

Tears spring to her daughter's eyes. "Please, Mommy. Don't be mad. It was so shiny. It looked so old-fashionedy and I wanted it for my time-travel machine. I was going to put it back after I used it, I swear."

Noa's shoulders shake as full-throated sobs come from her small body.

"Oh, honey, don't cry." Aimee strokes Noa's hair.

"I know I'm not supposed to do it, but I kept doing it, anyway." She lifts her chin. "What's wrong with me? Why am I like this?"

"There's nothing wrong with you. You struggle with something called *impulse control*. Do you know what that is?" The conversation reminds her of the unread evaluation in her inbox. Just one more thing to get to. "It's when you want to do something so, so bad. Like eat all the cookies at once. Or maybe draw on the wall with lipstick because it would look cool."

"I'd never do that."

"But you might want to. And impulse control is talking back to that little voice in your head and saying, *Well, hold on a minute. I know you really want to do this, but let's stop and think for a second if it's such a good idea.*"

"I have that voice, but I don't listen to it."

"That's right, and we're going to work on paying more attention to that voice. So, the next time you see something pretty or lovely, you'll be able to have the feeling of wanting to take it, but then when that voice kicks in, you'll listen."

"Is that how grown-ups are? They listen to the voice?"

Aimee smiles. "Sometimes. Some grown-ups are better at it than other grown-ups." Aimee looks at her watch and curses herself. This wasn't a smart time to bring this up. She's off her game with Scott missing. She should have waited until after school. Now they have five minutes until the bus comes.

"Honey." Aimee crouches down to Noa's level. "It's okay. I am not mad. We're going to talk about this when you get home from school."

"You're not mad at me?" Noa peers up at her.

"Nope, I'm not mad." Aimee smiles and pushes a tear-soaked clump of hair out of her daughter's eyes. "Now go get your backpack. We don't want to miss the bus."

She calls up to the twins, and they come bounding down past their sister and into the kitchen to grab their backpacks. Aimee corrals the kids and gets them outside. There's not a cloud in the bright-blue sky after the overnight rain. It's another perfect September day and the neighborhood is brimming with life. People heading to the cut-through to reach the metro, walking their dogs, kids rushing to the bus stop. It's isolating to Aimee to see how little impact the tragedies on this cul-de-sac have on their neighbors' lives, which go on as before while she struggles to keep things running smoothly and Gwen falls apart next door.

"What are you going to do with it?" Noa asks as she walks briskly beside her.

"I'll put it in an envelope and drop it off at the house. And maybe you can write a note, how about that?"

Noa nods. "Okay, but you said Cathy was gone."

It takes Aimee a minute to remember the story Detective Salazar spun that morning to explain why he was asking so many questions about Cathy. "Yes, but she'll be back," Aimee says as they arrive at the bus stop.

"Who is taking care of the kittens while she's gone?"

"Oh, another lady, a nice lady."

"I was thinking last night how if Cathy didn't come back then the kittens wouldn't have a new home. Mommy, the other things, you should put them in the envelope, too." Noa says that last part so fast that Aimee almost doesn't catch it.

"You mean the things in the box?"

"We should give them back to Cathy." She looks up at Aimee with her big brown eyes. "Do you think she'll be mad at me?"

"No, of course not. I think that's a good idea."

"I'm sorry, Mommy."

"It's all right, honey. See how much better it feels to tell the whole truth? Now, let's get you on the bus."

Noa runs onto the bus, but a moment later she's bounding down the stairs and running back to Aimee.

"Mommy, I remembered one of the things in the box isn't from Cathy's house. One of the things is from Cathy's car."

"Which thing?"

"It's a card with a fox on it. Now I told the whole truth. Bye, Mom!" She runs back up the steps of the bus and the folding doors hiss closed.

Noa waves from the window as the bus pulls away. It's only once the bus has turned the corner that the significance of what her daughter said hits her. *Cathy's car.* Cathy drove Noa home in her Subaru. Anything Noa took from the car would belong to her, and not to Jean Brewster. Aimee breaks into a run, nervous energy propelling her back to the house. Inside she rushes upstairs to her bedroom and grabs the shoebox, dumping everything on the bed.

It isn't a lot to hang her hopes on, but it is all she has. She sifts through the items that were in the box, looking for a card that has a fox on it. She finds a sterling silver teaspoon, a magnet in the shape of the Eiffel Tower, and a piece of lilac silk ribbon. Noa's been quite the little collector.

And then Aimee sees it, a card with a fox on it. She plucks it from under a dried rosebud whose leaves are disintegrating. She can see why it was appealing to Noa. The fox is hand drawn and wearing a jaunty ice-blue scarf. The Little Fox Coffee Shop. It's a loyalty card with seven of the ten holes punched out.

According to the address printed on the card, the coffee shop is located in Frederick, which is about forty-five minutes northwest of where they live, near the mountains. She and Scott have taken the kids up to Sugarloaf Mountain and then gone into Frederick to eat. It's a quaint town with Civil War–era buildings, filled with shops and cafés.

Aimee turns the card over in her hand. It's a long shot, but just maybe someone at this coffee shop knows something about Cathy Stocker.

41

Gwen puts Anton's journal in her bag and goes outside. She's halfway up Aimee's walkway when the door opens.

"Hey," Gwen says. "I was just coming to see you."

"Now's not a good time."

"Where you heading?"

"Frederick. It's a long story, but I hope I can find out something about Cathy."

"I'll come with you. Keep you company."

Aimee hesitates. "I don't know."

"That's what you said yesterday when you went to Cathy's house, and it was because of me—well, because of Sababa, actually—that we found Scott's car."

Aimee pauses and Gwen takes the opportunity to open the passenger door of her truck. "Anyway, there's something you're going to want to hear. I think I figured out what Anton was blackmailing Scott about."

"Fine." Aimee climbs in.

Aimee pulls the truck out of the driveway.

"Thank you for being there yesterday," Aimee says in a somewhat begrudging tone. "You were helpful."

"Of course. I want to help, Aimee. I want you to know that I will never forgive myself for not coming to you as soon as Anton said something to me. And I will do everything I can to make that up to you." Gwen adds, "Besides, I need to get out of my house. I'm slowly going insane in there. Can you tell me where we are going?"

"I found this." Aimee pulls something out of her jacket and puts it on the console between them.

Gwen picks it up. "A loyalty card?"

"Noa had it. Apparently, she's got quite the sticky fingers." Aimee lets out a short laugh, but it sounds fake. "I found her box of goodies the other day. She said it was all taken from *Cathy's* house. But then this morning she told me there was one thing not from the house, but from Cathy's car."

"This card."

"Yup."

"So you think where Cathy really lives must be close to where this coffee shop is?"

"That's the idea." She glances over at Gwen. "Too far-fetched?"

"Oh, I don't know. Sounds reasonable to me," Gwen says. "What are you planning to do if you do get an address? Barge in with your hedge clippers and demand answers?"

This gets a faint smile from Aimee. "I hadn't thought that far ahead."

"What about calling that detective? Detective Salazar."

Aimee scowls. "And say what?"

"Say exactly what you told me."

"I'd sound crazy."

"You don't sound crazy. And I'm not sure it's a good idea to go chasing after this woman. She could be dangerous." Gwen retrieves the notebook from her bag. "If I'm right, then I think I know who she is."

Aimee shoots her a sidelong glance. "What is that?"

Gwen turns over the black notebook in her lap. "It's Anton's. It looks like he was doing research for his next novel. The thing you should know about Anton, he likes to base his fiction on real people and real feelings."

"Go on."

"His first book, *The Last Cyclamen*, the one about the young

French-Lebanese woman who had a fling with an older man in Beirut before the war?"

Aimee shrugs. "I never actually read it."

Gwen laughs. "That's okay. Turns out no one in my family did, either. The heart of the story was this girl's coming of age back when Beirut was called the Paris of the Middle East. How one summer, an older wealthy man seduced her and she shed her sheltered religious upbringing under his guidance. And the guilt she felt in betraying her family's values, but how she was so enthralled by the glamour of this new world he was introducing her to. Only, all the best parts, the ones that showcased Anton's understanding of the human heart, the lyrical interior monologues that led one reviewer to say she couldn't believe how thoroughly Anton Khoury understood the female psyche—he didn't write them."

"Who did?"

"His mother. In her beautiful script in her journal. After she died, Anton didn't just mine it for inspiration, he copied her entries word-for-word."

"That's insane. How did you find out?" she asks as they pull onto the Beltway.

"I found the journal recently. He kept it all these years. Which is crazy. You'd think he'd burn it or something."

"So you never knew."

"No. Not until just now, after he died." Gwen takes a deep breath. "It must have haunted him, that he didn't actually write *The Last Cyclamen*. His entire identity was wrapped up in being a writer. Not just a writer, but a literary figure. But I still can't believe he didn't even tell me."

"He was probably embarrassed. Maybe he was worried you'd think less of him."

Gwen leans back and watches a semi whiz past them. If that was the case, he couldn't have played it any worse. There was a chance, however slim, that telling her the truth years ago would have brought them closer. But Anton couldn't even be honest with himself, much less her. "I guess both of our husbands were hiding who they really were."

"Is that what's in the notebook? Something about Scott?"

Gwen knows that if she answers this question, she will risk her friendship with Aimee. Their bond is already on life support, and what she's about to tell her might be the fatal blow. In the best outcome, Aimee will view Gwen telling her what she found as a show of solidarity. As confirmation that they are in this together, no matter how bad it gets. More likely, however, Aimee will be so upset by what she hears, so horrified by what Gwen has to say about Scott, not to mention what Anton was doing, that she will take her anger out on Gwen.

After all, a few hours ago, as Gwen pored over these interviews that Anton conducted, and then read Anton's fictionalized version of these events, she wanted to throw up. Her husband was mining a woman's grief, opening her wounds, and stirring up the ugliest feelings inside of her in the name of his art.

"Where should I begin? Basically, twenty-eight years ago, two guys in the fall of their senior year of high school went on a backpacking trip into the mountains of California. Neither ever returned. One of them was named Dexter Kohl, and the other Michael Finch. Anton somehow tracked down Dexter's mother and interviewed her. She is convinced that Michael killed her son on that trip and disposed of the body. She thinks that he fled the state and started over by changing his name. And she thinks the person he became is Scott Crowder."

Aimee pulls over and slams on the brakes. "What are you talking about? Scott's never been to California. He didn't live there."

"There's more. The mother's name is Cathy Stocker."

Aimee lets out a guttural scream. She slams the steering wheel twice with her palm. "Shit! Shit!"

Gwen sits very still, unsure of what to do. She's had her own earth-shattering revelations recently and knows there is really nothing that can be done. All she can do is stay and witness it, and help Aimee process it when she is ready.

"I am such a goddamn idiot." Aimee leans her head against the steering wheel.

"You're not an idiot. How could you have known? She had everyone fooled."

Aimee picks her head up. "To think Noa was there." She shudders. "What does she want from us?"

"Here, let me read you some of this." Gwen opens the book. "I have to warn you it's kind of choppy, because Anton is obviously jotting down notes as he is talking to her, but here goes. *Michael and Dex friends at the beginning of tenth grade when Michael and his mom move from New Mexico . . . inseparable from the beginning . . . both played on the baseball team.*" Gwen looks up at Aimee, who is staring straight ahead, her hands gripping the wheel tightly.

"Okay, so what?" She sounds defensive, and Gwen doesn't blame her. She's always put Scott on a pedestal, and now she's learning he's not as perfect as she thought.

Gwen continues reading from the journal, "*Police never found their bodies . . . witness heard gunshots on the mountain that day . . . witness left town, too . . . couldn't be tracked down . . . saw Michael on the mountain months later . . . sure of it . . . went to police . . . Ray McCready's guys harassing me.*"

"This is insanity! You want me to believe that Scott is a fugitive who killed someone and then changed his name? This woman is nuts. Where's her proof?"

Gwen looks up. "From what I can make of his notes, Dexter's mother claims she saw Michael on the mountain months after their disappearance, but when she called his name, he fled. When she tried to kickstart the investigation, she says this Ray McCready sent some guys to scare her. Apparently, McCready ran a big growing operation up there in the nineties. She dropped it because she was afraid for her life, she says. But then Anton stirred things up, calling and saying he thought that Michael Finch became Scott and started a new life in Bethesda."

"And how did Anton learn about all this?"

"I don't know." Gwen stares out at the mountains in the distance. "Maybe he learned something and went digging? He didn't mention anything about it in his notes."

"No, this can't be right. This is crazy." Aimee shakes her head wildly as if she can physically banish the thought. "I don't believe it. Scott is not capable of murdering someone."

"It doesn't really matter whether you believe it, if Cathy Stocker does."

"There's more to this story, there has to be. She's confused. She has the wrong person." Gwen puts the truck in drive and eases back onto the road. "It can't be Scott. She's mixed up."

"It might explain a few things, though," Gwen says. "Like what Anton was blackmailing Scott about, and why Cathy moved here and hired you. Look at the dates—Anton interviews Cathy several times in August. And then she moves here in September and hires you."

Aimee shakes her head in defiance. "She has the wrong person. I'm telling you. Although . . ."

"Although what?"

"She did tell me that she had a son. She said she lost him when he was young."

"She told you that?"

"Yeah, she had this framed photo of her and a little baby in her kitchen. She must have carried that photo to Jean's house with her every day and then taken it home every night."

"I'm not surprised."

"What do you mean?"

"From the interviews it's clear she wanted to find out what happened to her son. She wanted to find Michael Finch. And

I'm sure having a picture of her son with her motivated her. She was on a mission."

"What was her mission?"

"Justice. To bring the people responsible for her son's death to justice," Gwen says. "In these interviews she said she had given up on ever finding out what actually happened to Dexter. She had given up hope that anyone would ever be held accountable for his murder. Until Anton contacted her."

A few minutes later, Aimee noses the truck into the parking lot of a small strip mall. The Little Fox Coffee Shop is the last business, on the far end, just after the Knitter's Corner yarn shop.

"Here we are." Aimee cuts the engine.

Gwen gets out and takes a deep breath. The air is just a shade cooler up here than it is closer to D.C. In the distance, Gwen can make out the wavy line of the Blue Ridge Mountains. They are several miles from downtown Frederick, surrounded by farmland, and this little strip mall is the lone commercial post on the road as far as Gwen can see.

Aimee pauses outside the entrance to the coffee shop. "I don't know what to say in there."

"Why don't you let me do the talking?" Gwen says. "Do you have a photo of Cathy on your phone?"

Aimee pulls up the photo of Cathy with the kitten that Jean texted her yesterday and sends the pic to Gwen. The Little Fox is small and cozy. Leaning against the counter is a large blackboard with colorful lettering spelling out the specials, apple caramel cappuccino and oat chai latte. Gwen recognizes an Indigo Girls song playing from the overhead speakers and gets in line. The clientele is a mix of the usual coffee house habitués—a scattering of folks at tables with laptops open in front of them, maybe writing the great American novel, working on spreadsheets, or more likely watching YouTube. The only person in front of her is a burly man with a baseball cap who looks like he spends his days atop a tractor. Gwen waits as he orders a smoky latte, whatever that is, from a slight girl with pale-pink bangs that almost cover her eyes.

Then it's Gwen's turn at the counter. When Nova—the girl's name, according to the tag pinned to her blue apron—asks her what she wants, Gwen asks for a plain black coffee. After using her phone to pay, Gwen keeps the phone out and pulls up the picture of Cathy.

"I have a really weird question." Gwen smiles at Nova, hoping to disarm her. "I'm looking for my friend—her name's Cathy. She comes here a lot. Do you recognize her?"

Nova hunches her slender shoulders and leans toward the phone. "She looks vaguely familiar. Skim milk latte?"

"I don't know her drink," Gwen says. "Like I said, her name is Cathy. I'm worried about her. Did she come in today?"

A young man who has been cleaning the behemoth silver espresso machine steps to the counter. "Let me see." He's short, the same height as Nova, and has a tiny, pointed beard that reminds Gwen of the devil. "I know her! She comes in every morning. She was here, yeah."

"Oh my gosh, thank God. I'm Gwen. Cathy sometimes sits for us, and she's become like a part of our family, and well, she didn't come yesterday, and she has not been answering her phone."

"Oh." He scrunches up his face.

"I know. Not good." Gwen glances at his name tag. "And, Lance, is it? I know this might be an overreaction, but I just wanted to make sure she was all right. That she hadn't, like, fallen or something. Her family is back in California. She really doesn't know a lot of people here."

"Right, that's scary," Lance says, nodding enthusiastically.

"I thought about calling the police, but I don't want to embarrass her. Just, for myself, I need to know that she's okay. And I know she lives up here. She's mentioned this coffee shop, but I actually don't have her address."

"Hmm." Lance turns his head toward the glass pastry display as if inspiration might be found among the croissants. "Actually, I'm pretty sure that she lives near the construction of the new high school on Autumn Lake Road, because she was complaining today that it was so loud. She said there was a cement truck in the road blocking her way to the coffee shop this morning."

"Thank you, guys, so much."

"I hope she's okay." Lance smiles. "Don't forget your coffee."

Once they are outside, Gwen hands Aimee back the phone.

"I never realized you were such a good liar," Aimee says, raising an eyebrow.

"I prefer to consider it improvisation." Gwen takes a sip of the steaming coffee. "So? Let's go find the new high school on Autumn Lake Road."

42

NOW

After looking up where the new high school is being built, Aimee drives in that direction. It isn't hard to find, a monstrosity of cement and glass jutting into the sky from the flat of the surrounding fields. She slows down as she passes a hand-painted sign that reads:

PUMPKINS
HOMEMADE PIES
2 MILES AHEAD

"So, if the cement truck was blocking the road on the way to the coffee shop," Gwen says, "then Cathy must live on the other side of the school."

Aimee stares down the country road that dips and rises in the distance. "That's a lot of territory."

"Well, let's go slowly and maybe we'll see something."

Just past the school is a dense copse of trees, and then a clearing. Finally they come across a modest one-story house with a beat-up truck on the grass in front, but no Subaru.

"Should we knock on the door?" Gwen asks.

"No," Aimee says, pulling onto a dirt road to make a U-turn. "She wouldn't complain about the construction noise from this far away."

As she heads back toward the high school, Gwen grabs her arm.

"Wait, is that a road?" Gwen points to the right. Aimee hits the brakes, and sure enough, there is an unmarked road, its entrance almost hidden by the woods they passed earlier.

"We must have driven right by it."

Aimee directs the truck onto the bumpy dirt road, and after a while the trees are replaced by more farmland. A house appears, a one-story vinyl-sided rambler with a leaning carport. Aimee edges the truck up to the beginning of the asphalt driveway. "Look, there's a Subaru, under the carport. I think it's Cathy's."

"Maybe now's a good time to call the police," Gwen says.

"And say what? We found a Subaru?" She starts to get out. "No, I have to go in and see if it belongs to Cathy for myself."

Gwen unbuckles her seatbelt. "Then I'm coming, too."

"No, stay here. If you don't see me in fifteen minutes, text me, and if I don't respond, call the police."

"Ten," Gwen says, opening up her phone and starting the timer. "I'll give you ten minutes."

"Fine. But text first. Don't call the police unless I don't text back, promise?"

"I guess."

"Promise me, Gwen."

"Fine. I promise."

Aimee gets out and trudges up the driveway. In the tumultuous days since Scott's disappearance, she thought she had felt every single emotion there was to feel—anger, betrayal, grief, loss, vulnerability, despair. But this is a new one.

Fear.

A faded wood sign hangs next to the door proclaiming *Home Sweet Home.* The house has seen better days. Green algae grows thick on the house's siding, spreading upward from the concrete base. On the window to the right of the door a loose screen hangs on as if by its fingernails. A strong wind would send it flying, Aimee thinks. She knocks on the door and waits. From inside comes a shuffling sound and her whole body tenses, readying.

The door opens. A woman stands on the other side of the screen door. "Hi, Aimee," she says.

It takes a second to register that it's Cathy. The woman before her is much younger and fitter-looking than the Cathy she knows. Gone are the filmy Eileen Fisher clothes, the tight bun, the chunky glasses. This Cathy wears tight-fitting blue jeans, a flannel shirt, and boots, and her hair is braided loosely, hanging over one shoulder.

No one would mistake her for a librarian. She looks like what her dad would call *a tough broad*. "You don't seem surprised to see me," Aimee says, barely able to get the words out. Her bravado masks her nerves. Her heart is beating so hard she can feel it in her belly.

"I'm not, really. I was wondering if you'd track me down. Come in, please." She steps back, inviting Aimee inside. "You must have a lot of questions for me."

Aimee stands there a moment, looks over her shoulder to her truck. A part of her wants to walk back, climb in, call the police, and sit there to wait with Gwen. But mostly she's dying to get inside and confront Cathy. She has so many questions. She follows Cathy through a cramped living room to a small kitchen that overlooks an empty field in the back. The house feels heavy and dark. Even the big windows in the kitchen are no match for the depressing, dark-wood cabinets and mustard-yellow linoleum counters.

"So, this is where you really live?" Aimee pauses at the entrance, unsure if she wants to go any further.

"It's where I've been staying, but I'll be hitting the road soon." Cathy puts a kettle on the stove. "It's an Airbnb, but if you ask me, I'm being ripped off. The water pressure's lousy and it's drafty as hell. I'm going to make some tea. Would you like some?"

"Where's Scott?"

Cathy ignores this question. "What about your friend? The one in the truck? Would she like to come in and have some tea?" She picks up an aluminum tea kettle and takes it to the sink.

Aimee tries to hide her surprise. Had Cathy been watching from the window? "I think she's fine. Now, where is my husband? What did you do with him?"

Cathy smiles. "Are you here to rescue him, Aimee? That's very brave of you. You must love him very much."

"I do. I want to see him." Aimee senses that beneath Cathy's friendly words lies an undercurrent of threat. Whatever fury Aimee feels toward Scott for keeping her in the dark, there is something that stopped it from consuming her. Love. She loves Scott, and he loves her. Whatever lies he told her, she knows that wasn't one of them. He gave her Noa and Benji and Max. He gave her fourteen wonderful years. "I do love him. That's why I am here."

Cathy puts the full kettle on the stove. *Click, click, click*—she ignites the burner and a blue flame whooshes up, which she lowers. Cathy turns around. "Have a seat, Aimee. Then text your friend to come inside. Tell her everything is fine."

Aimee scoffs. "Why would I do that? You still haven't told me where Scott is. I could just call the police right now."

"And tell them what? You can call the police, but I haven't done anything illegal. As for Scott, he's not here. But he's fine." Cathy crosses her arms over her chest. "Now, if you want the answers you came here for, text your friend and tell her to come inside."

"Fine." Aimee picks up her phone.

"Not so fast," Cathy says, walking over. "Let me see what it is you're writing." She stands over Aimee's shoulder as she types. Once she's sent the message, Cathy takes the phone.

"I'll keep this for now." Cathy drops it in a wicker basket next to a wood-paneled microwave. "You can have it back when you leave."

A few moments later there's a knock on the door. "Tell her to come in," Cathy says.

"Come in," Aimee calls. "We're back here."

Gwen comes through the door and stops short when she sees the look on Aimee's face. "Is everything okay?"

Aimee nods, feeling guilty for dragging Gwen into this. But the desire to hear Cathy out overpowers everything right now.

"Put your phone over there." Cathy nods toward the basket.

Gwen looks to Aimee.

"Do you want to know where Scott is?" Cathy asks.

"Just do it," Aimee tells Gwen. "Please."

Gwen does as she's asked and takes a seat next to Aimee, just as the kettle begins to screech.

"Tea, anyone?" Cathy asks, pulling a mug down from the cupboard.

"Just tell me where Scott is," Aimee says.

"I can't get used to calling him Scott. Michael's his real name, but he's fine. He's running an errand. He should be back soon, and you'll be able to see for yourself."

"I don't believe you. I don't believe he's fine," Aimee says. "If he were fine, he would have gotten in touch with me. He wouldn't let me worry like this." She fights the urge to jump up and attack Cathy, to pin her down, pull out her gardening knife and press it against the woman's throat, get the truth out of her.

"You're a sweet girl." Cathy turns, holding the mug. "And you're a good mother. But if you really love him, if you really care about your children, you need to let him go. Forget about him."

"Why, so you can kill him?"

Cathy laughs sharply. "Kill him? Now why would I want to kill my own son?"

43

THIS PAST SUMMER

The beginning of August in Washington was a wretched, humid slog. Kai was away at soccer camp, and Marcus had gone to San Francisco for work. As soon as Anton and Lisa returned from Tampa, he sent the email to Scott using a computer at work that couldn't be traced to him, but there had been no response. Lisa was bored and lonely. If Scott wasn't going to take the bait and respond, they'd have to up the stakes. One lazy afternoon, when Gwen was at work and Anton's twins were at camp, Anton came to her house for a change.

"I cannot believe this whole Scott-slash-Michael Finch thing," Anton said after their second round of screwing. "It has the makings of a movie. Did you know that Michael Finch's mom and her boyfriend Ray McCready ran one of the largest illegal marijuana operations in the area? Before pot was legalized. The boyfriend's a real badass. Spent time in prison."

"How do you know all this?"

"Dex Kohl's mom. She's a wealth of information. She thinks this is why the police didn't look too hard at what was going on," he said. "Nobody really wants to go up into those mountains and start poking around. They've got dogs, machine guns."

"Wait, you've spoken to her?" Lisa sat up, trying to hide her alarm. "When?"

"I told her we worked together on the podcast. No big deal."

"How did you get her number?"

He looked at her sheepishly. "Your phone."

"My phone?" Lisa had to bite down on the inside of her cheek to keep from screaming. Her heart galloped wildly. "Why would you do that, Anton?"

"Why? Because she has a story to tell." He looked up at her with the innocence of a boy showing his mother the earthworm he is sure she will find as fascinating as he does. "She's very eager to get her side of things out there. I think I can help her."

"Help her how?" Lisa asked. "We're not actually going to turn Scott in." She threw off the covers and stood up.

He sat up as a smile broke across his usually sullen face. "Don't be mad. I've been inspired, Lisa, by this whole thing. For the first time in years, the writing is coming. Every day I have new pages. Do you have any idea what that means after years of feeling like I didn't have anything to write? Of starting things and having them go nowhere, or sending them to my agent and him telling me it's not worth pursuing? I finally found my inspiration. I'm going to tell this story, the story of a boy who commits murder and then reinvents himself to become the perfect suburban dad. I've already outlined and pitched it to my agent. He loves it, of course. He's been trying to get me to write something more commercial for years. I told him this is not going to be some popcorn thriller. I'm better than that. This will be an exploration of the dark side of humanity, but I'll use the mechanism of the thriller to showcase my lyrical writing, my insight into human behavior . . ."

Lisa turned away from him, repulsion growing inside her. He reminded her of a puffer fish, swollen with his own self-importance, making himself out to be bigger than he was. Didn't he realize that she knew what a petty, bitter person he really was? But the more pressing issue was that he might be jeopardizing their whole plan. The more he riled up this grieving mother, the more likely she was to take action. What if he slipped up and she found out that Michael Finch was living in Bethesda? It wouldn't be too hard. She had Lisa's cell number. And with Anton's now, too, a clever person would have no trouble tracking them down.

She looked out the bedroom window at the stillness of the neighborhood. The only movement was a rotating sprinkler on her neighbor's lawn.

If the police came looking for Scott/Michael, that would be a disaster. Not because they wouldn't get the money—she didn't really care about the money—but because it was bound to come out that someone had tipped them off. And that someone was her. Aimee would never forgive her.

She swallowed her anger and rearranged her mouth into a pleasant smile before turning to face him. Hers was a delicate operation. Yes, Lisa hoped to drive a wedge between Aimee and Scott, punish him for his misdeeds, but she had to be careful not to leave a trail that could be traced back to her. That would defeat the whole purpose. Anton's recklessness scared her. He was intoxicated by the secrets he was discovering. Like a young girl drunk on her first taste of champagne, Anton's inhibitions had loosened, and he was taking unnecessary risks.

"That wasn't the plan." Lisa sat on his side of the bed and caressed his arm when what she really wanted to do was smack him upside the head. He was being stupid, careless. "The plan was we were going to get some money. Remember? So we could start over?"

"Oh, sure," he said in a dreamy way. "That's still the plan, but why not get a book out of it as well?"

Because the more you dig, the deeper the hole gets. And we might fall in.

Lisa stewed over this development for the next few weeks. And not just because what Anton was doing endangered them both, but because she was beginning to feel used. Several times he declined dates with her, saying he was writing and didn't want to interrupt his flow.

The last weekend of August before school started was a scorching-hot day. After soccer practice, Lisa took Kai down to the neighborhood pool, where she found Aimee and Gwen near the diving well in the shade.

She joined them and spent an afternoon like so many others before, watching the kids, taking a dip, returning to her seat to chat. *It's lovely*, she thought, *to have this stability*. Gwen pulled out watermelon chunks from her cooler and passed them around and Lisa found her dissatisfaction with life momentarily abating.

She almost had a panic attack earlier in the summer when Aimee casually dropped that she was going to use Gwen as her emergency contact. "Oh, Lisa, I put Gwen down as the kids' emergency contact since you don't drive to elementary school anymore."

But today, baking under the sun, surrounded by the familiar rhythms of a suburban summer, Lisa felt reassured of her place in the world. Even Gwen wasn't bugging her as much as usual. Sleeping with Anton had satisfied something in her. She knew she could take him away, and that felt like enough. Who cared if she was never going to be a size four, or if her hair, unlike Gwen's, frizzed in the humidity? All she had to do when she felt insecure was remember being on her knees in front of Anton as he begged her to suck him off. She liked to make him literally beg. That could be enough. She could make some kind of internal peace with Gwen.

But she should never have told Anton about Scott. What were the odds that he would keep his mouth shut? He was writing a goddamn book about it. What a selfish, entitled little prick. He had claimed he was in love with her and wanted to start life anew. He jettisoned that dream pretty quickly once he smelled a book. She wasn't hurt that Anton didn't really love her, or that he wouldn't really leave Gwen for her. She never wanted that. But she was scared. Anton would want everyone to know about his genius. His desire for validation would outweigh his instinct for self-preservation.

They would both end up in jail.

She felt her face grow warm. Gwen would paint her as some kind of psycho. She'd control the narrative. Lisa wouldn't just lose Aimee forever. She'd lose Marcus and Kai, her standing in this community, and everything she'd worked to build. She might lose her actual freedom. She'd been so stupid, so blinded by hate, and so focused on revenge that she'd endangered herself.

"Is everything okay, Lisa?" Aimee asked. "You're kind of red. Do you need sunscreen?"

"I'm fine," Lisa choked out, bringing her hand to her face. She was burning hot. "I think I just need some water."

Gwen passed her a canister of Evian. Lisa took her glasses off and sprayed the mist over her hot face. The relief was instant. It had been a terrible mistake to involve Anton, one that she couldn't undo. She'd once viewed him as the solution to her woes, but he had become her biggest problem.

Lisa put her sunglasses back on and leaned back in her chaise, letting the sounds of splashing water and children's happy screams wash over her. A single thought occupied her mind— what was she going to do about Anton?

44

"Your *son*?"

The word seems to ricochet off the walls of the small kitchen and lodge inside Aimee's head, where it cracks apart the image of Scott she has held since she's known him. He lost his mother young, just like she did. It was one of the things that had bonded them. Now this woman is claiming it was a lie.

"I don't understand," Aimee says, a clash of nausea and heartbreak spreading in her belly. "Scott's mom died when he was in college."

"Is that what he told you?" Cathy's gaze is steel-eyed and steady. "No, I didn't die. After Michael left California, he cut off contact with me. Cut me out completely. That's when he changed his name to Scott."

"Why? Because he killed Dexter Kohl?" Gwen asks.

Cathy turns to look at Gwen, amusement in her eyes. "Someone's been talking to Dexter's mom. I assume that's where you got that nonsense."

"I don't think it's nonsense," Gwen says, pulling out Anton's black notebook from her bag. "My husband was the one who talked to Dexter Kohl's mom. She told him her name was Cathy Stocker."

Cathy walks over and grabs the notebook. She opens it up, flipping through the pages.

"Cathy is Dexter's mom. I'm not Cathy Stocker." She looks at Aimee. "My name is Jen. Jen Finch."

"So why were you using her name?" Aimee asks, incredulous.

"Well, she's not using it anymore," she says dryly. Jen Finch puts the notebook on the counter behind her and picks up the mug of tea. "Cathy is dead. The generator outside her trailer blew up about a month ago, right before I came here. She's the one who booked this Airbnb. She was planning to come out here and see for herself if it was really Michael. So I came instead. I mean, it was already paid for. Would be a waste for someone to not use it."

"She's dead," Aimee says, more to herself than anyone else. "You say her generator blew up? Was it an accident?"

"Oh, those old generators can be quite dangerous, you know." She takes a tentative sip of tea. "Such a shame. Poor thing died after three days of clinging to life in a hospital with third-degree burns."

Aimee feels herself shiver. She's not imagining it, there's a subtle glee in the woman discussing Cathy Stocker's gruesome death.

"I want to know the truth." Aimee's voice is tentative. "Was Cathy murdered?"

"Well, let's put it this way. She had a big mouth and she was pissing off a lot of people. We live in a small community. Not geographically, mind you, it stretches over many miles, but it's not that many people. I heard from Arlette that someone was looking into the disappearance of Michael and Dex, but I couldn't have been the only one who heard that. I visited Cathy. She couldn't keep her mouth shut, even after I offered to buy her a new refrigerator to keep her quiet. Nope, she was determined to drag all this out of the past and into the present. I told her it wasn't safe. I warned her. I told her there were people who would rather see her dead than stir up this hornet's nest. But did she listen to me?"

"So, she *was* murdered," Aimee says. "And you came here."

"I came because Cathy said she'd been talking to someone who thought Michael was living here. I had to alert Michael. I didn't plan to stay. I parked in your little suburban neighborhood one night. There was some kind of block party and I wandered onto your block. I saw you. I saw all of you. I told myself I was just here for a short visit—to warn him. But once I saw Michael with the kids . . ." She squeezes the bridge of her nose. "I hadn't seen my boy in so many years. Never even seen my grandkids. Being apart from him all this time has been hard. Once I saw him I couldn't bring myself to leave. I got curious. About you, Aimee." She stops and smiles at Aimee, and for a flash Aimee sees her the way she did when they first met—as a kind older woman, good with kids and cats. But then Aimee remembers that isn't who she is.

"I wanted to get to know my grandkids," Jen says. "And when I met you, Aimee, I really liked you. I could tell you liked me, too. And that time I got to spend with Noa, I wouldn't trade it. But last Tuesday I heard some news—they've issued a warrant for Michael's arrest. It's only a matter of time until they track him here. I had to warn him."

"You want him to run from the police?"

"The police?" She scoffs. "The cops are the least of it. I don't know how much Michael's told you about me, about our life in California."

"Not much, actually."

"Ray, that's his stepdad, and me, the people we know, we're not the kind of folks who go to the police to settle our problems, if you get my drift. What Michael and Dex did was stupid, and it cost Dex his life. But Michael can't come back to testify. It might be selfish, but him coming back will ruin my life. Ruin Ray's. If he testifies, it won't be safe for me and Ray to stay."

"Testifies to what? What happened exactly?"

Gwen gives a startled cry. Aimee looks up to see Scott walking through the living room toward them. She jumps up to meet him but stops just before throwing herself into his arms. A part of her longs to bury her head against his chest and squeeze hard. What she wouldn't do to be rocked back and forth in his strong arms, for him to kiss the top of her head.

But anger stops her. Everything that has happened in the past few days is now a barrier between them that she cannot cross. "Where have you been?"

The question is sharp. The gratitude that he's safe is lost in the fury that she has been keeping under control.

"I'm so sorry, Aimee, I really am."

Aimee wipes at her eyes with the back of her hand. "What is going on? Why didn't you come home? Why didn't you call me? Text me?" She makes a fist and slams it against his chest. "Do you have any idea what this has been like?" She hits him again. "How could you do this to me? Not come home?"

"He's never coming home, honey," Jen says. "He can't."

Aimee whips her head around, shocked. She is disgusted by the hint of a smile around the woman's mouth. "That is not up to you."

"Mom, please," Scott says. "Let me handle this. I want to talk to Aimee alone."

"Fine." His mother pulls a pack of cigarettes out of her pocket. "I'm going outside to have a smoke." She nods at Gwen. "Join me?"

Gwen looks to Aimee as if to ask if that's okay. Aimee nods her okay and then stands still, her arms stiff at her sides until the two women have left the house. Once the front door has slammed, Scott sits on the couch. He pats the seat next to him but Aimee chooses a threadbare chair nearby.

"I know I've been so selfish, Aimee," Scott says. "I know it must have been so hard—"

"Did you kill that boy?" she asks.

He twitches. "What? No, I didn't kill anyone."

"Dexter Kohl, right? That's his name?"

"You think I'm capable of murder?"

She chews on her lip, thinking about this. "No. At least I didn't think so. But I also didn't think you were capable of lying to me, *Michael*."

"I can explain everything."

"I also didn't think you were capable of leaving your family to wonder for three days if you were dead or alive. I deserve to know the truth. What happened in California? Your mom said something about testifying."

He runs his hands through his messy hair. He looks exhausted and run-down with the beginnings of a beard and shadows under his eyes. "My mom and me, we moved to California right before tenth grade. But I didn't kill anyone."

"Then what happened? Why did you change your name?"

"The truth is ugly."

"Please. Try me."

He stands up, thrusting his hands into the pockets of his jeans, rocking back and forth. It's a tic he has—can't stay still when he's nervous, just like Noa. "We were robbing some drug dealers, Dex and me. It didn't go as planned. Dex got shot."

"What does this have to do with a backpacking trip?"

"There was no backpacking trip. My stepdad, Ray, and my mom managed a farm about an hour away outside Garberville, near the top of a mountain."

"A farm?"

"This was before marijuana was legal. It was an illegal grow operation, about a hundred acres. My stepdad managed the trimmigrants—that's what we called the people who come through at the end of summer to work the harvest and make some fast cash."

"And you lived there? On the farm?"

He nods. "I did. And there was a lot of cash floating around that time of year. Trimmers worked nonstop for about five weeks, sometimes as much as sixteen hours a day. It's all they did. Then they got paid in cash. Not too many places to spend money around there. Dex and I heard my stepdad talk about a high-stakes poker game at another grower's farm. We knew there would be tons of cash floating around. We got the brilliant idea to rob it. We thought it was foolproof since they wouldn't go to the cops."

"And?"

"It went to shit immediately. We showed up in masks with shotguns and one of the players pulled a handgun. Dex shot him in the arm and the guy returned fire, killing him. I barely got out of there with my life. If that guy's gun hadn't jammed, I'd be dead, too. I took off running, and I ran and ran until my lungs were on fire. I didn't even go back to where our car was. Called my mom once I hit the highway and found a pay phone. She came and picked me up. She knew right away I had to get out of town. You can't go around robbing criminals and not have them come look for you."

"So, she sent you away? A boy was killed."

"You don't get it. I couldn't go to the police. Do you know what the felony murder rule is? It says that if someone dies while you are committing a felony, you can be charged with murder. You are just as liable as if you pulled the trigger yourself."

"But you didn't kill anyone," Aimee protests.

"That's the law. There are people on death row who were driving the getaway car when their buddy shot someone inside a bank. But I wasn't worried about that at the time. I was scared of the guy who killed Dex. I saw him do it, Aimee. He pointed that gun at me and I'll never forget that look in his eyes. He wanted me dead. I had to leave."

"So she sent you to North Carolina. To Aunt Kay."

"Aunt Kay agreed to take me in. She didn't really want me there, but at least she gave me a place to get my act together. I changed my name, finished my senior year. Spent a year at community college and then transferred to UNC. I've spent my whole life trying to make up for what I did. To be a good person."

"What about your mom? You just cut her out?"

Scott gazes at the picture window that overlooks the front yard where Jen stands with Gwen. "It might be hard for you to understand this. Your mom sounded like an amazing person. But my mom is different. She's deeply in that life. And I mean deep. Her boyfriend was a major player in the growing scene back then. I basically spent three years of high school surrounded by people in the drug trade. She wanted to get me out of town to protect me, but honestly, it was also to protect herself. She could have left with me. We could have started over together somewhere. But she chose the life over me. She chose my stepdad over me. So, yeah, I cut her out. But she cut me out first. At Aunt Kay's I had an opportunity to start over. I took it."

"The way you start over is by coming clean, Scott. Not by abandoning your family."

"Don't you get it?" He kneels in front of her, beseeching her with his eyes. "I'll have two choices—go to prison for the rest of my life or testify. That'll mean not just testifying against the man that killed Dexter but against all five men—including my stepdad—who were at that poker game. They didn't report the murder, either. And they got rid of the body. They've all committed first-degree felonies. Why do you think they killed Cathy? To shut her up."

"They have witness protection programs. We could go somewhere."

"Is that what you want? To cut ties with everyone you know, including your dad, and live under an assumed name in some random place? Is that what you want for the kids?"

"I want them to grow up knowing their father." She lifts her chin in defiance.

"They won't if I'm in WITSEC. And they won't if I'm serving time in California." Scott flinches. "I'm sorry, Aimee. I'm weak. I feel lucky to have met you, married you, had these great kids. It's more than I thought I would ever have. I'm sorry I've ruined it all."

"What about Anton? How does he play into all this?"

Scott jerks his head back. "Anton? What are you talking about?"

"He was blackmailing you. You're saying you didn't know?"

Scott stands up and stumbles back. "Anton? Where did you get that idea?"

"I talked to Jon Block. He figured out where the email was coming from. An account at a library on the American University campus."

"What? He didn't tell me that."

"I think he just found out. And then when I confronted Gwen, she confirmed it. Anton confessed to her the night he died."

"I can't believe this. I had no idea it was him. He was trying to talk to me that night. But I blew him off because I was meeting Jon Block. Holy shit. I need a drink." He walks into the kitchen. She hears the whoosh of the fridge as he opens it. He appears in the doorway holding a bottle of beer. "Want one?" He pops the top off the bottle with the edge of the counter and takes a swig.

Aimee glances at her watch. "It's not even noon."

"I don't get it. Why would he do that? Why would Anton blackmail me? And how the hell did he even find out about my past?"

"I don't know. But you paid him, right? A hundred thousand dollars. I've looked through the finances over the last few weeks. The money is gone."

"No, no. You have it wrong. I didn't pay him," he says. "I took that money out for me."

"You what?"

"I took the money out to help me run. I never paid the person blackmailing me. I never intended to. I didn't know Anton was the one who sent me that email or that text. I assumed it was someone from back in California. The person never gave me their name. I just knew that someone out there knew about my past and the clock was ticking. I withdrew that money for a getaway fund, to start a new life."

"You've been planning to leave us for weeks?" Aimee stands up.

"I know how it sounds—"

"How it sounds? You're a lying sack of shit, Scott. Michael. Whatever your name is."

She brushes past him to get her phone from the basket in the kitchen.

"Wait." He grabs her arm.

"Let go of me!" She wrestles free of his grip and steps back into the living room. "So what happened Monday night?" She spits the words out. "You just decided that was a good time to put your little plan into action?

"When I went to pick up Noa, there was my mom. She told me Cathy had been murdered. That people were already looking for me, and she and Ray had to go into hiding. She said the police were going to issue an arrest warrant. I had to run. I wasn't ready, but I left my car there and came here. I had to get new papers, social security number, passport, things like that."

"And what will you do once you have all those things?" She fights to keep her voice steady.

"I'll make my way to Ecuador. There's no extradition with the US."

"Clever." Aimee looks at the man in front of her. He has the same dark brown hair, the same green eyes, the same strong jaw as her Scott, but she doesn't recognize him. And it's not his ill-fitting jeans and sweatshirt, his unshaven face, or the bags beneath his eyes. His demeanor is different. He's harder, like he's been filed down in the past few days into something sharp. Maybe that's what happens when he's around his mom—he reverts back to Michael, the boy who thought robbing drug dealers was a good idea.

Or maybe Michael was always inside her Scott, and she just never wanted to see it.

"I can't believe you would do this to our kids," she says. "I thought you were the best dad in the world. I looked at other dads, and husbands, and I actually felt sorry for my friends because their husbands seemed so second-rate compared to you. I believed you loved us more than anything in the world."

"I do love you, Aimee. You and the kids. That's why—"

"Forget the lies you told me," she says, speaking over him. "Forget the mistakes you made when you were young—that's nothing compared to the mistake you're about to make. What you decide to do right now, right at this moment, will determine what kind of man you are. Not just what I think of you, but what your kids will think of you."

"You don't get it, Aimee. I'll be gone either way." He takes a step toward her. "You think it will be good for these kids to see their dad do time?"

"But you'll get out. Eventually. I mean, you didn't actually kill your friend, right? You might be able to make a deal."

"If I don't testify, I'll go to prison. If I do, I'll be killed."

"At least your kids, at least I, would know what happened to you. I can't believe you would let us suffer for the rest of our lives not knowing. It's sick." Aimee goes to the front door, puts her hand on the knob. "I'm not going to beg you. I'm all wrung out from worrying about you the past three days. From keeping our family together during this crisis. From believing in you and defending you." She pulls it open. Across the yard, Gwen and Cathy turn to look at her.

"Are you going to call the police on me?" he asks.

Aimee turns back to him, surprised by her own calm state of mind. The unraveling will come later, she is sure. In these past few days of catastrophizing, she imagined Scott in so many different terrible situations—wounded in a car crash, unconscious in a hospital, or kidnapped and held against his will. She hadn't entertained even for a second the thought that he would voluntarily stay away from her and cause her so much pain and grief.

And that knowledge is like a moat around her, one he won't be able to cross easily.

"I am going to go home to my kids. And yes, I am going to call the police. I am going to tell them every single thing that you told me. The rest is up to you, Scott."

45

Gwen turns as Aimee leaves the house and walks right by her without a word. She leaves Scott's mom sucking on a cigarette and hurries to the truck.

"Let's go." Aimee climbs into the passenger side of the truck, so Gwen gets in on the driver's side.

"What about Scott?"

"You drive." Aimee hands Gwen the keys. "I'd like to go back and scream at that woman, but there's no point. She's a horrible mother who ruined her son's life and he's still listening to her now."

"What's going on? Is Scott staying?" Gwen peers up at the house as if Scott might come running out at any moment, but the only movement is from Jen, who stands at the front door like a sentry, flicking the ash from her cigarette.

Aimee pulls her knees up to her chest, pressing her face against them. "Just drive, please. Just drive."

"Of course." Gwen starts the ignition and turns the truck around, heading back the way they came, past the high school with the earth movers parked out front. The clock on the dash says it's twelve-thirty. They'll be back in plenty of time for school dismissal. Gwen doesn't say anything on the drive home, but the quiet is fraught with tension. Aimee stares out the window, unmoving. She's a million miles away. It obviously did not go well with Scott, and as curious as Gwen is about what transpired between them, she wants to give Aimee her space.

It isn't until about forty minutes later, once they are off 495 and driving through downtown Bethesda, that Gwen dares break the silence. "I'm not trying to pry, but how do you feel?"

Aimee turns from the window. "I don't know how I feel right now. I'm so angry, I'm just so angry at him. But at the same time, I want him back. But the old him. Before I knew all this shit."

"Is he coming home?"

"I don't think so."

Gwen lets this sink in. She pulls into their neighborhood, a sensation of gloom overtaking her. The last few days have blotted out her good memories of this place, and she hates that. "Can I ask you—did you have a chance to talk to him about Anton?"

"He said that he didn't even know Anton was the one blackmailing him, and I believe him."

Gwen considers this. "So you don't think he was involved in Anton's death?"

Aimee gives her a sharp look. "No. Scott's not a killer."

"And you believe him?" Scott is, at the very least, a liar and a fugitive. He might even be a murderer.

"He was genuinely surprised that it was Anton. Yes, I believe him."

"But they were together right before Anton was killed. And with the blackmail, Scott does have a motive."

"What do you want me to say, Gwen?" Aimee's voice is shrill. "That I think my husband killed yours? Because I don't."

"I'm just saying—"

"Well, don't. Because I don't want to talk about it anymore."

"Fine. But are you going to call the police?"

Aimee scowls. "Of course I am. You think I'm just going to pretend to the police that he's still missing, and I have no idea where he is?"

Gwen pulls the truck up in front of Aimee's house and cuts the engine, unsure of what to say. Aimee seems to vibrate with anger. After a few moments of silence, Aimee takes out her phone.

"Why do I feel so guilty calling the police?"

"Because you still love him."

Aimee taps out a number on her phone. "Hi, Detective Salazar, this is Aimee Stern. I know where Scott is. He's at a house up near Frederick." She recites the address and hangs up. "It was his voicemail."

"I could tell."

She turns to face Gwen, looking weary. "Did I do the right thing?"

Gwen reaches out and squeezes Aimee's arm. "You did the right thing."

"Then why do I feel so crappy? No, don't answer that. I better go inside. The kids will be home soon."

Gwen recognizes the urge to be alone when she sees it. She's not going to stand in Aimee's way. She doesn't know what Aimee and Scott discussed when they were alone, but the fact that he didn't come home with her says everything. The two women get out, and as Gwen starts to walk away, Aimee calls her name.

"Hey, do me a favor—don't talk about this with anyone, okay? I mean, not yet. I know pretty soon it's all anyone will want to talk about. But until then."

"You got it." She hands Aimee the keys. "And when all this is over, you and me are gonna go on a trip where no one knows us, right?"

Aimee gives a little nod, but Gwen feels her heart sink. This feels like the end of their friendship. She wants to believe that they have a solid enough foundation that they can get through this. After all, she is one of the few people who can really understand what Aimee is going through. She watches to make sure Aimee is safely inside before she turns to her own home. As soon as she enters her house, she realizes that she left Anton's journal back in Frederick. She hesitates by the door, wondering if it matters, but decides to let it go. It is just one of the many things she's going to have to learn to live without.

She finds Barb in the kitchen packing a cooler bag with snacks and drinks.

"What's going on?" Gwen asks.

"I thought I would take the boys to Richmond tonight and keep them for the rest of the week. I'm going to be honest with you, Gwen. I don't think it's healthy for them to be here with you while you're in this state."

"And what state is that? Grieving?"

Barb purses her lips. "It's that attitude I'm talking about. The boys can pick up on it. What they need now are reliable, strong, positive adults in their lives. Your father and I can help. I thought we'd keep them over the weekend and bring them back next week for the funeral."

"The funeral?"

"It's all set. I've arranged it for next Tuesday at Gawler's. That will give Henri enough time to fly in from France. He's coming in Monday and leaving Wednesday. I've got him a room at the Marriott here in Bethesda; he doesn't drive anymore. This way he can walk to everything. There's that French bakery, Toot de Sweet, nearby. I'm sure he'll find their croissants passable."

Gwen lets all this sink in. Normally her mother's presumptiveness would rankle her. She hates Barb's sense of entitlement over her life. But she has to admit that Barb has a point. She needs help. She's barely holding on. "I guess so. I mean, thank you for dealing with all that. I really do appreciate it."

"You're most welcome. I assume you'll join us in Richmond. We could all use a little R&R."

"Of course, did you think I was just going to let you take the boys again?"

Her mother looks up from her packing, clearly caught off guard. "Well, that's settled, then."

They decide that Barb will leave with the boys now, and Gwen will follow later in her own car, once she's had a chance to pack up her things and get Sababa's crate down from the attic. Her parents are very particular about the dog. They won't let him stay in the house unattended without crating him. It's one of the reasons Gwen visits so seldomly.

She stands at the door and sees them off, glad to have a few hours to herself to process what happened that afternoon.

Scott may not have murdered that boy back in California, but he is wanted for a felony all the same. And his mother, what a piece of work, she had that hard-edge look to her. How the hell did she ever convince Aimee that she was a retired school-teacher, and a safe person to leave Noa with?

Gwen goes inside and grabs a vodka seltzer from the fridge. *Just one*, she tells herself. She needs it after the day she's had. She doesn't like to be too harsh on Aimee, but her friend has some serious lapses in judgment. Her husband is a wanted man, her babysitter a drug matriarch, and her close friend an adulterer.

The doorbell rings and she freezes.

"Hello!" a voice calls. She recognizes the nasal tone as belonging to Michelle J. She waits a few minutes until there is silence and then tiptoes to the front door to peer out. She can make out Michelle J.'s back as she turns the corner at the end of the cul-de-sac. When she opens the door, Gwen finds a basket the size of an infant's bassinet filled with fruit—pineapples, strawberry kebabs, clusters of grapes. She brings it in and sets it in the kitchen, pushing aside the several overflowing vases of flowers that have been delivered in the past few days.

This will be dinner, she decides, and finishes off her vodka soda.

As she pops a grape in her mouth, she replays the afternoon. Why did Anton want money from Scott? Was he planning on using it to leave her? She has so many questions she wants to ask him but will never be able to.

Outside the sun has set, turning the kitchen windows black. She has always hated the way uncovered windows at night make her feel so lonely. Growing up, the Buckley dining room had three French doors that looked out on the side garden. At night, she ate with her family in tense silence under the glow of the overhead chandelier, staring into the flatness of those three glass doors darkened by night. She felt like a specimen, easily observed by any passerby on the street, and it made her self-conscious and afraid. She gets up and draws the curtains.

She'd better start getting ready for Richmond.

Upstairs, she packs a suitcase, gets the crate down, and leashes up Sababa for a last walk before the long drive. She's halfway down the block when she hears the sound of footsteps behind her. She turns to see Lisa approaching, waving wildly.

"Hey, hey!"

Gwen turns her back on Lisa and tries to keep walking, but Sababa has found something pungent to smell and resists her tugging.

"Hey, Gwen—" Lisa, breathless, is beside her all of a sudden.

"I don't want to talk to you," Gwen says without looking up. "We're not friends." She finally yanks Sababa free and starts walking away.

"Fine. I know that. I know that you hate me, that you think I'm a terrible person," Lisa calls after her. "But you love Aimee, and so do I."

Gwen halts. She can't believe she's about to fall for this line, but she is. Aimee is her Achilles' heel with Lisa. She turns around. "So?"

Lisa takes a few steps forward. "I just want to know how she's doing. I called. I texted. She's not responding. I'm worried."

Gwen wrestles with her impulse to tell Lisa to get lost. But Aimee needs all the love and support she can get right now, and if Gwen's at her parents' in Richmond, Lisa will be the only one here to check on her.

"She had a bad day," Gwen says begrudgingly. "She saw Scott. And I don't think he's coming home."

"I'm confused. He's okay?" Lisa tilts her head, her thick black hair falling to one side.

"He's physically fine." Gwen hesitates, trying to find the right words to describe the situation. "But it turns out there's a warrant or something for him in California, so he ran." This barely scrapes the surface of the story, but she figures it will suffice for now. If Aimee wants Lisa to have the details, she can tell her later.

"That's crazy." Lisa covers her mouth with her hand.

"I guess you were right about it being a bad idea for Noa to go over to that woman Cathy's house, by the way."

"Oh no, is she involved in all this?"

"Yeah, it's very complicated. I'm sure Aimee will tell you."

"Thank you for filling me in," Lisa says. "Poor Aimee. I can't even imagine what she's going through."

Gwen yanks on Sababa's leash. "Well, I better get going. I'm driving to my parents' house tonight. I'm not sure if Aimee's sticking around here or heading up to her dad's. But maybe you could check on her."

"Oh, I will. Definitely. Marcus is gone this weekend, too. He and Kai are at a soccer tournament in Delaware," Lisa says. "Aimee shouldn't have to be alone at a time like this. Maybe I'll pop by with a bottle of wine. She may have just turned her phone off. I mean, can you imagine? Finding out your husband was wanted for murder all these years?" Lisa scrunches up her nose as if she's just smelled something rotten. "Hold on, do you think he might have, you know, Anton? I mean, if he has a history of violence."

"No. I don't."

At home, Gwen heads straight into the kitchen to grab her bag and car keys. She's ready to leave Nassau Court, maybe forever. But something is bothering her about her exchange with Lisa. It was as if Lisa was pretending to act how she thought an adult woman would behave, but there was some human element missing. And the way she was so excited to play nursemaid to Aimee creeped Gwen out. As if she had been waiting ages for this moment to step in and be Aimee's savior.

She's dragging the crate to the front when the doorbell rings. Gwen yanks it open to find Lisa on the stoop, holding a gold-colored box of chocolates. "These are for Aimee. She loves their sea salt caramels."

"What do you want?" Gwen asks, annoyance swelling within her.

Lisa slips through the narrow opening of the door, past Gwen, who is forced to move back.

"Actually, I was on my way out." Gwen motions to the suitcase and dog crate. She wants Lisa out of her house. It physically disgusts her to be near this woman, close enough to smell her sickly sweet perfume, to see the thick bronzer on her face. What did Anton see in her? "It's a long drive, and I want to get going."

"Right, sure! I'm heading to Aimee's in a minute." Lisa hoists the box, at least pretending to be full of good cheer. "I just wanted to talk to you for a second, you mind?" Lisa shuts the door behind her.

Gwen is startled by her boldness, and then it hits her. She realizes what was bugging her about the earlier conversation with Lisa.

I mean, can you imagine? Finding out your husband was wanted for murder all these years?

Lisa knew about Scott's past.

"How did you know Scott was involved in a murder?" Gwen blurts out. "I didn't tell you that."

Lisa bites her heavily glossed lip. "Well, fuck. I was hoping you hadn't caught that."

46

LAST FRIDAY NIGHT

Lisa was growing more concerned about what Anton might do. By the time the school year started two weeks ago, she was jumpy and unable to focus on anything else. *Stupid, stupid, stupid,* she would say to herself in the shower, hitting her head against the cold subway tile. Not enough to make herself bleed, or even to leave a mark, but enough to alleviate the pressure she was feeling. She had fucked up again. And this time she could lose so much. Her best friend, her husband, maybe even her freedom. Had she taken part in a crime?

Her relationship with Anton had turned sour. The last time they had tried to have sex was weeks ago, and he couldn't get it up. Lisa had spent a humiliating thirty minutes trying to get him hard, which left them both embarrassed and frustrated.

Neither of them had to say that this was the end. If she cared about him, she might have cried, yelled, reminded him of his declarations of love and his promises of a life together. But she couldn't muster the energy. They had used each other, and they both knew it. The only question now was whether he would do something dumb, something to jeopardize them both. Like actually try to publish a book about Scott. That would be disastrous. He didn't want to discuss the new book with her. He wouldn't talk about Scott, either. She was in the dark, panicking.

The next day, while Kai was at school and Marcus at work, she dialed Cathy Stocker's number. Maybe if she could find out what Cathy had been discussing with Anton, how much she had told him, she would feel better. The woman might have some insight into what Anton was up to.

She left a message, and when she didn't hear back, she tried again the next day. And the next. By Friday of that week, she had left seven messages for Cathy. Marcus came home earlier than usual that day so they could all grill at Aimee and Scott's. While he changed, Lisa emptied a carton of Caesar pasta salad from Whole Foods into a bowl. As she worked on the salad, she thought of someone else she could call: Arlette Fagin. She looked at the clock: it was two-thirty in California.

She locked herself in the downstairs bathroom and dialed. Arlette answered on the first ring. When Lisa began to introduce herself, Arlette interrupted.

"I really can't talk. This isn't a good time." There was no mistaking the hostility in her voice.

"Wait, please. Don't hang up," Lisa begged.

"I don't want to be involved in any of this, you hear? Don't use my name."

"I won't. I just have one question, and then I will never bother you again."

Silence and then a loud sigh. "What is it?"

"I'm trying to reach Cathy Stocker. We chatted last month, but she's not answering her phone. I just want to make sure she's all right."

"You haven't heard? Cathy's dead. They killed her, probably for talking to you and your friend. Now I'm not saying it's your fault. I'm not saying that you pulled the trigger. But you got her thinking and talking and ruffling quite a few feathers around here. Pressing on some old wounds that hadn't healed. And someone went and blew up her trailer. Now, please don't ever call me again."

The phone went dead. Lisa stared at it, shocked. A loud knock on the door made her yelp. She yanked open the door. "Don't scare me like that!"

Marcus held up his hands and backed off. "Sorry. I was just seeing if you were ready to go."

"I've been ready," she said. "I was waiting for you."

The three of them walked up the street to Aimee and Scott's, but Lisa's thoughts were three thousand miles away. She could picture an old woman in a mobile home among tall redwoods. *Blew up her trailer.* She needed to tell Anton. She had to stop him from going forward with the book.

As soon as they arrived at the house, Marcus peeled off to find Scott, ostensibly to help him grill. Lisa headed to the table where Gwen, Aimee, and Anton were sitting. She had felt Marcus pulling away from her lately. It was just as she was emerging from the affair with Anton. It was as if she had woken up from a coma and realized life had moved on without her. Where had Marcus's interest gone? Oh, he played at being a loyal husband, but something had changed. She knew he couldn't suspect her of cheating. He would never be able to swallow such an affront. Had he found his own little sidepiece over the past few months? It was hard to believe him when he said it was work that was keeping him so preoccupied. He even turned down sex a few times, even though their sex life had been diminishing over the summer.

". . . Cathy. Cathy Stocker."

Aimee's words crashed through Lisa's thoughts, shattering them. "What did you say?" She turned to Aimee.

Aimee gave her a weird look. "I said my new client's name is Cathy Stocker. Why? Do you know her? She lives out in Potomac."

Lisa pulled out one of the wrought iron chairs and sat down. She didn't dare look up at Anton, afraid of what his face might be revealing. "No, I don't know her. What were you guys talking about?"

"Noa. Cats." Gwen popped an olive into her mouth.

Aimee smiled. "Cathy has a cat that just gave birth, so sometimes Noa goes over there to hang out with the kittens."

"Alone?" The word comes out of Lisa's mouth like a shriek.

Everyone lapsed into silence for a moment, then Aimee laughed nervously. "Umm, sometimes. Cathy's a very nice person. And the kittens are adorable."

"You don't even know her," Lisa said. She felt like someone was strangling her. She'd never imagined that what she was doing might somehow come back to hurt Aimee or her children. "You can't just let your kids hang out with random strangers, Aimee!"

"Lisa, calm down," Gwen said.

Lisa whipped her head around. "Mind your own business, Gwen. This doesn't involve you."

Aimee stood up. "I'll get the salad."

Gwen stood as well. "I'll get the buns."

Lisa watched the two women walk inside the house. Behind her, one of the twins let out a sharp scream followed by peals of laughter. She looked at the kids, the four younger boys jumping on the trampoline while Kai and Noa played catch with Sababa. Despite the idyll playing out around her, Lisa felt unsafe. She knew that if Aimee discovered the truth, she would lose everything. Lisa got up and went to sit in the chair next to Anton. "Do you have any idea what you've done?" she hissed.

"I didn't know she was coming here," he said in a low voice. "Do you think she's here to track down Michael?"

"No, I don't think Cathy Stocker is here to do anything, because Cathy Stocker is dead. Someone killed her."

Anton's lip began to twitch. "That can't be true."

Lisa glanced at the kitchen window, where Aimee was watching from inside, and waved. She looked back at Anton, but this time she forced herself to smile. "Oh, it's true. She was murdered for talking to you."

Anton looked sick, like he might throw up. "If she's dead," he whispered, "who the hell has Noa been visiting?"

"I have no clue. But it's probably not very good, is it?"

"We need to tell Aimee," Anton said. "We need to tell Scott. Everything."

"No, we don't."

"We have to warn them. They deserve to know."

"Anton, we are neck-deep in this." Lisa looked up and saw Aimee and Gwen coming back outside through the sliding glass door. "We're not telling anyone anything. Here they come. Now plaster a smile on your face and keep your damn mouth shut."

47

"I knew it," Gwen says. "You knew the whole time that Anton was blackmailing Scott. You knew about his past. That's why you warned Aimee to keep Noa away."

"Can we go into the kitchen and talk about this?"

"What's there to talk about?" She watches Lisa walk past her toward the kitchen. She follows Lisa through the living room, past the dining room table, which is now empty of Anton's things. She stops short when she sees the two hideous pewter candlesticks Anton gave her back on the table. Barb. She must have pulled them out of the donation box and put them back.

Gwen makes a note to toss them later and enters the kitchen to find Lisa looking through her cabinets. "I forget. Where do you keep your alcohol?"

Gwen stifles a laugh. "You're delusional. We're not drinking together. I don't want you here."

"But you want answers, don't you? Aha!" Lisa bends down and opens the wine fridge. She stands back up, now holding a bottle of white wine with a rubber stopper in it. "Mind if I?"

"Do I have a choice?"

Lisa seems to glow from within, giddy with a strange energy. She grabs a wineglass drying on the dish rack and fills it. "God, I needed that," she says after a big sip. "You sure you won't join me?"

"You don't seem freaked out that I know. Aren't you worried?"

"About what?"

"That I'm going to tell the police. That I'm going to tell Aimee."

Lisa flinches and Gwen knows she's made contact.

"Imagine what Aimee will say when she learns that you were blackmailing her husband." Gwen takes a step forward, enjoying the way Lisa's eye has started twitching. "That you allowed sweet little Noa to go over to this crazy woman's house, a criminal, actually, and you never told her who Cathy really was."

"It wasn't my fault. Anton threatened to kill me if I said anything."

Gwen scoffs. "You're kidding, right?"

Lisa blinks twice, and as if by magic her face rearranges itself into one of fear. "I was scared for my life, Gwen." Her voice trembles. "He slammed me up against a wall. He put his hands around my neck and choked me." She looks away and sniffs. "He told me he would kill me."

"You have got to be kidding me. You seriously think anyone will fall for your act?"

Lisa grabs the wineglass and takes a swig. "Oh, I think so. If I were you, I'd be more worried about what people will say about you when they learn that your husband was a liar, and a criminal, and violent, too. That he threatened a woman's life. Are you an enabler, Gwen? That's pretty sick."

"You're a complete psychopath, aren't you? I never understood why Aimee put up with you. You're like a stray dog she felt sorry for—"

"Shut up, Gwen. I fucked your husband in this room."

"No, it's true," Gwen continues. "Everyone thought so. We all felt so sorry for Marcus, he's such a nice guy. We all talked about you behind your back, you know. How hard you tried. Always trying to get our attention. That leopard-print bikini at the pool? I mean, c'mon, Lisa. Pathetic."

"You're such a cold bitch. No wonder Anton stepped out on you."

"Hope you've enjoyed your life, Lisa. Because when I tell people that you knew, your life is over. Aimee will never speak to you again. You may end up going to jail."

"I'm not going to let you do that."

"Thing is, you can't stop me," Gwen says. "I'm done here. I'm leaving. You can stay and lock up."

She turns her back to Lisa and begins to walk to the front door. She's halfway through the living room when something strikes her in the back of her head. Gwen staggers forward, woozy, and collapses on the couch. She touches the back of her head, feeling something wet, and looks at her fingers. Blood. She looks up to see Lisa standing over her, one of the pewter candlesticks hanging by her side.

"What are you doing?" Gwen gasps.

"I can't let you tell Aimee." She steps closer. "I told Anton the same thing, and he didn't listen, either."

"What do you mean, Anton didn't listen?" Gwen blinks as the room starts to sway. "Are you saying—"

"I saw him follow Scott. I knew what he was going to do. He was going to tell him. He was going to destroy me. I had to stop him."

"You murdered Anton." Gwen struggles to stand up. She needs to get out of here. But Lisa stands between her and the door.

"You mean that cheating, lying, piece-of-shit husband of yours? You call that murder? I call that a service. I did you a favor! You're free." Her voice is shrill and there's a wild look in her eyes. "You should be on your knees thanking me, instead of acting like the bitch that you are." She raises the candlestick again, but this time Gwen bends forward and rams into the middle of Lisa's body, tackling her. They fall on the floor, struggling, and Gwen winds up on her back, Lisa straddling her. Lisa's hands are around her neck, and Gwen opens her mouth, desperate for air, gasping.

She tries to pry Lisa's fingers off but can't get a grip. Her right arm flails out to her side and hits something metal. The candlestick. She gropes around until she has it firmly in her hand and then swings it up, catching Lisa on the side of her head. Lisa sways, her grip loosens. Again, Gwen swings the candlestick, making contact this time with Lisa's forehead with a sickening thud. Lisa collapses on top of her, and Gwen pushes her body away.

She lies there for a moment, fighting to catch her breath. After a while, she sits up, dizzy, and looks at Lisa's crumpled form.

She puts two fingers to Lisa's neck, knowing before she does that there is no point.

48

Aimee is sitting on her bed, detangling Noa's hair, when the whoop of a police siren startles her. Red lights coming from the street outside bounce off the walls of the room. Her body quivers. She can't handle any more bad news today. She still hasn't processed what Scott told her this afternoon.

"What is that?" Noa asks.

"Hold on, sweetie." She pats Noa's head and goes to the window. Peering out, she can see two police cars arriving, followed by an ambulance. They pull up haphazardly, taking up much of the cul-de-sac, but it is obvious they are heading to Gwen's house. The relief she feels is slight.

"What's going on?" Noa appears beside her. She cups her hands around her eyes and presses them to the window. Max and Benji rush in, yelling about the sirens. They join their sister at the window.

"Is it Santa?" Benji asks, breathless.

"It's not Christmas." Noa looks up at Aimee. "Right, Mom? It's not Santa, is it?"

Every year around the holidays, the local fire station sends a truck through the neighborhood with someone dressed as Santa. Kids and parents gather outside their homes to wave as he rides by.

"No, it's not Santa." She tells them to stay by the window and keep watch, that she'll be right back. Aimee grabs a fleece and slips on her sneakers. It's a clear night, with a hint of a breeze and the cooler weather to come. Stepping into the street feels like stepping onto a movie set of action and bright lights. People rush about, confident of where they should go and what to do. She looks around to see if any of the other residents are here, but there's no one. Then she sees her older neighbor Paola on the other side of the ambulance.

As Aimee walks over, she sees Detective Salazar emerge from the chaos and approach Paola.

"Hi, Detective," Aimee says, aware she might be interrupting. "Did you get my message?"

"Ms. Stern. Hi. Yes, I did." He shoots a look at Paola, who is peering at him wide-eyed from behind immense glasses. Aimee interprets his glance as a question—*Do you want to discuss this in front of her?*

Beyond niceties at this point, Aimee pushes on. "And? Did you find Scott?"

He grimaces. "We have been unable to locate your husband. But we have a few leads. We can discuss it later. Right now, we have to deal with this."

Chastened, Aimee lapses into silence. What did she think he would say? She had hoped against hope that Scott would be there when the police arrived, that he would have changed his mind. She would be willing to forgive him eventually—she knew that in her heart—but only if he was willing to do the work. But instead he had run. Her chest tightens with the realization that it's over for them. He's not coming home.

"What happened here?" Paola asks.

"That's what we're trying to find out," Salazar says. "There was some sort of struggle inside, and Lisa Greco-King is dead."

Aimee digs her nails into the palms of her hands. This can't be happening. *The block is cursed*, she thinks. One by one its residents are being picked off.

"Dead?" Paola gasps. "Who did this? A burglar? Maybe it was the one who lives there, with the long blond hair."

"We're still figuring things out," he says, uncertainty in his voice. "Did you hear or see anything out of the ordinary tonight?"

"Tonight? No, all was quiet tonight," Paola says.

"No, nothing," Aimee says.

"And do you have any idea where Lisa's husband is?" Salazar asks.

"Yes," Paola says. "He took the boy to some sports event. I saw them leave several hours ago."

"Thank you." Salazar nods. "I better get inside. I'll be in touch."

She watches the detective duck under the yellow caution tape hung between two trees in Gwen's front yard and disappear into the house. She is struck by her lack of desire to check on Gwen. All she wants to do is retreat. She decides right then to pack the kids up and go to her father's house for the weekend. Get far away from Nassau Court.

"Tonight was quiet," Paola says quietly, as if to herself. "But things happen in the quiet, too."

Aimee turns to her. "I'm sorry. What did you say?"

"I see things. I may be old, but I see things."

"Like what?" Aimee asks.

"I see the Italian one go to that one's house during the day." She points at Gwen's place. "When everyone else is gone." Paola clucks her tongue. "Not so nice."

Within an hour, Aimee has packed the kids and several suitcases and is on 95 North heading to Baltimore. She's grateful that the kids are absorbed in their screens and can ride in silence. Her body is tired and her mind exhausted. She doesn't want to think anymore. She wants to stop her brain from chewing over the day's events, coming up with different ideas and angles, none of them satisfactory. There is no satisfactory answer. Scott is gone. Lisa is dead. And if she is to believe what Paola was implying, Lisa was sleeping with Anton, after all. She turns on the music, finds an '80s channel on SiriusXM, and tries to lose herself in the familiar melodies of Echo & the Bunnymen.

Deb is waiting for them when she pulls up and immediately commandeers the kids, offering them homemade cookies and a tour of the obstacle course her brother built behind the house. The kids run off, enchanted by the hundreds of fairy lights that hang from the trees in the backyard. She envies their innocence. At some point she will have to destroy it with the news about their father, but not tonight.

"I've got the kids," Deb says. "Why don't you go on in. Your dad's in the living room."

Aimee walks though the familiar kitchen, past the worn farm table she sat at for so many years, and into the living room. Her father is seated in his favorite chair, a book open in his lap—no doubt about World War II—and a tumbler of scotch on the table beside him.

She sits in the matching armchair across from him and watches his face as he removes his glasses and looks up, seeing that it's her.

"Aimee. What a wonderful surprise." Then he frowns. "I don't suppose you've got good news about Scott, have you?"

"If you pour me one of those," she says, pointing to the glass next to him, "I'll tell you all about it."

49

NOW

On Saturday morning, Aimee wakes up for the third day in a row in her childhood bedroom. She rolls over and looks at the other twin bed in the room, the way she did so many times as a girl when a friend slept over, but it is empty. Noa must already be up.

The house is too quiet, she thinks as she descends the stairs. In the kitchen she discovers why. Deb has left a note on the counter that Aimee's dad is at work but she's taken the kids out and they'll be back after lunch. The coffeepot is full and being kept warm. Aimee pours herself a cup and takes it out to the large screened-in porch in the back. From here, it is a quick walk down to Gunpowder River, which empties into the bay. Her mother had been an avid birder. She used to head out in the predawn hours to watch the sun rise over the water, keeping track of all the birds she saw. She'd draw them, adding dabs of watercolor, and leave them on the porch to dry, then tack them up to the wood railings with a thumbtack. None of that is left. All traces of her mother are gone.

Aimee curls up on the wicker love seat, cradling the coffee mug. She had thought Scott experienced that same loss of his mother, but it turned out to be a lie. Her phone vibrates in her pocket, and she puts her coffee down to answer it.

"Good morning, this is Detective Salazar. Do you have a few minutes?" His voice is brusque, as if he's walking fast. Aimee sits up.

"Yes, I have time."

"I'm sorry to disturb you on a Saturday, but I thought you'd want to know—"

"Did you find Scott?"

"Actually, your husband turned himself in. He is being processed at the Montgomery County Detention Center right now."

"Is he going back to California?" Aimee asks. "Will he stand trial?"

"He is going back to California, whenever transport can be set up. I don't know when. We'll find out more tomorrow. I just wanted you to know."

"Can I see him?"

"Not today, I'm afraid. Maybe Monday, after he's been arraigned. I'll see if I can set something up before he leaves for California."

"What about Lisa Greco-King? And Gwen? Can you tell me anything?"

"I guess everything I am about to tell you will be in the public record soon enough. We found trace amounts of Anton's blood on the front of Lisa's car, and on the underside of the front wheel. Clearly someone had tried to clean it but didn't do a great job. We believe she was responsible for Anton's death."

"Oh my God." She turns this over in her mind, flashing back to Anton's and Lisa's conspiratorial whispering on her back patio on the day that Anton died. "And Gwen? Is she being charged with anything?"

"No. Not at this time."

"I can't believe Lisa killed Anton. Was it to keep him quiet?"

"Well, that's the theory. That he was starting to crack under the pressure of blackmailing your husband. He was heading to Villain & Saint to talk to Scott. That must have spooked Lisa."

"So, what—she saw him following Scott, and drove there to cut him off?"

"We'll never know exactly how it went down, but that's the idea. We're closing the case."

* * *

On Monday, Aimee wakes up early to drive to the Montgomery County Detention Center in Rockville, about an hour from her parents' house. She dresses appropriately—after a little researching online she knows to wear a bra without an underwire and to bring a clear bag to hold her car key and ID. After going through a metal detector, she is led into a large modern room with metal tables and stools bolted to the floor. Small groups gather at the tables while guards stand at the periphery, watching. She sits at an empty table and waits, thrumming with anxiety. She slept terribly last night, waking constantly with panic attacks about how she would raise three children with Scott gone. The hour between three A.M. and four A.M. was spent wide awake, staring at the Maryland Men's Basketball 2002 NCAA Championship poster on her wall from high school as she went over how to make the mortgage work without his salary.

Finally, Scott enters the room wearing a maroon jumpsuit and heads straight over to her. She knows she's allowed a short hug at the beginning and another one at the end of the visit, so she rises.

They embrace for a few moments. She clutches his shirt, fighting back tears. She never thought she'd see him again, and here he is. He came back, after all. She pulls back, touching his face. "You shaved."

"Yeah, for court."

They both sit on the metal stools, holding hands atop the small table. A guard starts to walk over, and he pulls his hand away. "Sorry. We can't touch."

She nods, pulling her hand into her lap. "How did it go in court?" It seems easier to ask a logistical question than to pose the one she really wants an answer for—*Why did you change your mind?*

"It wasn't a real hearing. It was on video. I'm going back to California."

Aimee feels her shoulders slump. She is losing him, again. "What are you charged with?"

"Felony obstruction of justice. But my lawyer says that's just to get me back there, then they can charge me with something more serious. But he thinks I'll be able to make a deal if I cooperate and testify against the man who shot Dex."

"And you're going to cooperate with the prosecutor?"

"I'm going to do everything I can to minimize the time I spend in prison," Scott says. "That's all I can say. I'm really not supposed to talk about the case. How are the kids? What have you told them?"

"Nothing yet. That you're away on business. But I'm going to have to tell them the truth. Or something like it."

"Listen, Aimee. I don't expect you to stand by me. I really don't—"

"I haven't made any decisions."

"I understand, but let me finish. What I did was terrible, but I want you to know that what you said to me the other day had a huge impact. I thought long and hard about my life. I've done some things that land in the good column. I've done some things that land in the bad. Which column is bigger? Where has most of my life's energy gone? I'd like to think I've done more good than bad. Marrying you, being a father. Working on the software for diabetes."

"Does your mom even have diabetes?" Aimee asks.

He smiles. "Yes. She does. Type one, autoimmune. Anyway, in the end, the question I asked myself is: Who am I? Am I someone who can be trusted? I like to think that I am. That I have become a good person—fair, kind, compassionate. A lot of that is you, Aimee."

She looks away, feeling the tears coming. He has no right, she thinks, to be kind now.

"I was so blinded by fear when I saw my mom. It just pulled me right back to that night when she drove me to the Greyhound station, gave me cash for a ticket, and told me not to come back. I lived with that fear for a long time, and when she showed up here, it was all reactivated." He snapped his fingers. "I didn't handle it well. I'm not trying to blame her. But she was frantic. Said her life was in danger, so was Ray's. She told me I'd end up either dead or in prison if I didn't leave. I panicked. I should have been honest with you from the beginning. But I never thought I deserved you. I thought if you knew the real me, you'd run."

She turns back to him. "You never gave me that chance."

"You're right, and I'm sorry."

"But when you had the chance to run again, you didn't. You came back."

"I hope that counts for something."

"What about your mom?"

He shrugs. "She's gone. I don't know where. I wouldn't be surprised if I never saw her again, to be honest. In the end, she was more concerned about what my coming back and testifying would mean for her and Ray than what it would do to my life."

They talk until their allotted time is up. The goodbye embrace is longer, more difficult, because she doesn't know when she might get to hug him again. But she won't cry. She won't make him worry about her. She'll save her tears for later, even if she is overcome with grief. It doesn't matter what he did, she realizes, she loves him and wants him in her life. She knows with certainty that, whatever it takes, she will fight to get him back.

"I love you," she whispers in his ear.

"I love you more," he whispers back.

The wind is whipping up the trash in the parking lot when she leaves. She sits in her car for a good ten minutes, allowing herself to cry. Last week she was a typical suburban mom, stressed about balancing work and parenting, worried that Noa might have ADHD. Those concerns seem so trivial compared to what she will face in the coming weeks—explaining all this to the kids, figuring out if she can afford to stay in Bethesda, navigating the criminal justice system from afar.

She gets back on the road and, without even realizing it, finds herself winding her way through downtown Bethesda, toward her home. It's the last weekend in September, and a few overly excited neighbors have begun putting up Halloween decorations in their yards. Once news of what has happened on Nassau Court hits the media, she doubts she will ever feel comfortable trick-or-treating around here again. No, she thinks, as she pulls onto Nassau Court, they will have to move.

A news van is parked outside Lisa and Marcus's house, but it doesn't look like anyone's home. She can't blame Marcus if he left, another refugee from the chaos here. Aimee pulls up in front of her house, a plan formulating in her mind. It's only one month into the school year. Maybe she should pull the kids out and move back home with her dad for a while. There's room. She would save money. She gets out of the car. The plan is half-baked. She'll talk to her dad and see what he thinks. But she knows she won't be able to stay in this house.

After packing up a few suitcases and dragging them out to the truck, Aimee decides to see if Gwen is around. It seems doubtful. There is still yellow caution tape strung from the trees at the periphery of the property, although someone has cut it, leaving it to flap in the wind.

She knocks on the door and waits. No one answers, and she peers inside. Usually, Sababa comes rushing to the glass panel next to the door to see who's there, but it is still inside.

"No one's home."

Aimee turns to see a young man wearing a suit and a caked-on tan.

"Austin Byrd." He sticks out his hand. "Channel Five News."

Aimee ignores the hand and starts to walk past him.

"Hold up," he says as he jogs alongside her. "Are you a friend of Gwen Khoury's? What about Lisa Greco-King? Did you know her?"

Aimee stares ahead, ignoring him until she can get safely into her truck. She starts the engine. Was she a friend of Gwen's?

Did she know Lisa? *Good questions*, she thinks. Ones she'll be mulling over for a long time to come. She pulls the truck out, pausing for the stop sign at the end of the block.

Aimee looks in the rearview mirror. She can almost see them all—her and Scott, Lisa and Marcus, Anton and Gwen—seated on lawn chairs, watching the kids ride their bikes, drinking around a firepit on Halloween. It all seemed almost perfect at the time. Was it better then, when she was happy but clueless?

Yes. She would trade in the knowledge she has now to go back to those times.

But she can't. None of them can. Gwen and Marcus will have to rebuild their lives without their cheating spouses. Kai lost his mom, and Rafi and George lost their dad. And whatever the future holds for her and her own kids, it won't happen here.

She steps on the truck's accelerator, takes a hard right, and says goodbye to Nassau Court.

THE END

A YEAR LATER

Marcus comes into the room and offers me a mojito with fresh mint from the garden and garnished with a lime from a tree in our yard.

"Thanks, babe." I take the drink from him and aim the remote at the TV. "I kind of want to play it again."

Marcus laughs. "Twice wasn't enough? Anyway, aren't you meeting Aimee in South Beach?"

"No, I changed my mind. We're meeting at La Mar. I want to show her the best of what Miami has to offer. But you're right. I should go shower." I take a big sip of the drink and kiss Marcus deeply. "It went well, though, didn't it? I mean, I seemed sympathetic, right?"

"It rocked. You sounded great, and you looked hot."

My eyes shift past him to the azure waters of Biscayne Bay. *Great* and *hot* were not adjectives Anton would ever have used for me. If he had seen my interview on *Dateline*, if he had read my book, he would have offered hours' worth of analysis. Is it weird that I wish my dead husband could read the book I wrote about his murder, so we might have an intelligent discussion? No, I don't think so. We always want what we don't have.

I take my drink up the floating staircase to the main bedroom. The house I share with Marcus is huge, big enough for all three kids to have their separate spaces, although Rafi and George still insist on sharing a room. Anton's life insurance paid for it, and thanks to my book's success, and the speaking fees I can command, I won't ever have to work in a PR firm again.

Some might think it's gross that Marcus and I are together.

But spouse swapping is not as odd as it sounds. It happens sometimes when couples socialize a lot together—they fall for each
other's others. It's a story as old as time. There was that Canadian
country singer, Shania Twain. When she found out her husband
was cheating on her with her best friend, Shania ended up marrying the other woman's husband.

"I am actually grateful for what I've gone through and wouldn't
change a thing," she wrote in her autobiography *From This Moment On*.

"We slowly became very, very good friends," she had told a
talk show host about her new husband. "We had many months
of just trying to make sense of everything."

You could sort of say the same thing about Marcus and me.
We were both stunned and devastated by Lisa and Anton cheating on us. At least something good has come out of the whole
debacle. He really is my rock, in a way that Anton never was.

And now, I am finally getting to see my best friend for the
first time in almost a year. My favorite person.

When I arrive, Aimee is already seated at an outdoor table
overlooking the water and the sun setting over the Miami sky-
line. I would be able to spot her a mile away. With her slightly
frizzy brown curls, her freckled skin, and blue cotton shirtdress,
she stands out among the deeply tanned and the scantily clad.

"Oh my God!" I squeal, and she jumps up when I get close.
She gives me a hug and then pulls back, holding me at arm's
distance to examine me.

"My gosh, Gwen, you look ten years younger."

"Do I? It's living by the water, I swear." I sit down. It's being
free, is what I really mean. Not under Anton's spell, not under
my mother's thumb. That and a few units of Botox.

"I'm so glad you came down," I say. "I wasn't sure if you really
would."

"Of course. It's been way too long. I've been meaning to come
earlier, but I'm here now."

The waitress comes by, a slinky feline of a girl in a napkin-sized skirt and a tube top.

"Two pisco sours," I tell her, winking at Aimee. "And let's start with some conchitas and the cebiche clasico. Thanks!" Once the waitress is gone, I turn my full attention on Aimee. "The food here is to die for. I hope you don't mind that I'm ordering for us." I'm already buzzed from the two mojitos that Marcus made earlier, but I'm all nerves. I've missed Aimee so much. It's so much more fun to celebrate your wins with your best friend. But I know the last year has been tough on her, and I've tried not to push. I'm hoping that her being here means life is back on track for her.

"So, how are you and Scott doing?"

"We're taking it slow," she says. "He still has his own place. The trial starts next month, and he'll have to fly back to California to testify, of course. The kids love living near the Chesapeake Bay. And Noa is thriving in her new school. They are so good at supporting neurodivergent kids."

"You must be so relieved that he doesn't have to do any prison time."

"I am. We both are." Aimee leans back to allow the waitress to put down the drinks.

I hold mine aloft. "Cheers!"

We clink glasses.

"To your book. Such a success!" she says.

We each take a big sip. "Good, right?"

"Mmm." She nods in agreement. "I knew you had once wanted to be a writer, back before you worked in PR. But a whole book? Now, that's impressive."

"What, you thought Anton was the only one with talent?"

"No, it's just a lot of work."

"Between you and me, I hired someone, this quasi-successful thriller writer from Bethesda, to ghostwrite the thing. I mean, I gave her notes and lots of random pages, but she put it all together using articles and police reports. Stuff like that." I think back on some of the suggestions that she gave me, and some of the changes she thought I should make. "She helped me see that I had to make myself look bad at some points. I mean, exaggerate some stuff, you know, just to make it more believable. People don't like reading about perfect characters."

"Makes sense. Will you sign it for me while I'm in Miami? I have a copy in my hotel."

"Of course. Duh."

Aimee takes another sip of her drink. "Some of the things you changed, right?"

"Like what?"

"I mean, you can't really know that Lisa thought any of those things—about losing my friendship or being jealous of you."

"I sensed it, you know? It was intuition."

"And what you wrote about her sleeping with her college roommate's boyfriend, was that true?"

I shrug. "Poetic license. People like an over-the-top villain. And it turns out you can't slander the dead. Anyway, you can't hold that against me. The bitch was sleeping with my husband."

"True." Aimee laughs. "Yet, you also wrote things from my perspective, and you couldn't have known what I was thinking or feeling."

"I did my best, Aimee." I reach out and squeeze her hand. "I hope I didn't upset you. I would never do anything to jeopardize our friendship. This project was like therapy for me. I mean, it literally saved my life."

"Oh, well, having my life put on display for the world to see . . . Why would I be upset?" She laughs again. "The only thing is, a couple of details left me confused."

"Well, it's fictionalized."

"That's not it."

"Hmmm?"

"Like the journal, the one you found that had all of Anton's interviews with Cathy Stocker in it? In the book, you say you left it at the house in Frederick when we went to confront Scott's mom."

"That's right."

"But you didn't. You didn't leave it there. I saw you take it."

I blink twice. "I guess I thought it was more dramatic that way."

"Right. Except why would that be more dramatic? So, I started thinking, why else would Gwen write that?" She snaps her fingers. "Because she wanted to explain why she couldn't produce that journal later on. After all, I never saw it with my own eyes. You read to me from it in the car, but I didn't see it."

"What are you saying?"

"Just that I don't really know what was in it. Or in whose handwriting."

My heart starts to thump. "You're so clever and quick. I miss you so much. These airheads down here." I look around the restaurant, which is filling up. "Remember what it was like on Nassau when it was just our two families? I mean, before Lisa and Marcus moved in?"

Aimee nods. "Those were fun times."

"We shared everything. SAGA time! Right? I still have my #SAGA T-shirt. I don't wear it, of course, it might upset Marcus. There's no 'M' in SAGA. But it was amazing. It was crazy that you and me both had twins. It was like fate, we were meant to be friends."

"I thought it was interesting that you switched that in the book. You had Lisa and Marcus be the ones who were there first, when they were actually the ones who moved in later."

"Oh, well, I thought it added to the story." What did Aimee ever see in Lisa, anyway? She was tacky and loud and vulgar. But everyone thought she was funny and sexy like a cut-rate Sophia Vergara. I cringe at the memory of Anton practically drooling over Lisa when we first met in Aimee's backyard. Her boobs falling out of her top like that. I knew he wanted her, but I didn't think Lisa would take him up on it.

"Gwen, you were the one who wrote in that notebook, weren't you? Those interviews with Cathy Stocker that you read to me," she says. "It was your handwriting, wasn't it?"

"Does it matter?" I can feel myself letting my guard down. Maybe it's the alcohol, or maybe it's the thrill of having someone I can talk to. Aimee was there. She understands.

Aimee shrugs. "Maybe not. But it means that you were the one who was interviewing Cathy Stocker."

"What's the point of all this?"

"Curiosity. I want to know the truth."

"Really? The last time you went in search of the truth, you found out your husband was a fugitive who had robbed a drug dealer."

Silence, and then Aimee bursts out laughing. I join her. "Oh, Gwen, I miss you so damn much!"

My heart sings. There's nothing better than Aimee's laugh. "Me, too."

"Did you cook up this whole thing yourself? I mean, were you the one?" She grins slyly. "I mean, Anton? Lisa? They're not the brightest bulbs."

"What, you don't see Anton doing investigative journalism?" I giggle. "Well, he wasn't Bob fucking Woodward, that's for sure. He was so lazy."

"So you did. Good for you!" Aimee raises her glass. "Men can be so disappointing sometimes."

"Yeah? So you're not mad about Scott?"

"No, I'm grateful that you found all this out. You're a true friend. You were doing it to help me, right?"

"Yes!" I can feel tears of joy warming my eyes. "Thank you. I'm so glad you see it like that. You have no idea how anxious I've been about seeing you. I've always wanted to tell you, but things got so freaking out of hand."

"Did Lisa or Anton have anything to do with the blackmailing at all?"

"No. They were in la-la land screwing each other. I'm the one who sent the original email to Scott from American University. Anton had no clue, not until the day he found my notebook. We got in a huge fight about it. I had to tell him what was going on. He got so self-righteous with me, I couldn't believe it. That was the day we went to dinner at your place, and I heard him warn you. We got in a huge fight when we got home."

"But how did you, you know . . . ? I mean, there was Anton's blood on Lisa's car."

I laugh. "Oh my God, I didn't kill him. Did you think I killed Anton? No, I didn't do that. The police would have been all over me. They *were* all over me!"

"You mean Lisa did kill him? But why, if they weren't blackmailing Scott?"

I shake my head. I want to tell her, but it's not my secret to tell. "I can't tell you."

"Please, Gwen, I'm dying here." Aimee groans. Her hand goes to her neck, where she toys with the top button of her dress. Her skin is mottled pink, like it always gets when she drinks. She's such a lightweight. "You can tell me. The case is closed. There's nothing the police can do now."

"Well, what can I say? I wanted to kill the bastard when I found out he was cheating on me, again. But I couldn't. Then one night in the spring, I was walking Sababa, and Marcus was coming back from some event. He walked with me, and we just started confiding in each other. At first, we were just friends, two spouses being wronged, offering each other support. But then it grew into something else." I shrug, letting her fill in the blanks.

"You and Marcus, all the way back then? I had no idea."

"We were very careful. Marcus, poor guy, he felt so betrayed. Humiliated. I mean, so did I, but it wasn't my first time being cheated on. He was really devastated. Neither one of us wanted a divorce. He would have lost millions. We decided to help each other out. I'd take care of Lisa, and you know . . ."

"He'd take care of Anton. Wow. That's brilliant, Gwen."

"The night Anton and me got in a fight? When he went to your house, I knew it had to be then. I was waiting at the door when Scott walked Anton back over. He was shit-faced. He started blabbering about how he was going to go to Villain & Saint and find Scott and tell him everything. I went straight to Marcus as soon as he left and told him he had to stop him. I remember saying, *tonight's the night*."

"So he took Lisa's car to Villain & Saint? And he ran Anton down?"

I shrug. "I guess. I wasn't there."

"And Lisa? The night she came to your house?"

My skin begins to feel itchy. Something is off. "Why are you asking so many questions about the past?"

"Like I said, I want to know the truth, that's all."

The waitress arrives with our food and places it on the table.

"Do you ladies know what you'd like for dinner, or do you need a few more minutes?"

"A few more minutes," I say, draining my glass. "And another round of these."

Once she's gone, Aimee pushes the plate of conchitas away from her. "It looks good, but I've lost my appetite."

"Oh, come on, don't be that way."

She unbuttons the top of her dress, reaches inside, and pulls out a small black microphone, which she tosses on the table.

"What the hell is that?" I ask, recoiling.

"I think they call that a wire, Gwen." From the table behind her, I can see a well-dressed couple stand and head toward us. To my right, I also see two uniformed police officers weaving through the crowd.

"How could you trick me like this?" I hiss. "We're friends."

"Don't be mad," she says, lifting her chin in defiance. "Just think what a great ending to your next book this will be. After all, your readers deserve to know."

(THE ACTUAL END)

ACKNOWLEDGMENTS

I want to thank all the dedicated people at Forge for their continued support and their hard work. A special thanks to my editor, Kristin Sevick Brown, for her keen eye and insight. And I'm always grateful to my kick-ass agent, Katie Shea Boutillier!

A shout-out to my real-life, card-playing couple friends who taught me how to play *Pitch*—just a friendly game of cards. If any of my friends are wondering if I've based my characters on you, let me assure you that yes, I have.

Thank you to Julie, who lets me talk endlessly about plots on our long, winding walks and has never once told me she's cutting me off.

And finally, this book would not be possible without the love and support of my family. So thank you to my husband, John (whom I adore not solely because he's a grammarian who has saved my hide more than a few times) and to my kids, Theo and Roxy.

ABOUT THE AUTHOR

Before turning to fiction, AGGIE BLUM THOMPSON covered real-life crime as a newspaper reporter for a number of papers, including *The Boston Globe* and *The Washington Post*. Thompson is a member of Sisters in Crime, Mystery Writers of America, and International Thriller Writers, and serves as the program director for the Montgomery County chapter of the Maryland Writers' Association. She lives with her husband and two children in the suburbs of Washington, D.C.